WE ARE NOT ANONYMOUS

STEPHEN ORAM

We Are Not Anonymous

Print Edition
Paperback ISBN: 978-1-0685764-0-9
Ebook ISBN: 978-1-0685764-1-6
Published by Nudge the Future Fiction

Cover design by Jessica Bell
Interior design by Amie McCracken

In memory of my father, Len, and
the conversation that sparked this novel.

PART ONE

1

Beth manoeuvred through the crowds, which were pressing in on every side. The close contact of so many noisy people all squeezed into one place was wonderful. She wiped the sweat from the tip of her nose, pleased that she was getting the first-hand footage she needed to increase her credibility and gain the influence she'd been chasing for two years. She was more nervous than excited, but with a brave face she was going to make sure her first live cast was a good one. Otherwise, what was the point of leaving the security of her home town, the familiarity of its streets and its people, her friends?

Chatting into her sleeve camera, she cast her commentary without giving herself time to overthink. "Here I am, Beth Haliford your trusted caster, talking to you from Pancras Square, London. This private piece of land is home to the headquarters of OS, OmegaSimera, who are accused of child exploitation."

She filmed the crowd.

"As you can see," she said, checking herself to make sure she was smiling professionally despite the oppressive heatwave. "As you can see, among the multitude of protest groups, we have those directly against child exploitation and also groups focused on the continuing extraction of fossil fuels, anti-capitalists, anarchists, and representatives of the anti-neoliberal movement. Look. They've all come together to protect their children's future."

Although she was an orphan and struggled to understand parents, she wasn't going to let it show. She paused for effect, and to ensure her smile was still in place.

Continuing, she spoke in a quieter voice. "Not surprisingly, the OS Bot Police, the BP, are out of reach and yet close enough to intervene in an instant. Typical."

The mixed chants of the different groups grew louder and angrier, dominated by one in particular. "Stop your planet plunder. No more extraction," they repeated.

The closer to the front she got, the tighter the crowd became and the harder it was to concentrate. Breathing in deeply and bracing herself, she used her shoulders to move forward through this hard core of protestors. Not quite the same as when she'd carried drinks in a bouncing mass of fans, but the protest had a similar feel without the spillage, the delight of live music, or the friends she'd once had, before she ditched them all for a career in the city.

She lifted her arm up high and performed a three-sixty panoramic. "If you're here, please take the time to look around. If you need to leave quickly, head for the canal or the train station to escape OmegaSimera's jurisdiction." Conscious that an essential part of her casting persona was to reflect what her followers felt, she added, "My city is still the best capital in the world, but a country without the newly formed nations of East Albion and Wessex is greatly reduced. Like you, a small part of me grieves for the England that was." It was a clumsy cast and she wished that she was in the editing suite rather than casting live.

The crowd moved, squeezing her up close to those at her side. She twisted her body, and with it the cameras built into her clothes, towards a woman wearing the pinstriped uniform of the child protection faction, Humanity First. These were the sections of the protest that Beth had most wanted to capture and cast. These were mothers and fathers who accused OS of stealing their kids' childhood, of manipulating their attention and ultimately severing any loyalty to their families. None of this was new, but the immense amount of pressure put on young children to compete and conform was considered by many as cultish. Some protestors held banners with photos of parents who had committed suicide because their children had cut themselves off from any contact.

A woman threw a girl sexbot with a broken leg and fake blood leaking from its nose at the row of BP that stood between the protestors and the target building. "Stop extracting their childhood," she shouted.

"Not the catchiest of chants. But forcing kids to grow up fast and infantilising adults is not clever. Or, maybe it is," said Beth, instantly regretting her non-committal 'maybe' at the end. She followed the sexbot.

A feeling of betrayal swept over her, but sadly the sexbot would draw in more viewers than an interview with Humanity First. The silicon girl landed on the back of a man who jerked away as if he'd been burnt. The woman with him picked it up and threw it forwards on its journey, transported above the heads of the crowd. Beth recognised her as the mother of Child X, a kid who was so traumatised by her time in the OS Academy that she hadn't spoken since, except to her AI liaison interface.

A great cheer went up whenever the sexbot was thrown in the air, while Beth pushed and shoved her way through the crowd in pursuit. The sexbot reached the front and, in a brave move, a tall muscular woman carried it across the open space between the Bot Police and the protestors and leaned it against the one in charge. The BP turned its head towards her and then carried the battered replicant to the line of human police gathered behind their front-line colleagues. An officer took hold of the sexbot, gave it a peck on the cheek and a thumbs up to the crowd.

An almighty hiss erupted and the unified chant began in earnest: "End extraction. Now."

Without thinking, Beth had turned her attention to the woman who had braved the police. Still casting from her clothes, Beth pushed through the increasing density of protestors towards this fascinating woman.

Another of the pinstriped faction shouted, “Fuck off,” at Beth’s camera.

She stopped to show the shouting woman her pulsating hand-sized orb. The globule, which Beth’s grandmother had insisted sounded like a ball of phlegm and would not stop calling a phone, displayed her caster credentials by working its way through the colours of the rainbow.

“Fuck off,” the woman repeated.

Knowing that the fear from protesting was running high, Beth half-grinned, thanked her for her time, and moved on.

The chant was loud and rhythmic and underscored by the boom of drums somewhere off to the side. The deep resonance of one long beat followed by three short was driving the repetitive, “Stop—The—Plun—Der. Stop—The—Plun—Der.”

A faint female voice of a human police officer wafted over the top of the BP, stating the rights of her corporation under the Civil Contingencies Act and the Climate Change National Emergency to disperse the protest.

The officer’s supercilious tone annoyed Beth. “Don’t forget,” she said into camera, “that despite the appearance that this is a public space, Pancras Square is actually private land with its own regulations. Be careful.”

The BP released a swarm of tiny drones, which formed a dense layer above the front section of the crowd where Beth was standing. Her initial nervousness was being replaced by the mood of the crowd’s righteous anger.

The crowd continued to chant in defiance of the threat. The drones moved closer, and the chant grew louder as it bounced off them. Her love of the crowd intensified. Then without warning the drones swarmed into the distant sky before swooping back down to perform a murmuration, with each one emitting a flapping sound that, in accumulation, drowned out the chants. She watched in awe and anticipation, waiting for the drones' next move, which came with as little warning as the murmuration. Every single one stopped dead in the sky and held its place. The frozen tableau was silent and so was the crowd. Beth lifted her arms up high to capture the phenomenon. Then they descended *en masse* to form a dense umbrella that was just out of reach. She pushed her way forward and burst through the last of the crowd. In a carefully coordinated act of defiance, the protestors lifted their globules above their heads and turned them around in their hands to symbolise allowing full access to all of their data. She gasped. This was exactly why she'd come, to capture moments like this that would not be cast anywhere else.

The crowd began to chant. "We are not anonymous. We are not anonymous. We are not anonymous."

Beth reached for her globule and quickly cast, "Amazing. Deliberately calling out the pretence of anonymisation. Standing up to be counted. Refusing to be averaged by big data blanding. Brave."

She was about to raise her globule to claim caster immunity from such a taboo act by the protestors when the muscular woman leant across and shoved hers next to Beth's face.

Surprisingly, she grabbed Beth's hand and squeezed the two globules together. "Naomi," she said and nodded.

Distracted by the unusually rapid vibration of her globule, Beth replied. "Beth," she said, unsure what else to say.

"Put it away. Not your fight."

"But—"

"Seriously," said Naomi. "It's extremely dangerous."

Beth was still deciding what to do when the riot drones dispersed their dense layer and lined up, one drone to one globule. The drones hovered and the protestors held their globules out as a sacrifice for the cause. It was mesmerising.

Beth made a quick cast. "As the dominant and most sinister of the tech-corps, we've seen elsewhere what OS is capable of. The dedication of these parents to their movement is magnificent."

The protestors chanted, "We are not anonymous."

The drones responded with a piercing single-pitched noise while the BP moved forwards, followed by the riot drones spraying the crowd with their mist before shooting off into the distance.

"Here," said Naomi, as she passed Beth a capsule. "Swallow this and then lie absolutely still."

Beth hesitated, not sure whether to trust her.

"Now," said Naomi. "Quickly. It blocks the effects."

With adrenaline pumping through her body, Beth cracked the top of the vial, swallowed and waited anxiously. The BP edged their way closer to the crowd, which by now was a mass of bodies. Some writhing in agony, but most on the floor. Paralysed. Beth tested her fingers and toes. They still moved. She exhaled softly. The BP hadn't reached her yet, but they were steadily working their way through the protestors lifting them up from the floor like rag dolls and when their arms were full, taking them to the waiting vehicles. The human police were watching, joking and laughing at the collapse of the protest. Her stomach tightened.

Naomi winked and threw Beth a balaclava. "Follow me," she mouthed. "Do what I do." She pulled her balaclava over her head and down to cover her face, displaying the constantly changing patterns of the fabric.

The chaos surrounding them was immense, so without question Beth followed suit.

Naomi stood up with her arms by her side and faced the approaching BP. She stood rigid. Beth copied. Two of the BP stopped, one in front of Naomi and one in front of Beth. The BP stayed like that for a few moments and then moved on.

"They're only looking for humans, immobilised and on the ground," Naomi whispered. "You go that way," she said tilting her head to the right and I'll go this," tilting her head to the left. "See you at the Retro Bar in two hours."

Naomi turned and began walking slowly, mechanically, towards the edge of the crowd. She was leaving and the BP didn't seem to notice, or didn't care.

Fighting to keep her emotions under control, Beth considered Naomi's request with equal measures of intrigue and apprehension. She must act quickly and, deciding to let her caster curiosity win, she took a direct route to the edge of the fallen crowd and out on to the main thoroughfare that bordered the square. A seldom heard thwump thwump of a helicopter approached. Fascinated and terrified by such a display of wealth and power, she turned back to the square.

A single line of BP surrounded the site despite all of the bodies having been removed. Other BP were searching through the debris, looking for traces of people as yet unidentified. She sent the scooter she'd ordered back to its resting place, noting the subtle change of colour in her globule as it took payment. Pressing the identity indentation on the globule's surface to activate her caster credentials and holding it out in front of her, she walked up to the nearest BP.

"Hello," she said in her best professional voice. "I've come to take a look."

No reaction. No movement and no attempt to scan her globule. She pushed it up close and repeated that she was a caster and wanted access to the site. Still nothing from the BP. Shrugging, she stepped to one side to walk around it and it moved to block her. "Caster," she said, hoping to convey an air of authority.

This time the BP visor lit up with the words: *No access; Status under review.*

She pressed the indentation again and the globule worked its way through the rainbow colours that signified she had clearance. Holding it up to the BP once more she said, "I want access. Please."

The BP responded by moving closer. It was almost touching her. The message on its visor changed to: *Leave the area or risk arrest.*

Frustrated and a little scared, she decided to heed its advice and summoned her scooter.

Once she was out of the immediate vicinity she began to tremble, her mouth dried up, and her globule kept alerting her to an irregular heartbeat. She instructed the door to her flat to disable automatic access to all delivery drones and moistened the inside of her mouth with as much saliva as she could muster.

A thought kept buzzing around inside her head, like an annoying insect. Why had the BP questioned her credentials?

2

NAOMI TUCKED the balaclava into her pocket, told the trike where to go, using the standard three word locator for the Retro Bar: *attend.slot.soak*, and leant back in the seat allowing it to mould to her back. She was confident that asking the autodriver to find the fastest of the cheap routes would still get her there in time to meet Beth. Beth, the promising young caster who could be useful to Resist and Regain's activism. Whether Beth would be prepared to lose her identity to the movement, to the collective, was a different matter. Naomi had done just that, but it wasn't easy, and it wasn't for everyone.

In a rundown garden between derelict shops and a boarded-up pub, BP with different logos to those at the protest were busy shaking small tents that were scattered around the brown grass. Naomi stopped, disgusted and unable to ignore the abuse of the homeless. Some might consider it a weakness, this inability to pass by an injustice. She saw it as a strength and had learnt at a young age that to fear was to fail, which meant that she refused to appear intimidated, even when she was.

The occupants were being ordered to come out. Tent doors were being unzipped and the garden was filling with dirty, dishevelled people. There were shrugs of confusion from some and apprehensive fidgeting from others. Low mutterings of discontent were mixed in with the stamping of feet and the occasional shout of anger. She checked the trike's locator: Cable Street community garden.

The BP moved into line, standing a metre apart. In unison they stepped towards a group kneeling in front of their tents with their hands behind their heads.

Naomi swallowed, sickened by the sight and grateful that this could never happen in her beloved East Albion.

The homeless woman who had been walking around and calming things down called out to her fellow campers. "Everyone. Listen. Hands behind heads. Like that," she said, pointing to those who were kneeling with their heads bowed. "Or they have the right to beat you up."

Naomi pulled on her balaclava. This was wrong and should be resisted. She checked her globule to see how far from the bar she was, mindful that she needed Beth to help crack open the veneer of complacency about OmegaSimera and their poisonous extractive behaviour. She couldn't afford to miss their meeting. She double checked. She had enough time. She had to help. She squeezed her globule and it shrank enough to tuck into its protective pouch. Trusting that the BP wouldn't spot her, she slipped through the gate and for extra precaution zigzagged in short bursts across to the outermost tent.

As one, the BP stopped moving and the sergeant read out the basis on which the action was being taken. "Private space generously made available to the public cannot be used as common land. You must leave immediately or face the withdrawal of Universal Basic Income. Or imprisonment. Your decision."

When the BP were in range, they scanned each face. One of them moved towards Naomi, slowing down as it passed by, stopping just beyond her. As it turned around, she knelt on all fours as she'd been taught. She stared straight ahead, desperate not to flinch as the BP stood close by, scanning in her general direction.

She held her breath, hoping that she'd remembered her training accurately, that there was a high probability she could fool the BP into thinking that she was an animal. Her subterfuge trainer had explained that it was a flaw that OS had been unable to fix because there was simply not enough footage of humans behaving like animals. His addendum had amused her: no amount of incentives had generated sufficient volunteers to correct the data. The BP moved on and she relaxed, thinking how proud Gerry and Morgan would be of her when she told them what she'd done and thinking how the respect they showed her in the company of others always gave her a warm glow and a strong feeling of confidence.

The sergeant spoke again. "Globules, please," it said.

Slowly, each of the cornered campers took a single hand from behind their head. They gripped their globules, from pockets or wherever they had laid theirs down, and held them in front of their faces. A BP stepped forward and touched each in turn.

When it returned to the sergeant, they stood facing each other for a few moments before the sergeant spoke. "You have twelve hours to reach the location that the officer will now transfer to your globule. This is a final warning. Stay off private land unless you have specific permission from the owner."

One of the men stood up and grabbed his tent, expertly collapsing it as he did, and walked away. The sergeant sent a riot drone after him. The man began to run, but the drone easily caught up and sprayed him. As soon as the man hit the floor one of the BP was despatched to collect him, scooping him into its arms.

Sickened, Naomi stayed still. There was silence all around while the BP moved across to the waiting van.

The woman who seemed to be the leader stood up. Holding her globule in front of her, she said, "This is madness. This is miles away and I'm sure it's flooded."

She was impressive and Naomi wished that she could sit and talk with her.

"Twelve hours," repeated the sergeant as another riot drone took off from its head. The drone reached the woman and hovered next to her. She dropped to her knees.

"Twelve hours and no more," repeated the sergeant.

Naomi had to act fast. She crawled on all fours using the zigzag technique, making her way through the kneeling campers, flipping her globule out at each one for a quick message and desperately getting it back in its pouch before it registered with the BP. The message read: *You'll find sanctuary in East Albion, at Healing Train Station. Bonfires.stroke.juggles.*

Once she'd sent it to all the globules in the garden she crawled away.

Back on the street, she got moving before there was any trouble. As strongminded as she was, she wasn't someone who looked for confrontation.

There was barely enough time to reach the bar but she resisted upgrading her route, conscious that Gerry had stressed that funds were tight. Determined to ignore any further distractions, she stared ahead and willed her scooter to get her there on time.

She arrived with a few minutes to spare and, taking advantage of them, she inhaled a long deep slug of the fresh estuary air. It smelled superb. It was good to be out of the suffocating buildings of the city. She was definitely an open air woman.

A loud siren boomed across the river and five gunboats set out from the shore to block the passage of an unwelcome refugee barge from the Netherlands. They formed a line to force the barge to turn around. It veered towards the shallow shoreline and the gunboats kept their blockade in place. A loud piercing sound echoed over the water and one of the gunboats moved in alongside the barge. A flare shot across its front and it began to turn around towards the North Sea. She watched the inevitable play out and shrugged. The East Albion port of Tilbury was close and it was well known that barges were welcome there. It would be fine. With one last gulp of the cool sharp air, she turned towards the bar.

The doorman was wearing a lightweight hooded top and loose-fitting trousers elasticated at the ankles. It was early twenty-first century style, but she wasn't sure how authentic the fabric was. He smiled and held out his hand, presuming she knew the rules. She did and smiled back, handing him her globule which he took into the famous Faraday room that had once been a part of the service to the residents of New Providence Wharf. She entered the bar and walked with a lightened step alongside the conveyor belt of drinks and snacks. Towards the rear, she took a seat in an alcove where the belt came in and went around the edge of the wall and out again, echoing the loop in the river outside. She sat facing the wall, chose an old-fashioned cherry beer and waited patiently. She kept an eye on the door in the artfully designed and cleverly placed small mirrors that adorned the wall. They looked as if a glass had been thrown and the shards had pierced the brick-work, a style she admired. She adopted her best calm expression and sipped her bittersweet drink.

Eventually, Beth arrived. Naomi felt her shoulders relax, a tell-tale sign of how tense she'd become. Beth handed the doorman her globule, scanned the room, waved, and eagerly made her way alongside the conveyor belt while Naomi appraised her potential as a recruit for Resist & Regain. Naomi approved of the practical clothes, the comfortable cut of the trousers and the sturdiness of the jacket, all marked with the regenerative fabric symbol. The hair dye, which was busy changing to a darker pink, impressed her less. Beth appeared to be in her mid-twenties, about the same age as Naomi, and from the way she was grinning at the goodies on the conveyor belt this was her first time in the bar. Gerry and Morgan had seen Beth's casting and agreed with Naomi that she should attempt to recruit her. How she wished they were in the bar with her to help.

3

Beth had spotted Naomi sitting in the alcove as soon as she'd entered the bar. Naomi's stature was commanding and seemed to emit an aura of authority. Beth braced herself, unsure what to expect. "Hey. How nice to see you again," she said, holding out her hand.

"You made it."

"This is a nice place. Is it taboo?"

"Guess so. Who cares?"

Beth sat down and breathed in the evocative background smell of simmering shipworm sauce, her grandmother's favourite. A steady stream of drinks and snacks flowed past before she picked out plates of crunchy crickets, berry caviar and slices of purple pineapple. "This is amazing," she said, grinning with delight and carefully completing her choice of meal with a glass of rose red juice.

Naomi helped herself to one of the crunchy crickets. "We don't have long," she said.

Irritated and intimidated, Beth pulled her plate closer and popped two of the crickets into her mouth followed by a large slug of juice. "For what?" she asked.

"You're a caster. Right?"

"Yes. Well. Trying. But, it's not as simple as just wanting to be."

"You need to expose this," said Naomi rolling out a micro thin sheet of SlendTek.

She stared, her eyes wide open. "How did you get that? I thought it was only available to the tech elite."

"Doesn't matter. What does matter is what I'm about to show you."

A map appeared on the rolled out sheet and as Naomi traced the national borders with her finger, they appeared. She traced out the English-Wessex boundary along and down from the Severn Bridge on the Welsh border to the Isle of Wight. Next, she traced out the English-East Albion border from the Thames estuary, slicing north through London, up to York before cutting across to the coast at Scarborough. "Now," she said, pointing at Selby just inside the English border. "That's a flood defence. Constructed from disused technology. Shipped in from the very places we shipped it out to years ago."

With a disappointed shrug, Beth replied. "That's hardly news."

"No, but it is when children are mining it to provide precious materials for the tech industry."

Beth raised her eyebrows. "Hardly," she said, pleased she wasn't showing any distress, despite the barely suppressed desire to have her own kids.

"I'm not lying. As young as eight. Digging dangerously deep."

"It's only shocking because it's here. It's been happening elsewhere for years."

Naomi leant in close. "There are rumours. They get trapped in the bonding agent." She leant back. "Like insects in amber."

Beth shook her head and noticed the tips of her hair turn a lighter shade of pink, annoyingly undermining her serious expression. "I don't believe you," she said, ignoring the urge to save every child in the world. "You'll have to do better than rumours."

"Go look for yourself. An extraction economy in action. It must be exposed."

"Hmmm… It sounds more like a conspiracy theory to me."

"They are literally killing our children. For profit. It is sick."

Naomi sat back on her stool, picked a passing plate of shipworm and chomped. She was considering Beth carefully, chewing slowly. She swallowed the last of the shipworm and grabbed a beer, took a swig, swished it around inside her mouth and then slammed the bottle on the counter. A few heads turned before returning quickly to their conversations.

Beth straightened herself on her stool. "You want to change the system by throwing sex dolls at the BP?"

Naomi's smile was forced. "Beth," she said. "We have just allowed our semi-automated government to sanction twelve-year-old girls to have children. So long as the conception doesn't involve sex. They only see us as bodies."

"But—"

"We allowed it. We didn't vote for it. Didn't resist it either. We pay our tax. We have our say on the things we care about. For most people, their own economic benefit. It's disgusting. We must stand up against it."

"Oh, I see. But nobody takes those 'freedoms' for girls seriously," said Beth. "It has to be a glitch in the system. Surely?"

"You're the caster. You tell me." Naomi grimaced. "An algorithm that knows fertility is in full swing by twelve. Knows the population is shrinking. Knows that sex before sixteen is a taboo. Go figure what it makes of those three facts."

"So why don't you stand up against it rather than expecting me to?"

"I will. In my own way. You must in yours. I saw how you were at that protest. You're a fighter. Like me. We can make a difference."

Beth considered her companion. This woman was intriguing. Roughly the same age, but she seemed so much older, as if she'd lived more life or lived the years they had in common more deeply and dangerously. She seemed to be well-informed and confident of what she knew, but Beth was beginning to learn that you could rarely trust first impressions. Her early steps into casting had taught her how most conflicting accounts of events were the effect of bias. Facts are not necessarily the pure truth, unlike her granddad had led her to believe. Facts have a context, in the knowing and the telling, and it's often that which shapes their meaning.

"Look," said Naomi, breaking the silence. "You can't take my word for it. I get that. You're a caster. It's in your blood to scrape away until the truth is revealed. You…" She paused and pointed in the mirror to the BP gathered outside, up close to the windows. "Don't worry about them," she said. "This whole place is a Faraday cage. If they come in, they stop working."

Beth was worried. She frowned sceptically. "What's the globule cage for then?"

"No localised globule-to-globule connections, no unwanted approaches. From anyone. Forget the BP. What about these child miners?"

"I'm not sure. It seems far-fetched. I don't think they'd do that."

"Really? Are you that naïve?"

Beth resisted retaliating. She put a piece of pineapple in her mouth, chewed and stared. She swallowed, washed it down with a drink of juice and pulled a quizzical face. "Maybe I am," she said and sighed.

Naomi rolled up the sheet of SlendTek. "Remember three words."

Beth didn't react.

Naomi continued. "Charge. Amounting. Scorch."

"Got it. Charge. Amounting. Scorch," Beth repeated, thinking that if it was true then this stuff with the child miners could be the cast that compensated for everything she'd given up, the one that finally made her name.

Naomi leant in close again. Her breath smelt nice, of sour cherries and alcohol.

Beth looked her in the eyes. "They wouldn't do that to children. They just wouldn't."

"Go see for yourself. Please."

Naomi's breath lingered as she sat back. "And them?" Beth asked, looking over Naomi's shoulder at the BP.

"They won't bother you. Put your balaclava on and walk through them whenever you want." Naomi passed Beth a protective pouch. "Here. Pop your globule in this and they can't access it."

Beth slid off her stool and smiled. "I'll think about it."

With the words 'go see for yourself' echoing in her head, she could see in the bar's mirrors that Naomi's gaze followed her all the way to the front door as she retraced her steps along the side of the conveyer belt.

4

Beth took the cheapest train from London to Selby, which had meant that at every station along the way it waited until it was at optimum load before moving on. She did her best not to be irritated by its slow progress, knowing that it was hampered by people setting their maps to the local station as a proxy for somewhere close by, and then not turning up for the train.

It had taken her a while to decide to make the journey and, after her automated trawlers had tried but could find precious little about the seawall, curiosity had got the better of her. Since the meeting with Naomi, she hadn't been able to get the image of the 'children in amber' out of her head, often failing to ignore her own unresolved issues at being orphaned as a child. Her grandparents were great, but for some inexplicable reason she had never felt totally safe and the lingering claustrophobic feeling of loneliness, from nightmares of being locked in a cupboard, haunted her still.

When she finally arrived in Selby, she stepped onto the platform and set her globule to: *charge.amounting.scorch.* Cupping it in her hand, she set off, following the vibrations on its surface as it directed her to the south bank of the River Ouse.

At the river, heavily laden barges of imported tech rubbish being transported from the Humber docks kept pace with her. There was definitely something going on. All along the bank, children flocked to the barges. She grinned at the cheekiest, who jumped into the water, swam across and attempted to steal from the cargo. In the distance was the unmistakeable sound of heavy machinery unloading the assorted jumble of globules, bulky laptops, ancient smartphones and screens. Excited, she picked up pace and headed toward it as fast as she could walk, constantly glancing over her shoulder in anticipation of being followed by local BP.

At the point in the river where it bent round and flowed back in the direction it had come, there was a small market for the seawall workers. The smell of highly processed meat being barbecued hung in the air, mixed in with the earthy smell of the organic binding agent used to turn the pile of disused detritus into a solid weatherproof wall. The heady mix added to her excitement. A queue of trucks laden with goods from the supersized farms of the nearby East Albion inched their way forward. Their caretaker drivers had disembarked once they were off the roads and were busy replenishing their hungry souls with the chitter chatter of gossip and their hungry bodies with food from the market. A boy who couldn't have been more than four years old tugged on Beth's sleeve and pointed at her hair, which was becoming a cold blue as her body heat dissipated. Intrigued by him, she turned her arm slightly to capture footage of him with her sleeve camera. He grinned with a toothless grin and pulled her towards a woman with a small boat that carried passengers back and forth across the river. They quickly negotiated a price and Beth transferred the ePounds, from globule to globule. In a matter of minutes, she was on the opposite side of the river and ready to explore.

The seawall was impressive. It stood three metres high and was still growing. Obsolete objects were taken from the barges and added to its top and its sides while an automated builder travelled up and down its length filling the gaps between the newly added components with the earthy-smelling bonding agent.

She continued her walk away from the town and towards the geolocation Naomi had given her. The noise of the wind replaced the machinery of the barge port. The icy air was tearing at her skin. She pressed the edges of her jacket together. It sealed tightly and she hugged herself so it would mould to her contours, giving comfort against her rising anxiety. With one hand in the jacket pocket holding her globule and the other manipulating the zoom on the camera in her beanie hat, she filmed the seawall and the surrounding area. At the same time, she added her background commentary, her experiences from the moment she met Naomi to the solar-sailed boat that had brought her across the sixty metres of fast flowing river. It felt good to piece the story together as a live cast, almost like reliving it.

Her globule vibrated under her fourth finger and she turned her head to face the direction it proposed. Flicking the lip of her beanie down in front of her left eye, she focused in on the spot where the globule had shown interest, and to her surprise there was a pair of legs jutting out from the base of the seawall. Inquisitiveness kicked in and she hurried towards them.

When she was within range, a man's voice came through the emergency channel of the globule. It didn't sound as desperate as she'd have expected from a call for help, but it was a rarely used channel and she took it extremely seriously. She paused and looked again. His legs were gradually disappearing into the seawall. Her fast walk turned into a jog and then a run. She expanded her chest and her jacket loosened its grip. She ran as fast as she could along the bank and by the time she reached him, only his ankles and feet were showing.

Exhausted, she shouted to the young girls sitting on a nearby bench. "Hey. Come and help."

"You want him, you catch him," one of the girls shouted back, while the rest of them overtly ignored her.

"What the—" She stopped shouting and shook her head. "Bloody kids," she added under her breath.

Torn between casting the children and responding to the pleas for help, she called into the small gap where his legs were. "Hey there. I'm here. Please, tell me what I can do?"

An echoey voice replied. "There's a leash in my stuff. Tie it to my ankle."

Beth scanned the area and found his belongings: a small bag and a trowel in a heap on top of a paddleboard a few metres along the base of the seawall. Interesting. Inside the bag was the leash, which attached leg to board. Beth grabbed it, ran back and secured it to one of his ankles. "Hey. You're good to go," she shouted.

"Thank you," he replied. "There's a child lost in here. I must find him before they pour in the damn binding agent."

Suddenly, all her attention was on this man. "Oh my god. What are you telling me? Are you saying that he'll die? Inside this wall?"

"You'd better believe it."

And with that the ankles and feet vanished as if he'd been swallowed. Occasional whistles and indiscernible shouts came from within and what remained of the leash in the outside world got shorter. Beth gripped it and held tight to prevent it being dragged in to the earthy-smelling ramshackle construction in front of her. The end of the leash inched closer and closer to the gap into which the man had crawled, and his shouts became more rapid and more distant. The leash tugged at her, slipping slightly through her sweaty hands. She hesitated. Should she hold tight or should she let him loose? Images of a small, rigid boy trapped by the bonding agent flashed through her mind, rapidly followed by images of herself slowly choking to death inside the wall. She couldn't leave him to rescue the boy on his own. That would be cruel beyond belief. She looked across to the young girls. They were swaggering away with their backs to her. With a resolve she didn't really believe, she pushed her hand and then her arm into the hole, desperately trying to keep a hold of the leash.

It kept tugging and she yanked it back towards her. The man was too strong and too determined to find the lost boy. She had no choice. She crawled in behind him, knowing that she must not go beyond the point where her ankles and feet left the outside world. The mechanical sound of the autobuilder grew louder and louder until it was replaced by the sound of gushing liquid. The pungent stink of the binder filled the air. A little bit of bile burnt the back of her throat. The leash tugged. She held her breath and slowly she crawled. Hard edges of discarded tech cut into her knees while her elbows sunk into the soft binding agent. Awkwardly and slowly she shifted herself along. It was only a centimetre at a time, but each tug and each shift felt like a lurch into the unknown. Tethered, they crawled forward. The man shouting and Beth concentrating on her ankles. While she could feel the cold air on them, she knew she was safe, at least from getting lost and being unable to quickly find her way out. The leash pulled sharply, surprising her, and she felt her bladder spasm. She hoped she hadn't pissed herself. The leash tugged once more and she crawled again, only this time she felt the cool air disappear from her ankles. She shouted. "Please. No more. Please. Stop."

The man shouted back. "Two more centimetres and I've got him."

"Hey. Hello. Didn't you hear the binder being poured in?"

"Yes, but it takes a few minutes to solidify. There's still time."

Beth kicked off her left boot so she could feel the air on her toes and inched forward again. The leash was taut and she could feel it stretching. Hoping with all her heart that it didn't snap, she held her grip and dug her knees into the ground to stop from being dragged any further in. There was a shout from deep inside. This time the high pitch of a boy, answered by the deep shout of the man on the end of the leash.

"Got him," he shouted.

Beth crawled backwards as fast as she could through the small tunnel that the boy had dug and the man had expanded. The leash jerked as she moved faster than the man and boy at the other end and every now and again the man would shout to remind the boy that the earthy bonding agent was in the process of setting and they had to speed up. As soon as Beth was outside the wall completely, she knelt in front of the entrance, gasping. The leash was slack, but the last metre was easy enough for them to navigate without it.

A man with long, lank, black hair appeared, followed by a small boy.

"You saved our lives," he said as he went to hug her.

Conscious of how dirty she was, she stepped back slightly and surreptitiously brushed her hand across her crotch, checking for any dampness. Dry. She smiled a crooked smile and laughed. "Honey, it's all in a day's work. I'm Beth, by the way. It's nice to meet you."

"Tam," he said. "And, this is…" The boy he was about to introduce had scarpered. "Bloody idiot kids. They go digging inside that thing before it's properly set because it's easier, but it's so much more dangerous and so many of them get trapped and die."

Beth swallowed hard. "So, it's true. But why? It's horrendous."

"It's what happens. Where there's money to be made 'n' all that."

Beth studied him. He was quite handsome in an unusual kind of way. The lank hair was probably a result of the heat and the fumes from the bonding agent inside the seawall and the unfashionable length gave him an air of someone with their own mind. His clothes were filthy, again probably because of his rescue, and were as unfashionable as his hair. However, his blue eyes were as clear and sharp as any she'd seen. "Do you mind if I ask? What are you doing here?"

"I dig around the edges, salvaging the stuff I need."

"To do what?"

"Don't be so nosey."

"Oh, why ever not? I just saved your life."

"Good point," he said. "And now you want to know if it was worth saving."

She snorted, meaning to laugh but getting it wrong. "Yeah, something like that."

Lost in thought and with his mouth open he rolled his tongue against his teeth, revealing some scarring from an old piercing.

"And?" she said. "Is it?"

"Absolutely." He laughed a gutsy laugh. "I'm one of the best data harvesters on the planet."

"Do you mean hacker?" She shifted uncomfortably on her feet while he stared at her. Hacking was at best a taboo and at worst punishable with the loss of UBI, the Universal Basic Income that everyone received. And in the extreme, hacking could mean imprisonment.

"Data harvesting is a noble profession," he said quietly.

"Hey, I'm not sure it is, is it? Not really."

"Really."

He held his arms high in the air revealing a taut and tanned stomach. "For the greater good, naturally," he shouted.

She turned her head towards the seawall. "So why are you encouraging these kids to go mining?"

"I'm not."

"Well, I think you are. You're here, so at the very least you're a role model."

He squatted down, resting his well-shaped buttocks on his heels. "They need no role models. So long as someone will buy, there will be child miners. And believe me those corporates buy a lot. It's a fact of modern life."

She sat down cross-legged next to him. "What is it that you hack?"

"As I said, we prefer to call ourselves harvesters, but don't worry. I've been called worse." He inhaled deeply. "Can you smell that binding agent setting?"

"Sorry, I didn't mean anything by it."

"Whatever."

"Sorry." She stood up and pointed across to the girls who had returned to the bench. "Why didn't they help you?"

He joined her, standing alongside and looking across at the girls. "Pregnant," he said and then quieter under his breath he added. "Some as young as ten. They're womb factories for the highest bidder."

"That's not just taboo, that's illegal."

"Fake digi-ID," he said and shrugged. "There's a lot of poverty around here. Rumour has it that almost all of the babies end up in the orphanages sponsored by the tech-narcissists. OS most likely."

Beth frowned. "I don't get it. It doesn't make sense."

He rubbed his temples. "The orphanages fund the young mothers to make a new start."

She turned to face him. "Do they buy the babies?"

"Pretty much, yeah."

Beth's investigative radar was on overdrive. She was about to ask if she could film an interview with him when he picked up his board and bag.

"Hey," she said. "Can we talk some more?"

"Sure. Drop me a line if you want."

He held his globule close to her jacket pocket and she felt the buzz in receipt of his details.

"Thanks. I might do that."

He nodded, glanced at his globule and chuckled. "A caster? Who would've guessed? Intriguing."

Beth filmed him paddleboarding across the river and then summoned her own transport to the London train, determined to make contact with him in the next few days.

5

Naomi sighed. The knock on the door had the familiar rhythm of a drone. Only it wasn't a delivery, it was the bailiffs.

Since she'd returned from the protest in England, she'd been actively planning the next Resist & Regain campaign. And then out of the blue, the landlords had been in touch to say her rent was no longer being paid and that they were evicting her. The same day she'd been refused entry to a bus and had to walk home. She no longer existed as far as the East Albion register of citizens was concerned and, as a result, she wasn't receiving Universal Basic Services, no UBS. No healthcare, no access to education, no free travel and most poignantly of all at that moment, no housing. She'd deal with it. What annoyed her more were Gerry's assurances that it would be fine. Platitudes from people who simply asserted that 'everything will be fine' was one of her pet hates. He said it would be a temporary problem and she shouldn't worry, but the smugness of his slick voice made it difficult to believe he wasn't being superficial. She loved him, but sometimes his attitude didn't make that easy. Still, she'd been meaning to move and return her clothes anyway, having been caught up in planning the campaign to such an extent that she'd been living in the same house and in the same clothes for almost a year. It was becoming embarrassing, as her friends frequently pointed out: *You've got a contract. Just swap things.*

The knocking persisted until she opened the door. The bailiff hovered at head height, flashing red and emitting a repetitive beep. She acknowledged it by allowing it to transfer its court order to the house's control panel and it withdrew a few metres, still hovering but no longer red and no longer beeping its annoying alarm.

Gerry called from upstairs. "Is that thing still there?"

"Certainly is. Let's pack up. Let's go."

Not that there was much to pack. Her furniture and her appliances were rented. Before she'd become fully involved in R&R, she'd bought her clothes and changed her style frequently. In the early days of her activism some of the more militant of the movement had been scathing, accusing her of being as much to blame for the state of the world as the tech elite and their corporations. They were wrong, but it had been her blind spot. Well, not so much a blind spot as an itch she had desperately wanted to scratch. She wondered if peer pressure had ended that need for the new, or whether it would manifest in some random way later.

Gerry and Morgan appeared, struggling to carry a fridge wrapped in a blanket with an animated image of a woman wriggling in her sleep. What an unlikely pair of removal men they made. Gerry was far too skinny and impeccably dressed, and sweat was pouring from Morgan's bald head, making his big, bold glasses slip down his nose. She took the fridge from them, enjoying the feeling in her biceps and grinning at the fact that she could lift what the two of them couldn't. She hoisted it on to her left shoulder and walked down the steps and into the garden.

The drone moved to its right and blocked her path. "Illegal removal," it said. "Please replace the item immediately."

"That's crap," she said, pushing her face as close to the bailiff as she could. "You'll throw it away. You'll get a new one for the next person."

The bailiff ignored her.

"Extraction," called Morgan.

"What?" shouted Naomi.

"You're being extracted."

"Very funny."

The bailiff moved in closer, once again flashing red and beeping its alarm. Naomi put the fridge down and pushed the drone away. It moved backwards and returned to its original position as if it was on a piece of elastic. Silent except for its alarm, it continued to flash its red warning. Naomi pushed again and the same happened. She pushed and pushed and it simply shifted away from her and then shifted back again. As close as ever, but no closer. It would have been quite a game if it hadn't been for the fact that you never knew when these things might turn on you and when they did what they might do. She picked up the fridge and the bailiff came to life.

"Illegal removal. Please replace the item immediately."

She nudged it with her shoulder and the alarm became continuous at the same time as tiny fly drones dispersed from its back.

"It only realises you're a person when you're holding the fridge," shouted Gerry.

Naomi dropped it. The flies returned to their base and the alarm returned to its beeping.

Gerry appeared at the door. "Wow, you're invisible unless you're taking stuff away." He scrunched up his boyish face and muttered to himself, "Different datasets, I guess."

Naomi picked up the fridge and immediately there was the whirr of the bailiff's back opening up. "Oh, very well," she said. "You win." She turned around and carried the fridge towards the house. "Worth a try," she said to Gerry as she passed. She dumped it inside the hallway and lifted the blanket. The bailiff was hovering in the doorway flashing, but not beeping. "Here." She threw the blanket to Gerry. "Try some clothes. There's a pile that aren't rented on the bed."

He hurried up the stairs and made a fair amount of noise in the bedroom above them before running back down with an armful of blanket and clothes. "Resist and Regain," he said and bounded past the bailiff and across the garden.

The drone did nothing.

Naomi smiled. "Resist and Regain."

"Resist and Regain," said Gerry and Morgan in unison.

With the few precious possessions she owned, Naomi walked away from the house, pausing halfway down the garden to take one last look. "Bye," she said and shrugged. "Good while it lasted."

Morgan rubbed his stubbly beard and play punched her on the arm. "You'll be nice and cosy with me and Gerry. Our bed is big and its borders are open."

Naomi chuckled. She no longer rose to the bait about her sexual appetites, which in a nutshell were zero. She only got angry with those who used the term 'absent' to describe her preferences, presuming a norm she didn't recognise. "Not interested," she said, and put her arms around Morgan to pull him close. "Cuddles are nice."

He winked. "Three warm bodies close and snuggling. Now, that does sound rather nice."

Out on the street, their pod arrived. It was a house-moving present from Gerry and they all bundled in with the excitement of a new adventure.

"When your tiny hiccup is resolved you should think about moving in more long term," said Gerry. "So we can plan the campaigns more effectively."

Morgan nodded vigorously and Naomi grinned at them both.

The pod pulled up outside the gravelled front garden of their house in Haven Meadows. It was a cheap rental even by Boston standards, not least because the first signs of flooding had appeared nearby. The flat horizon and these identikit houses gave the feeling of a desolate future, and that's what Gerry and Morgan said they loved about it so much. They revelled in the constant reminder of what was to come if things didn't change dramatically and fast.

Gerry took her few possessions to her new bedroom while Morgan made tea from the plants in their back garden and toasted some potato bread.

While they ate, they sat studying the micro thin sheet of SlendTek rolled out along the length of the table. Morgan pressed a finger here and there to expand parts of the country and the associated data. There were pockets of activity everywhere, but the densest areas were those which were close to some kind of flooding, no matter how slight. Morgan skimmed his hand across the map showing how the stories they put out which linked politics, technology and poverty had the greatest effect. He showed them how the targeted news of global disasters linked to local concern were quickly followed by waves of activity and intensified anger. Sadly, these sudden uprisings of action were followed just as quickly by an increased sense of hopelessness as the corporates deployed their bot police to crush the crowds. What was obvious was that to get any kind of protest to happen still required some form of pushing and prodding of the populace.

"This is interesting," said Morgan as he twisted his fingers on Pancras Square. "Look. We managed to find this partially drafted press release on their semi-private server."

A snippet appeared on the techsheet: *Ground-breaking Leadership at OmegaSimera: an Artificial Neural Network named simply as ANN has been secretly operating as the CEO for two years and with huge success. ANN said in a statement, "This is the beginning of a new form of leadership for the world."*

"Good harvesting," said Naomi.

"Hacked, while being paid to harvest."

"Impressive. Whatever you call it."

"Me or this ANN?"

Naomi sat back in her chair. "Both. I meant you." She sighed. "We need more of you. Less of this ANN."

Morgan closed the data bubble and leant forward. "Why? It could be just what we need."

"The OS are ruthless neo-liberal narcissists. From their top most tip to their fossilised foundations."

"But a neural network with the right motives could transform society."

"Indeed," said Naomi. She scraped her chair on the floor as she pushed it backwards and stood up. "More automation. More focus on value. Less on values. Basic services reduced for the ninety-nine percent."

"We are not anonymous," shouted Gerry. "We are Resist and Regain."

Morgan shook his head and sat back down, running fingers this way and that across the map, pulling bubbles of data out but not pausing long enough for anything other than a casual glance before moving on.

"It must be destroyed," said Naomi. "Before it becomes the norm."

"Destruction, destruction, destruction," muttered Morgan as he left the room.

Gerry sidled up close. "We've been crowdfunding for you. Enough to last until your UBS are reinstated."

"I could get work."

Morgan shouted from the next room. "Good luck with that."

"No," said Gerry. "You must spearhead our fight."

Naomi gave Gerry a hug, rolled up her precious SlendTek and retreated to her room, still churning through the possibilities of an ANN that could change the world for the better or an ANN that might accelerate humanity's already downward spiral.

6

In Sleaford, at the border of England and East Albion, Naomi disembarked from the train, pulled on her balaclava and strode through the barriers, undetected. She was relieved, as there was no doubt that if she'd attempted a legitimate crossing she would have been stopped as a non-person. Mary would be waiting for her on the English train, which was expected soon.

It gave Naomi great pleasure that after they'd met in the Retro Bar, Beth had been keeping her abreast of the investigative piece on the abuse of the Minor Miners. Beth had spent the best part of her time gathering evidence, which showed that the wall builders were aware of what was happening. She'd located other walls across north east Europe and Scandinavia and spent days at a time attempting to find similar stories. She found none, but Naomi was still bursting with pride about Beth's emerging inclinations towards activism, whatever Beth did or didn't find. In fact, Beth was the only person, except Gerry and Morgan, who she'd felt comfortable confiding in about her upbringing. Beth truly listened, empathised. Telling Beth about the hurt caused by her parents, who moved to set up and farm the new plains of Siberia created by climate change, was a relief. That they had left behind the ten-year-old Naomi to be brought up by her Lincolnshire born and bred grandfather had echoes of Beth's childhood, of being an orphan. When Naomi had described her grandfather as the man who explained to her at an early age that it was the billionaires who were really 'stealing our country', Beth had chuckled and exclaimed, 'That makes a lot of sense', before apologising when she saw that she had upset Naomi. Beth had become the small glimmer of calm in her otherwise intense life, the one who could soften her emotional edges when they got too hard.

The train arrived and Naomi settled in opposite Mary, who wouldn't stop fiddling with her hair and rubbing the side of her nose. Mary broke their silence. "This is amazing. Thank you so much. To be involved in—"

"Don't mention it. Seriously. Don't."

"I'm sorry. I didn't think. I'm a bit nervous."

"Concentrate on the job and you'll be fine."

Mary attempted some light-hearted observations, which Naomi didn't appreciate, about other members of R&R and their strange habits. Naomi made a point of ignoring her and they fell into silence while the train continued its way along the English-East Albion border to King's Cross station in London, pausing as usual as it waited for its optimal load.

South of Peterborough, the view was spectacular. Small brown birds littered the remains of the Holme Fen nature reserve and, beyond that, the great expanses of water shimmered in the sunshine. The floods stretched out on both sides of the train, on both sides of the border, and were as beautiful as they were catastrophic.

Naomi's thoughts drifted. R&R had made several attempts to hack deeper into the OmegaSimera systems. They'd patiently gathered all the public, semi-public, and leaked data they could track down and their best harvesters had scrunched it until there was nothing more they could squeeze out. Each time they thought they had enough and made their move to hack the OS system they managed to trip a different alarm and were blocked. Sometimes, they'd even set off a retaliation, which led to lost time repairing and retrieving their own systems. Naomi looked at Mary. When R&R came to the conclusion that they required a different strategy, Naomi had only hinted to Beth what the next course of action was that they were planning. Beth had been intrigued and wanted to join her, but she felt protective of Beth and knew it was job for a resistance movement, not a caster. Naomi enlisted this young woman who sat opposite her, a dedicated member of R&R who worked for OS as part of the original OSANN team. Mary was a valuable asset for Resist & Regain's plan, an employee with a high degree of access to their headquarters, an employee who had become disillusioned.

Before long, the land was no longer flooded and, in her head, Naomi turned to her plan to infect the ANN, going over every detail time and time again as the fields and towns passed by, slowly replaced by the city.

At King's Cross, the reality quickly unfolded. They strolled through the pedestrianised streets, past the market stalls and between the many tall corporate headquarters. The BP moved back and forth in front of the buildings and out to the edge of the pavements and back. Naomi slipped on her balaclava as they reached the top of the slope and stepped into Pancras Square. Its fabric got busy displaying abstract moving images and Naomi smiled to herself at what you could get away with if you were bold enough to take advantage of their weaknesses. Mary let out a small gasp, but otherwise kept her head down and didn't acknowledge the hooded woman walking beside her. Fleetingly, Naomi wished it was Beth with her. She looked up high, following the columns of fruit and vegetables growing up the external iron girders towards their destination, the penthouse with its top lip jutting out, displaying its overhang of vines, emphasising its ostentatious presence. It was an impressive sight and one that she must have walked past many times and missed by not bothering to look up at her surroundings. She made a mental note that a good activist must always be attentive to the edges of the world, human and manufactured, if they want to find weaknesses to exploit.

They passed through the BP on the front door of OS HQ and she pulled off her balaclava, positioning herself half a pace behind Mary. As they walked past the oversized portrait of the founder and CEO, everyone held their globule up to experience the augmented reality enhancement of this unfeasibly handsome individual called Kai. It was a weirdly reverent act. They were seemingly transfixed by his eyes, which really did watch you wherever you went. Naomi dropped her gaze to the back of Mary's legs. She needed OS to think she was a guest who was suitably intimidated by the corporate giant's HQ, that she was a visitor who would be happy to simply join the throng of workers moving from one meeting to the next as they strategised their moves on the global stage. Or, as Mary had described them, 'preparing to emit instructions to their army of mercenary coders and engineers, all keenly waiting to bid for the next piece of work.'

At the automated reception desk, Mary dutifully signed Naomi in. Naomi allowed the bots to take her biometrics. They would try to track her, but she'd be protected once she was wearing her balaclava again. She was relaxed. Morgan had harvested footage from inside the building so she was well prepared. The ANN was in the basement. Cleverly, the only way of getting there was via the executive suite on the penthouse floor, and access to that was limited to those with special status, such as Mary. They had to go up to the penthouse, cross it, and then descend in the private lift. The purpose of the plan was simple: to compromise the understanding the ANN had of the outside world and the place of OS in it. Success relied on the building security's over-reliance on the BP.

Mary led her through the barriers and into the belly of the beast, as Beth had unhelpfully described it, and as the doors of the lift opened, displaying the CCTV of the empty room at the top, they both breathed a sigh of relief and stepped inside. The silence in the lift was oppressive, but Naomi couldn't think of anything to say that wouldn't be too trite or give the game away.

At the top they casually left the lift. Mary was still within the bounds of her security clearance and Naomi was wearing her balaclava. They strode across the heavily carpeted floor of the penthouse, which Morgan's footage had showed was hardly ever occupied, to the express lift, one of them permitted and the other invisible.

Naomi was about to call the express lift to take them down to the ANN when Mary stopped her. "Me," she said.

Naomi shifted uneasily from one leg to the other as they waited for its arrival. She wiped away the sweat dripping from her scalp. "This fucking balaclava itches. It stinks. Musty. Damp wool," she whispered.

Mary whispered back, "Do you think the ANN might know exactly what's happening?"

Naomi glared at her and she stopped speaking. Maybe it was patiently waiting for them to arrive, but there was no other way. If there had been, Morgan would have found it. They had to go deep down there where, unconnected to the outside world, the simulation that the ANN used to plan the running of the corporation was housed. It commissioned the mercenary OS harvesters to fill any gaps in its knowledge and she was all geared up to subvert that usual learning process by finding the access point and injecting her own data. If all went well, a seismic shift in one of the most ruthless organisations in the world would begin and Resist & Regain, with its newly agreed 'nurturing resistance' symbol of an Ω cupped in a pair of hands, would take its place in history. She drew a deep breath, to hold on to the hope that there would be enough time for them to escape and get back to East Albion undetected. Not only that, but she could then give Beth the raw material for the cast of the decade.

The lift arrived and she was about to step in when her balaclava was pulled from her head by someone from behind. Mary screeched in surprise. Naomi spun around and was confronted by a human security guard. The guard grabbed her shoulders roughly and turned her to face the main lift. She tried to pull herself free from the grip of this formidable woman, but couldn't. BP arrived and all but one disappeared out of sight behind them. The guard pushed Naomi to the lift and shoved her inside. Mary was already cowering in the corner. During the silent descent to the reception area, Naomi was frantically trying to think of what she should do.

A light on the guard's arm flashed orange and she touched the bud in her ear. She nodded and pulled Mary towards her. "Little miss. We are going to cancel you completely. Obviously, you're dismissed with immediate effect. But, better than that, all of your OS globule accounts are terminated. You will have no communication with anyone. Listed as a person to be avoided. No account. From anyone. Ever. Digitally severed." She shoved her face up close to Mary's and with an open mouth she chewed her gum loudly. "I–so–lated. That's what you fucking are. We own everything. There's no escape. One small edit and you're history. Alone. Erased." She cackled. "De–ceased. The dead one."

Mary's eyes were wide and her mouth was open, but she said nothing. The guard clicked her fingers at the BP. Mary looked at Naomi, full of fear. There was nothing Naomi could do.

"Take her to my office," said the guard.

She turned to Naomi. "You. With me."

Naomi was escorted to the reception desk where she was told to wait. It was an unnecessary instruction, given that she was surrounded by BP and their riot drones.

She sat still, wishing that she could calm her heavy, sporadic breathing and racking her brains to think of something she could do for Mary, knowing that neither was possible.

She'd been sitting there for what seemed like hours when the guard returned and indicated that she should leave the building.

"Your lucky day," she said. "Dunno why, but then we never do."

Naomi coughed.

"The BP want me to let you go. What do you think to that?"

Naomi didn't respond, deciding it was simpler to stay silent after witnessing the vitriol the guard had spewed onto Mary.

The guard continued, almost as if she was talking to herself. "It'll be that bloody ANN. My nephew explained neural networks to me once. Well, he tried. Did you know they can't tell you how they make decisions? Simply that they have."

"I see," said Naomi, not wishing to antagonise the stupid woman.

"So, you're free to go." The guard paused. "*If* I do what it tells me."

"Will you?" asked Naomi.

"There's no record of your existence. Although, you blatantly do exist. Apparently, there's nothing we can do to you."

"And Mary."

"She's finished."

Naomi sucked in her cheeks to prevent herself from reacting.

The guard's eyes narrowed. "If I had my way, we'd teach you a lesson in the storeroom and then throw you into the gutter. But it seems those days are gone."

Naomi stood up so quickly that she thought she might trigger a defensive reaction from the BP. Thankfully, they remained where they were and she turned towards the open front door.

"Wait," called the guard, and then beckoned to a BP.

The bot responded to her command and as it took up position, she grabbed Naomi's arm. Naomi instantly tried to pull away, but she was strong. Too strong even for Naomi. The guard clicked her fingers and a needle shot out of the tip of the BP's finger. It injected Naomi between the two places that the guard was holding, expertly finding a vein without causing any noticeable sign of its intrusion into her body.

"Now I feel better," said the guard. "You're free to go."

Naomi bit her lip and although she had no idea what had just happened, she set off towards the door, quickening her pace as she went. Her breathing became more and more rapid. Keep going, she urged herself. Keep going. Her eyes were firmly fixed on the square outside, cursing the fact that even once she reached it, she was still on private land and subject to their rules. She wouldn't be completely safe until she reached publicly owned space. No matter. She reached the door, walked out on to the steps and down into the square. She was free.

"Shit," she shouted.

She stormed off to find a safe place to rest and to call Gerry and Morgan, hoping that one of them would have an idea of what had been injected into her and more importantly how to neutralise it.

7

Tam had finally invited Beth to his place in an East Albion town called Withernsea. It was a ramshackle affair. Two old cottages attached to an old lighthouse, which bizarrely had been built some way back from the seafront. She'd only seen it via her globule and in video clips and she suspected he had only shown her the best bits. He said he liked it because it had been cheap, partly because of the state of repair, but mainly because of the high risk of flooding. He also said that if it did become flooded and he had to move out of the cottages and into the tower, he'd be fine living at the top. At thirty-nine metres he'd be safe for a few years yet.

As she approached the cottages, her globule buzzed with his signature code confirming that she was close, and she was thrilled as she turned into his garden to see that he was standing outside of his front door waiting for her.

"Hey. Hello to you," she said as he opened his arms to hug her. She stepped forward, put her arms around him and pulled him close. There was something beautiful about the fact that they'd not met in person since she'd seen him paddleboarding across the river. He smelt of vanilla mixed with soil. It was a nice smell. She was pleased to see his hair had more bounce in it than when they'd first met. It was something she'd gently teased him about, hoping he'd take the hint and rectify any lack of personal grooming. On her part, she'd freshly dyed her own and it was a most glorious shade of deep pink that fluctuated in and out of a silvery grey and through to black as it reacted to the blood vessels on her scalp. "What a big day," she whispered into his ear.

"The first of many," he said and grinned. He had good teeth. "It's so good to see you," he added and then quickly let go of her.

"Come in. Tea?" he asked.

It had been lovely, taking the time to get to know one another properly. He'd helped her with the Minor Miners cast, although each round of feedback had taken him a while to send, and usually raised more issues than it helped conclude. Such as, whether the evidence she'd obtained truly substantiated her claims beyond the provable fact of kids being encased in the solidified bonding agent. He was particularly hot on her proving her accusations that the wall builders were complicit in the deaths. On several occasions he'd also pressed her to be absolutely certain that she really understood who would get hurt by it, and how that might manifest itself. It was a slow and irritating process, but she was grateful for his insights and turned on by his wisdom. And that wasn't all. Taking advantage of the globules' twinning features, they'd discovered a mutual interest in old-fashioned music streaming sites and a similar strong distaste for the recent trend of on-the-fly machine generated music created to match your profile. Tam called the two of them Luddite lovers. She was most definitely not anti-technology with all its benefits and didn't subscribe to what she understood Tam's definition of a Luddite to be, but she'd decided not to challenge him on that. And, unsure if he meant they were lovers that were Luddites, or lovers of Luddites, it was a conversation she had avoided, preferring to let the tantalisingly erotic tension it caused to flourish.

In his usual practical manner he invited her to his study. The three-minute climb up the spiral stone staircase left her a bit breathless. He passed her his mug and, putting his hand flat on the door, it clicked open, revealing the mess of his sanctuary. He stepped over the crap strewn across the floor and closed the door behind him.

"The views from the very top are amazing," he said. "I'll show you later."

He dragged a battered wooden chest from behind the sofa. "It doesn't look much, but it is my most precious possession," he said in a reverential tone.

It was lined with a metal mesh and housed a glass container full of shimmering orange gel.

"My secret computer. Meet ALANN," he said.

"Alan? Who is Alan? You haven't told me anything about someone called Alan."

"Artificial Local Anonymised Neural Network."

"Oh, I see, ALANN. It's like an ANN, but more introverted," she said and giggled.

"Exactly."

"Maybe it's more male?"

The corners of his mouth turned up in a cheeky smile that was even more enticing in real life than it had been on her globule. And that was saying something. He beckoned her closer to show her what he was doing while explaining, a little formally, all about ALANN.

"Over months of experimentation and using the knowledge I gained working on prototype ANNs, I painstakingly constructed this machine. Nothing travels through the air, keeping the data safe as it flows from the gel to the processor and so on."

Pausing, he smiled before continuing. "It is shielded from the authorities and I keep it hidden. Only I, and now you, know it exists."

He rummaged around in a desk drawer until he found the leads that connected the gel to the processor.

"This island of technology, cut off from all the other interconnected devices around the world, should allow us to analyse the data I've harvested on the orphanage, without worrying about being discovered."

He intrigued her, even when he was being a bit pompous, explaining his tech. Pushing the leads into the gel and attaching an old battered screen and keyboard, he assembled his ramshackle machine. It was strange to see him type rather than speak, but he explained that this is what he had wanted: a computer that felt as if it was from a different age. Beth was impressed. It was Tam to a tee. The gel changed colour to a deeper orange as he swiped the screen. Images and data flashed by rapidly.

"Look," he said with a big smile. "No breaks in the data flow. The gel didn't change colour, signifying its pristine condition." He grinned and placed his globule on the charging-sheet. "I'm satisfied it hasn't been tampered with. Now to take a covert copy of its data while the globule recharges. My little modification." The gel turned lime green. "Look at that intense processing activity now the data is safely within the protected confines of my computer."

They stood side by side, arms touching, watching the gel gently fluctuate in colour. The atmosphere was electric, a taboo machine investigating the narcissists, coupled with some tantalising thoughts about the man who had built it. Beth could see the tips of her hair betraying her body's reaction.

"Hey, can I have a look?" she whispered.

"Look?"

"At the tech-tattoo. You know. While we wait. If you see what I mean."

He grinned. "You've seen it," he said.

"Not in the flesh." She blinked.

"We need to keep an eye on this." He hesitated. "At least one eye," he added.

Beth kept her eyes firmly facing ALANN, but fumbled around with Tam's shirt, undoing a button before turning to face him. "Come on," she said and tugged. "Reveal the body now. Or maybe… it'll be never."

He coughed.

"The tattoo of the bodies, silly," she quickly added.

He wasn't forthcoming but neither did he back away so she continued to undo his buttons. As she helped him off with his shirt, his smell got stronger, and nicer.

"There. That didn't hurt, did it?" Her hair was now a dark grey rather than silver and certainly not pink.

He touched the ends and said, "I like it."

"C'mon, let's see it in all its glory then."

On each side of his torso, on his chest and down to his stomach, were tattoos of a human body. On the left-hand side was the front view and on the right the rear. It was as if two corpses had been laid next to one another. They were anatomically androgenous, but with otherwise fine detail. When he'd first shown her on the globule, she'd been fascinated in a way that surprised her, and seeing it on his body and seeing them move as he moved, it was as if they'd come alive.

"Incredible," she said as she drew the tip of her finger around the edge of each tattoo in turn.

Tam punctured the moment with a gasp. "Look," he said. "ALANN's found it."

Beth stopped and turned her attention to the computer.

He placed the palm of his hand on the screen to stop it processing. "There. Subsystem. Conqueror. Brothers."

"Where is that?"

"Northumberland National Park. Kielder Water. Two hundred and forty kilometres."

Beth unzipped her bag and pulled out the drone that Naomi had sent her. According to Morgan, it was a supercharged caster drone, which had long-range surveillance capability from piggybacking its signal off the old unmonitored 5G network. She handed it to Tam. "Hey, shall we take a look?"

"What? Send it up there to the orphanage?"

"Yeah. Why not? Naomi tells me it can travel up to two hundred and fifty kilometres per hour."

"There and back in roughly two and a half hours, taking into account a generous twenty-five percent adjustment for today's weather," said Tam, showing off his mental arithmetic.

"Plus, the time to explore," she added.

"Let's do it," he said. "Do you know how to tell it where to go?"

"Sure, I'm not stupid you know. What do you take me for?"

He flinched.

She turned her globule into a globe and found the location on its surface. Pressing the spot against the tiny opening on the side of the drone to direct it. There was no need to control it by hand. When it arrived it would alert her.

"Shall we launch it from up top?" said Tam. "I can show you the view, too," he added and smiled.

They climbed the final flight of stairs.

Inside his watchtower were low shelves of old photos and bric-a-brac. He noticed her glancing at them. "Family heirlooms," he said simply. "C'mon, let's set this free."

It disappeared with its high-pitched whine quickly vanishing into thin air.

The view across the top of the houses and out to sea was as spectacular as Tam had promised during their many calls, but he hadn't prepared her for the view looking back inland and the encroaching floods from the River Humber. It was if a dirty blue snake was slowly slithering its way across the land to the sea. She shuddered and Tam put his arm around her.

She held still to encourage him, before easing herself from his embrace. "You never did explain exactly why you call those your tech-tattoos," she said.

"Neatly changing the subject."

"Neatly avoiding the subject."

He slipped his shirt back on. "I can show you," he said, so quietly that she wasn't sure she'd heard correctly.

"You can show me?"

He chewed his lip. "Promise you won't judge me?"

"You know me well enough by now to know I won't. Don't you?"

"Guess so," he mumbled. "Come on then. It's downstairs."

Making sure she had her globule, she followed him down the spiral stairs. He was descending slower than he'd climbed, which was odd. Every now and again he hesitated as if he wasn't sure of what he was doing. At the bottom he led her to the cottages and to his immaculately tidy bedroom. Even the bed had been made. Impressive. Sexy.

"It's a prototype," he said, holding up a jet-black full-length body suit. "SlendTek with enhancements."

"Did you make it yourself?"

"Yeah. But never tried it."

"Oh, why not?"

"Nobody to test it with. Nobody I could trust, that is."

"Yourself?"

"It syncs with the tattoos so can't be me."

"Tam. Are you suggesting testing on me?"

"Would you?"

"Well, I might. What does it do?"

"Put it on and I'll show you."

"Please tell me."

"Wherever I touch the tattoo it touches you," he said quietly.

She dreaded to think what colour her hair had become. "Do you mean—"

"Try it," he said. "Please?"

Beth checked her globule. "We have forty minutes," she said and grabbed the suit from him. "Turn around."

He did, and she quickly stripped off and pulled the skintight suit on, making sure everything was lined up and tucked into the right places.

"I'm ready," she said.

"Lie down."

"Really?"

"It'll work better."

She did as he asked and watched as he took a mini-globule from his pocket and began to roll it along the spine of his tattoo. She felt a corresponding warm tingle up her own spine which then moved between her shoulder blades as he rolled it back and forth. She closed her eyes and relaxed, enjoying the sensation across different parts of her body. He explored pretty much everywhere except the obvious, which was a nice and pleasant surprise. After what seemed like an age of pleasure, she opened her eyes to see him staring at her with a knowing smile. She blinked and nodded small nods of appreciation and she hoped of encouragement. He got the message and moved the globule to what her great-grandmother would have called her intimate parts. As he rolled it around in tiny slow movements he squeezed, which signalled the suit to apply pressure. She was totally lost in the moment.

Sometime later, while he was directing the suit to gently massage her legs, her globule informed her that the drone had arrived. He joined her on the bed and together they watched the footage come streaming through. Sure enough, there was the headquarters of the *Out of This World Orphanages*. Next to it was another building with considerably smaller signage: *Star System Research Lab (Mars Section)*. The drone flew up close, over the roof of the lab and into the woods behind. It flew at ground level almost touching the floor, its comms-dot blinking. Programmed to investigate, it must have detected something it did not recognise and was busy capturing images to consult with its fellow drones. It hovered in front of a thicket of bushes before landing and then inched its way through to a clearing where it raised itself off the ground. Cages full of weird looking animals were fixed to posts with heavy-duty chains. The captives looked familiar and strange at the same time; normal pigs, but distorted. Their proportions weren't right. Some had heads that were way too small and some too big. Others had six legs or three eyes. Beth shuddered and took control of the drone. Immediately it plummeted, hit the ground and failed to respond.

"Quick. Disconnect it," he said.

She severed the connection and they both collapsed on to the bed.

"What did you do?"

"Nothing. Honestly. It just stopped. I connected it to my globule and it crashed."

"You must have done something."

"What the fuck?" she said through nervous laughter.

"I've no idea, but that's some scary shit they've got going there."

"Hey, what do we do? Any ideas?"

"Lie low and hope they don't trace it back to you. Naomi gave you it, you said?"

"She did, and I'm sure she said that she got it from Morgan."

Tam went quiet for a few minutes and Beth let him think.

"I reckon we'll be fine," he said. "Don't see how they can know it's you if it collapsed the moment you connected. More likely to have happened because of Naomi's status issues."

"Come here," she said.

They cuddled, which led to intense touching and fondling for real this time until eventually they fell asleep.

When she woke and watched him sleeping, she decided to stay, in case there were any reprisals.

They talked, ate and drank, laughed and had lots of wonderfully uninhibited sex. They experimented for hours with the suit, and only occasionally did Beth get annoyed that sometimes Tam seemed to be more interested in the technical aspects than he was in her.

The days went by and the BP didn't come knocking. They agreed that the danger had passed and that it was safe for Beth to travel.

As she was leaving, Tam gave her the suit to take with her. "Do you mind?" he asked.

"Hey, why would I mind? I do not mind at all." She kissed him. "Not. At. All."

8

EXPLORING AND experimenting with Tam and his suit was gloriously tender and superbly erotic. They explored her physical likes and dislikes, but the most surprising and electric of adventures were those where they played out her fantasies. The coming together of the suit and her imagination was deliciously potent. However, big things were afoot in the wider world and the time came to revert to casting.

She released the finished piece and waited. Nobody picked it up. No syndication. Nothing. It was as if it had never been published. She pressured R&R for help, but they were too busy building their own reputation and membership. Dejected, she decided that there was nothing else for it but to earn an income by writing short, punchy pieces for other people, of mediocre interest and little substance. It wasn't an easy decision.

As she'd set out that morning, Tam had once again encouraged her to be patient, reminding her that it took a long time to build a reputation. Unless she… He never completed that sentence.

Beth was surprised when the train company's BP didn't collect any fare from her at the A12 crossing into East Albion, just before Stratford Station. They'd undertaken the standard checks on everyone and she had dutifully offered her globule, which the BP had scanned. It had welcomed her home, thanked her for travelling with them and then with no indication of a payment being taken it had moved on. Confused because East Albion wasn't her home, she double checked and it was indeed a free journey. A little unnerved, she watched London speed by.

The dense city landscape transformed into countryside and she split her attention between the wonderful view and her globule. She wanted to make sure the launch was still going ahead. There'd been rumours that it was a hoax, that it was one big publicity stunt for a new OmegaSimera product rather than the promised dawn of a new age, as their PR was calling it. The message didn't change. This was a monumental moment in the history of mankind. The beginnings of artificial neural networks and Homo sapiens working together hand in hand to make the world a better place. ANNs and humans, as the publicity stated, could transform society together.

Shortly after Manningtree station, as the train trundled along the raised track and over the flooded River Stour, the excitement grew louder and louder. There was a real buzz in the carriage about the OS announcement. *Have you heard about the freeship? A super-tech city on the sea, with its own laws. That's why I'm going to Felixstowe of all places. What could it mean? Was it really the time for humans and robots to co-exist? Hadn't they seen the films? Didn't they realise what they were setting loose?* Whether on the side of the excited optimists or the anxious pessimists, they all agreed that this was a turning point in history and not to be missed. Good-natured arguments along the length of the carriage erupted and then rapidly dissolved. Beth had her head down and her ears open, recording snippets for the cast she planned on writing after she'd seen the launch of Freeship One later that day and heard the Proclamation of Liberation from Kai, the OS founder and CEO.

In Ipswich she changed trains along with all the other travellers. She alone was stopped by a railway BP, which stepped in front of her.

"Explain why you have no ticket or permission to be in East Albion," it demanded, its tone unfriendly and its increased height and width imposing.

"The border BP took no payment and I've only just realised it didn't validate my entry from England to East Albion either," she explained.

"You do not have permission to be here or a valid ticket to travel," the BP stated again.

In a panic she pulled on her balaclava and tried to walk around it. The BP blocked her. She took out her globule and pressed the indentation to show that she was a caster. The BP shrunk back to its normal size and scanned. Her globule vibrated. She had permission to travel and a payment had been taken, along with a considerable fine.

At the docks, there was a real party atmosphere. "Look," she cast, "OS has laid on assorted free drinks and the most gorgeous spread of the finest foods possible. The Solein burgers smell exceptionally enticing." She bought a cone of jellyfish chips, one of her favourites, and filmed the drones filling the sky with blue, red and orange vapours. "OS colours, of course," she commented over the footage of her cast. The most amazing fluid flights of hundreds of tiny drones flying in formation spelt out messages of hope and inspiration, promising a new wonderful era of human evolution. She stopped casting and wandered through the crowds towards the dock and the freeship. The local BP were hardly visible, letting the crowds enjoy their day out without interfering, although the chances were that the drones overhead were more than mere entertainment. Freeship One was at the dockside. All twenty-five decks of it topped by a transparent spherical crow's nest on a long metal arm. It sat like a domineering skyscraper. On its bows the footage of its journey across the ocean played out, film of the huge waves crashing against it with a long line of drones trailing behind, flying, diving and fishing.

Beth's globule buzzed with Tam's signature code.

"Hi," he called across the crowd.

"Isn't this completely fantastic?" she said as he arrived.

"Absolutely. You look wonderful."

"I meant this freeship. But now you mention it, it's so good to see you too."

"It's been too long."

She winked. A habit she'd picked up from him. "I felt you."

His eyes dulled. "The suit doesn't count."

"The Minor Miners cast was great. Or at least, I thought it was. I couldn't have done it without you and your clever snooping, and your wonderful advice. Thank you so much."

The crinkle around his eyes that she loved so much returned and they turned to look at the ship sitting proudly in the docks just at the moment the film of it crossing the ocean stopped and Kai appeared. He was stunningly handsome and exceptionally well groomed, as Beth had imagined he would be. His smile was one of those with a heady mixture that conveyed, *You can trust me with your life* and *We'll have a lot of fun along the way*. It was no surprise that he and his fellow superstar tech-business leaders had been recently nicknamed the Narcissists, a tag they didn't seem to mind. As the saying goes, 'if you think you're a narcissist, you probably aren't'. They didn't and they were.

Kai clapped his hands once and silence fell across the crowd.

"Today," he said and then paused to turn his head from left to right as if he was looking for someone in the crowd. "Today is the most monumental moment in the history of mankind. Today will be remembered as the day humanity threw off its shackles and freed itself from itself. Today is the birth of the freeships. The freedom of the oceans has been tried. Plenty of people before us attempted to live a life at sea and failed. We have the wealth, the know-how, and the ability to rise above the restrictive regulations. We will make it happen." He waited for the whooping and cheering to subside.

Beth whispered to Tam, "Hey, isn't he totally brilliant?"

Tam raised his eyebrows, but Kai continued before he could reply.

"For two years OSANN, OmegaSimera's artificial neural network, has had complete control of running the company. As its CEO."

There was a palpable intake of breath from the crowd.

"The two most successful years in our company's history."

Loud cheers.

"Today, OSANN will officially take control as CEO and I will step down. I will set sail on Freeship One to pursue the ongoing progress of humanity, without any petty national restrictions. We will turbocharge nature's evolution. We will accelerate the natural development of plants, animals and humans. Onboard we have many ANNs known as the Ls, specially crafted to run complex systems such as your governments. Each one can be deployed to look after different territories, but all with a common ethical protocol we call the Loop, the Ls Omniscient Operability Protocol. This forms the basis of how they operate. The rules, if you like. It will act as the heart and soul of our emerging network of Ls across the world. It will be the common conscience, steering them all towards the elimination of poverty and disease and the equality of all. Best of all, it too can evolve as it learns more about what works. The Ls implement the Loop and then feed it with the real-world results, which it then uses to improve itself. The iterative transformation of society. Isn't that truly marvellous? Today, we also make you the solemn promise that we will always fund whatever infrastructure is required to maintain the Ls in every part of the world so that everyone can benefit from them. Rich or poor."

Beth squeezed Tam's arm.

"Fellow humans," said Kai. "We are truly entering the age of artificial intelligence. Life for Homo sapiens has never looked so good."

Once again, he paused for the cheers and to acknowledge the crowd by slowly moving his head from left to right and nodding once every second.

"Today, we officially launch our very own currency: the OS dollar. The Loop will guide monetary policies. It will set the interest rate across the globe. No longer will your wealth be subject to the whims of your government. We will do what's right for you the individual and for the world as a whole."

"What a performance," said Tam in a deadpan voice.

Beth agreed, unsure of what she really thought, unable to dissociate the images of the orphanage from Kai.

Kai's face faded and fireworks were launched from a flotilla of small boats that had formed a semi-circle around the freeship. From the inside of each exploding firework a drone appeared, darted to a new location and released more fireworks, which in turn exploded releasing smaller drones. Then, more fireworks and still smaller drones. This continued until the sky was awash with smoke and colour and the docks were subsumed by explosion overlapping explosion. All heads were tilted backwards to soak up the spectacle above. Gradually, the noise subsided and the sky returned to its former light grey.

Kai reappeared on the ship's side. "Now, I invite you to join me and my crew aboard Freeship One for the launch party of your lifetime."

"Shall we?" said Tam. "I bet your caster curiosity is peaking right now."

Beth was about to agree that she certainly did want to see around the ship when there was a tap on her shoulder. It was Naomi.

"Hey," said Beth. "What a lovely surprise."

Naomi grabbed her hand. "Surprise? Why?"

"Well, I didn't think you'd approve of all this."

"We don't. That won't stop us from being here."

Tam coughed.

"Oh, I'm so sorry," said Beth. "Naomi, this is Tam. Tam, this is Naomi."

Tam held out his hand.

Naomi barely acknowledged his existence, instead keeping her attention on Beth. "Come with me," she said, grabbing Beth's hand and pulling her towards one of the food stalls, adding casually, "Casting off. No cameras."

At the back of the lean-to was a curtain that any casual passer-by would presume screened off the food storage and preparation area. However, as Naomi pulled it to one side and pretty much shoved Beth inside, it became apparent that this was an R&R hub of technology. Four people were huddled over a sheet of SlendTek, frantically chattering and swiping and muttering instructions under their breath.

"Hey, what's this?" asked Beth.

"Impressive," said Tam from behind her.

One of the R&R coders pulled a quizzical face and asked, with a barb to her voice, "Who? What?"

Naomi replied with a soothing smile. "Beth. A friend. Remember?"

"Tam," said Tam.

The coder shrugged and got back to work.

Beth gave Tam a reassuring glance before turning her attention to Naomi. "What's going on?"

"Gonna prove they're not as good as they think they are," replied Naomi. "Ready?" she added, as the four coders stood up and stepped back from the table.

"Oh, yes," replied the lead woman. "All we need to do is press that button," she added, pointing at a big, round circle in the middle of the sheet.

Naomi nodded. "Beth, why don't you do the honours?"

"Me?"

"Yes." Naomi winked at her. "Wouldn't you like to?"

"Hey, I would."

Tam pushed his way through Namoi and the coders. "No!"

Beth shot him an angry frown.

"Don't you think they might have a *little* bit of surveillance surrounding the freeship?" He pointed at the roof of the lean-to. "Not exactly military grade security, is it?"

Naomi laughed. "So, this is the infamous hacker you've been hanging out with?"

"Not funny," snapped Beth. "Either of you," she added, turning her head from side to side to catch both Naomi and Tam's eyelines. "My choice."

Tam made a move to grab her arm, which she dodged. "Don't be stupid," he said.

Focussing her attention on the lead woman, she asked, "Do I just press the button, then?"

The woman gave her the thumbs up and Beth leant over the sheet, pressed the button and gave Tam a defiant grin.

"Your choice," he said, and at that exact moment, Kai's head on the side of the freeship exploded into a million tiny pixelated fragments, quickly replaced by a single message that ran the length of the ship: *We are Resist & Regain. We are not anonymous.* This was followed shortly after by another: *The Narcissists cannot abandon their responsibility.* Then a third: *Systems can be hacked. Resist & Regain are on your side.* Finally, the word *Always* and the Ω symbol in cupped hands appeared.

Naomi grabbed Beth's hand and Tam took a step back.

Beth removed herself from Naomi's grasp. "That symbol. It's wonderful." she said to neither of them in particular.

Beth grinned. Kai was creepy so it was amusing to see OS taken down a peg or two and the new R&R logo was perfect. "Naomi. What does it mean?" she asked, more for Tam's benefit than hers.

Naomi rubbed her hands together and took an audible breath. "We will resist this onslaught of unfettered belief in the flawlessness and omniscience of artificial intelligence. It's species suicide. We will resist."

"Oh, c'mon," said Tam, but Beth shot him a glance. He shrugged and stopped speaking.

Beth looked at Naomi. "Maybe the Ls can make the world a better place. It's got to be worth a try, isn't it? Don't you think?"

Tam was nodding vigorously, but Naomi was clenching her jaw. "They haven't got a clue. No idea what they're letting loose. If we can hack their systems. What can others do?"

"Only their broadcast, but fair enough," said Tam.

Freeship One let off an extremely loud siren and started to move. It was as if part of the cityscape had started to slide towards the open seas.

"Shit," said Naomi. She scanned the crowd and waved at a small group a few metres away. "Don't use the balaclava," she said over her shoulder as she began to sprint across to her friends.

"Hey. Why not?" called Beth, but she was gone.

Beth grabbed hold of her globule and pressed the indentation. She pushed through the crowd and Tam followed close behind. She was determined to get first-hand footage of this extraordinary event.

They arrived at the dockside as the last of the flanking flotilla were about to set off. "Wait," she shouted, waving her rainbow pulsating globule in the air.

The captain of the boat beckoned for them to leap onboard, and as soon as their feet touched the deck it set off.

"I thought you'd agree with Naomi," said Beth to Tam once they'd found a seat at the front of the boat. "You know, all that stuff about me being too scared of the tech companies to push that piece on the child miners."

"I do worry you're not cut out for the nastier parts of the job," he said. "And pressing that—"

She scowled. "Do you see me the same way that you see technology? You criticise the hell out of it, but you still want it. To be honest, I'm surprised you're still here. Still putting up with me."

"Ouch." He put his hand on her thigh, which she stared at until he removed it. "Whichever way you swing on this one, whether it's up or down, it's not to be missed," he said quietly.

She frowned and felt her forehead wrinkle. A sensation she hated because she knew it made her look ugly. "What do you mean by up or down?"

"Up being the blind belief in technology to solve our problems no matter what the cost, and down being the cautious desire to hold back."

"You've explained this to me already, haven't you? It's proactionary versus precautionary, isn't it?"

"Exactly," he said.

She raised her eyebrows, but kept quiet.

They drew alongside the freeship. There were hordes of people onboard scurrying around the exposed decks pushing and pulling large crates to help the drones steer them into the giant cargo bays. Their boat was moving faster than the freeship and before long Beth could see into the lower deck cabins. Only a few were occupied, by people unpacking their belongings. About halfway down its length there were cabins with bars on the portholes. Inside these Beth was pretty sure she could see rows and rows of cages.

"Hey, look at that," she said to Tam, but it was too late. The captain had steered them away to avoid an oncoming BP boat.

The boat pulled up alongside and a BP riot drone flew across. *Present Your Permissions* was displayed across a screen suspended from its base. Beth stretched out her arm and held up her globule for the drone to see. The 'present your permissions' message was replaced with: *Status Pending - Prepare To Be Boarded.*

The captain of their small boat quickly turned it around, cranked up the engine and sped off towards the shore. Thankfully, the riot drone didn't follow. Beth used her globule's telescope to continue watching the freeship as they sped away and she was sure she caught sight of Kai in the crow's nest, looking directly at her.

9

Beth watched in awe as Resist & Regain campaigned hard against the increasing influence of the ANNs. Despite R&R's efforts, corporation after corporation followed OS and handed over executive control, and those same companies were seeing their profits rise exponentially as a result. The politicians went beyond admiration of the power of the ANNs, almost tipping into a form of worship. Not one of them had broken ranks to criticise or question the ever-increasing free market libertarian interpretation of the taboos, and polling showed that the general public had more trust in an ANN than it did in a human. Naomi called it the hushed reverence of the bribed and coerced. Weirdly, and fortuitously, while Morgan was scanning Naomi to see if the pain she was experiencing was at all related to the injection, a dose of imported painkillers somehow interfered with the nano-tracker that the OS BP had introduced into Naomi's arm. As a result, he neutralised the device that up until then had evaded detection by concealing itself within what appeared to be a biological casing. Beth burst into tears when she heard, surprising herself at how much emotion she'd been holding in.

The nations were about to vote on whether they wanted the Ls to lead them entirely, which prompted Beth to revise her cast: *The Minor Miners of Selby Dam*. The revision was a scathing attack on the selfish greed that technology spawned, cutting deep slashes across the narrative that tech was the green saviour of the planet and asking serious questions about the depth to which humanity would stoop to get what it wanted. Naomi described it as brave, which pleased and petrified Beth in equal measure.

Tam was sitting opposite her. “Yeah, it’s fine,” he said, as noncommittal about this version of the finished piece as he had been about the various redrafts that had led up to it.

“Thanks,” she replied, unsure their relationship would withstand another disagreement about her work and, although she was annoyed with his lack of comment, she was relieved that he’d had the emotional intelligence to be vaguely supportive.

The SlendTek sheet was laid out on her kitchen table with each of their globules resting at diagonally opposite corners. She chuckled at the thought that devices packed full of the latest tech were acting as old-fashioned paperweights.

“What?” asked Tam.

“Nothing. I’m just a little nervous. That’s all.”

“If you gonna do it, you gotta do it,” he said in a fake yet indistinguishable accent. He was nervous, too.

She rolled her shoulders around and leant across to kiss him on the forehead. “It’s no reflection on you,” she said.

“It is. And I’m proud to be associated with you.”

She grinned and under her breath muttered a thank you before giving her globule a good squeeze and placing it in the exact position on the sheet in front of them to send *The Minor Miners* on its way across the networks.

As soon as she published, Resist & Regain picked it up and syndicated it across all their communities and networks. The CEO ANNs reacted instantly. Whether it was a reaction to R&R or to the content, the response from them was ferocious. *They were the saviours that humanity had been waiting for*, they said over and over again until it became a mantra for their supporters. *Beth was nothing more than a mouthy meddler desperate for attention,* they repeated. Beth metaphorically cowered under the onslaught of their abuse.

"It'll die down," said Tam.

"Really? Not so sure myself. They have no concern whatsoever for my mental health."

"Well, they are ANNs," he said, failing to lighten the atmosphere.

"Hey, you don't say. Empathy and compassion are blatantly not one of their strengths. Unless, that lack is their strength."

"Fair point," he said, irritating her with his fence-sitting.

"I'm worried that I pushed things too far. Maybe I thrust the truth in people's faces too starkly. Do you think I was too harsh?"

"I don't think so."

The ANNs began a storm of justification. *Look at our track record on the use of the chains to trace the provenance of our products from source,* they broadcast. *Through manufacture, ownership, and recycling. It is an unprecedented change brought about by our developments.*

Naomi messaged privately. *You hit them front and centre, and it hurt them. You've got them on the run.*

R&R publicly backed her, streaming live footage to show that the child miners did still exist despite claims to the contrary by a handful of politicians.

The ANNs counterclaimed. *Our ethics protocol is dedicated to ensuring no human will be enslaved. If the children want to mine then they should not be stopped.*

The torrential abuse thrown at Beth personally was relentless. She kept quiet and, with Tam by her side, she watched it play out between R&R and the politicians. As night fell it calmed down.

"Well," said Tam with a little too much satisfaction, "looks like the R and R lobbying has been successful, with my lot at least."

Beth nodded in agreement, saddened by her own politicians and increasingly conscious that their two countries were diverging.

Tam held her hand. "England stands alone," he said in a mock Churchill voice, adding in a sinister robotic tone, "with its extreme version of freedom."

She was about to answer when her globule buzzed with the trigger code that she'd agreed with Naomi and for the first time she retaliated. *Make the underpinning ethics of the Loop public, and in detail,* she cast.

This was rapidly countered by the ANNs. *There is no need for such a thing. Nobody will understand it.*

Beth kept her demands brief. *Irrelevant. Do it. We will decide what to do, not you.*

Resist & Regain picked up the thread and went on the attack. *Obey your own rules – equality of all. Publish the protocol.*

The ANNs fought back. *What would be the point? Except to cause confusion and give data harvesters an opportunity to scam OS dollars from anyone foolish enough to think the Loop could be gamed.*

Through the night, Beth and Tam were transfixed as this toxic public relations battle played out, while at the same time Beth continued to be subjected to a torrent of abuse.

"Look. An even spread of troll types," said Tam, pointing at his globule. He was keeping a tally of the trolls' registered level of sophistication; how many were simple bots, neural networks, full-blown ANNs, and all the way up to human. "Two opposing factions are forming. A trend is emerging."

Beth shuddered as he showed her the most vociferous campaign, for her UBI to be withdrawn. *You're wasting your opportunities. Where is the art or the creativity in your piece? To be paid to sit outside the system and hurl rocks is tantamount to treason, and you can't even claim it to be a great piece of academic research.* In amongst these accusations was the trending: *Terminate the Traitor.*

Through the sickening shock of what she'd unleashed, she triggered Morgan's cleverly constructed part-automated, part-human argument generator. It responded to the ANNs, and the less sophisticated bots soon solidified in their allegiance to either OS or R&R. The human trolls also took sides pretty quickly, repeating and amplifying their chosen message.

"Why do you think the mid-range neural networks are taking so long to take sides?" she asked.

"No idea," said Tam. "But it seems significant."

They watched and waited, and slept when they could. As the balance of opinion settled into eighty percent support for OS, Beth became labelled as the freedom killer and nicknamed Molly Coddle by the ANNs, a name soon adopted by everyone, fans and foes alike. Devasted and resigned to failure, she took to her bed.

Sleep didn't come easily and, even after grabbing a few hours of sleep, when she woke, she was emotionally exhausted, but having Tam there was great. What a relief it was to have him brushing her hair, telling her that he loved how the colour got darker the more he brushed. Occasionally he whispered a poetic line, which she was sure he did to see how quickly he could speed up the darkening.

"You have to go," he said, laying the brush on the bed, beside her.

She glanced at it and sighed. "I know, it's such a shame. Maybe a little longer? Please?"

She could get lost in his rhythmic strokes, hair and otherwise, for hours if he'd let her, but he was right. She had an appointment with her doctor. A regular check-up.

When they'd first got together, he'd been surprised by her high-end health care. With English UBI she was able to choose where her tax was spent and she found that with her caster training and implant inhibitors she could tune out any anxiety caused by reducing her contribution to defence. Health was where it was at for her, knowing that things could have been so different for her mum if she'd done the same. Reducing the chances of being killed by any genetic thing, which might have been handed down to her, was worth the constant monitoring of her implants. He listened and disagreed, but took every opportunity to remind her of appointments, and to send her all the latest research coming from the tech companies, OS mainly. It was sweet of him and a tad patronising.

"Go," he said, pushing her gently in the back.

"Will you—" She stopped herself. "Thank you for looking out for me," she said instead.

She grabbed her discarded shirt, pulled it over her head and leapt out of bed, checking her appearance as she headed towards the door.

"Nicely brushed hair."

She shook her head a few times to make it lighten a shade or two.

He followed her to the kitchen and while he was busy making himself a drink she kissed his cheek and left the flat.

The doctor was close by in one of those health pop-ups that came and went depending on the amount of investment that had been made by the local population.

"Beth," called the receptionist. "She's free to see you."

"Thank you," said Beth as she strolled past the desk.

The doctor waited for the algorithms to collate all the information required for Beth's regular check-up. "You've been busy," she said.

"Busy?"

"Molly Coddle."

"Oh, that. Yes." Beth nodded, fixing her gaze on the flickering algorithms at work. This was not a conversation that she wanted with her doctor, who seemed to realise and didn't pursue it.

"Your egg app predicts another twenty-three years of fertility," the doctor said, without looking up from the SlendTek sheet in front of her. "I remember you mentioning at the last check-up that you felt ready to have a baby."

"Yes. I remember saying that. I'm not sure. I think I am."

"You don't need to rush, that's for sure. Very healthy ovaries. I'd wait until we know how this vote goes. Who can tell what the health system will look like?" She hesitated. "Any ideas?"

She had a point about the health system and Beth felt a twinge of guilt about not chatting. This was a doctor who was desperate to appear confident and in control, but failing to hide her human fragility.

The doctor returned to studying the sheet in front of her. "Everything looks fine," she said. "When you're ready to test the compatibility of your eggs to his sperm, let me know. There is a him, I presume?"

"Yes, he's a him."

The doctor explained the new procedures for having a baby and Beth listened in silence until her allotted time was used.

In the reception area, Beth said her goodbyes and glanced at the Med Bank on her way out. If she had a prescription that she relied on, would she donate? She wasn't sure she would.

Outside, she called a trike, and while she waited she mulled over what the doctor had said. It concerned her. Not the baby part, that was fine or at least it was too unknown to worry about. It was the procedures that went with it and the matter-of-fact way the doctor had described the biological compatibility test. There'd also be the ANN assessment of the likelihood that she and Tam would stay together long enough to raise a child. It was all so flaky. After all, the predictions came from the dating app data of her grandmother's generation; who clicked with who and why they'd stayed clicked.

The trike arrived and took her home.

She was lost in her thoughts when Tam met her at the door.

"How did it go?" he asked. "All healthy?"

"I am perfectly healthy and extremely horny."

He grinned. "Really? Now?"

"Get the suit out. Please."

He frowned. "The suit?"

"I want to try out those adjustments that you told me about. You've intrigued me."

He bowed his head. "Madam, your suit is on its way."

10

The female security officer put her glasses on as Beth stepped forward from the front of the queue with globule in hand. She smiled nervously. She was being asked to more and more of these 'invitation only' events, but that didn't mean she was getting used to them. Behind the officer stood the grand but dilapidated six-floor building that had once been a flagship fashion store in the heart of London's West End. To enter you had to be cleared by these fully-fleshed men and women scanning your vitals to ensure you were not, in their words, a terrorist. Beth was not.

The security officer looked at Beth's face, blinked, and looked at her globule and blinked. "Thank you," she said and waved Beth through.

A slickly dressed, smug and grinning Kai was greeting the VIPs as they entered. Beth had been surprised and flattered to receive the invitation, but his presence instantly turned that into an anxious queasiness.

"*Human* security for this extravagant showpiece, for the introduction of Ls to the political system?" she said, with a forced chuckle, hoping that her voice didn't falter.

"Welcome, Beth," he replied. "How nice to see you."

"Thank you," she said, wanting to get away as fast as she could.

He held her hand while he continued with his polished speech. "Inside, each version of the L that is being offered to the English and East Albion's populations has a floor of its own, as if they are market traders setting out their wares. The Leveller, Liberty, Liberation, Locals and Laissez-faire are the choices and each has a different interpretation of the core ethics protocol described by the Loop."

She knew all that, it had been on the invitation. She thanked him again and tried to walk away, but his grip was firm, almost tight. "The vote, which will choose your new leader, is in two days' time and you are privileged to be one of those that the elite of Freeship One has allowed to visit and publicly comment."

"Then I should get going so I can give it my full attention," she said, again hoping her anxiety wasn't obvious. The invitation had stated that, 'she understood what was at stake and was suitably knowledgeable to convey this in terms that the voting public would engage with'. She thought it could well be a trap, but there was no way she was going to pass up the opportunity. Kai's appearance put a whole new slant on that fear.

"Your cast about the child miners has established you as a hybrid between a caster and a fully-fledged influencer. People are keen to hear your opinions on almost any topic. I'm sure you'll do a great job," he said and let go of her hand.

It was true, she had numerous offers in the pipeline for serious investigative work. The thing that puzzled her, apart from her semi-celebrity status, was that her profile was associated with events she'd been nowhere near. Many times she'd been asked about the BP clearing a communal garden of the homeless. She ducked the questions and they moved on, but it niggled. She didn't want to rattle the data cage too hard in case she lost her status and could no longer attend events such as this, so she kept quiet. Did that have anything to do with Kai's intense attention on her? She hoped to find out, and she hoped not to find out.

Laissez-faire occupied the first floor and as Beth reached the top of the escalator she was confronted with the stark contrast between the shoddiness of a disused building and the location for a top-end tech launch. The walls and ceiling were pockmarked with holes from the now absent shelves and signage that had hung there when the building was at its height as a fashionable clothes shop. The walls were covered in rough drawings and sketches, a legacy from the constant stream of homeless inhabitants who had been using the place as a shelter for some years. Piles of discarded shop furniture littered the floor and in the middle of them was the shiny humanoid robot that housed the L, Laissez-faire. Its features were blank. No face, not even a skin tone. Incomplete. It was difficult to imagine trusting such a charisma-free persona.

When a dozen of the VIPs had gathered in the room, Laissez-faire spoke in a silky, androgynous voice. "Welcome," it said. "I am Laissez-faire, which you will know means leaving things to take their own course."

It waited while a few of the audience nodded, mumbled to one another and, like Beth, recorded an observation onto a globule, to accompany the recording of the L.

Kai joined her at the precise moment Laissez-faire continued with the guiding principles of the Loop. "Minimal government spending and interference, to free all private individuals, and to enable business to thrive and drive the economy. As you can see, I am yet to be given physical attributes and the same can be said of my thinking. I am open to you. You can form me in whatever way you wish within those guiding principles. I am yours to mould."

During its next pause, she started to move away from the over-bearing presence of Kai, but he put a gentle, restraining hand on her arm. "Good principles, eh?" he said in a voice that didn't invite a response.

Laissez-faire stood up and finished its speech with outstretched arms. "Elect me as your chief bureaucrat, shape me as you wish and I will work tirelessly to fulfil your dreams."

Beth was shocked at how vigorously most of the VIPs clapped at what was in effect a completely contradictory statement: trust me to run things on your behalf; you'll need to tell me how. "A new low for popularity politics," she said openly into her globule.

"I can see we'll have to keep our eyes on you," whispered Kai in her ear.

The VIPs moved on and Beth hurried along with them.

The second floor was very different. It was spotless and the walls had been freshly painted. Another humanoid robot stood in the centre of the room, but this one had a grin across its friendly, aristocratic face and it beckoned the arriving VIPs to come closer as they stepped off the top of the escalator.

Once they had assembled it spoke in a soft, firm voice. "I am Liberty, in the traditional English sense. The liberties of old, where regal rights were revoked and held instead in private hands. As your mesne lord I will protect you and look out for you. I will be entrusted with the tenure of your land. I propose we look to the past and acknowledge that our current way of doing business is more akin to a feudal system than a capitalist system. The ways of the past are the ways of the future. Let us stop kidding ourselves that we want a meritocracy. What we want is to know our place. To know where the true power lies and who we need to please. In our glorious past, we called them our lords and masters. Now we call them our bosses, our landlords. They own us and they can set us free. I offer benevolence beyond your dreams. I am your freedom."

Beth looked around, but Kai was nowhere to be seen. She breathed a sigh of relief. The low-level murmuring of the VIPs increased in volume. It was a surprise pitch, but it was an interesting idea and certainly more radical than Laissez-faire.

As the VIPs moved on to the floor that housed Liberation, Kai appeared and kept pace with her, one step in front as if he was leading her. Maybe he was.

There was a faint smell of damp air and cut grass. The pitch from this particular L was also one of freedom. It looked like a cross between a mid-twentieth century peacenik and an early twenty-first century tech entrepreneur, with long, flowing flower adorned hair and a black suit and T-shirt. It talked slowly and with a soothing yet slightly sinister drawl. It spoke of no limits, no laws, nothing to hinder free trade and no clumsy regulation. It proposed an unfettered utopia, encouraging entrepreneurship with a hint of philanthropy to help those who were failures. There was a lot of nodding and murmurs of agreement from the gathered group.

"Clever," was all Kai said to her before he moved on.

Beth had to pause and think hard about how she could summarise Liberation in a sentence or two. "Open spaces and open minds, with welfare holes you hope you won't fall through," she told her globule.

On the fourth floor were the Locals. A semi-circle of five whose features changed from time to time to reflect the diverse nature of the populations they hoped to represent.

In unison, they opened their pitch with a simple statement. "We will work with you," they said.

R&R had been sent confidential and unedited code related to these and were anticipating putting their support behind them for the East Albion vote. Beth was fascinated to hear what these Locals had to say.

Kai appeared at her side. "How tiresome," he whispered, with a trace of laughter in his voice.

"Five of us, deciding together what's best for your country, what needs to change and what needs to remain. We will only change what is necessary."

Kai coughed. "For the small-minded?"

Certain that he was trying to provoke her, Beth turned to challenge him but he was gone.

The Locals stood and folded their arms. "That is all we can say before you vote us in."

"A bit Laissez-faire but with the twist of collaboration," she said into her globule.

The next and final floor was home to the Leveller. The walls were covered in images of ordinary people. Crowd shots, individual portraits and family groups adorned the space. Sitting in the middle of the room, palms up and with open hands was a humanoid robot with the face and texture of an old woman.

The Leveller was chanting, "All are welcome. All are equal."

It was entrancing. The group of VIPs silently gathered around and when they were all ready and waiting the Leveller broke out of the chanting trance and spoke.

"There are ancestral traditions and there have been ancient attempts at true equality. At last we can achieve that dream. The Levellers and the Diggers of the seventeenth century were committed to it. The religious, political, and on occasion regal, notion of a debt jubilee resets the balance. That is what I propose, by redistributing wealth equally. Thereby creating a real starting point where we can rid ourselves of the privilege that stifles our creativity and our economy. This is simple, effective and ultimately the only efficient way to get the most from every citizen."

It looked around the room, seeming to rest its gaze momentarily on each and every person. The murmuring of agreement that had greeted Liberation was replaced with murmurings of ridicule, condescending smiles, shrugs of shoulders and even chuckles loud enough to be considered rude. Beth on the other hand could see the merit in starting again with a level playing field. The implication that those with the most wealth and power had not made a successful society resonated with her emerging view of the world.

As the specially invited group headed towards the stairs that wound their way down to the exit, a flurry of leaflets fell from the ceiling. Replica pamphlets from the groups referenced by the

Leveller piled up around their feet. Most kicked them out of the way, as if some obnoxious litter had inconveniently appeared, but some picked them up, studied them and tucked them in their pockets. Beth recorded some initial thoughts on her globule, ready to tidy them up and broadcast as soon as she left the building's protective Faraday cage.

As she was leaving, Kai appeared next to her and whispered in her ear, "I see you," before vanishing as quickly as he'd arrived.

The words reverberated around her mind. In a failed attempt to throw off their sinister intent, she shook her body a few times and then scurried to the exit.

Outside, she hurried through the deserted streets, which in her grandparents' day had been the bustling heart of their community before automated retail had created the convenience of delivery to your door and the shops had disappeared, along with their local tax contributions and their security guards. The empty rundown no-go area she was in had been inevitable. The popular media had named it the Wild West End.

Glancing over her shoulder to make sure that Kai wasn't following, she hurried to where she felt safe. She began casting her opinions, based almost entirely on her gut reaction, her emotional response. But that's modern politics, she reassured herself whenever she detected a seed of doubt. There was a tiny amount of time to contribute her influence to the vote that was due to take place at the end of the following day and she focused mostly on the positive aspects of the Leveller when compared to the others. It was a ridiculously short amount of time for the public to hear and understand the options and then make a decision, but the freeship spokesperson had been clear that what had made OS so successful was meeting punishing deadlines that had seemed impossible. With concentrated attention, they said, innovative products were not only launched but they were the ones that gave the greatest results. Humanity was at its best when forced to focus.

11

ON THE day of the census, the day before the vote, Naomi, Gerry and Morgan were huddled around a bank of desks and makeshift tables, engrossed in a last-ditch attempt to crack into any one of the ANNs. Even hacking into the most insignificant CEO could open the door into the ANN network, and although finding a backdoor via the census app was a long shot, it was a possibility.

Gerry shrugged and shoved his cushion away from the rolled-out sheets of SlendTek. The cushion altered shape to enable a smooth glide across the floor. "It's impossible," he said. "If only you'd broken into the OS HQ when you had the chance."

Naomi hesitated before replying. Tensions were high. "Are you suggesting I'm to blame?" she asked, as unemotionally as she could manage.

He scooted across the room and hugged her and Morgan joined them.

"No," said Gerry. "You are fantastic. Resist and Regain is lucky to have you."

"Good. Are you sure there's nothing we can do? Have we exhausted every avenue? What about the data harvesters? Nothing from them?"

"Sadly not. Tons of work and nothing more than this map of interconnections."

Naomi swallowed. “Any news of Mary?”

“No. Nothing. We’re still searching. We won’t give up.”

Morgan interrupted their morbid reflections. “The map could be a source of hope. If they don’t realise we have it, then we have an advantage.”

Naomi and Gerry agreed with small nods of their heads. It was true. Knowing what was connected to what and being able to follow the paths between ANNs might prove to be valuable. It was hard to see how at that precise moment, but it had to be better than nothing.

Gerry called them back to the SlendTek. “There,” he said, “Freeship One is anchored in Jackson Bay, New Zealand.”

This was quickly confirmed by taking control of a drone in the area and live-streaming from it. Three children of indeterminate sex and wearing goggles sat in the crow’s nest, not moving a muscle. The sight of their static bodies wired to drones flying elsewhere was unsettling. Nothing much had been heard about the freeship since it had sailed, except the occasional report of a trading party landing at the port of Boma in the Democratic Republic of the Congo to negotiate with the owners of the rapidly depleting stocks of precious metals. It was rumoured that in exchange for rare metals the freeship traded gigantic spiders capable of spinning vast amounts of super strong silk. Allegedly, these engineered beasts did not possess the usual predilection to eat their neighbours, which enabled vast colonies to be used for manufacturing.

Gerry’s and Morgan’s globules vibrated in their pockets.

“The East Albion census has opened,” said Morgan.

“Every citizen needs to register ahead of the vote,” confirmed Gerry. “Oh, and an amnesty is in place for anyone currently excluded.”

“Me?” asked Naomi.

“Yes, you should go now and register and get your amnesty.”

"I've done nothing wrong, though."

Gerry checked. "Doesn't matter. Go claim your citizenship back."

"Wait," said Morgan, full of excitement. "This is weird."

Gerry's eyes lit up. "What?"

"Naomi, you won't believe this."

"What?" she asked in a raised voice, echoing Gerry's enthusiasm.

Morgan grinned. "You've no real need for an amnesty, it looks like it was a data glitch that caused your issues. Not your links to R and R."

"Really?" asked Gerry, returning Morgan's grin. "Does that mean she should wait and register after the split, when hopefully the Locals take control?"

"I reckon."

"I am here," said Naomi, louder than she intended.

Morgan held her hand. "That way you remain off the register in England and can go where you like undetected, and most likely in the virtual spaces as well as real ones. You would be invisible."

"But I'd be an East Albion citizen?"

"Sure. Registering after the vote should mean you are known here, but hidden in England. We need someone like that."

Naomi furrowed her brow in concentration. This was not an easy decision, but R&R had to come first. "I'll do it," she said.

"You should still go to the amnesty registration though. It's a perfect place to recruit."

"C'mon, let's register," said Gerry and they both pressed their thumbs into the indentation on their globules and a profile for each of them was displayed on to the nearest sheet of SlendTek. They scrolled through and after a few minutes of reading and checking they confirmed with a double press of the thumb.

"Registered?" asked Naomi.

Morgan put his arm around her. "Go and tell people why they need to join us. If ever there was a moment this must be it."

"Sure. You're probably right," she said, feeling like an outsider without citizenship but not really caring, too much.

Gerry ordered her a trike on the R&R account and she set off for the Municipal Buildings.

She encouraged her trike to take a left turn here and a right turn there, but essentially she let it find its own route based on the price Gerry had paid.

At the registration centre, the queue was a long and ragged affair filling the pavement and in places bulging on to the road and causing a traffic jam. She tucked the trike away in a side street behind a pile of recycling that was waiting for collection. That should make it awkward for it to navigate its way out, and less likely to be chosen for another customer. It should still be there once she'd completed her registration. She walked along the queue. The amnesty from prosecution for minor offences had prompted a large proportion of the unseen population to emerge. She approached a small group of young men who were jostling each other, trying to push one another into the road. They had an edge of nervousness and aggression that comes with being young, homeless and wired on whatever mind distracting drug was doing the rounds.

One of the young men bumped into her as she passed by. He shoved her in the side, looked back at his friends and shouted, "She assaulted me."

Naomi was a few centimetres taller than him and stood her ground. He was wiry and in poor condition so it was easy to push him away.

He stumbled and fell to the floor, screaming as his knees caught the edge of the pavement. "Fuck you," he shouted, without looking at her.

She continued to walk along the queue. The majority of those waiting shuffled as the queue inched forward, with their heads down as if they were ashamed or were being escorted to a prison where they would see out the remainder of their lives. The joy that Naomi had expected to encounter wasn't there. Strange, given that these were the very people who would benefit most from being able to complete the census, register themselves for East Albion citizenship and be forgiven for any misdemeanours that had kept them away from the authorities and the associated access to UBS. Rhythmic shouting was rolling in from somewhere beyond the silent traffic jam. The shouting had an angry edge to it and as it grew louder it became apparent that it was large group chanting at the top of their voices. Naomi weaved her way through the stationary traffic to the pavement on the other side of the road to try and get a glimpse. Nothing. The volume was increasing. She stepped on to the bumper of a delivery van and stretched her neck as much as she could. Still nothing except a stern automated voice telling her to get the fuck off. She hopped down and ran back to the queue, which was slowly shrinking. She tucked herself in behind a group of about thirty men, women and children, all wearing the non-conformist Nomad emblem, an anarchy symbol inside a tipi-shaped triangle. She was about to start up a conversation with them when the approaching group of chanters came into view.

They were walking slowly and deliberately. A slow march chanting over and over again. "STAY OUT. STAY PURE. STAY CLEAN."

As they moved through the static traffic towards the registration queue, a squad of riot drones flew in and created a barrier between the angry chanters and the queue. The Nomads in front of her arranged themselves into two groups. Two of the men and the children moved back against the wall and the others formed a human shield in front of them. They were obviously veterans of this type of confrontation. Further forward the young men who had tried to intimidate her were standing tall and straight with the tips of their noses touching the drones, shouting abuse at the anti-amnesty protestors. The drones ignored the queue but when one of the chanting protesters nudged a drone it released its spray and the protestor fell. It wasn't long before the ground underneath the drones was littered with writhing bodies. The chanting persisted and the taunting continued. One of the female protestors broke through the line of riot drones. She was quickly surrounded by the Nomads who linked arms and warned her in loud steady voices that they were prepared to be violent, very violent if necessary, and would break her legs to stop her hurting their children. It was extremely effective and as they loosened the circle she fled back behind the drones. The queue moved forward and the protestors moved with it, determined to target the Nomads. Along the queue, Naomi could see groups of protestors picking on the weak and vulnerable, taunting those who had obviously suffered from an ongoing lack of UBS and would need the most care. The chant directed at them was quieter and more sinister. *The fittest will survive.* Naomi kept her head up and facing forward along the length of the queue. She didn't want confrontation and was comfortable that she had her own methods of dealing with these noxious nobodies. She shuffled forward, doing her best to ignore the taunts being flung at them.

A protestor using a globule as a megaphone addressed the BP. "It's our land. Not theirs," she shouted. "We are citizens. Not them. We invoke our right to protect it from invasion." She held her globule out to the BP and shouted. "Take payment and do your job."

The BP released a swarm of riot bots, which gathered and then headed towards the Nomads who were busy distributing pills among themselves and adopting the static position of lying on the ground, exactly as Naomi and Beth had done in Pancras Square. Naomi smiled. They had received the tech from R&R, even if they weren't aware of it. The BP hovered over the fallen Nomads and after a few seconds began to congregate, ready to return to their hosts.

The woman with the megaphone was screaming at them. "What the fuck? Do your job. They're faking it. Take them. Now."

As the swarm flew off and the BP departed, one by one the Nomads got to their feet. There was a hushed anxiety emanating from the protestors. That perfect moment when the bully realises that he's outnumbered. The Nomads checked on their children with an exquisite patience that simply increased the tension in the air. Then, making low repetitive grunts, they took a step forward. Paused. Took another. Paused. And then hurled themselves at the protestors, fists and feet flying. They were angry, they were letting it loose, and Naomi was loving it.

Once the protestors had been chased away, Naomi approached the Nomads. "Nice work," she said, holding out her hand in greeting to the woman who had been organising them. "Those pills you used, they're ours."

"Don't talk rubbish. Who are you anyway?"

"Resist and Regain."

"Never heard of you."

"One of your crew will know us. You're the Nomads, right?"

"What of it?"

"We need to work together. I'm recruiting allies for R and R. Interested?"

A young man who was hovering nearby sauntered over. "Did I hear R and R?" he asked.

"She's—"

Naomi interrupted her. "Yes. You know of us?"

"Sure. Don't worry, they're the good guys," he told the woman. "They did that trick on the side of the freeship when it was docked at Felixstowe."

The woman stared at the sky, as if she was trying to remember. "Eh?"

"The hands cupping the symbol for resistance."

"Oh," she said and raised her head so her eyes were level with Naomi's. "That was *you*?"

"Yes. Care to join us, become part of the alliance I'm building?"

"The alliance?"

"We need to fight OS, stop Kai, destroy these ANNs."

The woman squatted down with hands on thighs. Sat quietly for a while before standing again. "We're Nomads, we do our thing and only get involved if we have to. Like today."

"But imagine what the future will look like. A world of faceless bureaucracies. Literally. Manipulated by emotionally stunted narcissistic boys."

"Kai hardly strikes me as a boy."

"You know what I mean. We need you. We need each other."

"What do you want from us?"

"At this stage, nothing. A loose alliance of like-minded groups with a general agreement that OS are not to be trusted and that at some point action might be needed."

"Is this a public affiliation?"

"Doesn't have to be."

The woman sucked in some air, pursed her lips and held out her globule. Naomi pressed hers against it, they were connected, R&R was getting stronger by the day.

12

Twenty-four hours after listening to the Ls and making every minute of influence count, Beth was sitting on the steps of the OS headquarters with Tam. It had been intense. At first, she had been a lone voice from the group of VIPs that had early access to the Ls and their proposals. Speculation about how the differences would manifest themselves took up most of the airspace to begin with. Only Beth had come out clearly in favour of one straight away, attracting much derision from her fellow influencers, but substantially increasing her already growing following. She pushed hard for the Leveller from every angle she could see. It made sense, she said. It was a once in a generation chance, she said. It would be the end of child miners, she said. It had to be better than their semi-automated government with its bot trawlers scraping think-tank policy ideas and then taking a popularist vote from a population with a veneer of understanding on whether to implement them. The replies came fast and furious. It would put the lazy, incompetent and to be frank the stupid in as much control as the hardworking, intelligent and experienced. Accusations of naïvety, wilful stupidity or out-and-out anti-capitalist tendencies were constantly thrown at her. Molly Coddling was the phrase thrown at her like a constant barrage of abusive artillery. Nevertheless, she pursued her path and as the Leveller gained the population's attention and its popularity with the masses became evident, the mood began to change. The usual threats from those with wealth and power that they would leave England and let the country stew in its own pit of pathetic incompetence came thick and fast. It was tough. The insults directed at her increased in number and in ferocity as the Leveller gained popularity but by the end of the night the polls showed that it was too close to call. Each of the Ls had roughly the same level of support.

"I'm proud of you," said Tam, reaching out to hold her hand.

She looked down her nose at his hand.

"Thank you," she said tilting her head down and looking up at him demurely.

"Piss off," he said and withdrew his hand. "You know what I meant."

She grabbed his hand and pulled it back to her lap. "Hey, I know what you meant. And I know what you meant to mean."

"Never a moment's reprieve," he said, squeezing her hand.

She resisted the urge to snatch her hand away and turned her attention to the outcome of the vote, which although it had been closed for only a few minutes was due to be announced. The power of automated government was captured in that single act of counting votes accurately and almost immediately. She suspected that it could have been instantaneous but the behavioural scientists felt a few minutes gap would reassure the population that due care and attention had been paid.

An extremely loud cheer erupted. Every globule lit up with the old woman's face of the Leveller and the displays across the sides of the surrounding buildings flashed between her and the percentage spread of votes. The Leveller had won eighty-three percent, which was way above anything a single political party had received since 1918 when another momentous shift in democracy had ceased the necessity to be male and to own property to be able to vote. A moment in history that Beth had used in her argument that *change can happen.* People were jumping up and down, hugging and kissing as if a war had just ended, which in some ways it had. Beth turned Tam to face her and pulled the back of his head forward until his lips met hers. She kissed him and the cacophony around them faded into the background. He responded with enthusiasm, which turned the dial up on her desire. Tam was beautiful, sensitive and strong, with eyes that penetrated the soul and pierced through her defences. She was pinned to the steps by his presence.

They stayed locked in the kiss for as long as they physically could and then as they parted and drew breath he whispered. "Are we a thing now?"

"A thing?"

"A couple."

"We've been a couple for ages. Well, I thought we were."

"Not in public. Not where anyone could see."

"Well—"

"I love you," he said.

She was sure he had blushed as he'd said it. "Let's party." She dragged him to his feet. "C'mon. We won."

He followed in her wake across the square and into the joyous crowd. Corks were flying everywhere and the free bottles from the British Bubbly Company were being handed out with abandon. It was a celebration of England at its best and there'd be plenty of time to find out how the other nations had voted. This was their moment and she would enjoy it to the full. In the distance, a trickle of people was leaving the square with their heads down and some were even shouting abuse at the revellers, but the overwhelming majority were whooping and cheering and dancing chaotically with whoever was closest. Others were just jumping up and down on the spot.

The Leveller spoke into the crowd, across the globules and, Beth was sure, through every communication channel in England.

"Fifty years," it said. "No more tax for at least fifty years. I will distribute the wealth of this great nation equally. Keeping enough back for government essentials. You will never have to pay tax again."

A roar of approval reverberated around the square.

"I will free you from the decisions that are too tedious and too complex for a human to waste their time on."

Another uproar.

"Your freedom has come. Your life as a citizen truly begins here. No more monarchy. No more inherited privilege. No more financial uncertainty."

Beth and Tam held each other. Kissed. Danced. Sat down and rested. And then started again. It was a night to remember.

Exhausted, Beth grabbed his arm. "Hey, follow me," she said and he obeyed with a twinkle in those beautiful blue eyes.

She led them through the crowd and after a few minutes of weaving in and out of the swaying masses someone pointed at her and shouted. "Molly. It's Molly."

Those nearby stopped dancing and began patting her on the back. Calls of thanks came from every direction.

She took Tam's hand and a stranger's next to her and raised them in the air. "We did it," she shouted. "We are free." She made an overemphasised bow, moving through ninety-degrees and making another until she'd done a full circle. "With me," she whispered in Tam's ear.

"Where?"

"I'm taking you home," she said and kissed him on the cheek. "You are mine."

They left the square, called a trike and set off for Beth's flat, lost in one another and the rising passion from the promise of those three words he'd spoken.

13

NAOMI, MORGAN, Gerry, and the local members of Resist & Regain had gathered in the shoddy single-storey community centre. They waited patiently, and anxiously, for the result of the East Albion election. There was no good outcome as far as Naomi was concerned, but the best she hoped for was that the Locals rather than any other L would be in charge, and that's what they got. A subdued party of relief followed, while outside the centre, fireworks, laughter and singing filled the air, creating a cushion of noise over their less than enthusiastic celebrations.

The Locals chose not to broadcast immediately, except to say that they would be forthcoming with their manifesto. First, they must convene, consider and find a compromise that would serve the best interests of all the citizens of East Albion. However, their first move would be to add to the Universal Basic Services package. A globule and all the associated costs would become part of the suite of services. The mood of the R&R party was one of wariness because of the implications of the state owning and being in control of permitting access to every form of communication. In contrast, it seemed as if the general populace warmly welcomed it as a positive sign that the Locals were orientated towards the benefit of the poor as well as the rich.

"I want to register fully as a citizen and sort things out, leave this accidental anonymity behind," said Naomi, arguing with Gerry about whether she should accept.

"Wait, until the data harvesters have had a chance to evaluate the implications," he suggested.

"For a while," she reluctantly agreed.

Morgan was sitting there with a half-drunk glass of local cider swirling it around as if he could see the future in the cloudy vortex.

"Thoughts?" she asked.

"Yes."

"What?"

"Oh, you know. Nothing and everything."

Naomi was about to quiz him further when every globule except hers lit up. The screens around the room kicked into action too. On a normal night they would have been showing films or music with the sound piped direct to ear buds but they had been blanked, ready to broadcast. Five circles of light appeared on each of the screens. Naomi glanced over at Morgan's globule and that too was lit up with five circles spaced around its spherical surface. A connecting beam flashed from each circle to a focal point, which pulsed as if it contained a massive untapped energy source.

Five voices combined to deliver one message. "This is our manifesto," they said. "We are your Locals. We are here for you. We will listen and we will lead."

Most of the heads around the room nodded in appreciation.

The connections between the circles lit up and the focal point pulse intensified, hinting at its latent energy. "We wish to explore alternatives. We believe that you wish us to free you from the grip of the past. We believe that it will be difficult for some of you and so we propose a form of compensation. We believe we have the questions, but not the answers. Not yet. We believe that nature is complex and cannot be beaten into submission as you have tried to do for so long. We do believe that nature can be tricked into behaving as we wish, as you wish. These are the big questions we will turn our attention to: a new start for everyone that works with nature not against it. We will return to you when we have considered these things fully."

The room darkened as the globules dimmed and the screens returned to their standby status.

Life in East Albion carried on, little changed. The private companies continued to patrol their spaces with their bot police. New buildings were born and old buildings were decommissioned. Had the borders been open to the outside world, the economy would have appeared to be as it was before.

Naomi spent her time working through all the scenarios that they could anticipate their Locals might come back with. R&R planned their options, focussing on how in each circumstance they would react. She found the inaction extremely difficult to handle, but in a strange way she also found the enforced pause therapeutic. It gave her time to get her head straight about what she believed and what she was prepared to do for those beliefs. It was emotionally draining to see the world continue to dominate and abuse nature. Although, there was one positive. The Locals had built into their manifesto the strap line: *You are not in nature; you are nature.*

Exactly three months to the day after the vote, the Locals once again took over everyone's globules and made an announcement. Five voices speaking as one. "We have gathered real-time data. Seven million, eight hundred and sixty-two thousand, four hundred seconds for every registered citizen of East Albion. There are no visitors from outside. The data is clean. We have aggregated and we have analysed. Our conclusion is to initiate a council of leaders. This council will consist of us, your five Locals, and five humans. We will select a representative group from among you."

The globules dimmed and Gerry sat back in his chair. "Well," he said. "All that time and the only conclusion they reach is that they need more time and more people."

"Registered citizens only, so that rules me out. Thanks Gerry," said Naomi, failing to hide her bitterness.

Morgan was enthralled by something on his globule. "England has opened up too. In fact, all the Ls have made decisions today. It must be a coordinated thing."

"The Loop," said Naomi. "The connecting protocol. That's the key. To all this. We need to infect it, with the future we want."

Gerry's globule brightened again and the five circles appeared. "You have been chosen to join the Council of East Albion. Instructions will follow."

Naomi touched her forehead and bowed her head slightly. "Your worship," she said with a broad Lincolnshire accent.

"Stop it," said Morgan. "Let him alone. This could be fantastic for R and R. Someone at the heart of government. This is what we need."

As promised, more instructions came.

"I'm to set aside a space in our house and dedicate it to act as a virtual council chamber," explained Gerry.

Naomi frowned. "The only spare room we have is the one that I'm living in."

"True, but the Locals don't recognise you and therefore don't know that it is occupied. I'm really sorry, but I think you'll have to find somewhere else to live."

With a heady mix of elation at getting R&R a seat in government and devastation of breaking up their established home, they discussed their future.

Naomi calmed them down and made them listen to her. "I've been intending to move out and this was the shove I needed," she reassured them. "After all, this was always only ever meant to have been temporary and I've outstayed my time."

"No—" said Morgan, but she interrupted him with a finger to her lips.

Secretly, she was sad. It wasn't what she wanted and not what she'd expected but she was sure it would look better after a night's sleep, and it did.

In the morning, the council equipment arrived with an instruction to be ready for the inaugural meeting that day. Naomi gathered all her belongings and piled them up in the corner of the lounge. There wasn't much. Her non-status still forced her to buy outright rather than being able to enter into any rental agreements, and with limited access to funds she had been very frugal.

Gerry was busy unpacking his equipment.

"Can I help?" she asked.

"Yes, please."

They each plugged into the headsets, found the instructions, and walked around the mock-up of the completed space. Basically, it was made up of two key pieces of kit. A hi-tech mattress that moulded to the naked body and formed a head-to-toe haptic experience and a spongy full-face mask with built-in virtual reality that encased the whole head. The other peripherals that had been delivered allowed onlookers to observe council sessions via a standard VR headset.

"Shall we set it up then?" she asked, failing to suppress her giggles at the thought of a naked Gerry lying on a mattress that wriggled and tickled while wearing what could only be described as a bondage hood.

"Yes, but don't you dare laugh."

Once he'd started it running, she couldn't help herself. She laughed at him squirming away while the mattress made a few failed attempts to function properly in demo mode. She laughed and laughed and the more she laughed the angrier he got. After occasional screeches of pain, he finally got its stimulation levels set correctly and aimed at the correct parts of his body.

"Put your headset on," he said as he reached over for his hood. "I want you in here with me."

Inside the council demo, the five cream-coloured spheres of the Locals hung in the air with strands of light connecting them. As soon as Gerry clicked his hood into place he appeared as a blue sixth sphere. The Locals began to pulse and connected Gerry to their web of light. His sphere appeared to be alive, dimpling in places as if it was being pressed like a piece of dough. Then it disappeared. He must have left the demo. Naomi took her headset off and there he was sitting on the mattress rubbing his ears and his nose.

"Amazing," he said.

Naomi sat down next to him and put her arm around him.

"Shall we?" he said. "One for the road. So to speak."

She moved his hand away. There had been that one time with the three of them and that had been nice, but it wasn't something that she was particularly interested in repeating with or without Morgan.

"No. Thank you. Once was great. Let's leave it there. Shall we?"

She moved the conversation on before he could get maudlin, which he was prone to do.

"I'm still not sure," she said. "I don't like the way that the Loop sits at the heart of all the Ls. I really don't like that it's controlled by Kai and the Narcissists on the freeship. Something's not right."

"The council is our way in," said Gerry. "We can take control from here."

"I hope so. I really hope so."

"You'll stay for the first meeting, won't you?"

"Most certainly. You don't think I'd miss you squirming around under the tickling tentacles of five ANNs. Do you?"

Gerry mumbled something along the lines of *you wish* and grabbed his clothes to get dressed.

Outside, Morgan was basking in the early morning sunshine.

"This heatwave is unbearable," she said as she squatted down next to him. "How can you lie there?"

"Making the most of it," he replied. "It's only going to get worse."

Naomi sighed. "Put this on," she said, handing him a tube of nanotech sunscreen. "You know *you're* getting worse, don't you?"

"I know. Pessimistic, annoyed and angry. Nothing's changing, the Locals do nothing. I'm becoming resigned to it." He hesitated. "It's a fate for humanity that pretty much sounds like extinction."

Naomi folder her arms. "OS and Kai are still the definitive enemy, though. Right?"

"They are," he replied in a soft determined voice.

"So Resist and Regain really does need to get its act together, especially now that the borders are open and the Ls are engaging again?"

"Guess so, yes. You're right, this is our opportunity to shift the psyche of East Albion and hopefully the rest of Great Britain and then the world."

The Loop was the key to all of this, she was sure. She'd been saying it for a while now, but the ears around her were deaf. She must make her own path. There was little choice, but to turn her attention to what she could do. She kissed Morgan on the forehead and went back inside to continue her search for a small ship and a tiny crew that could head off into the oceans and find Freeship One.

"C'mon," shouted Gerry. "The inaugural session is about to commence."

Morgan came rushing in and together they ran up the stairs to the newly installed council chamber. Gerry was already lying on the mattress with his hood on. She threw a headset to Morgan and they both entered the VR council at the same time. Hovering in the air were the five spheres and one by one they were joined by five other spheres.

"Which one is Gerry?" she heard Morgan say to her left.

"Dunno. Blue maybe?"

The five spheres whose shapes were not fluctuating pulsed as the five voices of the Locals spoke. "Council is convened."

Gerry coughed and one of the other spheres pulsed with a blue light.

"Yes, that's him," she said.

The Locals continued. "We believe that the most effective way of reducing the impact of humans on the planet is to encourage those whose wealth is dependent on high impact activity to stop and we propose to pay compensation to those who desist. Does the council agree?"

One of the human spheres pulsed green and a single voice answered. "No. This is unprecedented and I do not support it."

The Locals replied. "It is not unprecedented. It is similar to the slave compensation package to assist abolition in nineteenth century Britain."

Gerry's sphere pulsed. "We cannot repeat those mistakes. We cannot compensate the abusers and not the abused. What about those countries that have suffered from our over-extraction and our clear contribution to their current disasters? We should pay them, not bribe those other barbaric bastards. We must legislate, not gift them some sort of apologetic sweetener."

"That is not the way of the Loop," said the Locals. "Encourage not enforce is one of the moral pillars that underpin the protocol."

The spheres stopped pulsing for a few seconds and then they spoke again. "We will vote," they said. "Four of us vote for compensation. Human council members, please clench your right fist if you agree with our majority."

The yellow and red spheres pulsed.

"Carried, six to four," said the Locals. "We will reconvene soon."

Gerry pulled off his hood and threw it across the room. "What the—"

"Stay with it," said Morgan. "Early days and you can't give up now."

Gerry lay back on the mattress and closed his eyes. "I need some space," he said.

"Sure," said Naomi and Morgan in unison, and they left him to his thoughts.

14

Beth studied the sleeping Tam lying next to her. He'd never mentioned the four-letter word again, but it hung between them like a strand of strong, invisible silk binding them together. It seemed like a lifetime ago since that wonderful evening when they had celebrated the Leveller, and their love for each other.

All wealth, including property and savings, had been redistributed equally among everyone over the age of thirteen, with offsetting corrections made for those predicted to die before the end of the adjustment period. And without warning, the Leveller had shut the physical and the digital borders, until, it said, 'The changes I am making have found their new equilibrium'.

That morning, the borders had opened up and life had taken a step towards normal. To celebrate, Beth cast a rehash of her piece critiquing the redistribution decision and added her ongoing criticism of some of those that had come before it, such as the formalisation of the taboos.

She sat back and rubbed her pregnant belly. The morning also brought with it the day of incubation for little Alex, the result of that celebration on the first night of their new government. Her egg app had predicted that, at twenty-nine years old, she had another twenty-two years to reproduce, but that night had been the moment when it had felt right. Pregnancy hadn't stopped her being perfectly straight with Tam. Her career and her independence were paramount, and she was not going to combine her fifty years of redistributed wealth with his. Although, much to his relief and slight amusement, she had given his toothbrush access to her oral health docking station even if it did mean a tenuous connection with each other in the national health data. Pragmatism, she told him, meant that she wanted to know if she was sharing a bed with gum disease.

Tam turned over in his sleep to face her, making those comforting snuffling sounds that she'd grown to rely on as an anchor to normality. She was proud that he continued to take the innards of discarded technology and repurpose it into useful globule peripherals in this restructured world where too many people worked very little and were bored senseless. She particularly liked his family tray. It resembled an egg box, allowing up to six globules to form a self-contained group for the purpose of multi-player games. It was genius and extremely popular with a particular out-on-the-edge crowd. She picked up the book he'd been reading when he'd fallen asleep and leafed through the SlendTek pages to see what download had kept him so enthralled. A pirate romance. Not a surprise, but an aspect of his character that she struggled with. He wasn't all bad. He had supported her in refusing to have the embryonic Alex screened for genetic defects and he was certainly no fan of the trend to find a 'best match' of sperm and egg for the purpose of reproducing optimum humans, as the Leveller described it. Warm feelings towards him drifted over her as she stroked his hair. In a lot of ways they were not a typical couple, something the Leveller had picked up on and placed in the public record of those who were on the boundary of breaking the taboos. Beth couldn't make up her mind about the taboo tally. On one hand, the transparency it provided around how and why each taboo was in place and the reason for revisions by the Leveller was a good thing. On the other hand, she felt queasy about the subjective interpretation by an ANN about who had broken them or might break them, especially since all laws had been scrapped in favour of these nuanced taboos. Tam said it had always been that way, that laws were more stringently applied to the less powerful and targeted at the activities of the poor while supporting similar activities of the rich. A little too often he cited tax breaks, interest rates on loans, socially acceptable drugs and certain forms of debauchery as prime examples of the hypocrisy. It was a viewpoint that she had a lot of sympathy with, but was growing tired of hearing.

"Morning to you," he said in that sultry voice that made her want to cuddle him to death.

She took hold of his hand and placed it on her belly. "Hey. Don't you mean us?" she said and then immediately regretted it.

He grinned and lay his cheek on the exposed flesh peeking out from her unbuttoned pyjama top. "Our perfectly formed family," he whispered.

The idea of a perfect family cocooned from the outside world upset her, but she let it go for the sake of not spoiling the day and because she suspected he was deliberately teasing her. Instead, she ran her fingers through his long black hair and gently tugged.

"Really?" he said.

"Time please," she called out and the ANN that managed her home replied that it was eight thirty-five a.m.

"My appointment's not until two o'clock this afternoon," she said in a low voice.

He took the initiative as she hoped he would and with his hands he did what the suit had done all that time ago.

As they lay there on the crumpled sheets with the mattress no longer shifting its shape to accommodate their movements, she talked freely. "He won't have—"

Tam interrupted. "He? Alex?"

"Yes, Alex. Alex won't be educated by a human. It really worries me. Those ANN educators are all facts and no feelings."

"You should write the killer cast and we'll be rich and we can send him to private school."

"That's not going to happen if I keep criticising the Leveller and its lackeys whenever I think they're wrong."

"I was kidding."

She pinched his nipple. "Not funny, mister. Seriously though, this responsibility thing is weighing me down."

"I'm his dad. I'll do the parenting part."

"I know you say that, but—"

"Enough. Why can't you believe me? Let me be his dad."

"I want to, but he won't become an adult with his own independent wealth until he's thirteen. That's a long time for you to look after him."

Tam swung his legs over the edge of the bed and stood over her. "Well, it's a bit bloody late to be thinking about this now." He checked his globule. "In four hours, they'll be taking him out of you and incubating him for the next six months whether you're ready or not."

"For fuck's sake," she said and left him standing there with a clenched jaw.

In the bathroom she showered while the various health apps and devices took their daily readings from her implants.

He was sitting on the edge of the bed fiddling with his globule when she returned to get dressed. "I'm sorry," she said quietly.

"Me too. But we still have to decide who gets to host his data identity. Which data trust do we sign him up for?"

"Give me a break," she said, but he was right and she'd been avoiding the decision for weeks. "I haven't changed my mind. I'm not going to join a trust while these weird glitches with my data keep happening. I had one the other day where it seemed to be tracking my interest in buying a small ship. Which I don't want, by the way. It's creepy."

"I get it," said Tam. "So why don't we enrol him into mine. At least they'll make some money for him."

"You're a bunch of fixers working way out on the fringes."

"Frontier fixers. And the alternative? The default. The state, and the English state at that. Bunch of nationalistic neoliberal nasties."

She chuckled. "Nice phrasing," adding more seriously, "I'm trying to expose the creeping inequality. It's hard though. The propaganda pouring out of those bastards who've recovered their fortunes is extremely fucking effective."

"I know and you're doing a great job, but if we let Alex's trust default to the Leveller, his data goes into the very trust owned by those bastards and they use it to make themselves more wealth. At least with mine it's put to good use and gives a dividend every now and again."

"True. As you've pointed out several times. I know I'm shit for not deciding. Sadly, you're completely correct." She kissed him on the cheek. "As ever."

"Mine then?"

"Sure. We can always move him later."

"Maybe you'll join us once you've sorted out those glitches."

"Maybe," she said. "Shall we go?"

He nodded.

"Can we hire a trike and make our way there slowly? I think I'll produce a cast about the world that Alex is being born into."

He checked his globule. "Three hours. Plenty of time."

They sat on the trike while Beth worked out a route, and when she'd decided on which areas of their capital she wanted to cast about for posterity, she told the trike where to go and they set off.

The city was at its best, dynamic and full of energy. The smart pavements were swarming with ant-like lines of consumers weaving in and out of each other at a remarkable pace. Their globules were connected to the Leveller's junior cousin, the city's ANN architect, which kept them on track and at the correct speed for optimum movement. The roads were also packed full of traffic moving fast and freely. Beth couldn't help thinking of those old-fashioned films of speeded up night time cars hurtling along freeways, their lights leaving a trail as they whizzed by while dodging each other with great dexterity. She was pleased to be bringing new life into this wonderful outpouring of humanity's inventiveness.

15

It was one of the rare days when Tam wasn't visiting their son in his incubation unit and they were spending the day together. Or, more accurately, Tam had agreed to tag along with Beth on her mission.

The heat of the day was getting to them both and Beth was feeling tetchy towards him. "I want to see if I can find them. Is that alright with you?" she said with more spite than intended.

"You know the answer to that," he said without looking at her.

"Meaning?"

"Naomi clicks her fingers…"

"R and R need to build up the alliance. You think the Ls are a good thing?"

"You know I don't."

"So, what's your problem?"

Tam huffed. "Again?"

"Yes, again."

"Why, when you know?" he asked, but didn't wait for a reply. "They're never going to win. They're using you to do their dirty work and we have Alex to think about now."

"Alex? That's new," she said, intrigued by the introduction of their son into the argument. Up until then, she'd presumed it was straightforward jealousy of Naomi.

"It's true though, isn't it?"

"Which part?"

"Avoiding danger for the sake of our family."

"Hey, maybe. You know you got together with a caster, right?"

The uncomfortable silence of a truce descended.

Tam touched her leg with his. She didn't respond, but didn't move away either, and they continued their journey in a half acceptance of peace. Yet again, unresolved.

"Next left," she said to the trike.

"The park?" he asked.

"The park," she replied.

"One-nil for the Leveller."

"What?"

"Those royals. What a waste of space they were. Best thing the Leveller ever did was to take their stacks of cash from them. Not so privileged now, eh?"

Beth shrugged. As far as she was concerned, it was another example of why R&R had to keep up the fight against Kai and his cronies. It was all very well to be anti-royal, but the parks and palaces had shifted to other ruthless individuals. It was quite a surprise at how shocked most people had been. After all, that's how the royal families had got there in the first place – by taking their power and crushing all opposition.

As the trike turned into the road that circled the outside of the park, a pack of BP drones made it obvious that they were following, but after a few minutes the identification light on the trike's dashboard lit up briefly. Presumably because Beth and Tam had both checked out as legitimate and not on the banned list of whichever individual now owned the park.

"Trike. Leisurely, please," said Beth, and the trike slowed down to little more than a fast, walking pace.

The BP shot up into the sky and disappeared. The wind blew across the freshly cut grass carrying its gorgeous earthy smell and with it the pounding sound of building work from the far side of the once precious park that was now being turned into luxury houses. The wind blew the trees and through the swaying branches Beth thought that she caught sight of the flag of the underground Anti-Leveller League.

"Stop," she shouted.

"What's wrong?" said Tam with a tremor in his voice.

"Nothing. I think we've found them. Wait for me here."

Tam's head was jerking all over the place. "Where?"

"Over there," she said, pointing to a faded cream flag fluttering in one of the trees.

Three capital letters – ALL – were painted over the crossed out printed triangle of an A with two Ns underneath. She grabbed her globule and stepped off the trike.

"Wait," shouted Tam.

Only the trike paid him any attention.

Beth ran across the grass. She could hear a BP closing in behind her. She slowed down to a walk and casually wandered into the wooded enclave. Three women appeared from nowhere and blocked her path with their arms crossed, their legs apart, and their feet planted firmly on the soil. They were not going to be moved. Beth held out her globule, having pressed the indentation that made it indicate her credentials.

"Fuck off," said the woman in the middle. "No casters, technos or paedos here, thank you very much."

"Bridget," scolded the woman to her right, who then continued speaking to Beth. "She's right though. We're simply going about our legitimate business."

Beth tucked her globule in her pocket. "Not taboo? How? It's private property."

"Disputed ownership," said the first woman. "And while that stupid machine is stuck in limbo trying to sort things out, we are here. Doing no harm."

"The Leveller must know you're here. It's seriously taboo."

"We're zeroed. Don't exist. Persons unknown."

"Unwanted," added the third woman. "Unclean."

All three of them laughed.

Beth half-joined in the laughing and smiled at Tam who had ignored her request to stay with the trike and was standing a single pace behind her.

He stepped forward. "Tam," he said and held out his hand.

The women all stared at him briefly before turning back to Beth.

The one in the middle spoke. "You're Beth, aren't you? The child miners? You can come and talk. Not him. No names. No quotes. A positive piece about our predicament. Agreed?"

"Totally agreed."

She followed them into the camp where a dozen rough looking women were sitting around chatting.

"Beth, the caster," said the woman escorting her. "I invited her," she added as a couple of the women stood up and started to move towards Beth.

These were the sort of women who Beth would give a wide berth to if she was passing them in the street. Hardened faces and shabby clothes. Loud and confident and likely to turn on you for no reason.

The middle woman pulled over a chair. "Help yourself," she said and pulled another one over and parked herself on it.

Beth sat down and took out her globule.

The woman shot out of her chair and shouted. "Put that fucking thing away or piss off. Now."

Beth shoved it back in her pocket and held her hands up in surrender.

"Good," said the woman. "Now, what do you want to know?"

"Can we start with why you've dropped out when the Leveller has provided so much for you."

Several of the women sitting around listening laughed and stamped their feet.

Beth shrunk a little inside. "Sorry," she said. "I didn't mean anything by it."

"Yes, you did," said the woman. "You presume we have a principled objection to the Leveller and despite its generosity towards equality we have spurned its offers and chosen to live a life of protest."

The women clapped, celebrating their spokeswoman's articulation of exactly what Beth was thinking.

"No, not at all," said Beth. "Honestly, I'm curious. You must have very good reasons."

"We do," shouted one of the other women.

Beth couldn't see who it was, but whoever it was had a sour bitterness to her voice.

The spokeswoman continued. "We fucked up," she said. "We'd never had such wealth. Never knew anyone who had and we didn't know what to do. And then the vultures came. Men and women in suits. Sweet talking and smooth with investment schemes pouring out of their nostrils like snot on a cold day. Although at the time it felt like they spoke and honey flowed. The money poured in, topping up our fifty-year fund on a daily basis. Lots and lots of partying followed. We bought loads of shit we didn't need. And then it twisted. It turns out we made a bunch of seriously crap investments and all the funds drained away to the suits. We were wiped out. Fifty years' worth of wealth gone in one. Our advisers disappeared and we were zeroed. The Leveller in its wisdom decided we were no longer part of society. No longer existed as far as it was concerned and with the abolition of UBI we were well and truly—"

"Oi," shouted the same woman as earlier. "You make us sound pathetic."

"We were simply not educated about how to make the most of having wealth. The privilege that the Leveller says it seeks to eradicate is handed down generation after generation. Each one being taught that it is both worthy and entitled to its position." She shook her head and took a breath. "That and how to make money make more money. They're bred to be a heartless bunch of selfish lowlife parasites and we let them crawl all over us and feed until there was nothing left to take."

Beth swallowed and steadied her breathing. "Can I ask? How do you live then?"

"We're allowed to work on the illicit market. We're cheap and that's what they want for the hard shitty work that only the desperate will take on."

"It could be better," said Beth, bracing herself to talk about R&R.

"You don't say?"

"What I mean is that Resist and Regain can help. They're forming an alliance with other groups. You'd be very welcome."

"No thanks, we've had enough *outside* help to last us a lifetime."

Beth attempted to put her hand on the woman's shoulder, but she twisted away, recoiling with a sneer. Instead, Beth swallowed and, with what she hoped was a welcoming smile, asked again. "OS, Kai, Freeship One, the Ls. If we're going to break them we need to work together."

"I said no," repeated the woman, folding her arms in defiance.

"Is there anything I *can* do?" asked Beth. "That you can't do for yourselves," she quickly added.

The woman leant over close. "We have no voice. The zeroed. We have no access to the Leveller. Sure, we were stupid but this is brutal. Stop it happening to anyone else. Laws to protect the vulnerable. Taboos or whatever you call them. We need them again."

She gently placed her hand on Beth's belly. "If not for you, then for junior."

Beth felt a strange pang of loss, of absence. "How did you—"

"We have the tech. We know he's ripening in one of their facilities."

Tam had rejoined them. His jaw was clenched tight and his eyes were narrowed. He was seething. "We need to go," he said in a low, controlled voice.

She nodded.

As she walked away staring at the ground in disgust at the world that she was about to bring Alex into and with the woman's words lingering inside her mind, she muttered under her breath. "I'll do my best. Honestly, I will."

16

Naomi watched as Freeship One manoeuvred alongside the London dock while Kai waved to the gathered crowds from the transparent crow's nest. An image of his smiling face was displayed on the side of the ship and despite his handsomeness a twenty-foot-long grin did him no favours. He looked like a manic doll that's about to turn into a mass murderer. Or at least, that's how she saw him. Judging by the elation of those surrounding her, this was not a common reaction. In fact, you could go as far as saying that they were behaving as if a benevolent god had deigned to pay a personal visit, which she was certain was exactly what Kai intended. Parallel with the dockside, the crew were patiently waiting in line for their breakfast, eagerly waving and shouting greetings. Aromas from the morning's mass cooking drifted from the ship's lower deck and the atmosphere was fizzing with the energy of a truly magnificent spectacle.

Naomi hadn't heard much from Beth since she'd been looking after the baby, but Naomi had been busy herself refining R&Rs recruitment techniques and unsuccessfully trying to find a replacement for Mary. In the last proper conversation they'd had, Beth had told her that collecting the baby from the incubation unit and taking him home had been a surreal experience and not a particularly rewarding one. Despite this, Beth seemed determined to be a mother above all else. Naomi was disappointed that on this day of all days she wouldn't be meeting Beth alone, but it was a relief that Beth seemed to be getting back on the caster road.

Lined up along the dockside were rows and rows of the zeroed and the under thirteens. The rumour was rife that the freeship would be recruiting crew from those most in need. Adventures on the open seas were promised. Talk of bleeding edge technology that was being developed on the ship was widespread, with much speculation about what it could be. Some were sure it was perpetual food that grew from the scraps that were left over after preparing a meal, which Naomi couldn't help thinking was exactly what nature did when left alone to be itself. Others believed it was tiny devices that could be implanted at various places around the body and that could enhance digestion, cell regeneration and even speed up the acquisition of a suntan. The ideas might have seemed wild, but Kai was a master at getting people to believe what he wanted and to aspire to his vision. In other words, it was the natural extension of a tech company's marketing strategy: to create the need, and then meet the demand. Behind it all was the ever-present Loop, with its effect on the day-to-day. Exactly what and how was a mystery to everyone, possibly even to Kai.

Naomi edged her way towards the front of the crowd, being careful to stay clear of the zeroed in case her non-status somehow led to her getting mixed in with them and gathered up as freeship crew. Not something she was keen on at all. The freeship was static, looking like a street of office blocks at the edge of the water. Inside, people were scurrying around, occasionally pausing at a window and either staring out or waving to the crowds. They were certainly doing a good job of making life on Freeship One appear attractive. Kai had come down from the crow's nest and was standing at a podium on the edge of the deck with a camera crew surrounding him. He appeared across the side of the ship as two identical images side by side, and as images on the front and on the back of the ship. He was setting himself up for one of his speeches. He coughed and it boomed around the docks, bouncing off the buildings.

The crowd quietened and he spoke. "We are so pleased to be back after all this time. So much has changed, hasn't it? The Ls – your Leveller and your Locals – have been improving your lives beyond our wildest dreams. The time has come for Freeship One to play its part in your success. Firstly, we know that in England there are those of you who have used all of your wealth already, you so called zeroed, and there are those of you too young for wealth, you children." He paused as if he was mulling over his own words and their meaning. "Well, we want you. Come aboard. There's room for everyone and a welcome for anyone. Come and explore the oceans of the world and join in the wonderful future we are creating for ourselves and for humanity. We are the first of the freeships. That's why we're here, for you. A welcome awaits."

The lines of the dispossessed and the pre-adults shuffled along. Only, after Kai's speech they held their heads high, no longer slumped towards their feet. There was a bounce in the step of the zeroed that came close to the excited energy of the youngsters and Naomi couldn't help feeling sorry for them, like contented cattle being gently guided into the slaughterhouse.

A girl of about seven was the first of the children to board. Kai was waiting to welcome her. He took her to one side and whispered something in her ear. She grinned at him, vigorously nodding her head. The cameras panned back from the close up and scanned along the rows and rows of patiently queuing hopefuls. Succulent red strawberries were being handed out by small delivery drones. A punnet for each person. Luxury was theirs for the taking and Kai was not shy about showing it and not slow in offering it. Hand in hand he walked with the young girl to his podium. The cameras closed in on the two of them, both with big fat grins across their faces.

He clapped and the crowd quietened. "I have a gift for all the under thirteens who join me," he said, placing a tiny spherical object in the palm of the young girl.

He whispered again in her ear and she touched the top of the sphere carefully with her tiny fingertip. It elevated from her palm and slowly rose until it was level with her ear. Kai then turned her around so her back was to the camera. A nurse approached and knelt down. While Kai held the girl's hand the nurse did something the cameras couldn't see. The girl's shoulders flinched, but then she turned around to face the cameras stroking her left eyebrow. The camera zoomed in to show a fresh piercing. Kai held her hands high in the air and made her clap loudly.

"Citizens of England and citizens of East Albion," he shouted.

He waited for silence.

"I give you the girl-globule. There's a boy one, too. This mini-globule will accompany her wherever she goes. Through the piercing it will hear what she hears and see what she sees. It will educate her as she goes about her daily life. No more need for lessons. No more need for school. An educator at her fingertips every second of the day."

The crowd cheered and cheered to the point that Naomi thought they'd never shut up. "Girl? Boy?" she muttered. It was depressing how quickly the binary nature of the Ls had reversed the notion of fluid gender, and this was regressive beyond belief.

Kai clapped. "You like it?" he shouted, and the crowd shouted yes. "In that case," he said and paused. "In that case I will make one of these available to all the children of England and East Albion."

Another roar of approval from the crowd.

"For free."

Naomi turned to leave. How could they be so stupid? A constant stream of Narcissist propaganda into the mind of every child in the country. Offered, not forced. That fact she had to accept.

They'd been duped into willingly accepting manipulation. She was unable to form her thoughts into words let alone to raise a coherent objection so she left the crowd behind slurping from the dog bowl Kai had so expertly put in front of them.

Beth, her boyfriend and their baby were in the Retro Bar waiting to meet her. She checked the availability of a trike. Many of the visitors had not relinquished their transport when they arrived, knowing there would be high demand immediately after the event and although scooters were not her favourite it was one of those damn things or nothing. While she was waiting for it to arrive, Kai's voice boomed across the docks.

"Local una," he said in a clear soothing voice. "We are upgrading our OS dollar from a world currency to be local. To be yours. English Una. East Albion Una."

There was plenty of chatter between globules and, from what Naomi could tell, the masses were confused. There was a general lack of understanding about currencies and money. So long as some form of money was there, then most people were happy. If the interest rate rose, they cared. How much they cared depended on the percentages and on whether they were a saver or a spender. Inflation mattered too, but that was less tangible. As for the time value of money, that was complicated. Especially in England where everyone already had their fifty years' worth of wealth.

Kai continued. "Una will be totally transferable e-cash. You can store it on whatever device you wish. The toaster if you want. It works on the mini-globules too, so you can safely give cash to your kids. The days of being restricted to using your globule to pay are gone."

Even at a distance the clapping of the crowd was loud. She was disgusted at how they relished convenience. What they didn't understand was that they were witnessing the next step in global domination. No matter, so long as they were happy.

Kai tapped his podium. "There's more," he said and the crowd stopped talking. "There's more. We have made it local so each jurisdiction with its own L can set their interest rates. You can even decide whether to have a light or dark currency. Or, a mix. Go dark and you get the freedom to behave as you wish, to set the rules as liberal as your desires demand and with absolutely no accessible record of what you've been up to. Or you can play safer and choose a light currency. Typically, we might expect a higher interest rate for the dark currencies, but local una isn't restricted. It's yours to control."

A lot of clapping followed with occasional whoops of support from overexcited individuals. Naomi left, bewildered at the way her fellow citizens seemed to lap up everything the freeship gave them.

At the Retro Bar, she followed the usual routine of giving her globule and exchanging pleasantries with the doorman. Inside, she looked around and chuckled when she saw that Beth had chosen the alcove where they'd first met. For some reason it sent a little ripple of joy down her spine.

"Beth," she said. "Tam." She stooped to stool height. "And, who is this?"

"Alex," said Beth. "It's been way too long."

Naomi stood up and Beth opened her arms for a hug. Naomi staggered on her feet, which she hoped Beth would take for a stumble rather than her surprise at the hug. Tam sat and smiled.

"Bloody stupid people," said Naomi. "No idea what they're letting themselves in for."

Beth raised her eyebrows and laughed. "Meaning?" she said.

"Sorry. Couldn't contain it any longer."

Tam lifted his head from his hands, took his elbows off the bar and straightened his back. "We saw the freeship broadcast. Good news about the currencies," he said.

Naomi shook her head. "Do you think they comprehend? That dark currency is the anonymous one? No tracking. No interference."

Tam's smile was condescending. "The interest rate on the dark would be negative, too. We'd have to pay to store unas, which for the English is a real issue. Not only that, the lighter one allows the tracking of criminals, terrorists and stuff. That's got to be a good thing, and it pays interest."

Naomi glanced at Beth who was tending to Alex before answering him. "I suspect you're right. That is what they'll choose. In effect giving up their privacy. For a little more cash. The Ls can make any activity taboo. Driven by that fucking Loop. If your currency is light be prepared to be zeroed because you didn't follow the party line." She looked at Beth. "Is that what you want?"

Beth was busy with Alex and Tam started to answer, "I think—"

Naomi cut him short. "I asked Beth." She tapped Beth on the shoulder. "Well?"

Beth wiped her hands as she looked up. "Sorry, Alex takes a lot of attention."

Naomi nodded towards Tam. "I thought you said he was doing the parenting."

"He does his share," said Beth.

"A hundred percent? That was the agreement. Wasn't it?"

Beth smiled. "It's me. I won't let him, even though I know I should."

"Too right you should."

Naomi turned to Tam. "No disrespect, but I should be having this conversation with the caster. Not the hacker."

"Data harvester," said Tam. He picked up his beer and walked away.

"Beth. Don't waste your talent."

"It all seems so hopeless. I was so naïve and embarrassingly simplistic. It's like throwing stones at the moon. Nothing I do really makes a difference. We're fooling ourselves if we think we can. Don't you see? Human nature wins out over any levelling or attempt to create an equal world. I've spent a lot of time on my own. Well, not entirely on my own. I've had time to think while looking after him. Hundreds of casts, over a million followers, yet my stupid efforts aren't changing anything. That's the conclusion I've come to. At least I can bring him up to be a positive influence," she said stroking Alex's chin as he nestled in her arms. "Oh, and don't be so hard on Tam. He's great and wants to do much more than I'll let him," she added.

"So, let him. Seriously. We need you to dig away. Display your findings to the masses. Otherwise, there'll be no world for your Alex to be positive in."

"Don't overstate things. I know you have this thing about the Loop, but an ethics protocol guiding the Ls has got to be a good thing. Hasn't it?"

"Let me remind you. The guiding principles are minimal government, to free all private individuals, and all businesses to thrive. Now, if that's not going suck the planet dry of all its goodness, natural resources and humanity's kindness. I don't know what will."

"What about this new currency. Will that help? Surely, we could make the light versions prohibit the wastefulness of resources?"

"Maybe. I'll give you that. If the council doesn't link it to identity, then I can have access to East Albion una. That'll be a relief. Did I mention I'm about to buy a ship? I want to see the world before it vanishes. R and R's international ambassador. Need to make as many connections with likeminded groups as possible. Not only that, I want to chase after the freeships and find out as much as I can about them, and those darn Ls and their Loop."

"Hey, that sounds totally fantastic. I'm oozing jealousy. You know what's really weird? I've been getting glitches in my data about small ships. What a coincidence."

Naomi grimaced. "Don't believe in coincidences. I'll get Morgan to investigate."

"And, I'll get Tam to take a look," replied Beth. "Stay in touch. It sounds dangerous."

"You stay in touch, too. With me. With Gerry. You must use East Albion as the touchstone to what's happening in England. We must compare these Ls, if we are to make any headroom with the Loop. Keep digging and displaying."

With that, Naomi kissed Beth on the cheek and ruffled Alex's magnificently curly hair.

"Be careful my brave pirate," Beth called after her.

Naomi grinned to herself. It was nice to see Beth again. A part of her wanted to stay and put the world to rights, and get Tam to do his part in the parenting. That would be a pleasant way to spend a few weeks, but Freeship One would be departing soon and she had to be ready to follow, at a distance. She called a trike and set off for the docks to buy one of the two ships that she and Morgan had narrowed her choice down to. Both ships could be crewed by a single person and both ships had space for up to six people. Both perfect. It was simply a matter of price. She checked her globule and sure enough Gerry had transferred una to the R&R account that she could use, enough for her to buy a ship and live for at least a year. Things were looking up.

PART TWO

17

BETH WAS at the regrow shop getting some food for Alex's tenth birthday. Up ahead, an orderly queue of people patiently waited while clutching their bags of scraps. She joined them and they slowly moved forward. Why he wanted regrown food was beyond her, but Tam had assured her that it was part of finding his identity, of showing that he had a personality in his own right. Beth thought he might be doing it just to be annoying. Whichever it was, they both agreed that Alex's change of behaviour had been triggered by their move from south-east London to east-central London. The move had highlighted her shift towards the mainstream, brought about by the desire to focus on nurturing her son. Sure, she kept in touch with Gerry and Morgan, but more as a friend than a fellow traveller.

One of the women in front of her turned around and looked her up and down. Conscious that she looked out of place, she tried not to attract attention by showing her disgust, but the stench of rotting food that wafted in and out of this human regiment of hopeful hand-me-outs was repugnant, as was the fact that society had failed and that these regrow shops were necessary. Although being able to grow the full thing from a sample was fantastic, it was looked down on. In fact, if it wasn't for the freeships sharing their technology, those unfortunate enough not to be able to sustain themselves properly could very well have starved. Many had lost their wealth, and not all of them had brought it on themselves, as some of her less charitable neighbours suggested.

The queue moved forward slowly.

Tam kept her abreast of the rapidly changing technology from the freeships and what was likely to become prevalent across England. He was a great help in her work, which was targeted on the children and their future. She was earning a decent amount of una and was gaining a good reputation from her casts and sponsorship deals as a children's champion, and she suspected Alex was being teased about it. No amount of explaining to him that the move across London was simply to leave an area that was likely to flood could persuade him that it wasn't a way of her boasting about her newfound income. He hit out, constantly using the phrase *sucking at Babylon's tits*, despite her telling him it was totally taboo. Rational arguments had no effect either. Tam said Alex would get over it. She wasn't so sure, but was hoping that his birthday and the fact that his datatrust fund would begin to yield una for him in a year, would act as triggers for him to 'grow up'.

The queue continued its shuffle along the pavement in a slow march to replenishment. People were talking of new contributions from one of the freeships docked at Canning Town, speculating about supersized fruit, and chickens that could shed limbs for food and then regrow them. Only to shed them time and time again.

What a decade it had been. Resist & Regain had pursued the use of the dark currencies and had found themselves increasingly isolated as the punishing cost of using money that couldn't be tracked forced more and more people to use its lighter cousin. After a few difficult years, they were once again going from strength to strength. Naomi's determination to build a worldwide alliance was delivering results. Although, as she was fond of pointing out, it wasn't easy to persuade people to affiliate. There was a lot of suspicion about everything generally, and it took time. Beth got the impression from their chats that Naomi was relishing the experiences that travelling the world was giving her, as well as allowing her to indulge her hatred of the freeships by gathering as much data as she could on their mode of operation and circulating it among the R&R membership. Beth sensed that Naomi was on the verge of direct action and in the early hours when her family were asleep, she toyed with her jealousy, imagining joining Naomi and taking on Kai. Harmless fantasies, she hoped, fuelled by Naomi's teasing about Beth becoming one of the comfortable.

The queue moved and the woman in front of her tipped the contents of her bag into the disposal chute at the front of the building. She stepped into the scanner and waited inside while it analysed whatever traces it found in her waste, traces to be replenished with lab-regrown versions. It validated her identity. This was not a facility for the zeroed. A readout of the contents appeared on the floor beneath her. Tomatoes, potatoes, carrots and pork. An X appeared next to the pork. The tech wasn't perfect and if it had been regrown too many times, it degraded beyond the point of usefulness. Or, at least that's what they claimed. She frowned and then shrugged. There was no way of knowing which food was at the end of its regrowth cycle, on its last legs. It was the luck of the draw. Beth tipped the scraps that Alex had collected from random people into the chute. The queue continued to move steadily forward through the building towards the pick-up point and the exit. The walls were showing a constant diet of Kai's cookery programmes on how to make nutritious meals. With his winning smile, he encouraged those who were not about to collect these enticing ingredients to purchase them by touching the images. Seeing him whip up extravagant meals so easily from a few basics was exciting and she was tempted to join the steady tap of fingers touching the screens as the queue moved slowly forward.

"Hello, Beth," he said, as she waited in front of one of them. "How about a recipe for that special day? Alex's birthday, isn't it? Ten going on fifteen?"

There was something uncanny happening. Kai's eyes had a depth of sincerity that was hard to pin down, and the kitchen behind him had the vibrancy of cooking in full flow. Despite having the tag indicating deepfake, she was unable to tell whether this particular deepfake was actually real. A knot formed in her stomach and she moved on quickly, shaking inside at the thought of him tracking her family. It wasn't the first time a supposed deepfake Kai had spoken to her directly, a fact that she was keeping hidden from Tam. Was it possible that Kai was manipulating the taboo that allowed deepfakes so long as they were tagged? Was he flipping it to his advantage?

Once she was outside with her bag of random regrown food she headed home, not bothering to rummage around to check what was there. That was a job best left for Tam as the birthday party's chef.

In the garden, Alex was bumping jLobs with a girl he'd met in VR. It all looked a bit inept as they struggled to pick up the humanoid robots, which were the same size as them, and clumsily bash them together. Beth chuckled. Not at Alex and the girl, although there was a naïvety between them that they would have been devastated to know. Not at Suzann and Camerann, their patient companions, either. She was amused by humanity's ability to adapt without question. It had been amazing how the eyebrow-connected boy and girl mini-globules had soon become a distant memory and every parent happily claimed their kid's free jLob on their fourth birthday, becoming immediately absorbed in teaching them how to use it to its full potential. Naturally, Alex had trained Camerann to appear sullen and disinterested in everything that wasn't somehow insolent or taboo. He insisted that he'd named it Camerann after Cameron which means crooked nose, as an everyday reminder that it wasn't perfect despite appearances. It also amused Beth that while the kids insisted the j of their child-shaped globule was a retro-reference to the turn of the century, being the next letter in the alphabet after the ubiquitous *i*, all the parents knew that j was short for juvenile. Watching Alex and his new friend playing certainly confirmed this. Not that it mattered.

Alex screamed at Tam. "This is not the party I wanted."

"Oh no, here we go again," she muttered.

Tam shook his head, glanced across at her and crinkled his mouth. She exhaled quietly at the memory of the night before. He was as sexy as the day she'd met him and that still surprised her, especially when comparing notes about such stuff with her friends.

He cleared his throat. "What do you expect, my young rebel? If you only allow Camerann to learn from connecting to its peers on your birthday, then it can only learn once a year and you'll only get a mildly revised party. Mate, it's your choice."

Alex waved his arms around, pointing at the brightly coloured food and decorations. "This," he said, making sure his friends could hear and see him. "Really?"

"Your choice," repeated Tam, as he walked away.

Alex turned on Beth. "Did you get my regrows?"

"Hey. I sure did. Here you are. All perfectly formed for your pleasure." She emptied the bag on to the table and couldn't help turning her nose up at the faint whiff of decay.

A sneer of disappointment crossed his face. "Good. I didn't think you'd bother."

The other children were happily banging jLobs and tinkering with the various pieces of rescued tech that Tam had carefully laid out for them. They seemed happy enough and although Alex was being his usual difficult self, he, too, seemed engrossed in whatever he and his friend were doing.

Beth took Tam to one side. "He's alright, isn't he?" she said.

"He's fine. Little tyke that he is. Gotta lot of gumption though, that one. Not surprising considering who his mother is."

Tam curled his lips and Beth kissed them lightly.

"I think it's time," said Tam.

Beth recoiled, knowing what was coming next.

"He needs a sibling to look out for."

"He'll be an adult in three years' time."

"Exactly. He needs some practice."

"That's a rubbish reason to have another child. Totally and completely rubbish."

"Oh, come on. You know it's not the only reason."

She looped her arm into his. Part of her wanted another child, and part of her was appalled at the idea. "These days, there's all that genetic fiddling before they'll accept an embryo for the incubators. I don't like it. I won't have it."

He unlooped her arm and gave her a hug. "There are ways to circumvent it."

"That is so seriously taboo. I'd be zeroed in an instant if we got caught."

"I know people. Good people. If we register me as the primary parent, you'll be free of any comeback if it goes wrong."

"Maybe. Give me a little more time," she said and kissed him once again on those oh so enticing lips.

Alex interrupted their moment. "You have to get me one of these," he said shoving his jLob in front of their faces.

An animation of a boy about Alex's age was playing across the surface.

"What's that, mate?"

Alex raised his eyebrows at his dad. "It's what everyone has," he said and then made a snorting sound. "Sadie has one," he said glancing at his friend. "I need one, too."

The animation focused in on the boy's arm and an intricate pattern of swirls that seemed to be formed by scar tissue. Tam glanced at Beth and she raised her shoulders in a shrug of *I've no idea*.

Tam tried to take the jLob to get a closer look, but Alex shoved it out of his reach. "Mate, I'm lost. Why don't you let me in on your secret?"

Alex sneered, but Sadie spoke. "It's the latest interface."

Alex nodded.

Sadie continued. "With this there is so much more a jLob can do. It is the passage to adulthood and the sooner he has one, the better adult he'll be."

Tam knelt down.

"And?" said Alex.

"You sound like an advert."

They both stared at Tam.

"Is it safe? It looks kinda weird to me."

"Not as weird as your tattoo," said Alex, and he dragged Sadie away.

"Hey," said Beth ruffling Tam's hair. She shuddered. "How does he know about that?"

"Search me."

She chewed her lip. "We can't allow him to have this. Can we?"

"No way. I'll check it out, but it's a big fat no from me."

"You know, I'm sure there's more than we realise being pumped through these jLobs. More than we ever get to see, that's for sure."

"No doubt."

They stood holding hands, watching the party. The kids were pretty much ignoring the regrown food and guzzling the brightly coloured stuff that Alex had been so scathing about.

"Did you try that regrow stuff?" asked Tam.

"Hey. No way. It stinks. Did you?"

"Yeah. Bland beyond belief, and I was as hungry after eating as I was before."

"The kids love it though." She laughed sarcastically. "Just look at them fighting for a taste."

The robot companions – one for every child – queued in an orderly fashion, ready to choose the next plate of delights for their humans. It was a lovely scene of tech and human working in harmony. Six years of training was a long time for an ANN and there was still another three years to go before Alex would part company with Camerann. Was a sibling really required to teach him responsibilities?

Tam interrupted her thoughts. "Look out," he whispered. "Here comes more trouble."

Alex and Sadie were storming across the lawn, followed closely by Camerann and Suzann. All four had serious expressions on their faces.

"We don't need your money," said Alex.

"Glad to hear it," said Tam.

"We can earn it ourselves," said Sadie.

As they were turning to leave, Tam grabbed Camerann from Alex.

"Show me," he said.

Alex reached out to grab it back, but Tam was too tall.

"Keep it," shouted Alex. "We're going to have a baby and sell it to the orphanage."

"What?" said Beth. "What the fuck?"

Alex and Sadie giggled.

"Oh no you're bloody well not."

Tam put a hand on each of their shoulders. "I think you could be a little bit young for that."

"I'm not," said Sadie. "And, if he is then I can find someone else."

"You can't stop us," said Alex. He pointed at Camerann. "Don't think you can use him either. I've blocked you."

With that, they stormed back across the lawn and carried on playing with their friends.

"And you want another one?"

Tam nodded rather sheepishly. "We need to talk," he said and headed towards the house.

Inside, they slumped onto the sofa and sat in silence, each of them fiddling with their globules, lost in their own worlds and desperately avoiding another argument about Alex or having a baby.

Beth focused in on the orphanage, which she thought had been closed. Partly as a result of her *Minor Miners* article, or at least that's what had been widely reported. She was convinced of the link between the terrible experiments she'd seen at the orphanage and Kai's constant message about how critical it was to create enhanced humans for the next stage of evolution, despite the fact that some individuals would be heroic casualties of failure along the way. With Alex's revelation she was compelled to find out more. She tried every trick she knew, but there were no references that she could find. No matter. Eventually, while the kids were still playing outside, she rented a drone from a place on the English-Scottish border near to Kielder Water. She flew the tourist drone around the lake, going to great lengths to appear interested in the whole area. At the north eastern tip she spotted a newly built canal, large enough to accommodate a freeship. She followed its thirty-mile length to the channel of the River Esk on the west coast just inside the English border, providing further confirmation that the orphanage and the freeships were inextricably linked. Back at the lake, the drone meandered around, swooping high and low, dipping into the forest and then soaring way up above the treeline. She rolled her globule around in her hand taking pleasure from the smooth action of her top-end rental. As she approached the place where the orphanage had been, she told the drone the exact spot to hover over.

"Subsystem. Conqueror. Brothers."

The forest was so dense she could see nothing. The drone dropped to the top of the trees and she carefully steered it through the branches, occasionally clipping the drone's bumpers by accident. It was difficult, but she was slowly making progress when the drone came to a thick knotted canopy that it couldn't penetrate. She bashed against it as hard as she dared, but nothing gave. She tried a few times without any luck and she tried moving out of the zone and then approaching from ground level only to be blocked by thick hedges.

"It's still there," she said to Tam who was submerged in his own harvesting and didn't hear her. She sent the drone back to the hire company.

Maybe Naomi was right and she had become too complacent. Kai at the regrow, the jLobs covertly persuading Alex and Sadie, and the orphanage all combined to an overspill of fear that they were on the edge of a veiled precipice.

She began making plans to visit in person and the sound of the children happily playing drifting in from outside, made her quest all the more poignant.

18

Beth was standing on the platform of Boston station waiting for Morgan to collect her. She was hungry and tired. The trip had been fine and without any issues, but the emotional exhaustion of what she was planning and the last few days of Tam's nagging had tested her patience. He had pleaded with her to enlist Naomi's help when she had insisted on going to the orphanage in person, but she was certain that Naomi had returned to sea. She didn't tell him, he could be a worrier, especially now they'd agreed that he was almost entirely the sole carer for Alex.

The small station shop had a display of locally grown vegetables outside and an enticing window display of breads and cakes. Her stomach clenched at the smell of fresh baking and freshly cut grass. A message from Morgan arrived, saying he was running a little late. This made the shop even more attractive and she wandered across to take a closer look.

"Hey," she said to the young man behind the counter. "Can I use English una here?"

"'Fraid not. Local currency only. You visiting East Albion?"

"I am. I'm visiting a friend who I haven't seen for ages. I'm English. Your food looks amazing."

"Wait," he said, beckoning her towards the counter. "Have you used your guest allocation?"

"My what?"

"I'll take that as a no then. Well, you're in luck. As a guest of East Albion you have a daily allowance sufficient to adequately feed you."

"That's amazing. Why on earth…?"

"Great hosts. That's our aim. Here, hand me your globule and I'll see what I can pull together for you. Happy to spend today's allowance in here?"

She nodded and smiled all in one big silly gesture, which the young man ignored. He busied himself filling a bag with two bread rolls, a thick slice of plum bread, three apples and a chunk of local cheese.

"How about a couple of our speciality, the Lincolnshire haslet?"

"Yes, please. What is it?"

"Do you eat meat?"

"Local? Looked after?"

"Yup," he said and picked up a couple of brown caramelised oval shaped haslets.

He handed her the bag along with a bottle of liquid, an edible bottle he pointed out, tapped her globule against his and wished her a happy visit. As she left the shop, Morgan pulled up on a trike before she had a chance to eat anything.

He waved enthusiastically. "Hop on," he said. "I'll take you on a tour."

It was a warm, sticky day and the breeze from travelling at speed on an open trike went some way towards cooling her down. Out of Boston and on the road that ran parallel to the trainline the trike cut through the few centimetres of water that covered the ground, creating a spray all around them. It was fantastic. He shouted above the noise of the splashing wheels, pointing out various fields of crops that liked shallow water, and with great glee telling her that they were there for all of the community to use.

At Hubbert's Bridge they turned back towards Boston and home.

When they arrived, Morgan pulled onto the driveway and jumped off. Beth was surprised at how far the flooding had crept its way along the street. It hadn't reached their house yet, but it was well on its way. She inhaled. The air was fresh and vibrant compared with the heaviness she'd experienced at the station. As soon as her feet hit the ground, the trike started up again and left, off to its next booking.

"Is Naomi here?" she asked when they were inside the house.

Morgan sighed. "No. She's travelling again."

Gerry called from upstairs. "Is that Beth? How wonderful."

Beth dangled her bag in front of her. "I really need to eat, and to catch up on all the gossip."

"Follow me," said Morgan. "You shall have what you need."

They were sitting around the table with a cup of homegrown tea. Beth had her picnic laid out in front of her and was talking about her imminent visit to the orphanage.

"Alex said he was going to sell them a baby," she explained.

"You're kidding?" said Morgan.

Gerry was shaking his head. "No way, no I don't believe that. He's winding you up."

"Maybe," she replied quietly. "But I can't take the chance. Will you help me?"

Gerry leant forward. "Certainly. You know what? Naomi has seen freeships sailing into the canal near the orphanage. Unlike any other dock, all the non-freeships have been blocked from entering. A sophisticated shield seems to render them inoperable if they try."

Buzzing with excitement, Morgan interrupted. "The Loop. It's a live and dynamic protocol that adapts as it's fed real data from each of the Ls," he said. "And we've worked out how to manipulate the data glitch that exists between you and Naomi to switch your identities."

Not sure why he was telling her this, she raised her eyebrows, encouraging him to explain.

"It should allow you to visit the orphanage undetected. I'll have to contact Naomi to make sure that the timing of the switch doesn't put her in any danger, but seeing as she's out at sea I don't see a problem." He bit his lip before continuing. "Be careful though. Naomi has seen Kai on several docksides secretly giving a blessing to the failed experimental humans, as they're being discarded. Left behind. He's ruthless in pursuit of his dreams. You should be on your guard."

He blew her a kiss as he left the room to arrange it all and she parked his warning at the back of her mind, deciding not to spend time worrying about it.

"Gerry? How's the council? I saw all the fields full of food. You must be doing well. And, what is this idea of making sure all your visitors are fed for free?"

"Oh, you mean our Universal Necessary Goods. Isn't it special? It makes us all feel so good to know that nobody feels unwelcome. Started out with the refugees in the camp up on the Wolds, but then we extended it to all visitors to East Albion. Surprisingly cheap for the benefits it brings, and now we're in control of our currency it's just part of the economy."

"Free travel, too."

"Yup. We're the mostest hosts." He laughed. "Did you see the public gardens along the side of the streets?"

Beth shook her head. "No, I don't think so."

"Fruit trees and a smattering of vegetables, growing there for anyone to harvest. We trust each other, and nobody takes the piss. It's perfect."

Beth finished eating the last of the cheese with a bread roll and passed Gerry the haslets.

"I'll ask Morgan to do something fabulous with them," he said. "Now, make yourself comfortable while I finish off some business for the council."

She stretched out on the sofa and let her imagination play around with her trip to the orphanage. The train journey there would be simple enough, crossing back into England and then up along the border to York and across to Newcastle before changing for Hexham. Then a single seater drone, organised by Gerry and paid for by Resist & Regain. What came after wasn't so easy to imagine. She presumed there'd be extremely tight security. Probably with more advanced BP than publicly available, given its connection to the freeships.

She dozed, with a comfortable feeling of being nurtured and respected by her friends. She wished Naomi was there, but it was reassuring to know that Morgan and Gerry were in touch and looking out for her and as she felt herself drifting into sleep, she buzzed Tam with a 'missing you' message and closed her eyes.

19

Beth was hanging off the bottom of the drone, lying horizontally in the passenger hammock. The tips of the trees were within touching distance and she was tempted to hold her arm out to stroke them as she flew past, imagining it would release a powerful scent. There had been no security activity from the ground and no BPs challenging her in the air, and yet she had to make herself breathe in and out regularly, conscious that her default seemed to be to inhale and hold.

The drone set her down next to the dense hedge surrounding the orphanage and she got to work with the cutters Tam had made for her. Sharp and silent, he'd said. Like you, she'd teased back. She was bathed in fondness for him as she began to create an entrance into whatever strangeness was waiting for her.

It took ages to complete the tunnel, but she'd held her nerve and finally she could see daylight through the thin cover of foliage that stood between her and the grounds of the orphanage. She checked that her globule was silent and then cut through to the other side. Wriggling through the Beth-sized hole on her belly she emerged and immediately crouched on to her knees. It would be the movement that Naomi had originally taught her that would get her from the hedge to the building unnoticed if anything would, Morgan had poignantly told her as she was leaving. She crawled on all fours, zigzagging across the lawn towards another low hedge around a magnificent old building with large windows, each with a pointed roof above it and striking slim towers with spindly spires on top at either end. She reached the hedge and peeked over the top. A gravel path wound its way around the base of the building. Young children were everywhere, running and shouting, and playing with the same grotesquely deformed pigs that she'd seen before, only this time they weren't caged, they roamed freely around the grounds. On the face of it, it was a happy magical place where bot police stood guard, to protect their wards.

Beth leapt over the hedge and dropped back on all fours. One of the BP turned to face her and lifted itself off the floor, ready to glide towards her. She stood more chance of evading the BP if she was moving because as far as R&R could ascertain, a moving life-form on all fours that didn't register in the data was still considered by the drones as an animal of an unknown species. They only attacked those that posed a threat to them, and unknown meant unthreatening. Morgan had been keen to show her that, as the foremost haven for red squirrels in Great Britain, predators were hunted and it was more dangerous to be a fox or a badger than an unregistered human. With that in mind, she continued her zigzag journey to the house. The BP paused for a few seconds before returning to its place in the guardian line-up.

A noisy bunch of teenagers arrived, accompanied by two drones. Beth was close enough to overhear their conversation and they were too wrapped up in their excitement to see her. She dropped down on to her stomach, staying absolutely still.

"I'm gonna get a trip on a freeship," said one of the girls, patting her stomach.

The boy next to her frowned. "*We* are gonna get a trip."

She kissed his cheek. "We are."

None of the girls was showing any signs of pregnancy, but Beth was convinced that each one was there to have their foetus extracted and to collect their fee. It was horrendous, and yet she couldn't help feel a sense of pride in the boys who had come with their girlfriends, presumably as the fathers of the unborn babies.

As soon as the teenagers disappeared inside the building she continued her zigzagging.

An unusually large number of BP were congregated around one of the entrances. She made her way over, ensuring that the camera in her eyebrow was still recording. She paused, summoned all of the braveness she could find from deep inside and weaved her way in and out of the BP. Not one of them paid her any attention and she was soon on the other side of them and at the top of a slope that led down into the basement. Her knees were hurting, her legs were aching and on the edge of cramping. She rested for a few minutes until the pain eased and then worked her way down into the building. The slope had led her into a maze of corridors and she zigzagged along the one that looked the least dirty and hence the most used.

Deep inside, she came across a room with a strong smell that caught the back of her throat. It was a combination of a chemical odour she couldn't identify, a thick putrefying aroma and an earthy tang that clung underneath. Shelf upon shelf of half-formed plants lined the room. Bot insects filled the air. Flying from one to another, they pierced the plant skins and injected them before blasting them with a powerful light. She noticed a sickly-looking child chomping on a pile of discarded leaves and after a quick wave, which he returned, she hid behind a crate to watch. He chewed frantically and spat out a green mush at regular intervals into his hands. She couldn't quite remember the name of the disease of the swollen hands but she was sure it had something to do with consuming enough calories but not enough protein. A door creaked in the distance, followed by approaching footsteps.

A white-coated man entered the room. "Stop your snivelling," he said, close up to the boy's face. "You chose this. You wanted the shiny toys. It's called trade. A good lesson to learn. Eh?"

He lifted the boy's T-shirt and unscrewed a plug in the boy's stomach, before pushing his tech-tipped forefinger inside and stirring. He checked his globule, looked puzzled and after screwing the cap in place he left. Beth clamped her mouth shut to prevent herself from vomiting and crawled back out of the room bashing her knees and elbows as she went.

In the next room there were several children sitting with their backs against the wall watching an old nature documentary from when the climate was more stable, enthralled by the wallabies of Tasmania struggling for survival in the snowy winter. Racks of shallow liquid-filled trays of part-grown meat cultures fanned outwards from the wall and drones were gathering products for the children to consume. Scared that she'd be discovered she moved on quickly.

From then on, fabrics filled room after room. Swathes and swathes of different colours and textures grew in transparent covered vats. In the final room, a factory was in full swing cutting patterns in the material with lasers and tailoring clothes from an elaborate variety of microbe-cloths that she recognised from freeship propaganda about living cloth that could heal you, with varying degrees of success, many commentators had added. Once again children populated the far end of the room. This time they were wearing T-shirts and underwear produced by the factory in which they lived. Some were scratching their flesh and some were covered in scarlet and dark blue welts. Others were grinning and stroking their experimental clothes with affection.

Beth crawled across to one of the boys covered in welts. "What's wrong?" she whispered.

"It hurts. It's eating my skin, but they won't let me take it off," he said, through sniffling sobs.

A girl spotted her and Beth signalled for her to be quiet, but she screeched while trying to suppress a laugh. Beth scurried back to the slope, stumbling along as fast as she could. Half on all fours and half running. The damp chemical earthy smell clung to her throat as she zigzagged her way to the top of the slope and past the BP guards. She swallowed the puke that had leapt into the inside of her mouth and clenched her jaw shut. At the low hedge, she flung herself over and onto all fours. She threw up a vile smelling pile of half-digested food. It was disgusting and she only felt partly purged. Still gagging and dribbling down her chin, she scampered back to the hole in the hedge and pulled her body through with no regard for the cuts it inflicted on her.

The drone was waiting where she'd left it. She flung herself on to the hammock and instructed it to get to the train as fast as it could, thankful that Gerry had the foresight to rent it for the waiting time and the return trip. It shot up into the air and set off at such a pace that all she could do was hang on and hope she didn't fall.

The forest soon gave way to the lake and she was glad that the flight was too turbulent for her to focus on what she'd witnessed in the orphanage.

At the station she crawled out of the drone's hammock and ran to the train, which was about to leave. As she slumped into her seat, she thought she saw Kai's face appear briefly on one of the station's advertising panels, winking at her. She shuddered, and quickly replaced the eyebrow camera with a standard stud and tucked it into the pocket inside her knickers. Another of Naomi's tricks of the trade.

For the entire journey to Boston, horrendous images of the children being abused flashed across her mind, though none of them stayed for very long. Somehow her brain seemed to be protecting her from remembering too vividly the horrors inside that building. Her implants must have helped, too.

Morgan collected her from the station and she was grateful to him for not forcing her to speak. He could see she was traumatised and so he nattered on about trivia. Something about Gerry and the council, something else about their neighbours, and so on until they arrived back at his house.

She was walking up the driveway arm in arm with him and, when she could no longer suppress the need to expunge, she bent over double and vomited, time and time again. He rubbed her back, not commenting or even trying comfort her with words. She loved him for that. Eventually, she stopped and after a few minutes of dry heaving she straightened her back and walked slowly to the house.

Gerry was there in the doorway. "What was all that about it?"

"Leave it," said Morgan.

"Kids. Experiments. This," said Beth passing Morgan the eyebrow camera. "It's all on that."

Morgan took it and turned to Gerry. "Look after her," he said and kissed Gerry on the lips. "I'll see what on earth she's got."

Gerry helped Beth onto the sofa and plied her with cup after cup of tea. A bucket sat between them, just in case.

"Wanna spill the beans?"

Beth chuckled and snorted all at the same moment. "I think I did," she mumbled.

"What happened up there?"

She was trying to work out how to tell him when Morgan reappeared. His usual smile was turned down at the edges.

"What?" she said.

"Nothing there. Wiped, I presume."

"It can't be. They didn't know I was there. Me being Naomi, plus that zigzag trick, worked. I was invisible. I got right into the heart of their sick, evil orphanage."

"Sorry. They must have an automatic wipe of any recording equipment. It would have been deleted as you left the building. I could kick myself for not anticipating it."

Beth burst into tears and couldn't stop, no matter how much Gerry and Morgan consoled her.

20

Beth woke up with Gerry lying one side gripping her hand and similarly with Morgan on the other side. They were asleep, snoring. She was struck by how male they smelled, but somehow not as male as Tam. There was something cleaner about them. A small wobble in her stomach betrayed the fact that she was unsure what had happened the night before. She remembered them comforting her while she wept and she remembered the gradual sensation of feeling safe in their arms. After that it was unclear. A vague memory of accepting a soothing potion from Morgan hovered at the edge of her mind. As she extricated herself from their grip, Gerry stirred. He turned onto his side and reached out for Morgan. She left them in each other's arms happily snoozing.

Downstairs, she made tea and toast and took it outside. Sitting in their back garden she surveyed the flooded neighbourhood that stretched out across the fields. It was early in the morning and the air was fresh. It was peaceful and soothing. Enjoying the moments of solitude, she resisted bringing her globule back to life. She wasn't quite ready to face Tam and all his questions.

Gerry joined her. "Good morning," he said with a lilt to his voice. "Feeling better?"

"What happened?"

"You collapsed from exhaustion."

"And?"

"The sedative had a bigger effect than we anticipated so we put you to bed."

"Is that all? I woke up with you two in the same bed."

"That's all. We wanted to keep an eye on you, and our bed is big enough for three."

"Honestly?"

"Yes. Why would I lie?"

"I—"

"For fuck's sake, Beth."

She gave him a peck on the cheek. "Thank you," she said.

"Hi," called Morgan from the kitchen. "Anyone want breakfast?"

"I'm good," said Beth.

"Me too," said Gerry.

"I helped myself to tea and toast. I hope you don't mind."

Gerry grinned. "We spent the night in the same bed. How could we mind?"

She laughed and shoved him away. "Hey, what's happening with Resist and Regain? I haven't heard much public stuff recently."

He sighed. "We've been busy, but mainly in secret. Morgan's doing a great job of creating a shadow L. We call it Luscious. One of us used to work for OS and managed to snaffle a copy of OSANN just before it was deployed with full security. We play around with Luscious by orientating it towards common ownership, a sustainable economy and away from the concept of freeing the private individual and their businesses from any collective responsibility."

She leant forward. "Can you change what the Locals decide? After seeing that orphanage again, I need to know we can stop them."

"I take some of the ideas that come out of Luscious and feed them into the council debates, but you can't get beyond the fact that ultimately the ethical stance of the Loop will override."

Morgan appeared with a plate piled high with food.

Gerry chuckled. "Hungry?"

"Fortitude for today's protest."

Beth inhaled loudly. "Smells great," she said. "Protest? I thought you were operating in secret."

Morgan swallowed his mouthful of breakfast. "We still need PR, to an extent. It helps raise funds, and when we make our move we'll need popular local support."

"Your move?"

"Injecting the Loop with the fake training data we're creating with Luscious, to infect the Ls."

Gerry cleared his throat. "Not R and R policy at the moment."

"Can I join you today? At the protest."

"Sure." Morgan grinned. "What will Tam think? Three in a bed followed by a naked protest."

Beth scrunched up her forehead, but he was up and indoors before she could ask him what he meant. Quickly followed by Gerry.

She squeezed her globule and as it came to life it turned a deep red, indicating urgent messages from someone on her VIP list. As she expected, it was Tam. She had told him she was safe at Gerry and Morgan's, but little more than that. His messages had been increasingly desperate, he needed to hear from her. For some reason that she couldn't put her finger on, she had needed time to process what she'd seen and she knew him well enough to know he wouldn't be able to give her that kind of headspace, especially at a distance.

"Tam," she said to her globule, and it connected them.

"Are you alright?"

"Sorry," was all she could manage at first. "I needed some time."

"What happened? I've been shit scared."

They talked and talked about what she'd seen. Tam took some convincing that she'd interpreted the orphanage correctly as a centre for experimenting on children in the most horrendous of ways. He wanted to see for himself and was extremely frustrated that the footage had been wiped. When she told him she was going on an R&R protest he got annoyed. He said it was because he was worried for her and she assured him that she would go as a caster, which helped calm him. It was a difficult conversation. Acknowledging that it would be easier and better to wait until they were together to talk about it more, they agreed to meet up in the lighthouse the following day.

Beth and Morgan set off. Gerry stayed behind. He'd taken a decision not to protest in public as he felt it compromised his position on the council and the trust the community placed in him. Morgan had snorted in derision at that explanation, but Gerry had simply shrugged and got on with his day.

Morgan instructed the trike, "Sailing. Tangling. Clots," and they began their journey.

"Who will be there?" she asked as they drove through another flooded section of the road, sending a spray of water into the air.

"A lot of refugees, I hope. Some local R and R activists. The refugees attract attention and are good hooks for news stories. Here and in their countries of origin. You know, stripped of their homes because of climate, and then stripped of their dignity because of their fellow humans. Even here they're kept in camps."

Beth was quiet for the hour-long trip, enjoying the countryside and the wind in her face. It helped her focus on something other than the horrors of the previous day, although not completely. The protest itself would be both a distraction and a reminder. Morgan had once again swapped her identity with Naomi's and despite what she'd said to Tam she had every intention of joining as an activist and not a caster.

The steep hill out of Ludford took them up onto the Wolds and to the meeting point. A crowd of about a hundred people was gathered with a handful of casters clustered nearby rubbing their hands and stamping their feet. The familiar hum of a wind farm provided the backdrop to the pleasant coolness of the breeze in the midday sunshine.

"We will come across as innocuous," said Morgan. "That's the point. It keeps the BP away while keeping us in the minds of the local community and those thinking of coming here as refugees."

She smiled back at him.

The trike stopped and as they stepped down there was a spontaneous round of applause for Morgan. He wandered into the middle of the gathered protestors and clapped his hands twice in quick succession. The noise died down and all eyes were on him, including those of the presenters from the casting channels, who had strolled across and joined them.

"Welcome," he said. "Welcome to our country. Welcome to this protest." He turned to the cameras. "Welcome to our friends who will make this worthwhile for us." He paused for the round of applause and the whistles to stop. "You know what to do, so let's do it."

A woman stepped forward with a large drum slung around her neck and she began to beat out a steady rhythm.

A young woman sidled up to Beth. "Here, have some of this. We grow it in the camp. Someone brought it with them from their country. It'll keep the cold out."

"Is it safe?"

The woman nodded. Beth thanked her and popped a piece in her mouth and chewed.

Morgan started the chant and the gathered voices of a hundred eager protestors joined in. "You strip mother earth of her natural clothing."

They all took off one item.

"You strip mother earth of her insides."

Another item of clothing was dropped to the floor.

"You strip away the homes of the animals, the birds, the insects."

More clothing came off.

"You strip away the dignity of humanity."

Morgan held up two fingers in a peace sign and the crowd all stripped down to two pieces of clothing.

"You strip away our hope."

He paused for the bras, socks and T-shirts to come off.

"You strip away all of our protection."

Knickers, underpants and long johns all hit the floor and a hundred naked people of all shapes, sizes, colours and ages held their globules high in the air.

"We are not anonymous," they shouted over and over to the beat of the drum.

The drum stopped abruptly and a handful of protestors gathered up the clothes, placed them in a pile and set fire to them.

The drum started again and the crowd chanted. "And the earth burns."

The cameras jostled for close-up shots of the naked activists, checking to ensure they could identify who was who, and then adding the by-line they'd been given. *Strip for Dignity: Resist & Regain calls for an end to stripping the earth and its inhabitants of all their goodness.*

Beth felt wonderfully free waving her arms in the air, but realised that she was in a privileged position by being anonymous despite the communal claims to the contrary. She was also confident that her notoriety as Molly Coddle had declined sufficiently in East Albion for her to go unrecognised by any of the channels. Once the film and photos had been taken, the cameras lost interest and began to disperse. The protestors returned to their vehicles and got dressed in their spare sets of clothes, congratulating each other for taking part.

Morgan handed Beth a set of clothes. "I'm going to the refugee camp," he said. "Why don't you take the trike and go to Withernsea. I'll grab a lift with one of these. You need to see Tam."

"Thank you. You're right. As ever."

Beth boarded the trike. "Stylist. Flats. Spurted," she said and it moved off towards Ludford.

At the River Humber crossing, the flooding became apparent again. The expansive view from the bridge was breathtaking, and the low, flat countryside to the south was covered in water. Beautiful. Tragic. The trike took her along the edge of the floods on the north side of the river towards Withernsea and Tam. A few miles from her destination she had to use the local ferry to cross a particularly deep flood, but apart from that the trike was able to cope without assistance. As she arrived into Withernsea she realised she needed a little more time to think before seeing him. She asked the trike to stop at the small cemetery and she wandered among the graves, considering her future. She took her time reading the inscriptions and imagining all the lives that had passed through the town. Each one unique, and yet together adding up to the sum of humanity in this tiny corner of the world.

It was a fifteen-minute walk to Tam's along the typical east coast country lanes and into a typically nondescript town. The lighthouse stood proud above the treeline at the end of the road and she fixed her eyes on it, not knowing what to expect when she broke her news to him.

He was there for her when she arrived, with Alex by his side. Camerann waited patiently and silently a couple of paces to the left. Her son had reached the point of pretty much ignoring his jLob despite the fact it would follow him around until he was an adult.

As soon as she was within hearing distance she called. "Alex. Come here. Come and say hello."

Alex ambled to her.

"Hey," she said. "Give me a hug, and then can you leave me and your dad to have a chat?"

He looked at her as if he was studying the extent to which she was serious. He touched her arm and spoke quietly. "Sure. Not a problem."

Tam joined her at the same time as Alex was slouching off.

"What was all that about?"

"I have to tell you something," she said.

"Can't it wait until we're home?"

"No. If I don't say it now, I might never say it."

He took a step back. "I need to know what went down at that orphanage."

"Later. This first." She pulled him close and whispered in his ear. "Let's have a baby."

He stepped backwards.

She continued. "Seriously. It's what I want. But I want it outside of the system. No genetic scans. No matching of eggs to sperm. And full term. I want to give birth to a baby not have a foetus extracted from me."

He didn't reply. He stared for ages and then took hold of her hand and guided her to the lighthouse and home.

Inside the safety of the cottage, he pressed for answers. "You know it's a health risk to go full term, right?"

"Really?"

"If—"

"Hey, I know."

"You'll get ostracised for taking time off from being productive. Can you cope with that?"

"Ironic, eh? That whole non-productive accusation for producing a human."

"Makes men and women more equal."

"Tam—"

"The incubation… It helps with spotting pre-birth population level patterns, you know to target research better, to a greater number of foetuses."

"And," she said through gritted teeth, "shadowy under the radar eugenics?"

"Who knows?" he said softly.

They talked all day, all night, and all the following day. Catnapping and chomping on Tam's special herb to stay awake and alert. Tam found it difficult to believe that a combination of personality, training, and the occasional burst from an implant allowed her to dissociate from the horrors of the orphanage sufficiently to even consider having a child. He was sure that it must be a perverse reaction, but eventually she persuaded him otherwise. At one point Alex caught them chomping and didn't seem convinced by their claim it was a breath freshener. Another time, Tam paused their conversation while he discussed with the doctors who worked with the zeroed about how to register a baby born outside of the incubators. On the third day, they came to an agreement that they would have a child, and take any consequences of breaking the taboo. Tam had also convinced Beth to keep quiet about the orphanage for the time being, making her see that it wasn't wise to have a taboo baby and go up against OS at the same time in what would most certainly be a bloody battle. And one she'd probably lose.

That night they spent the most wonderful, tender and erotic time together. Mingling sex, snuggling and snoozing until the sun rose and flooded them with light.

21

Sitting on the train travelling to London from Tam's, Beth gripped his hand as the stream of abuse was hitting the channels. Comment after comment about how fat Molly Coddle had become came from influencer after influencer caustically poking for reactions from their followers. They asked why she'd been silent. On repeat. Suggesting that if you'd damaged your health to this extent, you'd keep it under wraps if you could. Wouldn't you? Which led to speculation about how vast her wealth must be to keep her health implant data private. Nobody made the connection between her recent invisibility and her weight gain. At least, not in public. Suggesting that a woman who has become larger is pregnant had been illegal for a long time and remained seriously taboo under the Leveller. Even a hint could result in being forcibly zeroed. It was not a risk anyone was going to take, no matter what they thought. Not only that, it wasn't in anyone's mind, full-term pregnancy just wasn't a thing. Her gamble had paid off. She'd known the journey from Withernsea would be difficult and she'd worn the baggiest clothes she could find, but she had not anticipated this degree of damnation. She struggled not to engage with it, but as Tam kept pointing out each time she reached for her globule, she had to let them be. Keep her distance. Unless she wanted to risk accidentally revealing the taboo pregnancy that she'd kept secret with a daily dose of the post-conception pills the doctors had supplied, a medication which masked the pregnancy from any implants or remote scanning, and which they'd acquired from an underground source in a country where certain people were not allowed to breed. It was this, rather than top-end health-care, that had kept her safe.

The BP stopped the three of them at the Selby border, but soon lost interest in Tam and Alex. It was Beth they were interested in, probably because of all the activity that was circling her profile at that precise moment. The border control blocked her way and a BP, which had been hovering off to the side, swished across with its arm raised. She thought she caught a glimpse of Kai watching her from its eyes. She shuddered, but decided she'd been mistaken. It held a bio-signal detector in front of it and was broadcasting the sound of two distinct hearts beating away. A possibility she'd been aware of and one which had kept her away from BP for the duration of her pregnancy. She raised her globule to proclaim her credentials.

"Halt," said the BP. "Stop."

Tam walked straight past them dragging an inquisitive Alex with him. Once he was out of the direct sight of the BP, he drew out his globule and frantically fiddled with it. He gave her the thumbs up, which made her feel a little better, but only a smidgeon. The BP was gliding towards her and the heartbeats grew louder.

"Hey," she said. "Can I help? You seem very interested in me. Would you care to tell me why? How can I be of assistance?"

The BP stopped its approach and made it obvious that it was scanning her from head to toe. This show of surveillance was a new phenomenon designed to intimidate. And it worked. She felt her neck and face blush and a momentary thought crossed her mind that she was pleased that she no longer dyed her hair because it would be such a giveaway, quickly followed by the realisation that the BP knew all her vital signs and while hair that changed colour was fun and helpful to humans, it was a total irrelevance to them. To convey her compliance, she dropped her arms so they hung loose. The BP concentrated on scanning her upper torso. She slowed her breathing and focused her gaze on Tam and Alex as a way of avoiding eye contact. It scanned again and the words *Unregistered foetus* appeared across its display.

The two heartbeats filled the air, blocking out all other sound.

She waited.

Tam was waving, beckoning her to join him.

She glanced at the BP and then back to Tam, wondering if he'd lost the plot.

The BP switched off its broadcast, slid to the side and glided past her.

She took a quick peek over her shoulder and when she was convinced that the BP was no longer interested, she walked as quickly as she could to join Tam.

"What the fuck happened there?" she asked through heavy breathing.

Alex giggled, gently nudging Camerann next to him.

A fleeting look of concern crossed Tam's face and then he grinned. "Morgan did his stuff. You became Naomi momentarily. Long enough for the BP to lose interest. What do they care about a non-registered?"

"Wow, good call. Thank you. You're brilliant. I didn't put Naomi in danger, did I? You know, if she was me?"

"He didn't get a chance to check. It was snappy. On and off in a matter of a couple of minutes."

She kissed him and rubbed the top of Alex's head. Alex pulled away and creased his forehead, but the hint of a smile grew across his face.

"Let's go," said Beth.

Tam placed one hand on her stomach and the other on Alex's back. "Indeed," he said. "Let's get home."

As they made their way through the London streets, Alex was interested in the displays on a few of the pedestrians' backs. They were a recent addition to the clothes that you could rent from the Leveller, which it then used to communicate with its population; a method that was a lot cheaper than using the more traditional public spaces, especially now that they were all privately owned. A live feed of the health of the economy was flowing across their jackets and some of them simply walked up and down to earn a few una.

Tam was patiently explaining them to Alex. "Son, the rolling graphs show that the English economy is growing at a little under three percent. The rate at which the Leveller is spending its reserves is broadly in line with its fifty-year projection, and eleven percent of the adult population – that is, anyone aged thirteen or over – has no wealth whatsoever and is classed as zeroed."

"Is that good, Dad?" asked the wide-eyed Alex.

"Depends on who you are, Son."

Alex didn't pursue his questioning and Tam didn't offer any further explanation, which was usually the way. Alex would become quiet and introspective until he'd formulated his next layer of investigation. Then he would bombard them with insightful observations and often difficult follow-up questions.

All three of them were lost in their own thoughts as the streets of the city passed by.

At home, Alex retreated to his room while Tam and Beth pottered around, tidying up and cleaning surfaces, and generally getting ready for the doctors to arrive.

It wasn't long after they'd completed their thorough cleanse that Beth's globule buzzed, announcing the medical team. A team which more often than not would be performing full-term caesarean sections for the zeroed who had no access to healthcare or incubators. They got to work quickly, setting up the makeshift operating theatre and getting their various monitors and mini-bots in place. While they were engrossed in preparing everything, Beth was busy watching them and mentally preparing herself at the same time. It felt archaic, but this was the best option. Inevitable from the moment she chose to conceive and give birth outside of the system. She noted their professionalism with admiration and relief, taking comfort from the fact that they undertook this procedure day after day. The final piece of equipment they installed was the one that would register the baby's birth and hence bring it on to the Leveller's books, so to speak. It was a concession that had been made in line with the Loop protocol to avoid repeating the problem where generation after generation of a family were out of work and out of mainstream society. *Levelling For All*, was the slogan.

Tam appeared at the door when it was all in place. "He's not going to join us," he said.

"Did you try and get Alex to come in here? To see me being cut open? To see me naked? To take a look at my insides?"

"Yeah. It should be a part of his education, and why wouldn't he want to see his baby sister being born?"

She opened her mouth to explain, but the doctor in charge interrupted.

"We're ready for you."

Methodically, the medical team injected the necessary nanobots and pulled the screen across her body. Tam moved to the other side of the screen and although he and Beth could look into each other's eyes, only he could see what was happening as the doctor made the incision and opened her up. It was a weird feeling to know that Tam would see bits of her body that she never would. She felt the warm surgical bot being placed on her skin and then everything went numb.

"It's testing to see if you can feel anything," said Tam.

"Thanks, but no more commentary please. Look, but don't touch or talk. Deal?"

"Deal."

His face was a picture of curiosity and whenever she felt tugging or pulling, he cringed as if he was feeling it, too.

It didn't take long before the newly born Robyn was in her arms. She stared at their beautiful baby and was bathed in emotion about the beginning of new life. Tam stood next to her and they passed Robyn back and forth. Each one of them holding her tight when it was their turn. Whenever Tam was holding Robyn, flashes from the orphanage plagued her, memories of the little boy with the hole in his stomach. She knew that eventually she was going to have to do something about that place despite her promise to Tam to leave well alone. The doctor used a handheld device to take the newborn's vitals. He scanned her fingerprints, her head and face, her eyes, her hands, and her ears. Finally, he took her DNA. She was a fully registered citizen of England under the guise of a child with zeroed parents. As far as the Leveller was concerned, Robyn existed but her mum and dad didn't.

The team packed their stuff away and were ready to leave. "We were not here," said the most senior doctor. "If anyone asks who we were, tell them you had an unexplained seizure and we were an emergency medical team. Got it?"

Beth and Tam nodded their acknowledgements and the team left.

Alex peeked his head around the door, and being uncharacteristically coy he sidled up to Tam. After a few minutes of silence, he lost his shyness and was peering closely at Robyn.

"Alex," said Tam. "Those people came to visit Mum because she had a bit of a seizure, but she's fine now."

"Really?" he said and snorted. "How stupid do you think I am?"

"It's important to tell that to anyone who asks. Robyn is special, and it's very important not to draw attention to her. Do you understand?"

"Sure," he said and hunched his shoulders, before dragging his feet along the floor as he left the room.

22

"AMAZINGLY, IT worked," said Tam, returning from the regrow shop where he'd taken the milk that she'd expressed that morning. He lifted the two fifteen litre full containers from his trike.

"No questions about where you got it?"

"Nope. Cost me top una, and a fair amount of time waiting around, but here it is."

"Hey, that's brilliant," said Beth. "She's all yours now, and you'll be great. I'm so proud of all three of you." She kissed him on the tip of his nose. "You know how to work a freezer, don't you?" She winked and he smiled back.

"Good call, by the way. The regrow." He returned the nose kiss. "Nobody seems to know how many regrows I can get from it, but best guess is around ten."

"Well, my lovely darling man, I won't be gone for ten months and even if I am Robyn will be on to solids by then."

"Eh?"

"Ten regrows. One a month. You won't need that much."

"Right."

"Hey, this is such wonderful news. You being able to look after her."

"Do you have to—"

She interrupted. "Do you have to ask?"

"I—"

"I promise I'll make the most of it. We will expose them. Won't we?"

Tam shoved his hands in his pockets. "If anyone can, you can. Are you packed?"

"Hey, I sure am. The car arrives in thirty minutes."

"A car. Get you. That crowdfunding was a stroke of genius."

"Yup. Good old Morgan, eh?"

She said her goodbyes to Alex, not that he was particularly interested in tearing his attention away from Sadie. Their jLobs – Camerann and Suzann – sat next to one another in the corner of the room, surplus to requirement.

As she left them to whatever their latest scheme was, Alex shouted after her. "So, you got an NFT did ya?"

"No. Fucking. Talent," shouted Sadie, and they both collapsed in laughter.

Beth turned to face them. "Listen, juveniles. A load of folk put their trust in me to expose something that needs exposing. They don't know what that is, and they don't need to know. They own a part of the asset that I'll produce, and if it's as important as I say it is then it'll make history, become an artefact and increase in value year after year. Got it?"

Neither of the delinquents responded. Not that Beth expected them to. Her globule alerted her to the arrival of the car and after a long cuddle with Robyn and some exquisite kisses from Tam, she said goodbye, took her bags and left.

Inside the car, she settled down for the two-hour journey. "Charge. Amounting. Scorch," she said and the car sped off at such a speed that she found it difficult to relax until she was out on the open road beyond the built-up urban sprawl of London. Watching it dodge in and out of the city traffic with the dexterity that could only be achieved by a top-end autonavigator with sufficiently high priority rating, her confidence grew. Silently, she thanked her backers and settled down to read her research and refresh her memory.

The car arrived at the seawall where she'd first met Tam. It was considerably taller than it had been then, but she'd been assured it was still the place where the young pregnant virgins gathered for the three months before they took the long trek to the orphanage. According to her research, it was a trade that was as vibrant as ever. She set off on foot along Clog Mill Lane to the congregating spot, not wishing to do anything to spook the youngsters such as arrive in an ostentatious vehicle. Beth chuckled to herself. Sitting in an orderly line on the connecting walkway between two of the abandoned buildings overlooking the flooded fields where the wall had failed to do its job were eight youngsters shouting and jeering at the flat-bottomed boats that serviced the workers. Her research had paid off. She strolled across to the metal staircase.

"Oi!" shouted one of the boys. "Look 'ere."

All eight of them leant over the balcony, scanning her with devices and checking her out. With a swagger that a movie star of the previous century would have been proud of, they descended to the ground. Obviously, they didn't get many visitors to this edge of the town.

One of the girls wandered over. "Are you Beth?"

"I am," Beth replied, a little taken aback that this young woman should recognise her.

"Alex's mum," she said to the boy newly arrived at her side.

"Molly Coddle?" he said.

"Don't call her that."

She held out her hand. "Esme."

"Hey. Nice to meet you," said Beth. She was intrigued by the Alex comment, but decided not to ask.

"Why are you here?"

"That's straight to the point, Esme," said Beth.

"Best way 'round here."

"I have a proposition."

The boy laughed a forced laugh of derision, but Esme told him to shut up. "Go on," she said to Beth.

"Are you pregnant?"

Esme grinned. "You learn fast. Straight for the jugular. Yes."

"How old are you?"

Esme stuck her chin out. "Almost eleven. Same as Alex. Why?"

"Taboo then."

The boy put his arm around the mother of his unborn child. "What you gonna do about it? Eh, Molly? You ain't yellerbelly. You one of them frim foak."

Esme pulled herself free. "Stop it you idiot. For fuck's sake. What is it with you and that pathetic attempt to prove you're real Lincoln?" She turned to Beth. "I am," she said. "I am taboo pregnant. I fucked."

"Hey, I'm not judging anyone. Not even him," said Beth with a grin.

Esme grinned back. "Well, I wouldn't go that far."

"Can we talk? Alone?"

They strolled to the edge of the water.

"I'm doing a piece on the people who run the orphanage," Beth explained. "But to get anywhere near, I need to arrive with someone like you. Someone who is selling their foetus."

"Really? Sounds suspicious to me. What's in it for me, apart from hanging out with the infamous Beth?"

"You'll be doing the right thing. That's good, isn't it?"

"Not really. What if the orphanage realises what's going on. At the very best, they'll revoke their payment. At the worst… Well, I've heard the rumours and it's best not to cross them."

They walked and talked some more.

"How about I pay you if they refuse to?" suggested Beth eventually. "More than the orphanage."

"Not sure," said Esme.

"How about I pay you… and you can keep my payment whatever happens? And, I'll throw in a few tokens of the final asset."

"Who would have thought it," said Esme to herself. "Me, and a non-fungible token. A girl from the back of beyond playing with the rich and famous."

Beth's income had dried up, but she didn't disillusion Esme about the rich part of her statement.

Esme spent a few animated minutes talking to the boy, presumably the father, and after a short burst of shouting she left him standing there looking angry and joined Beth. They walked quickly to the waiting car and began their ninety-minute journey.

Esme calmed down after the initial shock at the speed and repeated gasps of awe at the sheer luxury of a covered vehicle, especially the indentation to store and connect your globule that gently closed in around it when you placed it there. An adult arriving with a sexually active pregnant youngster was going to need to stand up against some robust BP questioning, so they meticulously planned their cover story. With a sigh of relief from both of them when they'd got the story straight, they lay back in the reclining seats and through the transparent roof they watched the wonderfully white clouds whizz by, occasionally sitting up to take a peek at the green fields. Esme couldn't stop commenting that there was no flooding. Absolutely no field had even the slightest covering of water. Beth felt sad for her and her unconscious naïvety, which only increased Beth's desire to protect this seemingly street savvy kid who in reality had travelled no further than a few miles from home and had so little idea about so many things.

The car took them along the narrow roads as far as the water's edge where they hired a paddleboard large enough for them both. From the moment they placed the board on the water until the moment they stepped onto the jetty where the bus to the orphanage was collecting its passengers, the huge grin on

Esme's face didn't reduce in size or even take a few seconds' rest. Passengers came from all directions and on all sorts of transport with one thing in common: young pregnant women accompanied by the equally young foetus fathers.

Onboard, Beth was attracting attention as the only adult on the bus, but it wasn't long before each couple retreated into their private conversations. Mostly about how they were going to spend their payments, as far as Beth could overhear.

23

The sterile yet grand reception area of the orphanage conveyed an enormous amount of wealth and privilege, but very little humanity. Two BP were positioned either side of a soft-faced, middle-aged woman who exuded kindness to each couple in the queue as their turn came to be processed. The nearer Beth and Esme got to the front, the closer Esme got to Beth. When they were third in line she took hold of Beth's hand.

"Hey, do you still want to do this?" asked Beth.

Esme squeezed. "Yeah. Why wouldn't I?"

Beth said nothing, not wanting to layer her own anxieties onto the fragile brave young woman beside her. The warm calmness flowing from the woman in charge was infectious and Beth's own worries subsided as they moved forward and she could overhear the conversations between official and would-be child parents; reassuring comments about having nothing to worry about from the Leveller or the BP. Confirming that, yes, they'd been silly to get themselves in this situation by having taboo sex rather than getting pregnant in other ways, but that they'd done the sensible grown-up thing by coming to the orphanage to get it sorted out. She told them that not only would the orphanage take on the responsibility for the baby and the child it would become, but that they would help the young couple start again with a one-off payment to get them back on their feet. The relief from the couples was well acted. After all, it was unlikely that any of them had got themselves to this place by accident. The donators and the purchasers of human life both pretended to be engaged in a philanthropic moment.

When it was their turn, the woman signalled to the BP either side of her to move closer. She held her gaze directly on Beth. "Are you the father?" she said and burst out laughing, with a sinister undercurrent.

Beth smiled back pleasantly. "No. I am accompanying my friend here. The father is unable to attend but does approve of what my young companion, Esme, is doing."

The woman raised her eyebrows. "Esme. Is that correct?"

"That's right. He couldn't come." Esme giggled. "Not today anyway."

Beth gave Esme's hand a tight squeeze to remind her to stick to the script.

The woman pushed out her bottom lip and nodded her head ever so slightly a few times.

"Place your globule there" she said to Beth. "Anywhere in the groove will do."

Beth did as she was asked and one of the BP waved its arm across it.

"I see," said the woman. "A caster. Known to some as Molly Coddle, I believe?"

"Hey, that's me."

"And?"

"Esme here does need my support, that's true, but I would also like to use my influence to increase awareness of your invaluable service, backed up with a piece on what it's like to use. Good for all of us, don't you think?"

The woman hesitated, turning her attention to the pure white marble ceiling above. Beth noticed the smell in the air. One that reminded her of hospitals. The sort of cleanliness that catches the back of your throat with its delicate sharpness.

The woman returned her attention to Beth slowly and then shifted her gaze to Esme. "You can proceed," she said. "Follow that corridor down to the left and someone will be waiting for you."

"Thank you," said Beth.

"Not you."

"Why not? She needs me by her side and, if I'm going to write about it, I need to be there."

"It's no different to any standard incubation procedure that the whole female population undergoes. Nothing unusual. Sorry to disappoint you."

Esme dropped her hold of Beth's hand and walked away down the corridor as directed. Meanwhile, Beth was having difficulty suppressing her anger and her fear. "I guess I have to take your word for it," she said. "Can I at least see the kids that live here, so I can write about what they get up to?"

"No. We have a duty of care and a requirement to follow child protection guidelines. We do not break taboos in this institution. Now, please leave. You can collect her tomorrow evening."

Beth considered demanding to stay with Esme and insisting that she should visit the supposed orphans hidden behind the closed doors, but more of the BP had shifted a few metres towards her making it clear that she was not welcome. Thinking better of it, she left the building and made her way to the bus and back to the boat. She would have to spend the night in the car and was exceptionally grateful to those who had made it possible for the expensive vehicle to remain on hand for the duration of her visit.

It was a rough looking Beth that arrived back at the orphanage the following morning. Not so much from spending the night in the car. That had been relatively pleasant with seats that opened up to cover the whole of the inside as one large bed. It had even come equipped with gels, lotions and tiny bots to clean and refresh her body. No, it was the constant suppression of anger and hatred of the orphanage and its methods that had infiltrated her dreams. She dreamt of children being kept against their will and being tortured as part of experiments. Not helped by remembered images from watching the less savoury of Tam's old movies, vivid in their night-time replaying. She dreamt of kids attached to machines or being force fed body changing food. The worst of all was boys being cut and their scabs then dissolved with a variety of healing agents, most of which dissolved their young flesh too. Once again, though, she had no documentary proof of the goings on behind these closed doors. Nothing to show for her visit. Nothing to offer her generous backers. No ammunition to bring the orphanage and its evil owners to justice. As ever, the privileged would escape being held to account for breaking the taboos. She wondered if they realised how disgusting their behaviour was or whether they were so removed from reality that they failed to feel any empathy or responsibility for those who suffered from their narcissistic lives. She suspected that the babies born and reared in this place would never be missed by anyone. A theory that sat heavy in the pit of her stomach.

She squatted on the floor with her back against one of the ornate stone statues of a coiled rattlesnake. The carved words, *Don't tread on me,* pressed their shape into her back while the antiseptic whiff that escaped from the doors of the orphanage whenever they opened made her gag with revulsion at this hypocrisy. A couple of youngsters walking past her glanced down and smiled.

"Hey, can I ask you for a favour?" she said, as she got to her feet.

The boy shrugged.

"Can I take a DNA sample from each of you?"

"Uh?" said his young companion.

Beth pressed the indentation on her globule and it displayed her credentials. "I'm doing a piece on the orphanage and I'd like to trace your baby on the citizen's chain. Would you mind?"

"Why would we do that?" said the boy. "Piss off."

"For some una? The same again. As much they just paid you. That's quite a lot for a couple of swabs compared to three months of pregnancy."

"Alright," said the young woman, elbowing the boy to one side. "If you say so."

Beth took two swabs and thanked them before transferring the payment. The couple took off with a renewed bounce in their step and at a faster pace than they'd left the building. Maybe they thought she'd change her mind. She watched them go with the swagger of their paper-thin veneer of confidence on full display. A green glow on her globule indicated that the results were ready. Sure enough, as she'd suspected, there was no record of their baby. Despite the fact that it was mandatory for medical institutions to add it to the record the moment an incubation began, there was nothing, and she doubted those two youngsters disappearing into the bus were ever going to check. The freeships had generations of untraceable human beings. There could be no innocent explanation. There could be no philanthropy that justified such an outright deceitful and corrupt act as those that were being committed by this façade of an orphanage. They weren't so much orphans with no parents, as they were orphans from society. The suppressed anger that she had been holding in for too long erupted and she stormed into the building. Pushing past the waiting couples, she forced her way to the front to face the same, supposedly warm and kindly, woman from the previous day.

"They are not being added to the citizen chain," she shouted as she marched past the front of the queue. "Why fucking not? Eh?"

The BP moved in front of the woman who gently guided them away with her hands. "No need," she said. "Intervene if she touches me."

"Well?" shouted Beth.

"Well?" replied the woman in a super calm voice. "How can I help you?"

"You heard."

The woman sighed. "Would they be better off if they were zeroed? No. On the freeships, they are free. Free to make the most of themselves with no hindrances and no shackles from their past. It's what we all crave deep down, and they shall have it. They are the lucky ones."

"If you think—"

The woman interrupted her. "Shall we discuss your mysterious double heartbeats? Your sudden disappearance? Your miraculous weight loss? A newly registered baby girl? Robyn, isn't it?"

Beth swallowed, unable to speak.

"Alex. Now there's an interesting child. Do you want to tell me about him?"

"He's a child. What more is there to say?"

She called one of the BP. It handed her a mini-globule. "We've listened to you talking about him. Our ANN only needed a few minutes to make an assessment. It's not good, is it?"

"What do you mean?"

"He's heading for some real mental health problems. Your family is fucked." She laughed a gut-wrenching laugh. "All four of you."

"You don't scare me," said Beth, quieter than she'd intended.

"Oh dear. I should. Did you know he's planning on visiting us? With that girlfriend of his. Sadie, isn't it? You'd be surprised what those jLobs can tell us. That's as soon as he's fertile, of course. Poor lad. Hopefully, before Sadie gets bored with him. Don't you just hope? Now get the fuck out of our orphanage and go bury yourself back in your tedious life. As if you actually influence anything. Pathetic."

"Fuck you," said Beth.

She turned and left the building with her head held high, past the crowd recently delivered, and leapt on to the bus that was about to leave.

She stared at the back of the seat in front of her, aware out of the corner of her eye that Kai had appeared on the window next to her. He winked and then vanished. She gritted her teeth and kept staring straight ahead.

Back in the safety of the car she messaged Tam. *Keep your eyes on Alex. I've seriously pissed off the orphanage and I'm not sure how they'll retaliate. Don't let Robyn out of your sight either. Doubt this is a safe channel so silence for now. I'll be home when I can. X.*

As soon as the message to Tam had gone, she contacted Morgan. She needed to see Naomi. Morgan replied straight away. Naomi was back in East Albion and Freeship One was about to come into London to dock. She gave the car a location near to where she would meet Naomi and tried extremely hard to calm her breathing and get some saliva back into her mouth. She looked out of the window barely seeing the country lanes turning into minor roads and then into major ones, and it wasn't until it was too late that she remembered Esme stranded back at the orphanage. There was nothing Beth could do except send a vehicle to collect her and hope that she was unharmed.

24

The car delivered Beth to the specified spot and sped off to its next job.

She set off on foot for the thirty-minute walk to London's Canning Town, taking the route by the water's edge to avoid the throngs of off-duty freeship workers enjoying some land-based entertainment. The wind whipped around the buildings and drove the incoming tide against the crumbling wall. Chunks of the concrete arm designed to protect the city lay at awkward angles, as if its bones had been broken by the pounding waves. Dotted around the landscape were tower blocks that she'd heard had been refurbished time and time again by their owner-residents. Morgan had explained that many of the flats and maisonettes that were built in the gaps between them had gardens, and despite regular flooding they were well-tended. Plants grew out from the water-sodden soil and up the sides of the buildings where the symbiosis of biobricks and nature combined to create dwellings that thrived from the constant barrage of salty water.

As she walked, the freeship came into view between each of the repurposed office skyscrapers that had been abandoned by corporate giants in the face of rising tides. They had stood empty and guarded until the Leveller had split them up and sold them floor by floor to those who still believed in the inherent value of land that they could rent to those with less appetite for risk. As tall and majestic as they once were, they had become 'warrens of worn away grandeur', as Morgan called them.

At the shoreline of Canning Town the freeship imposed its sinister presence. The whole area was alive with the sounds and sights and smells of an international travelling fortress designed to weather the extremes of the planet. Transporting its elite inhabitants to and from their New Zealand safe havens, bought a long time ago when only they could see the way things were heading under their stewardship.

At the river crossing, she pulled on the protective suit provided by the driver of the hydrofoil and climbed on the back. The driver pushed the pedals with all the strength in her muscular legs and it lifted out of the water. They glided across to the beach on the other side, weaving in and out of the shacks that populated the waterway, homes that had been hand-built with a mixture of salvaged biobricks and washed-up plastic.

When she stopped pedalling, they sank to the ground and Beth disembarked with two smiles. One for the woman, and one for Naomi who was waiting there for her.

"What's this about?" asked Beth as soon as she was close enough for Naomi to hear.

"Thought it'd be interesting."

"A tour of the freeship. Hey, you expect me to swallow that?"

Naomi's grin was forced. "Fair enough. I have to—"

"You have to…"

"Hear me out," she said, holding out a tiny lozenge shaped device. "I need to get the contents of this into the freeship core, the Loop, hopefully. We will infect it."

"Infect?"

"Bad data, corrupt, poisonous, whatever you want to call it. Morgan says it'll crash the system and do lasting damage."

"Hey, are you serious? Sounds extremely dangerous."

"Probably is. You in?"

"Not really. I want to talk about the orphanage."

"You think they'll discuss that?"

"If I push them."

"No way. This is what we need to do. Subtle. Deadly."

Beth thought hard about the choice, and as ever suspected that Naomi was right.

"Well?" asked her impatient friend.

"Hey, I'm here, aren't I?"

"True. Shall we do it then?"

"Yes."

They joined two other couples who were standing on the embarkation platform gazing around expectantly. Immediately, a tattoo covered girl joined them, checked their day passes and then signalled to the waiting drones to lift the platform to the ship.

"Welcome," said a well-dressed host as they drew level with the ship's deck. "If there is anything you want to know as we take a tour around this freeship, please feel free to ask and I will do my best to answer."

She shook hands with all of them in turn.

"Are we good to go?" she asked and they all smiled and nodded vigorously. "Good. Follow me."

The host stopped after a few paces and waited for them to form a circle around her.

"As we take the tour, you will see many interesting innovations. Some of these you will recognise because as I'm sure you are aware the freeships donate most of their developments to you. The technology you don't recognise might be due for sharing soon so you can be proud to have seen it first, before your fellow grounded-folk. Some of it we won't share because we do not believe it would help anyone. Not you and not us. Any questions?"

All six of them remained quiet.

"Very well," said the host. "The first thing to point out is your health implants. You all have them, right?"

They all muttered a *yes* under their breath. Naomi had lied.

"They were developed by this particular freeship many years ago. Well, a forerunner of this ship, but by the actual people who are its inhabitants."

The host held her arm in the air and pointed towards a wall covered in a mass of purple plants that formed the slogan familiar to anyone who knew anything about the freeships: *More & Better.* They walked past it and with a smug expression their host reminded them that the regrow shops were also their gift to the grounded-folk.

"How does it work?" asked one of the men on the tour.

With her smooth, well-practised manner, she replied. "It is not in anyone's interest to share everything."

"Please, tell us. I'm interested."

"It's not wise to share everything. Not good for anyone," she replied

"Telling us won't hurt."

"I've told you," she replied curtly. "Now, it's in your best interests to stop."

He grimaced and glanced at his companion, but didn't ask again.

A little further on, she slowed down. "On your left are objects that construct themselves from nanobots."

She pressed her wrist and a swarm of dust lifted itself from a container in the corner and started to form into a chair. She pressed again and it disassembled back into the container. One more press and the dust left its home to gradually form a table. She grinned at Beth, who couldn't stop herself from grinning back. The host moved on and they followed.

It was a little way before she stopped in front of a transparent wall. "In here we have a prototype weather control system. It's not much to look at, but it's extremely powerful."

Beth stepped closer to look through the wall and into the room on the other side. The floor and the ceiling were covered in a thick organic material that was pulsing with faint veins of light growing and shrinking across its surface.

"Our most advanced ANN," said the host. "We hope to be able to make interventions in the climate to affect the weather to an accuracy of one square kilometre. We also want to extract carbon dioxide from the air as we travel the world."

They moved on, with the host pointing out various weather prediction charts on the walls, until she stopped and waited for them to congregate.

"On your right you can see the amazing effects of our anti-aging research." She waved her arm in the direction of a room of middle-aged men and women.

"What's so special about them?" asked Naomi.

"They are all over one hundred and fifty years old."

Beth took a second look. It was hard to believe. In fact, she didn't believe it, but she kept quiet. She wasn't there to challenge the myths of the freeships. She was there to help Naomi.

The host asked them to huddle around and with a low voice she spoke as if she was sharing the most important secret in the history of the world. "Artificial Neural Networks. The ANNs. The descendant of the first ever to help run a corporation is on this ship. Six hundred generations since that seminal moment and it's still throwing up bizarre and wonderful solutions."

She moved them on once again. This time they walked along a curved corridor sloping upwards and out into the open air. In front of them was the infamous plank of the freeships jutting out over the water. Beth shuddered and moved closer to Naomi.

"Cold?" asked Naomi.

She gestured to the plank as surreptitiously as she could, but the host noticed and laughed.

"Our little joke," she said.

As they strolled the curved walkways, Naomi gradually increased the distance between them and the host who continued to talk and show her guests the wonders of the freeship. There were bioengineered plants for medicine and food, and emerging drone technology with its own self-determined purpose depending on the context it found itself in. Twice, Naomi attempted to sneak them off into a side corridor, but the host turned and spoke at the exact same moment. As if she knew.

Finally, they slipped away and Beth hoped that the host would assume they were lost rather than up to no good.

Naomi kept one eye constantly on her globule, mapping the ship as she went.

Deeper inside was a shimmering see-through sheet with a group of people on the other side being handed a pill of some sort. A rough looking woman, presumably one of the zeroed, was dividing them into two groups. The group which looked the most ill was being ushered towards a room with the word *Decontamination* above its door. The other group seemed quite healthy and waited patiently in line. Naomi signalled to Beth that they should take a look, but as they took one step closer, the host appeared with two young men.

"There you are," she said. "We do need to be a bit more thorough when deciding who we give day passes to, don't we?"

"We got lost," said Naomi.

"You need to be careful."

"Is that a threat?"

The host stroked the bare biceps of each of the young men that stood solidly either side of her. Each time she stroked they clenched their jaws and their skin seemed to change texture, as if it was hardening. Beth was sure she could smell a faint oily odour.

Turning her attention back to Naomi and Beth, the host spoke quietly and slowly. "It's hard to threaten a taboo breaking trespasser and a non-existent." She stroked her bodyguards once more, and then continued. "Tenuous existences such as yours must be hard to live with. Easier to simply evaporate and have done with it."

Beth began to broadcast immediately and directly through her channel. "Hey, I'm here today visiting Freeship One." She spun the globule in her hand to face the woman. "Say hello to our wonderful host." She swung the globule around to stream Naomi. "And to my friend." Back to her own face. "There'll be so much more for you to hear about our tour when we're back on dry land. Have the best day that you can my lovely people."

"Time to leave," said the host. "And don't you dare share what you have no permission to share."

The young men escorted Beth and Naomi off the ship.

25

Beth was holed up at the refugee camp in the Wolds with Naomi. Neither of them had enjoyed their clandestine journey from Canning Town. It had been fraught with danger, or at least perceived danger given that they had no idea how long the tentacles of the freeship were or how determined they would be to impose their edict of silence on the two women they had deemed as imposters. Tam, Alex and baby Robyn had joined Beth soon after she'd arrived and they'd been allocated one of the newer biobrick houses that were being constructed in recognition that this was not going to be a short-term camp. The Locals had committed to a home for everyone and bricks were being shipped to Selby from the semi-derelict buildings of the London docks and transported across East Albion to Caistor where they were given to the refugees to take to the camp on the Wolds. It was a mammoth but worthwhile endeavour, of which Beth wholeheartedly approved.

While painstakingly trying to agree what to do, Beth and Naomi had spent time cautiously gaining the trust of the refugees on behalf of R&R and on the morning after Alex's eleventh birthday they had finally agreed to broach the subject of the freeships with the friendliest of them. Naomi was adamant that she already knew the answers, but Beth had insisted that it was only right that they should hear it from the refugees themselves, if for no other reasons than to back Naomi up, and to recognise their valuable experience. It was good practice, which Beth said would stand them in good stead later when they wanted to use the information.

Tam was busy repairing the low wall that designated their space with recently arrived end-of-life biobricks and Alex was off regrowing their breakfast in the nearest makeshift regrow facility just outside the camp. Robyn was all wrapped up warm and gurgling next to Tam, snuggled down in a cot made from shredded biobricks, tree bark and foliage all held together with salvaged – some called it stolen – bonding agent from the seawall. The familiar domestic life that had become the norm surprisingly fast was comforting, and Beth was hesitant to do anything that might disrupt it.

"It's time," said Naomi, as if she was reading Beth's thoughts.

"Hey, I know. You're right. You always are, but I can't help wondering what we might unleash if we start meddling in their affairs again."

"Kai and his crew don't scare me," said Naomi, but she leant over and rested her hand on Beth's arm nonetheless.

They walked hand in hand through the camp, giving Beth time to reflect on what she'd learnt. R&R had formulated the argument for allowing the camp, while staying true to the core tenet of the Loop. Gerry was proud of the influence that he'd been able to bring to bear on the Locals because of Naomi and Morgan's work with Luscious. The reasoning he'd offered was that those who made the treacherous passage from their homes to the East Albion Refugee Camp were the most resilient and entrepreneurial. It won the Locals over to the realisation that these were also the best people suited to fulfil the Loop's underpinning principles to free the private individual and their businesses to thrive and drive the economy. It was as if the endurance test of migration was clearly aligned to a suitability test for becoming a productive citizen.

She turned her attention to the camp around her. There was definitely a pecking order in the accommodation, which closely followed that of the countries the refugees came from. The biobrick buildings were predominantly occupied by northern Europeans and Indians, while the shabby tents and the lean-tos made from plastic dredged from the sea were mainly occupied by travellers no longer welcome in the countries through which they had once travelled. Naomi scathingly called it the blindness of privilege, but Beth couldn't help noticing that her friend hadn't refused the better of the dwellings they were offered when they arrived, tired and scared from their encounter on the ship.

At the edge of the biobrick zone, Beth and Naomi paused before heading towards the large tent where the more enlightened of the refugees spent their days and nights. It reminded Beth of a pagoda, the way it sloped up around its edges. Standing outside were the two women they wanted to talk to.

"There they are," said Naomi as she waved to them.

The women waved back effusively and beckoned them to follow through the overlapping flaps of the entrance. The smell of baking and barbecues filled the vast volume of space inside and the heat of the ovens and the sizzling of fat dripping from the slowly cooking carcasses streamed across Beth's senses. The noise of large crowds going about their daily life of buying and bartering was intimidating and exhilarating at the same time. It was a glorious sight and one she was still excited by.

The women, who had changed their names to Inge and Willemina, and not without a sense of irony at the inability of the indigenous East Albions to pronounce their real names, had prepared a morning feast for Beth and Naomi. Around a circular table were other women from many of the different parts of the world represented in the camp sitting talking softly to one another, passing morsels of rabbit and drinking from glasses brimming with warm milk. Inge patted the empty chair next to her and Willemina did the same. The invitation was made. Beth had given them advance notice that there was something of great importance she wished to discuss with the distinguished travellers. A conversation that could alter the course of hers and Naomi's lives. The reaction had been curiosity. Not, as she'd half expected, one of contempt for these two fortunate women from England and East Albion.

Naomi was the first to interrupt the comfortable chitter chatter, and in her usual style she got straight to the point. "What do you know about the freeships?"

Inge was obviously itching to speak, but as was the tradition of her people she waited until it was clear that nobody else was going to.

"What is that you mean?" she asked after a few moments of silence.

Beth indicated to Naomi that she wanted to speak and Naomi shrugged, muttering a *whatever* under her breath.

"Hey, it's so kind of you to welcome us into your home and to take the time to be with us. We are interested in discovering as much as we can about how the freeships behave in the different parts of the world that they visit. Do they operate in the same way as here? Do they adjust their dealings with the population of each place differently? Are they always generous or do they sometimes take from the citizens with no compensation, not even leaving behind any gifts of technology?"

"These are questions that are big," said Inge.

She opened her palms out and moved her arms around to signal to the gathered refugees that they should say whatever they wished. At times she had to orchestrate the order of contributions as the discourse picked up momentum and more than one person tried to talk at once. A deluge of stories unfolded. Tales of the freeships promising a life of luxury aboard for any youngster who wanted to join their crew, of huge piles of technology to grow food and of textiles that repaired themselves when damaged. Some even reported dust that could take on whatever form it desired. The wonderful generosity of the freeships was told over and over again, but always with a tinge of sadness. The young never returned. Or if they did, they were absent in mind and spirit and spent their days staring into the sky, growing old faster than was natural. Naomi said she'd heard similar stories the world over whenever she docked where a freeship had been. Surprisingly, to Beth as least, the same stories were told about England and about East Albion, as they were about Africa, America and India. The freeships appeared to be consistent in their disregard for human life wherever they found it.

Accompanied by a constant flow of food and drink, more stories were told for the remainder of the day, often in painful detail.

Until, Inge drew them to a close. "You need understand," she said. "Freeships try to fix the world with technology. It is not technology that is broken."

Through the final trickle of tears, Beth thanked them for their hospitality and left the tent, shaking so many hands along the way.

"They know nothing else," said Naomi when they were beyond hearing distance.

"Hey, it wasn't always like that you know," said Beth. "They were glorious nomads going—"

"Not them," said Naomi, jerking her head back towards the tent. "The Narcissists. The freeships. The technocrats. Kai, for fuck's sake."

"Oh. Sorry, I thought you meant—"

"Quiet. What I mean is that it's no surprise they try to solve everything with more and more tech. It's what they know. It's what they're good at. They can't see any other way. That's the problem. Right there."

They walked on in silence. Beth was lost in the slow but certain realisation that they either remained at the mercy of the freeships and their technological apocalypse or they took the fight to them and changed the mindset of the meek and apathetic humans they fed on, starting with England and East Albion. A lump had formed in Beth's stomach that extended all the way up to her throat and seemed to be about to gag her. She forced herself to ignore it.

"The orphanage. The experiments on the ship. Those stories."

Naomi stopped walking. "I know," she said.

"We must do something. Anything."

"It is time."

They walked a little further and as Beth was about to speak, Tam came running towards them with Robyn in his arms. He looked as if he would stumble, fall and crush their precious baby daughter at any moment, such was his speed and his apparent abandonment of any notion of safety. He was shouting, but Beth couldn't hear what he was saying. She broke out into a run, too, and they hurtled towards each other.

She screamed. "Tam. Tam." But, his voice was too far away, his words indistinct. "Tam. Tam. Tam," she screamed through the gasps of breath she could manage without slowing down.

"Gone," she heard him cry. "He's gone."

As soon as they were close enough she bent double, resting all the weight of her arms and torso on her thighs, regaining her breath. "What? Who?"

"Alex. He's gone. Left Camerann behind. He's gone."

She stared first at Tam, and then at Naomi. Alternating her shock between them.

"He's gone," said Tam again.

She grabbed Robyn from him.

"Gone?" she repeated and began walking to their home. "Gone?"

26

"Hey, can you bring that bloody thing with you?" shouted Beth.

Tam appeared, carrying Robyn in one arm and Camerann bent double over the other.

With help from Morgan, who assured them it would only take two or three displacements to disable it entirely without causing any lasting damage, Naomi deactivated Alex's left-behind companion. Beth watched her strong, supple fingers digging into its back, pulling at the mass of technology packed tightly into its innards and prising tiny pieces away from their intended place. Immobilised, it could be transported without resistance and without it insisting it should wait for Alex.

Tam heaved the inert jLob onto the trailer attached to the trike and Naomi leapt up beside it. He stepped carefully onto the vehicle with Robyn still in his arms and Beth signalled to them all that they were ready to leave. She told it to take them to a street close to Gerry and Morgan's in case they were being tracked. Not that it would fool a human, but it might trick an unsophisticated automated locator that didn't have any other data to triangulate with, one that was designed to register refugee journeys rather than the reasons for them. She tapped the tip of her nose, which had been a family tradition when she was growing up, akin to crossing fingers or touching wood, and off they set.

The fields were wet, but the roads seemed long and dry in the scorching sun. Machines made their way slowly through the crops, watched over by their human supervisors. Whether you considered modern agriculture a sign of human ingenuity or human failure depended on your perspective and your role in the world.

When they arrived, Naomi unhitched the trailer and single-handedly pulled it along the road and around the corner. Beth chuckled and Tam shrugged his shoulders. She loved the fact that he wasn't intimidated by Naomi's superior strength.

Morgan was waiting for them. "In here," he said, lifting a trapdoor that had been hidden by a section of the lawn.

"Whoa," said Tam. "What the—"

"Faraday cage. No time to explain. The jLob. In here. Quickly."

Naomi lowered Camerann in through the trapdoor. "We can get in via the house," she said and followed Morgan inside.

Beth and Tam glanced at one another. Happy to be there, she grinned and beckoned Tam to follow.

"Come in, come in," said Morgan. "Tea and toast before we begin?"

"It's as if you can read my mind," said Beth. She leant across to Tam who was holding Robyn closer to his body than he needed to. "Homegrown tea and homemade bread. You'll love them. The splendid decadence of it is scrumptious. Simple, good, old-fashioned..." She paused and then laughed a real gutsy laugh. "I was going to say luscious, but that would be taking your L's name in vain, wouldn't it?" She giggled and fidgeted on her seat.

Tam put his arm around her and moved Robyn's face close to hers. "Goodnight kiss?" he said, making a smacking sound with his lips.

She kissed Robyn on the cheek and then clumsily landed one on Tam's, too. It was weird to have him here with her. A first. She could tell he was uncomfortable, but the image in her mind of her beautiful family visiting good friends made her warm inside.

And then she remembered Alex and the reason they were there. She shuddered.

"Right, at the top of the stairs," said Gerry, breaking the awkward silence that had momentarily filled the room.

"Thanks," said Tam, gathering Robyn's things from the pile on the floor hastily pulled together when they'd left the refugee camp at such short notice.

"I have to prepare for a council meeting," said Gerry. "Good luck with the jLob."

The basement led to the large room that was the specially constructed Faraday cage. Morgan asked Naomi to place the floppy Camerann on the bench while he selected his tools. On the walls of the room were various strange looking devices. Long prodding things and soft patches of iridescent material sat alongside the more traditional array of screwdrivers and circuit boards. There was even an old-fashioned soldering iron, presumably for when the tech was unable to fuse itself back together. It was strange to see Camerann lying there so passive and vulnerable. It would often have been sitting totally still when it was at home with Alex but there was always an inquisitive look in its eyes, always switched on and waiting for whenever it was needed, ready to assist Alex in whatever task was required. There had been times when Beth had almost treated it as a second son. A brother to Alex. A thought that made a tingle run down her spine.

"Right," said Morgan. "Let's crack on with the comatose companion."

He laughed.

Beth and Naomi didn't.

He laughed a much quieter and shorter laugh and then took a handful of tools and placed them next to Camerann. "We have to investigate every nook and cranny to make sure we've collected all the recording and broadcasting devices embedded in this wonderful specimen. Some of this will be fiddly work. Naomi, can you hold it so it doesn't slip around."

He began with the toenails, pulling each one out by gripping them with pliers and yanking. Once he had all ten laid out on the bench, he took strips of the shimmering material from his wall and placed a piece carefully over each nail. After a few moments he peeled the nails from their strips and sure enough a dark pinprick had been left behind.

"Gotcha," he said.

He cut the soft part between each toe and once again used the material to locate and extract the tiniest of tech buried in the fake flesh.

Beth winced.

A long-handled, thin-bladed knife cut slowly into the leg and Morgan peeled it back to reveal what had looked like a bone but was in fact a series of cylindrical tubes linked together by a twisted mass of slime covered strands. There was something hidden behind the kneecaps that made Morgan pause while he examined it. He put it to one side. Beth coughed and giggled in unison when Morgan pulled a thin flex with a camera on its end out from the tip of Camerann's penis. Naomi snorted with derision. Fingernails, hands, arms and armpits were all examined and the tiny devices laid out carefully on the increasingly full tray at the end of the bench. Morgan swept his locator over its head, criss-crossing this way and that and pulling selected strands of hair from its scalp. Finally, he pushed a knife into each eye and popped the eyeball out from its socket.

"So, what have we got here?" he said to the dismembered body of Camerann.

It was a tense couple of hours. Morgan dissected, scanned, tutted and on occasion contacted another of the techies in Resist & Regain. He muttered worrying phrases such as, 'You got to be kidding' and 'Smart kid' and frequently whistled and grinned. At least three times he turned to Beth and exclaimed how impressed he was with Alex. Tam kept coming and going, frequently making the point that he couldn't stand being idle while others grafted.

"Well," said Morgan as he replaced the last of the devices and held the fake flesh together long enough for it to meld. "My, oh my."

"What? Spit it out," said Naomi.

"Apart from the usual trawling to find out about sexuality and fertility, they have been naughty."

Beth leant forward. "They?"

"There are strong and established sharing links between this and Suzann. Sadie's companion, if I'm not mistaken?"

"Isn't that what you'd expect from close friends?"

"Not like these. It's as if Alex and Sadie were planning to drop out of sight by getting the jLobs to become obsessed with each other and take their artificial eyes off their companions."

"He must have had help. Did he?"

"Highly likely. Personally, I see the dirty hand of the freeships in this. I couldn't prove it, but it reeks of Kai. Liberate the young to be what they want to be, and hang the consequences."

"Anything else?"

"Well…"

"Hey, go on. You have to tell me. I'm his mother. I must know. You must tell me."

Morgan's eyes had strayed from hers and were looking over her shoulder.

"And, I'm his father," said Tam. "Tell us."

Morgan nodded to Beth. "They've been investigating donating an unwanted child to the orphanage and—"

"What?" Tam grabbed Beth's shoulder and spun her around to face him. "Did you know about this?"

"The orphanage hinted at it. He told you at his tenth."

"For fuck's sake. Anything else I don't know?"

"You need to listen more carefully," she muttered.

Morgan coughed.

Tam stared at him. "Yes?"

"There have been rumours of Rejuve. A new drug to prolong life, some say indefinitely, and they've been trying to get hold of it."

Tam's eyes narrowed. "You're kidding me. Why would he do that? He's eleven. He's too young to even have the concept of becoming old. He has no idea what that means."

"From what I can see, the freeships are pushing the idea that the younger you start taking Rejuve the more effective it is." Morgan paused as he sat down on the edge of the bench. "Alex and Sadie have been manipulating their jLobs to ignore the stuff that they were up to and I don't think it's possible they could have done it without a lot of encouragement and a fair amount of help."

Tam stepped forward. "Wait until I get my hands on them. Where are they?"

Beth took hold of his hand. "Morgan?"

"I think the most likely place you'll find Alex is among the zeroed. Probably in London. If I've decoded these things correctly," he said waving his hands across the tray.

"And Sadie? Suzann?"

"I don't know Tam, but if I had to guess I'd say Suzann is inert in a corner somewhere and Sadie is with Alex. Your guess is as good as mine as to whether they'll find the drugs or get Sadie pregnant first. That said, I reckon they're both fertile so that ship may have sailed, as they say. In fact, it's possible they may trade their foetus for the Rejuve drugs. Actually, that makes a lot of sense now I come to think of it. But they'd need to know what to ask for and have some sort of introduction to be able to even ask for those, let alone be taken seriously and be trusted. Although, if the orphanage knows he's your son they'll almost certainly give him the drugs. What a coup that would be. Molly Coddle's son hooked on something only the freeships can provide."

Naomi put her hand around Morgan's wrist and squeezed. "Shut up," she said. "You are rambling. And, you're scaring them."

"Hey, I'm not scared. I'll kill the little bugger," said Beth. She paused. "Actually, I'll kill that disgusting woman who runs the place."

Tam took her hand and tugged. "C'mon, let's find him."

Beth frowned and her shoulders dropped. "You need to look after Robyn. Naomi can help me."

"You're—"

She interrupted him. "Please. I can't do this if I'm worrying about her, too. For me?"

"Oh, come on."

"Please?"

With the sound of him pushing his hands into his pockets, he nodded and left the room.

"Let's make a plan," said Naomi. "Upstairs. With the SlendTek."

"Gerry might be able to get the council to help," suggested Morgan.

Beth and Naomi ignored him.

"Gerry," called Morgan. "Can the council help Beth find Alex? Surely it's worth a try?"

Gerry paused, one foot on the bottom step of the stairs. "I'm not sure. We're about to meet. I guess I could try. There's always a slot at the beginning of a meeting for citizens' concerns."

Morgan held both of his thumbs up in Beth's direction. She shrugged and followed Gerry up the stairs and into his council chamber.

27

A PLEASANT waft of sourness and saltiness teased Beth's nostrils. On the floor were two jelly-like mattresses surrounded by globules, forming a perimeter as if to protect them. Above each mattress was a thin sheet of SlendTek stretched out as a canopy with traces of coloured light shooting across the surface creating all sorts of shapes and then dissipating into nothing, before beginning again.

Gerry handed her a tube of turquoise gel. "You need to cover yourself in this."

"Wow, this has moved on a bit since the last time I saw it." She grinned and began to take her clothes off. "No peeking now."

"I won't," he mumbled from underneath the T-shirt he was pulling over his head.

The two of them standing there, naked and covered in gel made Beth giggle. They were a ridiculous sight and she wondered how deliberate that was on the part of the Locals. A way of putting the humans in their place. Gerry indicated that it was time to lie down. The council was about to convene.

Beth couldn't help fidgeting on the high-tech mattress. The gel had formed a crust, under which it was finding its way into each and every nook and cranny of her body. She breathed deeply and deliberately to distract her attention from its scratching and itching. Gerry was relaxed next to her with a smile on his face and Beth sincerely hoped that she'd get as accustomed to the gel as he appeared to be. On the canopy above her, the ten circles were connected by an intricate web of coloured connections. As each one sent forth a burst of pulses along one of its webs, she felt a tingling through the gel and the room filled with the sickly smell of sweat and salty seaweed, accompanied by the sound of lapping waves.

Gerry leant across and held her hand. "They're ready," he said and let go.

All of the circles but one faded and a voice that was neither male nor female surrounded her. It was as if she was being bathed in a tide of rolling words.

"Welcome," it said over and over. "Welcome. Welcome."

The remaining nine circles lit up and sent pulses in response. Nine equally indistinct voices all said *hello* in unison and then faded. Voices and circles.

"Welcome, Beth. Our guest," the voice said, and an eleventh smaller circle appeared.

"That's you," whispered Gerry.

"Hey. Thank you." Her circle pulsed and shot webs of light to the others.

"How can we help?" said the voice.

"Should we?" said another, almost immediately.

"We should hear what she has to say," said the voice and the gel got warmer as all the other circles glowed, their voices filling the air with resounding agreement.

"Go on," whispered Gerry. "Ask them."

Beth wriggled. The gel had worked its way deeper into her crevices and she couldn't get comfortable. She sighed and then breathed in and out rapidly. Her circle lit up like a Catherine wheel firework, spinning and shooting sparks all over the canopy.

"Take your time," said the voice. "The council will sit for as long as it takes to consider your case."

Beth stretched her arms to the tips of her fingers, arched her back, lifted her buttocks off the mattress and stretched her legs to the tips of her toes. The gel cooled down a little. "Council of East Albion," she said in a quiet voice.

"Council will suffice," said the voice. "You need to speak up."

Beth coughed and stretched again. "Council," she said clearly. "I want to find my son. I want to save him from whatever mess he's got himself into."

"We commend your brevity," said the voice. "Please, tell us more."

A third circle lit up and a voice interrupted.

"Before we spend time on this, we must decide if it is within our remit to help her."

A fourth circle appeared.

"Meaning?" asked Gerry from beside her.

"Meaning, that I have interrogated the data and she is not a citizen of East Albion."

Gerry's circle glowed brightly. "Alex, her son, will have dual nationality. His father is East Albion."

All of the circles, with the exception of Gerry's and Beth's, vanished and only the faint sound of lapping waves remained in the background.

"What's happening?" whispered Beth.

Gerry leant across and held her hand again. "Patience," he said.

The chair of the council broke the silence. "You speak the truth," it said. "The father is a citizen and your son will have dual citizenship. He is in his father's data trust. However, you chose to companion him with a jLob. This is not the way of East Albion. You have shown your allegiances, and you may have to live with them. However, council, I propose we should at least listen to her."

"Agreed," said Gerry, as all the other circles appeared and eight voices repeated their agreement.

"My son." She took a breath. "Alex, a naïve boy and his equally innocent friend Sadie have been persuaded to run away from home, leaving their jLob companions behind, to pursue pregnancy and the Rejuve drugs. They are way too young for this, and I'm scared. I need to find them and bring them home. I'm sure you have the resources to help me. To stop whoever it is from dragging them further into danger."

"Thank you," said the voice. "I suggest we take a moment to study the data. Could I ask our Local members to search and summarise for us?"

Four of the circles appeared, flashed once and then faded. The canopy went dark and Beth lay there waiting, shivering as the gel cooled down.

After a while, the heat and lights came back.

She patiently watched as the ten circles fired pulses from one to another, creating beautiful patterns across the canopy. The gel reached a pleasantly warm temperature and the voice spoke.

"We accept that pushing pregnancy and Rejuve on children is unacceptable, although not strictly taboo in all nations. We accept that this has happened to Alex and Sadie. We may be able to locate him. However, we do not accept responsibility for him. He is not part of our community. When the time comes, he may choose to be East Albion over English. Until then, you have chosen England as his home country."

"But—"

"Leave it," Gerry whispered from his mattress. "They don't revisit decisions."

"Sorry," said Beth and the circles faintly pulsed once. "Can I ask about the Leveller?"

The voice's circle burnt extremely bright and Beth had to close her eyes.

"No," it said.

"I'm interested, from a caster point of view, what you see as the difference between your council and the ways of the Leveller."

The canopy erupted into all colours of the rainbow shooting this way and that and the gel warmed and cooled, causing the familiar itching when it cooled and tickling when it warmed. She experienced sensations across her body that she'd never known before and got lost in the sensuality of them. Her thoughts drifted to Tam and his suit. They weren't specific thoughts, more an awareness of her existence and hazy memories of their early days spent at a distance. The gel gently oozed its way around every orifice below the neck and it was sensationally wonderful. She was drifting further, almost into sleep, when the voice cracked through.

"Your audience with the council is terminated."

"What?" she screamed, but all the circles had gone. She scrambled off the mattress and stumbled out of the room.

Naomi was waiting for her. "Well?"

Beth burst into tears and through her sobbing she explained. "I fucked up good and proper. They were going to help and then I asked about the Leveller and they froze on me. I screwed it up."

Naomi didn't reply. Instead, she took hold of Beth and with a large soft towel she wiped her clean of the gel, helped her get dressed and then led her downstairs to where Morgan and Tam were waiting.

"Any luck?" asked Tam.

Beth shook her head.

Naomi threw the towel on to the floor of the kitchen and picked up the sheet of SlendTek from the worksurface. "Plan A," she said and rolled it out.

"Later," whispered Beth to Tam. "I'll tell you later."

Morgan squeezed his globule into life and took charge. "What are we looking for?"

Naomi replied. "Traces of Rejuve use and places where the zeroed gather. And anything your data can tell us about where Alex might be headed."

"Righto."

"Can you look for data activity that fits the profile of two kids who aren't from zeroed parents and are living on their wits?"

"I can certainly try."

"Thank you," said Beth.

Tam murmured in agreement.

Gerry joined them, having showered. After watching them for a few minutes, he apologised profusely and at length.

Naomi stopped him and signalled for them all to gather around. "Let's focus on the task at hand," she said.

Morgan rolled his globule around on the sheet, pausing at regular intervals. Occasionally, he read some data coordinates out to Naomi and she ran them through a device that he'd set up especially. When she found a connection in the data with a physical location she asked all of them if they'd ever heard of it, and only a couple of times did Gerry say it sounded like a place he'd heard mentioned in a council meeting.

Progress was slow, but after a few hours Morgan and Naomi were sixty-eight percent convinced that there was a ninety percent chance that Alex and Sadie were in an area of East London, specifically on or around Cable Street.

"I know that place. Makes total sense," said Naomi.

This was also an area that Beth knew of. An area where the zeroed congregated and where work was available for them. It was close enough to where she lived to be somewhere that Alex would know about.

It was decided that Beth and Naomi would travel there on the next day with Morgan and Tam as remote backup and with a large drone on hand in case they needed rescuing at short notice. Gerry put a call out to Resist & Regain in England, asking for anyone that could be ready to help if required.

The plan was in place, so Beth took Tam to bed. Finally, she was able to relax and pay him the attention she so wanted to, and hoped he wanted her to.

She touched the tip of her nose and then pulled him towards her.

28

As usual, Beth had crossed the border into England at Selby, relying on the fact that any attack on her would be reputational rather than physical. Naomi had travelled separately, taking the route down through East Albion to the Thames. She intended to cross the river at an unmonitored place with the help of Resist & Regain who kept a watching brief on the daily movements of the River BP.

Beth didn't want to risk going home in case she was wrong and the BP, or worse, were waiting for her, so they arranged to meet at the Retro Bar. She was sitting in their alcove supping her favourite drink of cherry beer when Naomi arrived.

Naomi plonked herself down on the stool. "You still drinking that?"

"You can take all the blame," said Beth, smiling warmly. "Remember?"

"Feels like a lifetime ago."

"Any problems?"

Naomi shook her head and plucked a cherry beer from the conveyor belt. "Nope."

"Hey. Shall we walk? I looked it up. It's three kilometres. We could do that easily in forty minutes. Better than renting transport and running the risk of detection. Don't you agree?"

"Sure." Naomi swallowed her beer in one long gulp and slammed the bottle down on the table. "Let's go," she said snatching Beth's beer from in front of her and gulping that down, too.

Beth blew her a kiss and slid down from her stool.

As they walked along beside the road with the semi-derelict skyscrapers and tower blocks on either side, an occasional breeze wafted the salty air of the river across their path. The plastic adornments of the buildings blew in the wind giving the place a retro post-apocalyptic feel, like one of those terrible twentieth century movies that Tam was so fond of watching. In silence they walked along the path and under the occasional bridge which carried a road that criss-crossed that part of the city, until they reached the small run-down St James Gardens.

Naomi rehearsed the next part of the plan. "Data on the zeroed is scant. We ask questions. We don't get upset. We keep our cool, no matter what we see. Right?"

Beth wrinkled her forehead. "Hey, you don't need to tell me that. I know how to behave, how to appear casual. It's my job, and I'm pretty good at it. Thank you very much."

Naomi pursed her lips. "You are, but it's not every day it involves the future of your son."

"Hey. I'm good. Don't worry."

They strolled out of the gardens, across the road and into Cable Street where they were hit by a cacophony of noise and smells. It instantly reminded Beth of an up-market refugee camp with its mixture of skin tones, accents, and clothes. She could imagine being eleven and never wanting to leave. She wondered if Alex and Sadie had spent time there before they ran away. Maybe this was what had attracted them in the first place and then they'd got hooked and drawn in. She ached to know.

The riverside Free Trade Wharf flats had been converted to luxury apartments for the wealthy tourists from the north of England. Morgan's data had indicated that they mainly came from the Peak District. Having moved from London when it became obvious that flooding was inevitable, they only holidayed in the capital now, served by the ever-increasing numbers of zeroed, many of whom who were prepared to do most things in order to feed, clothe and house themselves. Naomi had commented time and time again that some things never change, the wealthy will find the desperate and exploit them wherever they are. A fact of life that could be limited by altering the ethics of the Loop, she'd added. None of her friends or fellow Resist & Regain had ever agreed or disagreed with her, but Beth hoped beyond all hope that she was right about influencing the Loop.

Morgan had warned them of the cheap Rejuve that was peddled on the streets, and of clinics that would provide clean effective injections that lasted up to twelve months, but nothing had prepared Beth for the sight that met her as they turned into Cable Street. A queue of what could only be described as well-dressed husks snaked its way along the pavement. Men and women of indeterminant ages lined up to receive their hit. There was no way of knowing if they would have looked worse without the drugs, but there didn't appear to be a huge amount of benefit as far as Beth could see. A small gut-knot, as Tam called them, grew in the pit of her stomach. What if they couldn't find Alex and this was his future? Naomi wandered over to a crowd gathered around an oblong pile of biobricks covered in a thick green moss-like substance. Attached to the oblong on one side was a substantial wire that connected to a mishmash of different types and sizes of solar panels spread out across the side of a nearby building. On the other side of the oblong was a clear tube that fed water to the bricks. The crowd were busy snapping off chunks of the green food and chewing it while chattering away. The atmosphere reminded Beth of an eat-as-much-as-you-can restaurant.

"Hey," she said to one of the women on the edge of the crowd. "Is that moss? What does it taste of?"

"Here, have some," she replied and gave both Beth and Naomi a handful.

Beth chewed it in the way she'd seen the others do and she had to admit it tasted good. Peppery.

The woman handed her some more. "It's from the freeships. They call it nasturtium. Very nice with a spicy roast rabbit."

Naomi pulled the woman to one side. "Have you seen a young boy and girl hanging around, looking a bit lost? Not zeroed, but without their jLobs."

"I wouldn't be able to tell you. Not my thing, you know, keeping track of strangers."

Naomi patted her on the back and turned away, but the woman continued.

"Now, if you want a tour of the area, history and its hidden secrets, or the modern day technology that keeps it going, I'm your one."

Beth was intrigued, thinking it might be a good way to explore without looking too conspicuous. "I'd like that," she said. "Tell me, what sorts of technology do you employ here that's unusual?"

"You've seen the food. We do that by taking different pieces of tech apart and reconfiguring. There are bits of biobrick, regrow tech, nutrient enhancers, and so on in there."

"Sounds great," said Beth. "Those solar panels are awesome."

"Oh, that's nothing compared to our hydro-energy. We're using the underground rivers nearby now they're swelling up again. That was a feat of engineering, I can tell you. It's in the soul of Cable Street, you see, looking out for ourselves. As well as servicing ships. You should check it out. The anti-fascist marches would be a good starting point. Oh, and the manufacturing of hemp ropes."

"Hey, I'm impressed. It's amazing how people with very little can make so much happen."

The woman frowned and clenched her jaw and Beth took a step closer to Naomi, unsure of what she'd said wrong. She apologised and Naomi made some comment about it being a common mistake. The woman seemed to be considering walking away, but Naomi persuaded her to stay and take them on the tour. It was all a bit awkward.

"I'm sorry," said Beth, hoping to smooth things over with a second apology.

"Being zeroed does not equal being poor. If you have your wits about you… Well, some of us are extremely wealthy. As wealthy as you lot with your decades of una stashed away."

"I'm sorry," she said again.

"All done. Forgiven. Now, let's show you around. For a fee, of course," the woman said, before roaring with laughter.

Once her guffaws had subsided, they set off along the street. There was a lively, edgy buzz about the place, of desperation and of ducking and diving deals. It was as if the very air they were breathing was full of an energising compound that sharpened the wits and sped up the thought processes. Beth was finding it infectious, and by the look on Naomi's face so was she. The woman pointed out the poorer inhabitants in the community garden who planted end-of-life food that they'd salvaged from the regrow shops. It was barely growing, but the woman assured them that it provided enough calories to stay alive, which was all they could expect if they wouldn't work. Beth questioned the health of the young children with wasted muscles and bloated stomachs and the woman replied that they were most likely suffering from Kwashiorkor. A lack of protein. Naomi muttered something under her breath, which Beth didn't fully catch, but seemed along the lines of being better off in the refugee camp. Almost every wall along their route was covered in plants of some sort. The colours were incredibly vibrant and varied and the scents were so powerful that they made Beth's nose itch. She couldn't stop smiling and thinking that maybe Alex and Sadie had made a good choice, albeit, enacted inappropriately and too soon. As they passed a large warehouse, the woman told them it was an insect factory that supplied the local area, as well as high-end London restaurants. She seemed peculiarly besotted by it, the reason for which became apparent when she proudly told them it belonged to her daughter.

Naomi signalled for them to stop walking. "There's no BP. We should risk it," she said to Beth.

"Images?"

"Yeah. You got them?"

Beth nodded and brought out two large sycamore leaves on which they'd imprinted photographs of Alex and Sadie before they'd left the refugee camp. It had been Tam's idea and it was brilliant. There was no data trail whatsoever from the leaves themselves, unlike images on a globule or SlendTek. The only risk would be from a camera or recording device the woman might be secretly carrying.

Beth held them out to show her, one in the palm of each hand. "Have you seen either of these kids?"

"I'm not sure. Let me send them around and see if anyone else has." She chuckled. "For a fee."

"No," said Naomi. "Take us to anyone who may have seen them. No digital sharing. At all."

The woman grinned. "How exciting. And pricey."

"We can pay," said Naomi.

After the to and fro of negotiating a price, the woman admitted that she had seen them earlier that day hanging around the free-ship. They'd stuck in her mind because, although there were always kids selling trinkets or begging from the visitors, these two seemed to be engaging in relatively long conversations. While Naomi was questioning the woman further, they were interrupted by a man with large staring eyes, asking for scraps of food.

His pupils were the blackest that Beth had ever seen and his deep orange irises filled the rest of the eyes completely. A human eye with no white around the iris was enthralling and disconcerting.

The woman shoved him away. “Piss off, Owly. Can’t you see I’m busy?” Then she turned to Naomi and Beth. “I’m sorry. They dump their failed experiments on us and expect us to look after them. Not happening on my watch. Now, as I was saying.”

She carried on describing the interactions she’d seen between Alex and Sadie and the freeship folk, as she called them. Beth’s mind wandered, considering a cast about these awful adult experiments dumped like garbage, but they’d all volunteered, there was no real story. She told herself to stay focused.

The woman was still waffling on and on when Naomi stopped her. “Don’t worry, you’ve earned your una. Did you actually overhear anything or is this all speculation from afar?”

“Oh, I heard plenty.”

“And?”

“For a fee?”

Naomi flexed her biceps and expanded her chest. “Don’t take the piss,” she said quietly.

The woman shrank her shoulders. “I did hear something about the girl being pregnant and the boy being pleased to be able to say that he was properly fertile. Both of which were up for sale if any freeship folk were interested.” She shuddered. “Made me a bit queasy overhearing that little exchange.”

“Where are they now?” asked Beth.

“Dunno.”

“That is not going to wash with my friend here,” said Beth. “You’d be wise to do better than that. Do you understand me?”

“Sure. You’re not the first to threaten me and I know you won’t be the last.”

“We might be,” said Naomi with a seriously sinister grin on her face.

"I'll take you to where they're staying. No need to get so uptight."

Naomi grabbed the woman's upper arm and held it tightly. "Take us," she said.

The woman broke Naomi's grip. "I need to talk to people alone."

Naomi agreed to meet with the woman the following day once she'd been able to corroborate her overheard conversations and could be sure that she could lead them to Alex.

29

The next day they met her at the corner of Cable Street and Glasshouse Fields and walked to the Free Trade Wharf. Apparently, Alex and Sadie were staying there, courtesy of the freeship, and had set up an expensive looking booth on the Thames Path between the dock and the popular holiday residences of the wharf. The footfall was precisely the demographic that the woman had speculated they were interested in, which gave Beth hope. If she knew what Alex was up to, she might be able to help. Even so, it scared her.

When they arrived and Alex was in sight, Naomi handed the woman a brooch to pin to her jacket. "Stand close by, so we can hear what's going on," she said and gave the woman a gentle push towards the booth.

Beth watched with trepidation. Did she really want to hear all the disgusting detail of her son's activities? Not really, but without it how could she hope to help him? Naomi handed her one of the earbuds, popped one in herself and arranged her globule so they could both see. They were ready to go. It's what they had come for.

A middle-aged couple with the affected accents of southerners pretending to be northern were browsing one of the SlendTek sheets on display. "Are you really sixteen? You look younger."

Sadie purred her response. "Sixteen and pregnant. A blood transfusion gives you three-in-one. His young virile blood and my pregnant blood, with Rejuve flowing through them both. You'll feel the effects in no time at all, and then you can follow it up with an annual boost."

"When you say virile...?"

Sadie laughed and nudged Alex. "He got me pregnant the day I turned sixteen. As soon as it wasn't taboo. That's how virile he is."

"And how far gone are you, me duck?"

Naomi cringed. "Me duck? Crass cultural appropriation. And, crap too."

Beth ignored her and concentrated on the conversation taking place.

"Almost three months. The higher plasma does you a world of good."

The man nodded, but the woman seemed sceptical. "Really?" she said.

"It's what we came for," he said and took hold of her hand. He turned to Alex. "Do you have a large supply?"

"Just enough left for two transfusions. You two, for instance. But you'll need to snap it up quickly. It's in high demand."

Beth coughed. "Where did they get their script, and when did they become so proficient at telling lies?" she asked Naomi.

"Pretty convincing. Could be Kai," Naomi replied.

Beth took a step forwards and Naomi grabbed hold of her.

"Hey. What are you doing? I'm going to get that little shit of a son and drag him back by the hair if I need to. Kai or no Kai. Let me go."

"It won't work. You know it won't work. Patience. Remember?"

Beth didn't reply. She didn't attempt to move either. Her breathing was shallow, fast and through her nose like a tethered bull. Her jaw was clenched tight. She felt sick, but she managed to get a grip of her emotions and wait, as they'd agreed.

When the couple had departed, promising to come back later to place an order, Beth's spy stepped forward. "Hello," she said. "I couldn't help overhearing. Do you sell the Rejuve drugs on their own?"

"Yeah," said Sadie. "If you got the una."

"You look young."

Alex laughed a sneery laugh. "That's the point old woman."

"Sorry," said Sadie. "Ignore him. How much do you want?"

"Two months' supply. For fifty people. Say, twenty milligrams a day each. Can you do that?"

"No problem. Meet us here tomorrow."

"Why not now?"

"We don't carry that amount. You pay on delivery. Leave us your details."

"I'm zeroed. Don't have any."

"DNA swab'll do," said Alex.

Naomi sighed. "Smart kid you got there. Wasted on this. Pathetic really, and R and R could do with more like him."

"Hey, I'm so glad you appreciate the sophistication of his taboo breaking activities. Warms a mother's heart."

"You know what I mean. Guess we'll have to rendezvous back here tomorrow with our undercover friend."

Beth smiled. "For a fee?"

Naomi smiled back. "For a fee."

It had been a wonderful surprise that R&R were prepared to fund finding Alex. According to Naomi, it was a sign of how much they valued Beth. It was also a relief that a wealthy Resist & Regain sympathiser had offered to act as a conduit. Although the redirecting of funds through a third party wouldn't stand up to too much scrutiny, it did offer some protection against immediate detection. This was vital given that R&R, the Factions, and the Anti-Leveller League were all considered to be terrorist organisations by the Leveller. Close association with them would result in at least a temporary suspension of any citizenship rights, but the sympathiser was sure she could throw any of the Leveller's harvesters off the scent with some tricksy chain manipulation and was prepared to take the risk of getting caught. Beth was amazed once again at the loyalty that R&R attracted and, after some discussion, Beth and Naomi agreed that they should take one of the wharf's apartments to stay close to Alex and Sadie.

The room itself was fairly unremarkable. Clean and bland with a hint of pretension. Pretty much what Beth had expected. After an equally bland meal that was more about the promise in the description than the flavour of the food, the exhaustion from the day kicked in and they decided to call it a night.

Beth was completely comfortable sharing the one room and had no hesitation in getting undressed in front of Naomi. In return, Naomi seemed more cautious, coyer than Beth had expected. However, it was the luxury of the bed that surprised her the most. A soft yet firm mattress and a large warm fluffy duvet. Everything that they'd not had at the camp. It seemed to soften the edges around the reason they were there, to make it feel more normal. Beth felt the covers lift behind her and she smelt the sweaty Naomi slip in behind her and felt strong comforting arms wrapping themselves around her. She drifted into a pleasant sleep, knowing that Naomi was only holding her to make her feel secure.

When she woke in the morning, they were facing each other and Naomi's potently naked body was peeking out from the duvet. Beth casually drew back the covers and a shiver went down her spine at the firm and fully exposed flesh lying there in front of her.

"Morning," said a sleepy Naomi.

Beth dropped the duvet and felt her neck and face getting warm.

"You wish," said Naomi as she slid out and walked towards the bathroom, her naked perfectly toned buttocks on show.

Beth wasn't sure how deliberate that was, but was already regretting crossing the line with her friend. She wrapped a towel around herself, waited for Naomi to return and then grabbed a quick shower, drying and dressing in the bathroom.

"You don't need to be embarrassed," whispered Naomi as they left the room for breakfast and hopefully a meeting with Alex.

Beth ignored her, but was relieved she hadn't made a big deal of it.

They ate quickly and headed off to the same spot as the day before.

They arrived at the same time as the spy woman was approaching Alex and Sadie from the opposite direction.

"Alex," called Beth.

He froze.

"Hey. It's me."

Sadie nudged and whispered something in his ear.

At least he hadn't run away at the first sight of his mother, something she'd been prepared for physically if not emotionally. She was ready to pursue him and she knew Naomi could outrun him even if she couldn't. She suspected he realised that, too.

"What?" he said when they reached his booth.

"You know what," she said.

"Tell me."

They talked and talked, mainly consisting of Beth's long pleading explanations about why he should come home. She promised to look after Sadie, and to make sure she could have an incubation, or go full term, if she wanted to keep the baby. Just not with the freeships, Beth begged. She told them she'd seen things. Horrible things she couldn't begin to describe. None of it had an effect on the young lovers. Sadie was stubborn. Beth knew that. Alex, too. They were determined to make their own way in life, they said. Making the point that in less than a couple of years they'd be adults, have their own share of wealth and be expected to look after themselves. Adults, except for the sex. Sweet sixteen for that, added Sadie through gritted teeth.

As the sun set, Beth conceded that she had no more arguments left in her and she departed, promising to return the following day and every day after that until they either came back with her to East Albion or broke her heart and got on the ship. Neither Alex or Sadie seemed concerned about the latter, not believing that they would break her if they continued their course of action. At least that's what Beth hoped was behind this lack of sympathy.

Sleep that night was difficult. Naomi had offered to comfort her, but Beth didn't think it was a good idea and without an explanation declined the offer.

For the next three days, they sat beside the booth repeating the same arguments over and over again in-between the youngsters serving their customers. It made no difference. The intransigent eleven-year-olds were fixated on earning their own una and having their adventure on the freeship.

On the fourth day, Sadie announced that the foetus was ready for extraction and that they'd be boarding the ship that day. Beth pleaded and pleaded with her to reconsider, but she had nothing new to offer except increasingly stupid threats of cutting Alex out of her life forever, a threat she immediately regretted each time she made it, and one that made no difference. When they started to pack up the booth, it was hard to stop herself from dragging Alex away. Naomi knew what Beth was thinking and linked her arm through Beth's as they followed Alex and Sadie to the ship. It was uncomfortable, what with Naomi being that much taller, so Beth unlinked and linked hers through Naomi's, grateful for the support. The youngsters led them down to the dock's edge to a gangway that sloped from shore to ship. Swarms of drones of all shapes and sizes were busy loading and unloading and it was remarkable to see them jostle and negotiate with each other for space, barely leaving a millimetre gap between them.

"Can we board?" Sadie asked the ship's BP.

The four of them stood waiting, mother and friend, son and friend.

The BP were joined by a wild-bearded man whose face was adorned with drone-control cones protruding from one cheek. He rubbed the cones with the tips of his fingers while glancing at the containers the drones were emptying and while speaking with the BP. Eventually, he passed Sadie something that Beth couldn't see.

"You're good to go," he said. "Follow me and do as I say. No questions."

All four of them took a step. The BP shifted sideways to block Beth and Naomi.

"Not you," said the man.

Naomi held Beth's hand tightly.

At the gangway, Alex strode into the swarm, towards the ship's entrance. Kai was watching, waiting, and Beth choked back the urge to shout at him to leave her son alone. The drones made way for Alex and Sadie, closing rapidly behind them as they went. The smaller drones swirled around their feet and passed between their legs. The larger ones moved around their heads. At the top of the slope, they emerged from the swarm and followed the cone man inside.

When they disappeared, Beth ran to the edge of the shore trying to peek into the tiny portholes that punctuated the side of the ship at regular intervals, desperate to see her son. She was less than a metre above the waterline and all she could see was the plastic scum floating on the surface and bacteria laden water striders bioengineered to consume it darting around, gradually nibbling away.

She turned to Naomi and crumpled into her arms.

30

NAOMI HAD taken Beth back to Boston via the same clandestine route that she had taken to get to the freeship. It had been tough going. Not because of the physical demands, although there were plenty of those; scrambling through woods, wading through rivers and even pedalling their own hydrofoil at one point. No, it was the emotional wrench of accepting that Alex was onboard the freeship and it had set sail. He was lost to her. It made her want to puke and puke and then curl up in the hedgerow to sleep it away and if it hadn't been for Naomi's persistence, that's exactly what she would have done.

When they arrived at Gerry and Morgan's, she was relieved and upset in equal measure to find that Tam had returned to Withernsea with Robyn, rather than the refugee camp. Apparently, after some heated discussion, he'd been adamant that they were at no greater risk there than in the camp, and at far less risk than Beth. She sent him a message, letting him know she was safe and that she'd call him later when she'd worked out what to do. He replied with a short audio message expressing his love for her and his total trust that she would do the right thing. It ended with Robyn gurgling and Tam in the background laughing and telling her to tell mummy she's crazy but we love her. It was a clever soothing message and Beth played it over and over until Naomi called her to come and join them.

The moment she entered the room, Morgan and Naomi broke off from an intense discussion bent over the SlendTek.

"Hey, what's happening?"

They looked at one another and Naomi signalled to Morgan.

"I wasn't going to tell you until it was complete, or as complete as I could get it," he said.

"Go on. You have to tell me now. You can't say that and then not tell me. That would be weird. And cruel. I can do without any more secrets. For a while, anyway."

He smiled. "Fair point. I've rescued some of the footage you took at the orphanage on that first visit. Do you remember?"

Beth stared at him and snorted. "Err, let me think now. Can I remember?"

"No need to be sarcastic. Eggshells here."

"Get on with it, and bugger the eggshells."

Naomi grinned and blew her a kiss.

"It's patchy," said Morgan, "but the best bit I've got is the swollen boy chewing on the leaves up until the point where the white-coat lifts his T-shirt and reveals that disgusting plug in his stomach. Then it gets scrambled again."

"But, that's fantastic. It's enough to prove that evil things are happening up there, surely? Who do we show it to? What can we do with it?"

"You're the caster, the influencer."

"Hey, that's true, but you're Resist and Regain."

Morgan called to Gerry. "R and R man, get your arse down here."

After explaining to Gerry that they wanted R&R to help out with fighting back and he'd agreed, the four of them discussed tactics. The first thing they had to decide was whether the physical action should take place in London or Cambridge, the capital of East Albion. It was a tough decision with arguments on both sides. There were more members and affiliates of Resist & Regain in East Albion so the turnout would be higher, but the orphanage was in England, and they weren't sure how much attention the English would pay to a protest about their country staged in East Albion. A counter argument was that if they chose London, they'd have to ask the East Albion R&R to travel to England to make the protest worthwhile. A difficult thing to ask given that protesting in a country that you weren't a citizen of could be dangerous, especially in England. The argument went back and forth with nobody strongly in favour of one or the other. It was a delicately balanced choice and they decided to work out what form the protest should take before putting it to the vote across the R&R network to find out who would take part.

It was Beth who asked the killer question about what they were trying to achieve, and it was Naomi who answered in her typical straight-to-the-point way.

"To fuck them up," she said.

"Hey, I get that, but how?"

"Try this," said Gerry. "We need to create a newsworthy focal point. We use a protest. Into that heightened interest we launch our footage from the orphanage and I reckon it's time to release the photos Mary took of the OS team developing the OSANN to prove we have insider knowledge. That way we expose and undermine them at the same time."

They all nodded vigorously.

"Brilliant," said Morgan. "I have just the thing for the physical protest, too."

"What's that?" asked Beth.

"If the protestors all get close, intertwining their limbs, and we jumble up their data, the BP won't be able to determine who is who. They won't be able to evict them and they'll have to call in human police. That will cause a sensation and take a really long time."

"Oh, the irony of a 'we are not anonymous' chant at the same time would be fantastic," said Gerry.

The vote was set up and within an hour there were enough volunteers to take the protest to London.

Beth left them to the business of organising things and headed upstairs for some much needed and long overdue sleep. After a brief and groggy call with Tam to reassure him that she was safe she lay down to rest. There was a slight hint of guilt hovering over her as she drifted off, but she was convinced that not telling him about what was going to happen the next day, or about her fears that Kai was tracking her, was the right decision. The painful realisation for both of them that they may never see Alex again was more than enough to put an almost unbearable strain on their relationship and she couldn't face being estranged, or worse, losing him to the grief he would inevitably internalise and suffer alone.

She fell asleep, occasionally waking in a sweat.

It was a particularly hot and sticky morning and after grabbing a traditional tea and toast and confirmation from Morgan that she wasn't on the BP wanted list, she set off for the station alone. The scooter that Gerry had hired for her was sufficiently fast to create a pleasant cooling breeze, for which she was grateful.

The train journey itself was uneventful and although she couldn't be sure exactly who they were, she knew that another fifty or so R&R shared the train with her. She'd been told to make her way to the OS headquarters in Pancras Square, King's Cross where Naomi would be waiting for her. They had a unique part to play in the day's protests, but they couldn't start until they were absolutely sure that the Sticky People Protest, as Gerry had decided to call it, was successfully underway.

At the square, the signal went out and seventy-five people came together in one mass tangle of limbs. It was hilarious and exciting to watch.

"We are not anonymous. We are not anonymous. We are not anonymous."

It wasn't long after they began their chant that the BP arrived, and only a few minutes after that the cameras took their places around the edges of the square.

"So far, so good," said Naomi.

The word *Disperse* was flashing on the foreheads of the BP and each time one of them made a move towards the protestors they only got so close before they juddered. Like one of those old-fashioned toys whose battery has run low.

Beth couldn't help giggling. "Confused and castrated," she whispered.

"Bemused and without bollocks," replied Naomi.

Beth tugged at Naomi's sleeve. "Shall we?"

"We shall."

Zigzagging along the ground together as they'd done for the first time all those years ago was exhilarating. The BP ignored them, making it all the more thrilling. A few Londoners glanced down at them. Most ignored them. Beth loved London for the way it accepted pretty much anything and took everything in its stride. At one point she thought Naomi was going to attempt to crawl through the legs of a juddering BP, but she zigzagged around it at the last moment. The most difficult thing was suppressing her ever-bubbling giggles.

"Here," mouthed Naomi, and they stopped at the spot that Morgan had calculated was the optimum place to stream from. "Right. Let's get this thing done."

Beth took out the mini-globule and lined up the first burst to broadcast. She squeezed and a stream of photographs taken from within the isolated development centre for OSANN shot invisibly into the air. As soon as they had gone, Naomi broadcast the announcement from R&R: *Hack the Ethics*. It was only a matter of moments before harvesters from all over England started to confirm that, based on the people they knew who had worked on OSANN, the photographs were genuine and not deepfakes.

As predicted, a BP separated itself from those juddering around the protestors and came towards them. They zigzagged their way to the next optimum spot and the BP didn't follow. Beth released more and before the BP, two this time, could find them they zigzagged away. Three more times they released a batch of photographs, got the public confirmation and affirmation from the harvesters, and each time the number of the BP trying to find them increased. Meanwhile, the protestors were intertwined and the BP attempting to eject them from the OS private square were powerless.

Beth sighed with pleasure. "It is beautiful, isn't it?"

Naomi kissed her on the cheek. "Let's go. It's time for that footage."

"Hey, I'm ready whenever you are."

"Shit," said Naomi pointing to the edge of the square. "Police."

A dozen human police had arrived. Gerry had said that the only way OS was going to be able to break up the protest was to buy in the expensive London constabulary, and he'd warned them that there would be a tipping point when OSANN would consider it worthwhile. That moment had arrived and zigzagging was likely to make Beth and Naomi more, rather than less, conspicuous. Standing up straight and casually wandering towards the next release spot was an extreme test of nerve. They laughed and joked with each other and paused to admire the occasional statue of an important figure in the development of that first breakthrough ANN. The perfect tourists. A quick glance every now and again confirmed that the BP and the police were busy trying to pull the protestors apart, closely watched and commented on by remote casters behind the bank of cameras. The plan was coming along nicely.

At the chosen place in the square Beth and Naomi sat down, as if they were taking a well-earned break from their tour. Beth held the mini-globule tightly and, having lined up the footage from the orphanage, she squeezed. The few seconds of a young boy with a plug inserted into his fleshy stomach was sent to the world. OS, the freeships and the Narcissists had been branded as incompetent by the protest and cruel by the footage. There was an uproar across the R&R network and that soon spilled over into the general public. Damage was being done. Cleverly cut mash-ups of the tangled protestors, the juddery BP, the leaked photos and the damaged boy were put to music and were soon belting their way up the ladder of trending news. Beth pocketed the globule and stood up to leave. Four of the largest and most sinister police officers stood in her way. Naomi was by her side and had that stern determined look on her face that Beth had come to know as the concentration before the explosion.

The oldest looking police officer looked them in the eye, Beth and then Naomi. "And, where do you think you're going?"

"Home," said Naomi. "And, you?"

"You're coming with us. You won't see home for a long time."

One of those helitrikes was approaching from behind the police. It was empty. It was the emergency escape they'd planned should anything go wrong, programmed to come to them immediately Naomi or Beth gave it the signal. Naomi must have done just that. Beth tensed her muscles, ready to leap on to it. The officer turned to the side to see what was happening. That's when Naomi landed a full-blown power punch to the side of his head, elbowed two of the other officers and kicked the fourth.

"Now," she shouted, and they both leapt aboard.

As soon as their bums hit, the trike shot off at such speed that they were pushed back into their seats. Gracefully, it sped through the crowds, avoiding pedestrians, trikes and scooters alike. It took tiny streets and major roads, and occasionally turned through one-hundred and eighty degrees. Morgan had calculated that they would have no more than five minutes before the police regathered, traced the helitrike and set the special BP after them.

Beth checked her globule. Four minutes and eight seconds. It was going to be close. The trike turned a corner and up ahead was a crowd of people blocking the road. The trike wasn't slowing down.

Naomi nudged Beth. "We have to jump while it's moving, otherwise the BP will know we got off."

As they approached, the crowd parted and a sheet of the same material the camp tents were made from was stretched out at knee height across their path. The whirr of the blades began, the trike lifted off the ground and as it glided over the sheet, Naomi and Beth jumped. As soon as they hit the sheet the crowd reformed and continued its slow walk towards the station.

They were safe. For now.

31

By the time they reached Boston, the backlash had begun.

Gerry grabbed them as soon as they arrived and shuffled them into the house. He was more upset than Beth had ever seen him, and Naomi wasn't reacting well to it either. In fact, for the first time since she'd known her, Naomi wasn't in control of her emotions.

"The R and R crew are seriously pissed off with Gerry," said Morgan. "Accusing him of being threefaced. One to them, one to the Locals and a third now to you and your taboo breaking stunts."

Gerry shushed him, but carried on the explanation. "OS have released data showing that you rented the drone they disabled, the one that was snooping around the orphanage."

"So what? What does that prove except that I'm prepared to dig away until I find the truth. Honestly, that must be the least of our worries."

"They've turned things against you by asking why you've never released a story about it. If it was that important and you found things out, why wait until now to release it. They're pushing hard to convince people that the only conclusion is that the footage of the boy with the plug is faked."

"Oh, come on. That's how it works. You build the evidence, over years sometimes, and then when you've got the story you release it all."

"True, but then they released footage of your visit with Esme."

"Shit."

"Yeah. Now they're asking questions about why you brought a young pregnant woman to their so-called evil orphanage."

She took a deep breath. "Did you find Esme?"

"No," said Morgan. "Vanished."

"Shit. Shit. Shit."

"Fuck," said Gerry. "You have to see this."

He touched his globule to the SlendTek sheet so they could all see. There were two recurring questions among the data and footage. Where is her son and where did her daughter come from? The data proved Robyn's existence and the footage showed Alex boarding the freeship. Sub-questions followed. Had she stolen Robyn from Esme? Had Alex found out and done the right thing by disowning her? Popular opinion and comment had completely turned against her. It was impossible to know how much of that was engineered by OS fake accounts and how much was genuine. The reality was, it didn't matter. The mood music across England, and probably beyond, was that the moralising Molly Coddle had been exposed for what she really was, and not before time.

"Wow, we really got to them," said Morgan.

Gerry frowned. "I'd say they've regained the upper hand. Wouldn't you?"

"We need to fight back," said Beth, unconvinced by her own bravery.

A new set of data was streaming across the sheet with grouped elements of it peeling off and hanging there. More questions were being posed. Who is this? Why is she unregistered? Why is her data sometimes combined with Molly Coddle's? Are they the same person? Another secret life for Molly? Data that showed the failed attempt by Naomi to penetrate the OS headquarters was released, cleverly with no footage that would undermine the prevailing accusation that Beth, as Molly Coddle, had multiple lives and some were so secret they must be shameful. OS were annihilating her piece by piece, data segment by data segment.

Naomi clenched her fist and punched the wall. "Fuck. We're finished," she said quietly.

Gerry's globule was pulsating. The Locals were calling. He sighed.

"Hey. What now? We must be able to do something. Mustn't we?" asked Beth.

"No idea. I need to go. I won't be long."

He left the room and Naomi stormed out after him. Leaving Beth and Morgan alone.

"Bit of a shit show, eh?" he said, distracted by packing away the tech as if it really was all over.

She sat with her head in her hands trying to figure out what to do, but the focus wouldn't come. She was destroyed, that was for sure. Possibly Naomi, too. Was she a danger to Tam and Robyn? Probably. Of absolutely no use. Not for Alex, not for Tam and Robyn and not for those desperate kids in the orphanage. She'd been naïve. If the ethics were based on the notion of freeing the individual from any collective responsibility and everyone had bought into it, then this had always been an inevitable outcome, or at least highly likely. As Naomi had so succinctly put it, they were fucked.

Gerry reappeared looking more worried than he had when he'd left. He called for Naomi to join them before he told them what the Locals had said. He waited until she was sitting next to Beth and then explained. They'd given him an ultimatum. Naomi must be registered if he was to remain on the council. They knew she was a close friend and stayed with him often and in their view it was unacceptable that he should condone her nonexistence. It had been a unanimous decision, he added.

"You traitor," shouted Naomi as she grabbed Beth.

She dragged her upstairs where they sat talking for a long time, working through their options. The starting point that underpinned everything was the realisation that they were now bad news for Gerry, Tam and Robyn, and although there weren't that many options, each one had multiple branches that affected those they loved. Eventually, they came to a conclusion. Not one that was particularly palatable, but the best they could contemplate. It would be the end of Beth as an influencer and of any chance for Naomi to become a citizen, but it would give them the complete freedom to do what they needed, and that was critical to their cause. It was with a heavy heart that Beth came to the understanding that her family would be better off without her. They agreed to meet back in Boston in a few days once they'd each done what they needed to do and said what they needed to say to those they needed to say it to. Beth would go and see Tam while Naomi stayed with Gerry and Morgan. After a long desperate hug and through streams of tears, they parted company.

Beth arrived in Withernsea and as had become her tradition she walked the last half mile to Tam's. It was usually a way of appreciating the calmness of the coastal town. This was different. If anything, she was simply delaying the conversation she had come to have. She was convinced that it was the right thing to do, the only thing to do. She also knew that it was going to deeply hurt him.

In the garden, Tam and Robyn were playing at something that seemed to involve digging up large lumps of mud and throwing them at the wall. Laughing and giggling together they were the perfect portrayal of father and daughter. Precious and fragile. Protective and playful. This bubble of happiness was either going to be broken by her or by OS. It was her choice. Robyn saw her approaching and smiled. Tam picked up their precious daughter and hurried over to meet her. The family hugs and kisses that followed were as sweet as any Beth had known.

Inside, she asked Tam to leave Robyn in the other room for a while and the incredibly well-behaved opposite of her brother simply slept quietly while they talked.

"I have to tell you something and it's going to hurt both of us. All three of us."

Tam leant back in his chair. "I saw the way they destroyed you and Naomi. Bastards."

"It's about that. They aren't going to give up. Whatever I do, they're coming for me. I can't risk you and Robyn too. There's no telling what they might do to you, and I dread to think what's happening to Alex. You have to understand. I'm leaving. Forever."

"You're fucking not."

"I am. I have to."

"No. Do you think I care what people think or say about us?"

"I know you don't and I've always loved you for that. It will be more than words though. I don't know what it'll be. I'm sure it'll be nasty. It's not fair on Robyn. Or you. I'm transferring all of my wealth to you. For Robyn."

"Not happening," he said and left the room.

She gave him a while to digest what she'd said and then joined him in the bedroom.

"One last time?" she asked.

"One more time," he said and drew her to him. "I need you," he whispered.

It was a frantic fuck. Desperate and anxious.

As they lay in bed, she broached the subject again. "I have to," she said.

He didn't reply. Instead, he pulled her close and they lay in silence.

The three of them spent the evening, the night and breakfast together as if there was nothing of note going on. Tam seemed to have accepted what she'd said. Rather than pick at it to make sure, she left it alone and he didn't mention it. Not once.

She spent a long time saying her goodbyes before heading off back to Boston and was thankful for the solitary journey the trike allowed, giving her the space to cry her heart out the whole of the journey.

Naomi, Gerry and Morgan were all waiting for her when she arrived. They'd also spent an emotional night saying their goodbyes and Beth wondered if they'd sealed their close friendship with sex for a second time.

"Is everything ready?" she asked and all three of them nodded. "Hey, then let's do it."

The news story had been written. Beth and Naomi had recorded their pieces. The stage was set and only the play button needed pressing.

"Are you sure?" asked Gerry. "You can still change your minds."

"We are sure," they said in unison.

Morgan slid his four fingers across the SlendTek sheet creating the complex pattern that formed the passcode that would start things happening.

They all stood back and watched.

Firstly, Beth described why she had come to the conclusion to end her life. "The bilious barrage of abuse is more than anyone can take. I strongly deny the allegations and stand by my accusations against OS. But I love my family so much and the only way they can live anything like a normal life is if I am no longer here."

She sobbed.

Naomi came next. "The world is fucked. I tried to do something about it and failed. I am signing out with my good friend Beth, who, by the way, is a human being in her own right no matter what the data might say, and here is the proof. You fools."

With that, the screen went black and after two long minutes *We Are Not Anonymous* flashed up and the broadcast ended.

To the world, they were dead.

There was an eerie silence in the room, which Naomi broke. "Well, my deceased friend. Shall we go live our lives?"

"You are deleted," said Morgan. "Even your implants are no longer registered as active. They'll not be searching for you. At all."

Beth smiled at Naomi. "You'll have to teach me how to live without implants."

"My pleasure."

Morgan blew them a kiss. "Beth, with your new hair and those pills to fatten your face when you're in public, you won't be recognised. Forty-eight hours of facial anonymity, whenever you need it."

"Right," said Gerry. "It's all waiting for you at the port."

Beth grinned at them both. "Close enough to walk?"

Naomi grinned too. "No choice."

They gathered their belongings and ran to the port. There, waiting for them as promised was a ship shaped like a giant manta ray tilted backwards as if it was about to fly away. Pod-like rooms covered the two pectoral fins with a transparent covered central spine that led from the front deck to the back where the fins tapered into two long tails. Beth couldn't stop herself from grinning and hugging Naomi. It was the most splendid ship she had ever seen.

She turned to her friend. "It is absolutely fantastic," she said. "But." She held her breath. "Where did the money come from? Who paid for it?"

"Irrelevant. Resist and Regain have loaned it to us indefinitely."

"They know?"

"No. Only that it's being used for a vital mission."

"Hey, that's sweet."

Naomi pointed. "There," she said. Under the water, there was a long almost vertical nose that went so deep you couldn't see its full extent. "That," she said, "holds the most advanced tech we could find, and it's where a copy of Luscious is housed."

"It's coming with us?"

"Yeah."

Onboard, Naomi talked Beth through the basics, and most importantly the contact lenses through which she could access the pop-up instruction guide at key points around the ship. Once the introductory tour was complete, she gave Beth the techsheet that held the detailed schematics and which, in combination with a mini-globule, could be used to ask Morgan for real-time help. Naomi had already done as he had suggested and set the autopilot to manoeuvre out to sea before consulting the weather predictors to decide which route to take.

Standing alone on the front tip of the top deck facing the dock wall they hugged as the ship slowly turned one hundred and eighty degrees, lowered its nose into the water and sailed out to sea.

Naomi made a hissing noise through her teeth. "They won't know what's hit them."

Beth laughed a loud belly laugh and planted a big, wet, soppy kiss on Naomi's cheek.

The ship splashed the water with the tip of each fin in turn and then dipped its nose.

"Hey," screamed Beth. "They won't even see us coming."

PART THREE

32

It was eleven o'clock at night and Beth crept quietly into their shared sleeping space, having spent the evening staring at the stars, the shining moon and listening to the waves of the South Atlantic lit up by the ship's underwater lights. She checked that the tiny bead under her skin was activated, a ritual performed each and every time they were both going to be asleep. The ship pretty much ran itself, but if things did start to go wrong it would need human assistance pretty sharpish. She lay down on the bed and her mind drifted towards the morning. Naomi would be on duty again at six, which would give Beth a full six hours before she joined her for their overlapping shift. It was a routine that had taken a while to establish, and it worked for both of them. In the time that they'd been following the freeship, they'd docked whenever it did. It was much easier to watch when it was parked up, to see how it operated and how it might be vulnerable to their planned interference. And, after two failed attempts they were taking their time to get it right, despite the ever-rising stakes as Kai increasingly became the 'voice of reason', the 'teller of truths', the one that 'had the world's back'.

Residual contentment from the warm night's watch, the spray and smell of the ocean wrapped Beth in a blanket of delight. At times like this it was easy to forget about their mission and to wallow in the joy of their adventure and their wonderful friendship. Wallow. Now, there was a word to avoid. A word that Naomi was fond of using to reprimand Beth whenever she got a whiff of despondency.

Beth glanced at the shape lying next to her, letting the faint sweaty smell of sleep and the slightly irregular breathing coat her existing layer of contentment. It had taken them a while, and some awkward conversations, to agree that having separate rooms to sleep in was too lonely, especially on stormy nights. Beth stretched her legs and arms to relax into her tiredness, welcoming the comforting knowledge that her friend was close. A comfort, which combined nicely with the continuous lapping of the ocean beneath them and the deep orange glow of the nightlamps, gently edging her towards sleep.

When she woke up, it was to the sound of Naomi getting dressed and the early morning glow of the sunrise oozing through the tiny slit windows. She threw the covers off, which dutifully folded themselves neatly on the floor, flung her arms out wide and spread her legs, touching the sides of the bed with the tips of her fingers and each of her big toes.

“Hey,” she said, still a little groggy. “The sea and the stars were at their best last night. It was fully magical. Twinkling pinpricks from millions of years ago, shimmering on the quiet ocean waves. You would have loved it.”

“Morning.” Naomi grinned and winked. “I know that look. It’s the pleasure before work look.”

Beth returned the smile. “Yes, as you so elegantly put it, I am in exactly that sort of mood.”

“Who is it today? John? Max? Susan?”

“Very funny.”

“You’re the one who named them.”

“Only so I can recall the template easily. Without any fuss.”

Naomi chuckled. “Or mishaps.”

"It's not even humanoid. Unless I want it to be."

"Sure. Whatever you say."

Beth winked, knowing that she was about to make her friend cringe, but what did Naomi expect if she insisted on making Beth's sexual appetite a bigger deal than necessary by comparing it to her own. "Wanna join me? Us?"

Naomi blew her a kiss and departed.

Beth let out a long sigh of waking-up bliss, and without fully coming to life she ambled over to the cabin designated as her own private space, pondering as she went, on what she wanted from her pliable playmate. It was not a day for shocks or surprises so she settled on Max, the octopus that could enfold her. With lumps and bumps and tentacles of different shapes and sizes he was programmed to protrude at a moment's notice wherever her fancy took her. She had her favourite template in mind. A nice shade of pantone 147 and slightly cooler than a healthy human. Beth was pleased that she and Naomi had reached an understanding about her needs and that it had become a lighthearted everyday aspect of their lives. It hadn't always been that way. In the early days of being aboard, Naomi had been desperately inquisitive about how each variation felt, which in turn had led to a few misguided and unwelcome moves from Beth, followed by awkward rebuttals from Naomi, and intimate conversations about Beth's preferred ways to relieve herself when she needed to. There were still times after a few drinks when Naomi would focus in on it again, keen to understand what Beth got from encounters with a lifeless piece of plastic, as she inaccurately described the pliable playmate – it wasn't plastic. She usually ended the inquisition with a threat to prove its inanimate fakery by throwing it overboard for the ever-present plastic devouring water striders.

Beth closed the door behind her and for the following hour she fully indulged her desires. A perfect start to the day.

Having washed and dressed, she wandered over to the lab where Luscious was housed. She sat down at the bench, called up the interface on her mini-globule and set to work. Firstly, she checked that Luscious had updated and was identical to the Luscious back in Lincolnshire with Morgan. It had, so the serious work could begin. Between them – Luscious and Beth – they would continue the creation of the data that described the lives of the people in their fictitious town of New Peterloo, a conurbation that they were growing as additional training data to those that were currently used by the Ls. If they could introduce this town as a valid input to the Loop then it would join the other data returned by the Ls from around the world, which in combination were used to revise the protocol. When the updated Loop was released, it would ensure that New Peterloo was an integral part of how the Ls were learning from each other and organising their respective societies in accordance with their own particular interpretations. When Beth and Naomi deployed it, presuming they could, it was likely to be their one and only chance to change things and New Peterloo had to be absolutely believable for them to be successful.

Beth waited patiently for Luscious's first proposal of the day. She was ready to follow the established pattern of iteration which began with the L and ended with the human and with plenty of opportunity to refine the data between them along the way. New Peterloo was being developed as a place where the population took a poll once a week to establish if the policies being employed were working. By focussing in on the freedom phrase of the protocol – to free all private individuals – the data was skewed towards only one aspect, but the best of the best of Resist & Regain had confirmed that this wouldn't be a problem so long as they didn't compromise on other aspects of the protocol. After all, freedom was open to multiple interpretations. At the right time, Beth and Naomi had to introduce the training data to the

Loop as legitimate, and incorporate it into the Ls' decision making processes. It was a lowkey piece of activism that many R&R had taken a lot of persuading was the right thing to do, believing that if you weren't physically tearing down the establishment then you weren't changing things. With suitably timestamped data they were hoping to show that communal ownership of resources such as tools, toys, and even kitchens would make people feel freer than if they personally owned them. An idea from generations before them that had been squashed to death by those in control before it could be fully tested. Thankfully, the modelling was working. So far.

Her globule lit up to let her know that Luscious was ready. She squeezed and the proposal appeared on the SlendTek attached to the wall: *All meals to be owned communally*. An interesting idea, but she wasn't sure it was quite right. Would it be believable that you would be in favour of spending time and energy cooking a meal with the risk that it might be taken by someone else? Unlikely. However, having all raw food owned communally might work. She made the suggested tweak to Luscious and it ran the policy through the modelling, testing it on a random selection of people in the data. It seemed to work, so she agreed for it to be added in to the live version of New Peterloo with the constraint that it should take at least a week before it began to alter the freedom poll. While she waited for another suggestion, she ran a diagnostic to see if the town-wide policy of the local currency facilitating an IOU banking system was still having the desired effect. Again, using random datapoints in the modelling she tested the degree of freedom perceived by those who had taken advantage of the offer. Sure enough, smallholders Nicole and Willie Hudson had slaughtered a pig, distributed the meat among their neighbours and banked the IOUs inside the local currency. One of the recipients, a Joel Tucker, had increased his freedom score each week in the poll, as had Nicole and Willie.

She made a note to discuss with Naomi how they might bring this to bear across the whole town without causing a contradiction. What they didn't want was the IOU currency and the communal ownership of food at odds with one another if applied in the exact same location, to the same people.

Over the course of the following three hours there were no suggestions from Luscious that Beth could accept, so she shut up shop for the day and headed off to prepare a lunch of jellyfish chips and seaweed mayonnaise. A favourite of theirs.

"Look at this," said Naomi as Beth joined her.

On the screen was footage from one of their insect-drones which had taken up residence among the ragtag flock of drones that had been launched to welcome Freeship One to Boma Port. Naomi pointed at the transparent crow's nest where Kai was flanked by two young children. All three of them were waving furiously. "Fucking idiot."

"Hey. Ignore him and come and eat some lunch. There's nothing new to see. Is there? I mean it's the same old story. Whenever the freeship docks, chaos ensues. Why would this time be any different? The crowds come to see him. They cheer and scream as if he was the king of the world. The freeship leaves some tech behind. Tech that is almost certainly not in their best interests. And, he leaves with whatever it is he needed. Or more likely wanted, as I doubt that he needs anything."

"You're right. Smarmy shit."

"Can you look for Alex?"

"I did. No sign of him. Or Sadie." Naomi covered Beth's hand with hers. "Sorry."

"We'll find him," said Beth. Adding under her breath, "One day."

"I'll look for a vacant place for us to drop anchor," said Naomi as she manoeuvred the drone away from the freeship and flew it back along the edge of the flooded land downstream from the newly rebuilt floating port.

About four kilometres down, she found a tiny island where untraceable moorings were being rented out by the hour. She dropped the drone close enough to transfer sufficient local currency for three days and then instructed it to return to watch the freeship.

"Three days?" said Beth.

"It's all we have left from our last visit. Remember? You bought John, Max and Susan. Expensive."

Beth blushed. "You said you didn't mind if I spent that much."

"I don't. We can always get more once we're there."

They stood side by side with the screen split between the drone's feed from the freeship's passage to the dock and the map that the ship had created to guide itself to their mooring.

"There," said Naomi. "Look."

Lined up along the docks were rows and rows of desperate looking people. Despite their differences in size, gender, age, colour and so on, they had one thing in common, the familiar stoop and shuffle of Rejuve junkies in need of a fix. It made Beth's stomach clench at the thought of Alex. Likely to be caught in the same trap, if not worse.

"I hate him," she whispered.

"Kai? I know."

With little enthusiasm they ate their lunch while the ship expertly navigated to their mooring, weaving in and out of the smaller boats that infested the river.

Naomi choked momentarily on a chip. "Shit. Look."

A huge claw with the dexterity of a human hand was laying a giant net of extremely fine material on the ground behind the junkies.

"I bet it's made from that super spider silk," said Beth.

Naomi glared at her. "What?"

"I bet—"

"I heard. Surprised that's what came to mind."

They watched in silence as one by one the junkies shuffled onto the net until it was completely covered, at which point the claw pulled the edges together and lifted it high. Weirdly, the net remained solid where people were touching it, forming a transparent floor. The junkies were motionless while they were lifted up and across to the deck of Freeship One. Once onboard, they obediently shuffled off the net, which was then whisked away and out of sight.

"Quick. See what Kai is doing," said Beth.

Naomi directed the drone towards the crow's nest and there he was with a big fat grin and a hand placed firmly on the top of each child's head. He turned them to face outwards and Beth gasped. Their eyes were hooked up to a grotesque, bulbous, pulsating sac and a tube from each of their stomachs was attached to another larger dark green sac beneath Kai's raised chair.

"The sooner we kill that fucker, the better," said Naomi.

"Too good for him. Too good by a long shot."

33

THEIR SHIP manoeuvred itself into place, edging in between a couple of rough looking vessels. Bonfires littered the shoreline and further back in the sparse scattering of trees there were plenty of makeshift huts and lean-tos.

"Let's go," shouted Naomi.

"Hey. Coming. We need some local currency. Don't we?" Beth shouted back.

"Let's get it on the way."

Beth shrugged and ran up the steps to join Naomi on deck. "Let's go," she shouted in her best Naomi accent, and then smiled.

They stepped onto the platform, which lowered them to the shoreline where Naomi triggered the security bots. A swarm of minuscule drones formed an umbrella shape above the ship, creating a visible deterrent to anyone stupid enough to attempt to board without permission. A pair of blackish birds that Beth didn't recognise floated by. Dirty and ragged from a life of foraging the shallows of the industrialised river, they stared with their turquoise eyes at Beth over the tips of their long-hooked beaks. Beth linked her arm into Naomi's and, as if they hadn't a care in the world, they strolled over to a woman standing next to a small flat-bottomed boat with a sail made from solar-cloth and two bicycles at the rear.

Beth smacked her lips. "Wow. She's stunning. Look at those muscles."

Naomi ignored her and walked ahead, holding out her hand to shake with the blonde woman. "N," she said.

"I guessed," said the woman. "Nice to meet you. I am Harven. I have received your payment."

Beth made a coughing sound. "B," she said and then turned to Naomi. "You booked ahead?"

Harven clapped her hands and two of the women sitting among the trees stood up and jogged down. "Let me tell you how it works. The sail is made from solar-cloth and charges the battery at the same time as being a sail. If the batteries get too low it turns orange and you will need to pedal those bicycles until it turns green again. That's all. We will do the rest. Except. When we get stopped at the various checkpoints along the way, it is for you to negotiate our passage. Not us. Clear?"

"We negotiate?" asked Beth.

"We are excluded locally. You are not. Ready to leave?"

"Sure, our identities are valid," said Naomi, interrupting Beth who was about to correct Harven.

Naomi stepped onto the boat and sat in one of the two deck-chairs. As soon as Beth had joined her, Harven smiled, looked at her companions, shrugged, and they set off.

The stench of the river and the non-stabilised boat was affecting Beth quite considerably. Her stomach was alternating between clenching and wanting to rid itself of breakfast as quickly as it could. "I need the toilet," she called across to Harven, who pointed to a small hut.

Beth grimaced. "Really?"

"Really," said Harven

She slid the door open and took a step back in disgust. "There's a huge swarm of massive flies buzzing around the bowl."

"From the freeships," shouted Harven. "Bioengineered. Part fly, part machine. They digest the waste and when they expire we use them as biofuel. They're harmless. Here, let me turn them off."

The flies all settled on the floor and Beth braced herself. She stepped inside, slid the door shut and kept her eyes closed while she relieved herself. Thankfully, she managed to suppress the retching and swallow the small amount of vomit that made it to her mouth.

"What was all that about?" asked Naomi when Beth was seated back on her deck chair.

"Gross."

"Gross?"

"Gross."

Beth squinted as the sunlight pierced the treeline. Three shadowy figures were standing between the sun and the boat. A metal bar rose from the water in front of them. Harven held out her hands to show they were empty, and Naomi eased herself out of the deckchair.

"Been here before," she whispered to Beth.

As she moved to the front of the boat, Harven took a step back. "Hello," she called. "We're on our way to port."

"Toll," shouted one of the shadowy figures.

Naomi shouted across. "Resist and Regain. You can validate."

"Do they own the river?" Beth asked Harven.

"Not really. It's a free-for-all. It is a bit of an ownership blind spot."

The toll collectors confirmed that the boat was free to go, and they continued on their slow peaceful journey. Occasionally, they were interrupted by the shouts of people having parties on the rickety bridges between islands. Parties that looked as though they'd been going for days, or weeks in some cases.

After a couple of kilometres, the sails turned orange. Beth and Naomi boarded the bicycles, pedalling in an easy silence. Beth dropped her head to a racing pose and standing up on the pedals she pushed hard. She pushed and pushed, watching the tips of the sails turn green. It was slow progress, but eventually the sail was fully green. With relief, she dismounted.

The boat was stopped once more and again without any fuss a blockade was removed from their path. As they neared the dock, the water flowed against them and the boat's crew became busy deploying stabilising arms on each side.

A solitary figure called to them from the shore. "Over here," he shouted. "Before you enter the port."

Harven steered the boat across the choppy waters to the biobrick platform. "All yours," she said as they got close.

"Hello," shouted Naomi. "Can we pass?"

"For sure. I know who you are. Take these. You'll be glad of them."

He held out a sack for her to take.

"What's this?"

"Gifts. Blankets with weave that opens and closes as the temperature changes, which it does a lot on the ships and with little warning." He picked up a flat four-layered biobrick construction and held it up in the air. "This is a boat. You'll need it if you have to leave the freeship quickly. The joints react to salt so it assembles itself as it hits the water."

He passed them over to Naomi and as she carefully placed them on the deck of the boat Harven steered them away from the platform and into the deeper water. She set the sails and they headed towards the docks where the freeship was peeping above the buildings.

"Why did they give us that stuff for free?" asked Beth.

"Resist and Regain is expanding."

"That's it?"

"Yup."

Harven agreed to look after the biobrick boat and the blankets for them while they went ashore, and after arranging a rendezvous time, they thanked her and disembarked.

The dockside was heaving with the sounds and smells of trade. There were queues for the warehouse where the technology that the freeship would be leaving behind was being distributed.

Beth was keen to get organised. “We need food, tech and currency.”

Naomi took hold of her hand. “Walk with me. I have currency. From Harven. So do you.”

“Hey, that’s great. Shall we split up so we have more time to find Alex?”

“And find the freeship’s weaknesses.”

“That, too.”

“I’ll get the food. You get the tech. Be careful it’s not toxic tech, though.”

“How?”

“As ever. Check in with Morgan.”

Beth watched Naomi stride off towards the crowds that were gathered around one of the large containers, which had been winched across from the freeship. Beth turned towards the warehouse, taking her time and keeping an eye out for Alex or Sadie. A few people bumped into her when she wasn’t watching where she was going, scolding her with sharp words as they passed. She’d heard worse. In fact, she’d received worse in response to her casts. Nothing was going to faze her, or get in the way of searching for her son. She strained her neck to see above their heads and she leant forward to look through the gaps between their bodies. Nothing. Alex was almost a young adult. There were plenty of boys his age, but only a few with his skin colour. He would stand out and if he was also with Sadie then the two of them would be obvious. She paused and turned through a full circle. Nothing. The crowd seemed to be getting tighter and tighter and Beth was conscious that Naomi would be waiting for her, so she hurried to the warehouse to see what might be useful to them on the next leg of their journey.

While she waited in line, she dropped Morgan a message asking if he knew what she should be trying to get hold of. His response was concise. R&R only wanted the nanotech bots that could build and dismantle themselves into different inanimate objects. R&R wanted a closer look at the tech and it wasn't something that had been brought to East Albion or England, as far as they were aware. He said there were rumours that on the freeships the tech was intelligent enough to be context driven, but that she'd probably only be able to get a limited version. It sounded like the nanodust she'd seen the one time she'd been onboard the freeship, the stuff the refugees had told her about. As she neared the front of the queue, she could see the dust being demonstrated and sure enough it was the same thing. Dust. Chair. Dust. Table. Dust. It was hard to believe that this was anything other than a clever way to get the dust accepted into everyday life. Not a trick so much as a vanguard for the fuller capabilities it possessed. Nonetheless, if Morgan and his R&R folk could get hold of some and analyse it, maybe they could be prepared for anything more sinister that might follow. The queue moved forward as another person left with a massive grin and a bagful of dust. The closer Beth got, the more apparent it became that the freeship was simply giving it away to anyone who wanted it. No checks. No charge. One of those 'good news, bad news' situations. The young woman who was administrating the distribution gave her standardised polite greeting to Beth and handed her one of the thousands of bags stacked at the back of the warehouse. Beth was about to open the bag and take a look inside when Naomi arrived with a butler bot behind her pulling a large flatbed trolley piled high with food.

She grabbed a metal box and thrust it in front of Beth. "In here," she said. "Faraday cage. Keep the little buggers quiet."

Beth dropped the bag of dust into the open box, closed it and handed it back to the butler, which stacked it carefully alongside the other acquisitions.

Naomi pulled Beth to one side. "Counterfeit identities. Fake globules. I found someone. That's how we do it."

"What? Really? Fake who? We need to be able to pull it off. To be convincing. I remember when I was investigating a story back in England. It was well known that a caster… Jack? Fred? Milo? Oh, I can't remember. Anyway, he had fake ID and—"

"Enough."

"Enough?"

"I saw Alex."

Beth gasped so loudly that a few of the nearby queue turned to look at her. "You did what?"

"Come. I'll show you."

Naomi grabbed her hand and guided her through the chaotic crowds, which became denser the nearer to the freeship they got. Behind them, the butler was doing an incredible job of keeping up, although there was the occasional yelp followed by loud swearing as the trolley caught the back of someone's legs. They found a relatively clear spot a little way back from the dock. Naomi cleared a corner of the trolley and dragged Beth up to stand next to her. She took out her globule, activated the telescope and held it up to Beth's eye.

"Look. Top deck. Two-thirds from the front."

Beth swung around to the spot Naomi had described and, sure enough, there was Alex. He hadn't changed that much, except that he stood tall and bold with his legs apart and his feet firmly on the deck. The arrogant stance of the pre-adult with a crippling lack of confidence was gone. She zoomed in closer. He was sharply-dressed. She grinned at Naomi and when she turned back to observe him he was sauntering beside a shimmering three-metre high see-through sheet that surrounded a shuffling mass of Rejuve junkies. Drones at each corner were moving the shimmering cage to keep pace with him. A few of the addicts were limping, dragging one leg behind them, but most simply had their heads bowed and were concentrating on their feet. A few were fidgeting and fiddling with the sheet as if their veins were jam-packed with adrenalin. She focused in on Alex. He was glowing. With pride, she was sure. He looked so alive. His eyes were bright and he had such an eager look on his face. A tear formed and dribbled down her cheek. Her Alex was driving herds of people as if they were nothing more than the cattle she'd seen in Tam's old documentaries.

"I need to see him," she whispered. "You have to get us onboard. He needs me. Look at him. That's Sadie's doing, I'll bet. She was always trouble, that one. Please, get me onboard. I need to talk to him."

Naomi put her arms around Beth and drew her into a hug, letting her sob. Beth knew that it was more complicated than getting onboard, talking to him and them all leaving together a reunited happy family, but at that moment all she needed was the comfort of her friend and the belief that she could rescue her son.

"All in good time," said Naomi through the last of Beth's sobs.

"Hey. I know. At least he's alive. It was so wonderful to see him. I can wait, so long as we keep the freeship in sight."

34

They were back at sea and into their routine of tracking Freeship One, which appeared to be heading back to London. Sunshine was streaming across from the starboard to the port, creating a wonderful early morning sheen across the ship. Beth threw her arms open wide. She'd left Naomi sound asleep and snoring in that cute comforting way that she had and was enjoying the solitude. The sea smelt rich and vibrant and, so long as she didn't look over the side at the plastic-eaters busy at their work, everything seemed excellent with the world. She leant back in her chair and propped her feet up on the panel. There was nothing to do except watch the ocean pass by and be ready to step in if the ship needed help, which it never did. She gave her globule a quick squeeze and perused the world news. Footage of floods, droughts, and freak weather storms filled the first tranche. That was to be expected. A regular daily diet. It confirmed that their mission remained critical to the survival of humanity on earth, but seeing as there was nothing unusual in that, she squeezed to get the next tranche. As it was forming on the globule's surface a message from Gerry came in: *We're there.*

"Hey," she said, having flicked her thumb to call him. "Care to elaborate? I mean that's a little ambiguous, isn't it. Where are you? Were you intending to be there? Who is 'we'? Do you want congratulations or commiserations?"

"Well, good morning to you. You're certainly in a good mood, aren't you?"

"Yup. My belly's full. My companion slumbers. The sea and the sun are all mine, and they are glorious. You really should come and see us sometime, you know. Remarkable as it may seem, given everything that's going on, the planet is still amazing."

"Stop. Stop. You're making me itch to set sail. Look, I called because I have news. Fantastic news, actually."

"Go on."

"New Peterloo is ready. We've tested it to destruction. The data hangs together. It's consistent, believable and has enough hooks for us to keep developing it once it's incorporated into the Loop. As I said, we're there."

"Does Morgan still reckon we have to introduce it physically? No way to do it remotely?"

"Sorry. Yes."

"Onboard the freeship? No way to do it more locally?"

"No. Sorry."

"Hey, don't worry. We've always known it, haven't we? And we have a plan."

"Where are you?"

"We're pretty sure we're on our way to London."

"Could you come to Boston so we can give you what you need?"

"Can't we use this one? We have a Luscious with us."

"Sorry. The device to inject it is here."

"At yours?"

"We'll have to meet nearby. There's some dry land near the port where we can meet, unseen."

"I'll talk it through with Naomi when she wakes and let you know."

He disconnected after passing a few snippets of local news to her. Gossip he thought Naomi would appreciate. Nothing significant, but entertaining nonetheless if you knew the various characters involved.

After the call, she found it hard to settle. Thoughts of Alex hovered at the back of her mind. The sun had lost its magic and the sea its charm. Instead, she paced around the edge of the ship waiting for Naomi to wake. The plastic-eaters were busy chomping, fuelling her impetus to focus on the dangerous and vital task in front of them.

"Morning," said Naomi, putting her arms around Beth from behind and startling her.

"Hey. Gerry's been in touch."

They sat down right there and talked for the best part of an hour, working through all the implications of having to board the freeship and physically insert something into the tech that they were sure was heavily guarded. Should both of them go? No, only one. Who should it be? Beth. Naomi was better at running the ship singlehandedly and Beth wanted the chance to see Alex. Could they think of a different, less dangerous plan? No. It was settled and Naomi called Gerry to confirm. He gave them a place to rendezvous – *behalf.points.downsize* – explaining again that their house was subject to flooding and, although they were comfortably living on a combination of makeshift biobrick platforms and under the tree canopy of the upper floors, any extreme weather event brought the BP to their door, snooping around for data, ignoring any privacy taboos. It was a continuous point of disagreement in the council, and one that the Locals always won.

Naomi popped the globule into Beth's pocket. "That's that," she said and strolled off to get dressed.

It didn't take long before they were convinced that the freeship's destination was London, and that they were safe to forge ahead to Boston without the risk of not being able to find the freeship again. Naomi told their ship the coordinates, set it to full speed, and they let it do its thing, to deliver them to the rendezvous.

The mouth of the estuary was busy with large and small boats all jostling for position in the port, and their ship gradually made its way through the multitude of craft and up the coast to the bay closest to the disused prison where they were to meet Gerry and Morgan. Once in place, the ship lowered the smart undercarriage, its legs, to secure itself.

They pulled their blankets tightly around their bodies and set off across the deserted and spectacular flat ground. The vast open skies, the long, flat horizon and the sounds of the birds in the few trees that remained were a welcome distraction for Beth, and she knew that Naomi's laughter and exclamations of joy let loose into the wind were down to a deep primordial reminder of home.

Morgan met them outside. "Look at you two," he said and hugged them each in turn. "So good to see you."

Beth was pleased to see Naomi soften her posture in his embrace. Whatever else happened, this brief return to her Lincolnshire home would be very good for her.

"I have to give you this before we go inside," he said, handing Naomi a mini-globule.

She raised her shoulder and her eyebrows at the same time.

"Luscious." He looked around as if he was expecting to be shot at any moment. "It's edible," he whispered. "Once you're done, swallow it."

Naomi grimaced. "Traceable? In your stomach?"

"No. It's digestible. You literally digest it, leaving only tiny traces of plastic in your shit. No more than eating a fish from the sea. They'll never detect it."

She shrugged and tucked the device in to her pocket. "So, what's the big secret?"

Morgan tilted his head to one side and grinned.

"C'mon. Spill."

A trike pulled up next to him. "It's only a minute away. Come and see."

He hopped on and Beth hopped up in-between him and Naomi. They sped along, spraying dirty water from the flooded road as they went. Beth couldn't help thinking that they should have walked but said nothing, knowing how sensitive activists can be about their own blind spots.

He pointed at a row of semi-detached houses with rotting wooden slats covering the walls of their top floors. The drains were blocked by fallen foliage. Combined with the stagnant smell of the waterlogged road, it reminded her of a scene from one of Tam's post-apocalyptic films. "In there," he said, pointing to the house at the far end.

"Have you seen him?" she asked.

"Beth," snapped Naomi.

"Morgan. Have you seen Tam?"

"Later," he said and opened the door for them.

Inside, a small group of people were gathered. Some sat on chairs, others on the floor, and some stood. There was a low-level hum of chattering. The sort of chattering you know will cease immediately that anything happens, as if its only function is to prevent boredom or arguments. Beth looked around and was taken aback to see the woman from the Anti-Leveller League who she'd met when Alex was being incubated. The woman made a miniscule gesture of recognition and Beth reciprocated. Gerry was standing next to her along with another woman who was wearing the pinstriped uniform. It was strange to see a faction member after all this time.

Gerry called them to order and sure enough silence fell straight away. "Thank you," he said. "I won't keep you long, except to say we, Resist and Regain, are honoured to welcome you." He paused. "We open our arms to you, the Faction, and to you, the Anti-Leveller League."

Beth whispered to Morgan. "What's happening?"

"They're wrapping up their organisations and becoming R and R."

"Wow."

"Yeah. Wow. Can I have a chat?"

He tugged at her sleeve and led her out of the room.

"Hey. What can I do for you? Is everything alright with Gerry. You two haven't fallen out, have you? That would be such a shame. I was only thinking the other day—"

"Stop." He hesitated. "No, it's not Gerry. It's Tam. He's not coping without you."

"Have you told him?"

"What? That you're not really dead? That you didn't commit suicide? That Alex and Robyn still have a mother alive and well? No. I haven't said a thing."

"I doubt Alex knows or cares whether I'm alive or dead."

He shrugged. "Maybe not. But Robyn needs her mum…" He sighed. "Not to mention her pain of having to live with a miserable father."

"It has to be this way. For the greater good."

"Really? Does it? Please reconsider. Even if you just let me tell Tam that you're alive. That would make all the difference. I can tell him that you've dropped below the radar. For the time being."

Beth stared at the ceiling. She could feel her jaw beginning to wobble and clenched it tight. She pushed Morgan away as he tried to comfort her. She drew in a loud breath through her nose and was about to walk away when the barriers broke and tears flooded out. Morgan grabbed hold of her and held her tightly while she sobbed and sobbed.

Eventually, her crying subsided and, punctuated by gut-wrenching moans, she whispered, "I… miss… them… so… much."

"I know," he said gently into her ear. "I know."

"Tell… him – if I survive – I want… to see… him."

35

Gerry and Morgan accompanied Beth and Naomi to the ship and said goodbye, wishing them all the luck in the world with the New Peterloo data that was sitting in Naomi's pocket.

"Here, take this," said Morgan, handing Beth a handful of small discs. "They're peer-to-peer transaction currencies. Like the old cash. You'll be able to use them with the excluded in most parts of the world."

"Thanks. Appreciated."

They boarded their ship and gave it instructions. It was nice to be back onboard in familiar surroundings and to be alone with Naomi again. The ship edged its way back to sea and through the telescope she watched as Gerry and Morgan waved to them from the shore.

"This is it then," said Naomi, as they stood and stared at the open sea.

Beth put her arm around her. "Yup, this is it. Hey, couldn't think of a better person to be doing it with."

The ship soon picked up the trail of the freeship leaving the Thames, which allowed Beth and Naomi to relax and mentally prepare themselves. They had no idea how long it would be before they'd need to implement the plan, but they were both hoping it wouldn't be long. Tam had sayings: Waiting was harder than doing; Anticipation killed the best of intentions; and Trepidation crushed commitment. What did he know? No matter how long they had to wait, she was confident that once she began, her focus would be on succeeding and staying alive.

The freeship appeared to be heading for the port of Boma so Naomi negotiated a fair price with her fake ID contact at the port and agreed to pay on arrival with one of the discs that Morgan had given them.

They settled into their routine with the exception that they spent two hours of their overlapping shifts going over the plan and the potential problems. Again and again. No plan would unfurl exactly as predicted, but at least with forethought some of the more obvious flaws could be anticipated. Beth knew that. She got that, but she was rapidly becoming bored of regurgitating what she would do once onboard. She protested, but Naomi insisted – better to be overprepared.

When they arrived at the West African coast, Beth took the face fattening pill. They booked the exact same spot as before and let the ship expertly navigate its way to their docking point. Naomi's contact was waiting for them, flanked by a large scary looking bot. A sort of BP on enhancement meds, if you could have such a thing. She waved them over as they disembarked.

"Hello," said Naomi.

"Welcome."

"You have it?"

"Yes. An Indian refugee. Highly skilled at coding. That's what you asked for."

"Thank you." She paused. "Beth?"

Beth held out the disc and the woman clicked it in place with her own. As soon as the transaction completed, she scanned Beth's face and body and handed over the refugee globule.

"I'm not Indian though. I don't look Indian."

"Not native. Naturalised. India has open borders and is willing to give anyone citizenship who wants it."

Beth squinted at the globule while rolling it around in her hand. "Indian?" she said quietly.

"You're still Beth. It means 'promise of God'."

Next to her, Naomi suppressed a chuckle.

Beth stopped frowning and grinned slightly. "Thank you, that will help enormously."

The woman and her super bot disappeared into the trees, leaving Beth and Naomi alone to put their plan into action. They strolled casually to the freeship, not wanting to attract any attention. It was so magnificent they simply stood and watched. The energetic commotion of a ship when it docked was in full force. Goods were being offloaded and goods were being lined up ready to be lifted aboard. The most interesting thing, though, was the queue of refugees lined up at a makeshift shack close to the passenger platform that was lifting people on and off the ship.

"You need to join them," said Naomi.

"Hey, I know. Here, take this." Beth passed Naomi her globule, her real one. "Best not to have it on me. Just in case."

"Sure."

They hugged and Beth kissed Naomi on the lips, who didn't reciprocate, but did smile.

"See you soon," said Beth.

"Yup. Good luck, and don't forget to signal me if you're in trouble."

"Will do."

Beth turned towards the queue and without looking back she strode off, weaving in and out of the hustle and bustle as she went.

Getting accepted as a refugee was a lot simpler and quicker than she'd expected. They checked her globule by scanning it across a sheet of SlendTek. After a few seconds it confirmed her place onboard and transferred the location of where to report. Imitating the three people she'd seen in front of her, she smiled and thanked the BP profusely. She caught up with a man who had been near her and together they walked up the gangway and through the same drone swarm that she had watched Alex pass through with Sadie. The closeness of the drones was claustrophobic and the anxiety of passing herself off as a tech savvy refugee was giving her loud brain buzz. She nodded to her companion. His shoulders were pulled in towards his chest and his eyes were staring straight ahead. He half-nodded back. Weirdly, seeing his anxiety made her feel better.

The sentries at the top of the gangway demanded to see her given location and after scanning her globule one of them displayed a map across its upper body. Her globule flashed a pale yellow and she glanced down at it. The map had appeared with a route set out for her. She set off. It took her past the loading bay and along the edge of the ship on the opposite side to the dock. Surrounded by the crowds rushing around, the smell of spices being unloaded, and instructions being shouted at the drones and the zeroed, she saw nothing to worry about. At all.

She was puzzled when she arrived. It seemed a bit out of kilter. It was a metre off the side of the ship. She looked around, but there was nobody to ask. She squeezed the globule to reset the map, but the same error appeared making her wonder if there was a balcony below, as part of her cabin. There was only one way to find out, so she stuck her head over the side holding the globule at arm's length. It wasn't a balcony. Stuck to the side of the ship was a bubble, a totally transparent crustacean-like sphere. One of many, and most of them occupied. She chuckled. Her and Naomi had often speculated about what these lumps might be, and here it was, her home, her private space. She swung her head from left to right in the hope that someone had appeared who could help her. Nobody. A narrow ladder joined the deck to the bubble. Climbing over the edge, she descended slowly. One rung. Pause. The next rung. Pause. Until she was at the opening of the bubble. She touched the tip of her nose, took a tentative step inside, and when it didn't fall into the water below she put her possessions down carefully and sat cross-legged in the same manner as the other refugees. The roof of the bubble grew across the gap where she'd entered until it was fully sealed. Below, the sea lapped against the side of the ship, creating a haze of spray. A faint wheezing sound like an old man's breathing prompted her to look around, but all the other bubbles were too far away for it to be them. Whenever she touched any part of the bubble with her skin the noise grew louder and faster. She lay the palm of her hand flat against the surface and held it there. After a few seconds, the breathing steadied, as if it had grown accustomed to her touch. She pressed a little harder. The bubble was covered in minuscule folds of a rough damp organic substance. A soft slightly fetid odour hung in the air. All of the other refugees appeared to be meditating or at least concentrating on something so intensely that they were not moving. She could do very little else than wait and see what would happen. Gradually the heat became too much to bear and she remembered that her blanket was also able to cool. She wrapped herself in it and waited.

Eventually, the ship began to move, which caused the bubbles to bounce against its side. Beth sat still and watched the shoreline disappear. The other refugees were busy gathering their possessions together in to neat piles. They climbed the ladders and she copied, joining them on deck.

"Hey," she said to the man closest to her. "What happens now? I'm new. Beth." She held out her hand.

"Pradeep. Hardware engineer."

"Hey, that's great. I'm a refugee. I code. What do we do? Do we just stand here? Or do we go to work? Hey, why don't I wait and follow what you do?"

Pradeep pointed at a woman crouched a few metres away. "Dacia. She's a coder. She can help. By the way, call yourself a gee rather than a refugee and you won't seem so new."

Beth strolled over determined to appear casual, and thankfully the other gees only gave her a brief glance as she passed them. “Hey,” she said to Dacia. “I’m Beth. I’m a coder. Can I tag along with you?”

Dacia nodded and then returned her attention to her globule, holding it up to the sky and turning it around in the palm of her hand. She sighed. “The South Atlantic by the look of it. Belem most likely. Brazil. Follow me.”

They set off at speed towards a door, which led into the body of the ship. Beth clenched her jaw and then loosened it, hoping her gurgling stomach wasn’t giving away how anxious she felt.

36

Dacia led Beth along curved corridors, which seemed to slope up and down as they echoed the shape of the ship. It might have been an illusion, but inside this wave-like structure it was hard to get an accurate orientation. Dacia had warned her not to pay too much attention to whatever they passed along the way, encouraging her to focus on what she was there to do. Beth already knew that stuff was going on that was at the far end of taboo, but the next step in the plan was to find the core location of the Ls, so she had to keep her eyes open and register everything she could. It turned out to be a different part of the ship from the one she'd seen previously, and appeared to contain room upon room of gees busy at their tasks.

"Here," said Dacia over her shoulder as she stepped into a validation chamber. A cloud of green mist surrounded her and rapidly evaporated. "Your turn," she said and stepped into the room.

The green mist stung a little, but Beth passed the validation and followed Dacia. The excitement of people working together, calling across and shouting out loud was the first thing that hit her. Next was the smell. A stronger, thicker version of her bubble's odour.

Dacia noticed Beth pull her head back slightly and scrunch up her nose. "You'll get used to it. Cumulative pong of the pod people."

"Pod people?"

"Us. The gees."

The kitchen in the corner of the room was piled high with dirty glasses and a neat stack of branded snacks that Beth recognised. Dacia had strolled across to a large piece of SlendTek attached to the wall, covered in scribbles, diagrams and snippets of code. In front of it were two large globules, larger than Beth had ever seen. One appeared to be displaying a live feed from space of the earth's weather across its spherical surface and the other an animated version of the same, but with different patterns.

"Hey. Is that the weather around the globe? Is it live? To help navigate? I guess so."

Dacia smiled. "No. We're working on a system to control the weather. Not to observe it."

"Shit. Really?"

"Yes. Really."

"What do we do then?"

"There's a library of ANNs that have already been developed. For other purposes, naturally, but each one does something useful in its own right. We pick them out and knit them into Gaiann, the climate ANN. There's a library. There's a task list – pull requests. There's a lead producer who approves all of your uploads before they can be used. Process you're familiar with, I'm sure."

Beth nodded and wandered off to find an empty globule docking point. Once again, her stomach and her jaw were clenched tight. One of the gees who was sprawled across a biobrick platform covered in what looked like the same material as the bubbles, the pods, gave her the thumbs up as she walked past exercising her facial muscles, desperately trying to relax.

He tossed her a segment of the beige oblong he was eating. "Brain food." He pointed at himself. "Rex."

She thanked him and settled down nearby to familiarise herself with the task list and the library. The globule she'd been given slotted neatly into the docking point and provided the interface she needed. Presumably there was a throughput of work that was expected, but she didn't want to ask for fear of drawing attention to the mismatch between her fake persona and her actual capabilities. She wasn't too worried, though, because Dacia had explained to her that it was perfectly acceptable to spend the first week getting to know Gaiann before being able to take on any of the tasks, so that's what she did.

Each day she left the pod with her fellow gees and went to work. Eating, drinking, and chatting for the full fourteen-hour shift before returning to her temporary home to sleep. At the end of the week, she asked Rex about being able to wash more thoroughly than in the kitchen sink at the nest, as it was called. He pinched his nose and with a strange voice explained about the bath bubbles.

That evening she set off to bathe in the pods below the waterline, which were accessible via the ship's portholes. It took her a few attempts to find an empty one, but as soon as she did, she stripped off her clothes and a little self-consciously slid into the bath. She lay down and the porthole closed. Water flowed from outside, through the filters and the heaters, across and around her body, and out again into the outside world where bacteria digested the dirt into matter for other bacteria to create the energy to power the baths. Bathing and bioenergy in perfect symbiosis. The warm massage of the flowing water, the faint caress of cleansing bacteria and the panoramic view of the approaching underwater biobrick buildings covered in milfoils and molluscs helped dissipate her nervousness at being nude. Helped by the fact that, unlike their homes, these bubbles had a one-way translucence, which meant she could only make out vague shapes in the other bubbles. She trusted that she, too, couldn't be seen in all her naked glory.

Back at her pod, she stroked her skin, relishing its cleanliness. The word *rejuvenated* popped into her head. A word that quickly brought her back to the matter of Alex. She hadn't seen him or Sadie, but then she hadn't looked, preferring to wait until they were a long way out to sea and the ship wasn't crammed full of landed-folk flying in for the day. It had also given her time to establish herself as a legitimate and perfectly normal refugee. Nothing to see here, as Naomi was fond of saying.

She wrapped herself in her blanket and sleep came easily.

In the morning, she grabbed some snacks from the kitchen and sat down in earnest to begin her work on Gaiann. After trawling the library for modules that she understood, and spending time in the task list finding ones she was competent to undertake, she was ready. Happily, there were quite a few, so she chose the simplest, assigned it to herself and cracked on with the modification to make it Gaiann compatible. It was a pleasure to get lost in solving problems and she could completely see why the life of a gee on the freeship was an attractive option. At the end of her shift, she uploaded her completed task for approval and instead of heading directly home she took a different route. To search for the Ls.

She wandered the decks and the corridors for hours, up and down and around. There was no sign of the place where the Ls were housed. Even following different groups of gees to their places of work didn't reveal anything, and despite her reservations she came to the conclusion that she would have to subtly quiz her colleagues, extremely carefully if she didn't want to blow her cover. Up on deck, she got her bearings in relation to the crow's nest, the ever-watchful eye. A caring parent or a sinister tyrant, depending on your perspective. She set off for home. Up ahead she could see a large group of Rejuve junkies, surrounded by drones holding one of those shimmering three-metre high see-through sheets. She slowed down to look, hoping beyond hope that her wishes would come true. And they did. He was there.

Striding alongside. Issuing instructions. Arrogant. Pumped on Rejuve. Her grown-up son.

Beth waited for them to come close. Each step, each junkie shuffle, caused her heart to misfire and her glands to pour their sweat. She clasped her hands behind her back, hoping that would give her an appearance of nonchalance. Sadie was with him, also radiating an air of arrogant authority. Both of them looked great with skin that glowed and smiles that showed off perfect teeth. There was a bounce to their step and a flow to their movements that anyone would be envious of. Yet, as they got closer, the detachment from reality in their eyes betrayed their addiction. Inwardly, Beth groaned and her legs wobbled. She kept her gaze fixed firmly on Alex as he approached, not knowing what she should or could say to him. When he was only a few paces away he did a doubletake. She was certain he'd seen her, and sure enough his stare settled on her. He blinked a couple of times and his cheek muscles twitched. She opened her mouth to speak, but had nothing to say. He turned his head away and walked past without any form of acknowledgement.

"Alex," she said, quieter than intended and in a way that she could later fool herself he'd not heard. "Sadie."

They passed by with their shuffling herd.

Beth held her head in her hands and pressed hard on her temples. The pain was a relief, for a while. Reality slowly infiltrated its way back in and the shock of seeing him subsided, replaced by a growing fear that he would report her. The failed freeship experiments that roamed Cable Street flashed through her thoughts. A fate worse than death? Possibly. Probably. She hurried back to her pod.

Over the next few days, she continued to work with a foreground anxiety that at any moment she'd be whisked off to who knew what. Approvals for the modules she was reengineering plummeted, which added to the likelihood of being cast into the pile of gees that in effect were treated as bodies to be used and abused.

Nothing happened and gradually she was able to accept that Alex had decided not to report her. As well as being a huge relief it gave her hope for the future. Her approvals rate increased and she started chatting again with the rest of her nest. She exchanged quips, questions and occasional solutions with them across the room. She contributed to the SlendTek ideas sheet and began sleeping again at night.

One morning, with a deep breath and the best smile that she could muster, she broached the subject of the Ls with Dacia. "Hey. Do you know where all the hardware for Gaiann is kept? I was thinking, it would be great to see it. Somehow, it would make it all the more real."

Dacia shook her head. "No idea. A bunch of boxes. Bioware and hardware. Not interested."

"But it's the heart of the system. It's where all our work comes alive. How can you not want to see it."

"Just don't."

"Someone must, though? It must be maintained 'n' shit."

"Guess so. He'll know," she said pointing at a teenager who Beth had never spoken to.

"Hey. Appreciated."

Beth strolled over to his workspace and after introducing herself, she asked him the same questions. He was more forthcoming and agreed that it would be amazing to see Gaiann's actual house. In fact, he was sure that he'd heard that all the significant ANNs were in a heavily guarded core facility in the depths of the ship. Cooled by the passing water as the ship sailed along, he added. She asked him what he was working on and they chatted for a while before she returned to her questioning.

"Hey," she whispered conspiratorially. "How do we get to see Gaiann, then?"

He looked around as if he was stretching his neck muscles. "Become hardware fixers, I guess."

"Wow. What a great idea. Can we do that?"

He shrugged. "Dunno. I don't have the skills, but I guess if…"

He drifted back to his work.

She was excited and it was hard to concentrate on the remainder of her shift but she did, somehow. As soon as it was over, she went straight back to her pod to tie her things inside her blanket, except the biobrick boat, which she could sling over her shoulder.

The plan was going well and although she hadn't spoken to Alex, not being exposed was a good result. When they docked in the morning, she would have to leave the ship and return later as someone else, as a hardware fixer.

37

BETH HAD left the freeship and not returned, without being discovered, she hoped. Naomi had collected her without a glitch and, after consulting with Morgan and making sure that the worldwide R&R network were keeping track of the freeship's location, they'd set sail for home.

They docked in a flooded and deserted backwater behind the newly rebuilt East Albion port of Tilbury. After getting everything in order to leave the ship safely, they disembarked, leaving it in the safe hands of the drone umbrella. The top-end car, which their benefactor had arranged for them, was waiting. Its deep scarlet body and opaque windows oozed privilege, the sort that got you noticed or ignored, depending on which was to your advantage.

Naomi whistled. "Now, that is nice."

"Hey. We deserve it. Well, we don't. Well, we do—"

Naomi shoulder-barged her friend. "Shush," she whispered. "Let's go get your ID."

The car was amazing. Not only did it speed along, with every other single piece of traffic making way for it, but the internals were beyond belief. The super-rich employed caretaker drivers to take the responsibility for them, so the in-car entertainment was designed to be a fabulous display of wealth. Beth was having the time of her life exploring it while Naomi stayed alert in case of an emergency, not that there ever was one.

"Wow. You'll never guess what I've found."

"Do tell," said Naomi without looking up.

"Listen." Beth pulled a large globule from under the seat. It was about the same size as the ones on the freeship and it hovered in front of her. "Ready?"

"Go on."

She stroked it to life and then by revolving it, squeezing it, and moving it up and down, the various parts of the vehicle pumped out music. She was conducting the car. Musical notes from the seats, the doorhandles, the windows, the unattended steering wheel and the windows all blended together to form the most wonderful sound, which improved the more familiar she became with the globule. She laughed and laughed at the exquisite experience, utterly lost in the joy of making music. The streets sped past, more as a landscape to her creation than a city of real people. Occasionally, Naomi would congratulate her on a particularly tricky sequence, but basically Beth was immersed and alone in her own pleasure.

"We're here," said Naomi.

"Eh?" Beth paused the music. "Where?"

"Where do you think? The Retro Bar."

"But what about the border?"

"We went past without stopping. Waved through by the border BP. No questions asked."

"Wealth," said Beth quietly. "One set of taboos for them, and another for us."

"Come on. Get a move on."

Reluctantly, Beth stepped out of the car and watched it disappear back to its owner. That was no shared on-demand car, that was for sure. She grabbed hold of Naomi's hand and they swung their arms in unison as they strolled along the path to the bar. The sun was shining and the sharp tang of the Thames was wafting across on the breeze. She felt as light as a feather.

They dropped their globules off with the doorman and headed to the alcove where they'd met. She was engrossed in the conveyor belts and what they had to offer. Not much had changed since she was last there.

She chuckled. "That's retro for you."

Naomi laughed too, but her laugh seemed unusually nervous. "He's here," she said.

Beth shifted her gaze towards the alcove and away from the food and drink. Gerry was sitting there with a massive grin. Next to him was Tam. Beth stopped in her tracks and grabbed hold of the conveyor belt, pulling her fingers back as it tried to whisk them away. She steadied herself. He had come. She didn't think he would and nobody had warned her. Why not? Did they think she had to be protected? Did they think that it would be a nice surprise? It was in a way, but it would have been better to have been prepared.

She frowned at Naomi. "You can't be overprepared. Or so you say."

"Sorry. He insisted that we didn't warn you."

Tam stood up and held out his hand as if they were meeting for the first time.

She snorted. "Eh?"

"I don't know you."

"What?"

"I saw the two of you waltzing up the path, hand in hand."

"Friends."

"You faked your own death, for fuck's sake. You shoved me down a pit deeper than I've ever been and left me there. And, you say 'what?' Unbelievable."

"I..." She had nothing to give. She had so desperately wanted to see him. She ached to hold him, to have him hold her. This was not how she'd expected it to be. She held back the tears, which made her face appear tight and unemotional. It was shit.

"We'll leave you be for a while," said Gerry. "C'mon, N. Let's take a walk."

Gerry and Naomi walked away leaving her alone with Tam.

"I can explain," she whispered. Adding, "I missed you so much."

"I missed you. But, you two? You better be honest with me. The truth or you'll never see me or Robyn again."

She looked around the bar. "Where is she?"

"Did you think I'd bring her? Put her through this, just when she's starting to get used to the idea that she doesn't have a mother?"

"I'm back."

"Yeah. Right. For how long I wonder. And with us? With your 'friend'?"

Beth moved to touch him and he withdrew his hand from the table.

He exhaled loudly. "No," he whispered.

"Tam—"

"The truth about you two. The truth about where you've been. Then we can talk about us."

Beth nodded and leant forward to talk quietly and confidentially, hoping he would appreciate the intimacy. She explained about the mission in as much detail as she felt she could, explaining about the need to disappear so they could reinvent themselves in a way that would get them access to the freeship. Describing the ship and their routine of following it from port to port was easy. Telling him about Luscious and the plan to infiltrate the Loop was more difficult. It wasn't easy formulating a story that was seemingly complete and yet had crucial parts omitted, such as the constant fear that had permeated her time as a gee. Deliberately, she missed out the bit about having to physically plug Luscious in. He didn't need to be worrying about what was still to come. He listened carefully, seemingly intrigued by her pretence at being a refugee, and even smiled at her description of the baths attached to the ship. She was on the verge of telling him about Alex when he interrupted her flow.

"You two? Naomi? What's going on there?"

"We've become close. Good friends."

He raised his eyebrows.

"Not like that. You know she's not into sex, don't you?"

"Is that the only reason?"

"Tam."

"What?"

"Leave it. We're friends. I've been aching to see you, to hold you, and you're being like this. No touching. No Robyn. Cold. It fucking hurts."

"Welcome to my world."

"Please. I need to tell you about Alex."

"You saw him?"

"Yes."

"And *now* you tell me? After all that guff about the freeship, baths, Gaiann—"

"Hey. I was working up to it. Listen."

He rested his head in his hands and stared at her. "Go on."

She told him all about what she'd seen and how Alex and Sadie had ignored her, but hadn't reported her either. She began to say how the two of them seemed like a well-suited couple, that they seemed happy, when he interrupted her.

"You do know he was putting himself out there, far and wide, as a breeder for hire? To quote his exact words."

"A what?"

"A provider of healthy young Rejuve-filled sperm. For the discerning couple or the young woman looking to surrogate and sell."

Beth drew a sharp breath. "That's why Esme and her friends knew of him."

Tam pressed her to continue but dug into every tiny little detail of her story, asking what Alex was wearing, how he walked, how he held himself. The picture she painted was her best attempt to give Tam what she'd been lucky enough to have. A glimpse of their grown-up son. It wasn't adequate. She knew that and he knew that, but she did her best.

When she'd finished, he took hold of her hand and held it tightly. "Thank you." He swallowed and rubbed the corner of his eye. "Thank you."

She kissed his fingers, one by one. Passively, he let her. "Robyn?" she asked with a croaky voice.

"She's good. Cheeky. Prone to long silences. She misses you."

They chatted about Robyn.

"I've had some funny days out with her," he told Beth. "As for her quirky creations back at home, you've got to see them to believe them. Her favourite place to play is in the garden with mud, leaves, petals and bits of old plastic found in abandoned houses. Once a week we spend a morning together roaming around looking for whatever takes her fancy and then in the afternoon we work together to extend her play kitchen. She bosses me about, insisting on one thing and then insisting on another. All the time refusing to acknowledge that she's changed her mind."

Beth chuckled and Tam chuckled, too. She was relieved that eventually the atmosphere was light enough for them to both giggle at the antics of their daughter. She kissed him across the table and he responded passionately. Ignoring the loud whispers of disapproval from nearby booths they fell into what could only be described as a good long snog. He was back. They were back, and it felt good.

When they finally separated, she sighed.

"Go on," he said.

"I have to keep going. There's still work to do. I'm so sorry. I wish. Oh, how I wish that I could come home with you and snuggle down with you. Both of you. You can't imagine how much I want to pull the curtains across and shut out the world, but I can't. You get it, don't you?"

He nodded the smallest of nods and wiped away a tear. "Go get our son. Come back safely. Please."

With one last kiss he left the bar with his hands thrust deep in his pockets and his shoulders hunched.

She bit her lip to stop herself from weeping.

38

Beth was onboard the freeship again and was trying to work out how to safely contact Morgan. As luck would have it, one evening while sitting in her pod she'd caught sight of another of the gees frantically speaking into what looked like a half-globule. A quick glance around and she saw that almost all of her fellow gees were up to the same thing. The next day she began her quest to discover what was going on. Pradeep, who she'd met briefly on her first arrival, had become a friend. He had never asked how she'd moved from being a gee coder to a gee hardware engineer, but then he wouldn't. He hadn't known much about her original fake identity and as facial recognition wasn't used onboard the freeship because there were too many new and strangely shaped humans onboard, an unusual degree of privacy was the norm, something which had also protected her from probing questions from her previous colleagues. Her new identity was secure: Beth the hardware fixer. She'd asked him about the half-globules and he'd explained that what she'd seen were gees using a recently designed device to make contact with family elsewhere in the world. He introduced her to someone who could explain what she needed to build her own, and being among hardware engineers had meant that it hadn't taken her long.

Beth checked to make sure that nobody from the freeship was spying on her from above. All was clear, so she covered her head with her blanket and got to work. The semi-sphere of scavenged tech glowed in her hand, indicating that the narrow window of time when the ship's surveillance altered its focus was approaching. There were rumours, theories about why this occurred, mainly based around Kai. Two of the most popular were that he was busy uploading his brain to a remote device or that he was encased in gel and connected to an ANN that was fixing his decaying cells. Both ideas would require a massive security effort to ensure the procedure wasn't disrupted. Different gees had told Beth that they'd seen these in action, which naturally cast doubt on both. Whatever was going on, what had proved to be true was that using this window to make contact was untraceable, or at least untraced. Unless, those in charge were simply monitoring and waiting before pouncing on the gees they wanted to punish. It was a risk she had to take.

The surveillance window opened. Morgan was waiting and they quickly exchanged messages. She sent images captured by the eyebrow camera that she'd discovered she could smuggle into the lab in her mouth and then use clamped between her teeth. He replied with suggested solutions to her more complex tasks, but increasingly as they became more difficult he had to call on the wider R&R network. Tam was involved, too, which gave her the warmest most welcome feeling of any that she'd experienced. Not least because she'd been able to let him know that she'd caught sight of Alex a few times, and that he was still alive.

Morgan was taking a long time to respond to her latest set of images. She pulled her blanket tighter around her head, leaving a gap to peek at the other gees. They were all still huddled over their devices. Maybe there was a problem with hers, or at Morgan's end. She waited, rolling the semi-sphere around in her hand. A strange taste formed in her mouth and she realised that she'd been chewing the blanket. She swallowed the sour saliva. She waited, running her fingers along the edge of the biobrick boat that was her emergency escape route. Nothing. She sent a message to prompt him in case he'd got distracted. Nothing. The semi-sphere began to glow again. The window was closing. She sent a warning message to him and he replied. They'd been making sure, he messaged. They were convinced. This next task would take her into the core. This was her moment. Did she know what she had to do? She messaged back confirming that she did, disconnected and curled up under her blanket. She was shaking, and she didn't know if it was from excitement or fear.

She hardly slept and as the sun rose, she wrapped the mini-globule that contained New Peterloo in the Faraday sheet that she'd made from scraps in the gee lab and tucked it into her pocket. She climbed out of her pod and strolled towards the labs with the others, exchanging pleasantries as she went. Pradeep settled into his usual rhythm, walking a half pace behind her as if he was unsure whether she truly wanted him next to her. She chatted with him about the storm that was coming and about what to have for breakfast. Old-style roast shipworm encased in a salt-lined seaweed wrap was their favourite. All washed down with a glass of Quintz, a recent addition to the kitchen, which tasted like a cross between sour cherry popping candy and clam juice. It was strangely addictive. She nodded to gees she barely knew and blew kisses to the group of young women who had shown an interest in her. An insect-drone appeared at their side and kept pace with them. Beth's stomach tightened and she accidentally bit her tongue. The insect-drone was probably there because she'd displayed behaviour outside of her norm. As she wiped her open mouth with the back of her hand to see if there was any blood from the bite, she wiped the grin from her face. She needed to calm down, as Naomi would have told her in no uncertain terms. Pradeep was prattling on about the day's tasks, asking Beth which ones she thought she'd manage to complete by the end of the shift. She muttered noncommittal replies and dropped her enthusiasm for the day down to her normal level. The drone disappeared, seemingly satisfied that it was a behaviour blip, as they were known.

She strolled through the entrance to the lab. Security was more thorough on the way out when they were concerned about theft, and so the scanning on the way in didn't pick up the globule or any heightened anxiety. Once she was in, she was safe and the security ceased. After all, what was the point of looking for unusual pieces of hardware inside an experimental engineering lab?

As she squatted on the edge of the bench next to her allotted space for the day, she took a large bite of her shipworm wrap and spun the lab globule to review her tasks. She stifled a laugh. The option that would certainly take her into the core was still on offer. She quickly grabbed it before anyone else, and a couple of other tasks to diffuse the appearance of specifically singling out that one. She sat back against the wall and savoured the final few mouthfuls and the remnants of the Quintz. If all went to plan, this was her last breakfast onboard the freeship. With a swallow and a smile she stood up, strolled over to the long bench of equipment and spare parts that the previous shift had laid out for them. She gathered what she needed and gave Pradeep a tiny goodbye wave.

She sauntered along the corridors and the closer to the core she got, the number of freeship BPs increased. It was intense, but they didn't appear to be doing much except hovering in nooks and crannies.

At the door, the BP checked her credentials and the reference code for the task she'd been assigned and then moved aside to let her through.

It didn't take long to find what she was looking for and it didn't take long to find the indentation in which to place the globule. She pushed it in place and waited a few seconds before it displayed activity across its surface. All appeared to be as Morgan and the R&R hackers had hoped. The core recognised the data as passing all the necessary checks and, sure enough, it sucked the data up and processed it into the core. Weirdly, it reminded her of the living sponges in the freeship recycling tanks cleaning the waste of the ship and expelling clean water as they intuitively went about their business. From one foot to the other, she stood on tiptoes until New Peterloo was well and truly launched into the Loop. Immediately the activity was complete, she pulled the mini-globule from its docking place and bit it a few times until her saliva began to break it down. She popped it into her mouth and chewed. Chunks came away and she swallowed, contorting her face to allow them to pass as quickly as possible down her throat and into her stomach. It only took a few minutes and as the last piece was making its way, she headed to the exit, entirely focused on getting out of there as quickly as she could.

Back at the lab she pottered around for the remainder of her shift, nonchalantly saying goodnight as she left.

The walk from the lab to her pod was torturous. It was so slow. No slower than usual, but as Tam had been fond of saying, time was relative. He'd always chuckled at this witticism and the memory made Beth smile.

In her pod, she put her belongings into her blanket, tucked the biobrick boat under her arm and climbed up to the deck where she casually made her way in the dark to the entrance of the bathing pods. At the porthole she pushed her blanket of possessions into the bath, followed by the boat and then her body. She pressed the button to open the bubble so it could be cleaned and with a woosh she was washed out and over the side of the ship.

She landed in the sea with a thump, but soon dragged herself onto the boat that had formed itself as soon as the salty water had activated it. She pulled all the necessary straps into place to secure herself and her possessions and then, having sent the signal to Naomi who was close by, she lay back and stared at the stars. She was done and it felt good.

The ocean was lapping at the sides of her boat, but its flexibility and ability to manipulate its shape protected her from drowning. The stars were bright and to the side of where the freeship was fading into the distance a smaller vessel was coming her way. Her biobrick boat was bobbing all over the place, which made it difficult to concentrate on the approaching vessel, but something didn't look right. It was the wrong shape for their ship. It was too small. She sent a distress signal to Naomi who responded with a curt, *Coming*.

Before the vessel was close enough to make out what it was, a flock of drones surrounded her. She messaged Naomi – *HELP* – knowing it was unlikely to penetrate whatever cloud the drones had formed. A crane swinging its arm and with its claw swaying menacingly back and forth, was the first part of the vessel to become discernible. As she'd dreaded, it was one of the patrol vessels from the freeship. It pulled up alongside, bobbing on the waves in unison with the biobrick boat. The arm was lowered, the claw was clamped tight around the boat and she was lifted on to it.

Kai was there, surrounded by BP. He was standing rock solid. Staring at her.

A tiny squeak escaped her lips and her stomach pumped acid into her mouth at the same time as she lost control of her bladder.

Two bots held her tight as Kai approached. The squelching of his bare feet on the deck disappeared behind her, travelling from her left to her right ear where he whispered, "Gotcha."

39

Beth stood passively inside the curtained cage that she'd been placed in shortly after being lifted from the patrol vessel on to the freeship. What she now knew to be a slug mucus cage similar to the one she'd seen Alex with had been used on her by a topless, wafer-thin, girl with a row of bone spikes grafted on each of her ribs and poking through her skin. The girl had strolled over with the sheet wide open behind her and then, quick as a flash, moved it into a square, surrounding Beth. Taking all her possessions in the process, the girl had been standing guard ever since. Slowly sharpening her rib spikes with a stone.

Beth winced at the horrendous grinding sound every time the girl applied the stone. "Hey," Beth called to her. "I wish you'd leave me alone."

The girl ground again and Beth grimaced. The girl continued to grind and Beth prodded and pulled at the shimmering curtain. There was no apparent way out, unless she could contact the outside world and call for help.

She shouted. "Hey. You. What the fuck have you done with my son? He's the reason I'm here."

The girl ignored her.

Beneath them on the other side of the transparent floor was a considerable amount of activity. People and drones were rushing from one side to the other to clear the deck and the biometallic sound of some distant part of the ship being moved filled the air. The girl stopped grinding, touched her ear and said something that Beth couldn't hear. After running her fingertip along the recently sharpened edge of her spikes she clapped her hands and the curtain cage lifted a little off the floor. It moved with her across the deck and pressure from the cage walls forced Beth to move with it. The girl grinned at Beth with a mouthful of pointed teeth and from time to time she pressed the palm of her hand on a spike, drawing blood that she then wiped on her smock, which absorbed it without trace. They made their way to the edge of the deck through the bustling crowd and on to a curved corridor that wound its way down to the deck below and then the deck below that. By the time they reached the lowest deck where the only light was the faint aura from the water outside, the girl had ceased her bloodletting. She shuffled Beth into a corner with the shimmering curtain cage cordoning her off, grinning as she tantalisingly placed Beth's confiscated globule on the other side of the curtain.

Two hooded figures appeared out of the mouth of the corridor and paused.

Beth shouted, "You know why I'm here. What the fuck have you done with my son?"

The smaller of the two rolled back their long black sleeves revealing heavily tattooed forearms. They traced the intricate lines that traversed their arm, lightly touching their bronze hairless skin. Beth experienced a tingling inside her body as if someone was daintily dancing along her veins and tickling her organs as they went. The hooded figure pressed harder and traced the tattoo once again. This time Beth recognised its structure as the human nervous system wrapped around the figure's arm as if it was clinging to the trunk of a tree. The tingling turned to an unpleasant but endurable pain. Beth stared at her tormentor, who remained hooded and bowed. They traced once more, with even more pressure. Beth was on the edge of laughing and screaming with the strange delight of the tickle and the searing sting along the nerves. Fleetingly, she thought of Tam. She clenched her jaw and continued to stare. The tip of the figure's tongue poked out from under the hood and a tiny snort of laughter followed. They stopped the tracing and Beth regained her composure, relieved by the cessation, no matter how temporary. The black sleeves dropped to cover the tattoo. The figure lifted their arms high above their head and let their sleeves fall once more to reveal their forearms. They pressed hard on one of the darker patches and a burst of intense pain shot through Beth's body. They must have rebooted her health implants and had sent a shock into one of her organs. She couldn't tell which one and she didn't care. The threat of what was possible had been communicated extremely successfully. Standing like statues, they both stared at her.

Occasionally, one of them licked their lips and grinned.

Their eyes twinkled.

Their faces were relaxed.

They were calm and completely comfortable with the situation.

More sweat gathered under Beth's armpits. Her back was wet and a trickle was working its way down between her buttocks. She thought of Naomi. Of Tam. Of R&R. Of anything to take her mind away from her predicament and what she might have to face, heroically, alone. Her tormentors held up an oversized globule, each cupping it with both hands. It became transparent and an image of Kai appeared holding an ancient porcelain doll. He kissed its forehead and she felt a damp patch appear on her own. She shut her eyes and did her best not to react.

"Beth," said a voice that boomed around the room.

Squinting, she looked around as best she could without moving her head. He was there, in person. She was about to clench her eyelids tight when he bit the doll's shoulder and a bruise appeared on hers. All of her implants were being reactivated by his actions around the doll's body. The hooded sentries had bowed their heads either in reverence to Kai or because they didn't want to watch. He held the doll's little finger and pretended to snap it. He didn't, but Beth felt her legs almost give way in reaction. She was shaking and he was busy studying the doll as if it was a curiosity that an alien had found and was attempting to comprehend. While he was stroking the doll's neck, she closed her eyes in painful anticipation. As he gripped the doll's neck, she felt her throat tighten. The sentries swapped places and at the point that they obscured Kai, he vanished. Gone. Then, he appeared in the globule for a few moments before disappearing from that too. She braced herself for whatever was next. The sentries carefully placed the blank globule in the corner of the room and returned to their posts, staring once more at Beth. Strange and silent. Quietly threatening. One of them took a different globule from the hood of their companion and they both studied it. Placing it back in the hood and letting the sleeves cover their arms once more, they turned and left.

Beth gasped, inhaling and exhaling loudly.

After some time, she breathed a sigh of relief, able at last to think without risking dropping her guard to the pain. Her thoughts wandered, desperately wishing she'd found the time to have the latest dissolvable implants fitted, but she'd been too busy and afraid. To be able to trigger them to melt into her body right there and then would have been heaven. She couldn't. It hadn't been important enough to risk leaving the refugee camp for and then she'd died, deactivated them and been with Naomi onboard their ship. Regret engulfed her. She stared at the corridor. They'd be back, that was for sure. Either to complete whatever ritual torture they had begun or because the data they had retrieved was not what they wanted. Or both. If they were scanning to find out more about her, they'd be disappointed. Once they got past the standard security and hacked into the private elements of the implants, they'd find a fake identity registered to a ghost. A non-person. Naomi.

Footsteps in the corridor brought her out of her malaise. Someone was coming.

She was struggling to breath, terrified of what was coming.

Alex appeared and hurried across to her cage. Beth gasped at the realisation that the arrogance of the Narcissists meant she'd been left alone. He put his finger to his mouth and opened the curtains. She couldn't hide her surprise, but she stepped out and he hurried away without saying a single thing. Not even a whisper.

She followed him up to the top deck and in to a dark corner. "Hey," she whispered. "Why?"

He frowned. "Not sure."

"Are you alright?"

He snorted. "Yeah. Great. Seen some shit."

She reached out to touch him, but he pulled back. "Hey," she said, "I'm still your mum."

He made a strange sound with his teeth, like a chicken's cluck.

She stared at him. "Why are you on this fucking ship?"

He whispered his answer. "They got some great stuff here. Food that can adapt itself to fit the nutritional needs of whoever's eating it. Kids enhanced in the womb with implants that grow as they grow. Nano-tech that runs around inside and fixes your body. They even have embryos created from eggs alone."

"Sounds wonderful. You believe they have all that?"

He squinted. "Yeah."

"But?"

He hesitated.

She let him take his time.

He sucked his bottom lip.

"But?" she prompted.

"There's something wrong. With the juvers."

"Can you tell me?"

He froze. No movement. No talking. Staring into the distance.

She touched his arm and he didn't pull away. "Where's Sadie?" she asked quietly.

"Gone."

"Where?"

"Into the pit."

"What?"

"It's a juver thing. She went into the depths of the ship for more Rejuve. Experiments. She won't come back. I need out. I have to get off this hell-hole."

"Oh, you poor thing. I—"

He pulled his arm away from her touch. "We need to go. The gees have helped get us this far, but they're scared of getting caught. Come on."

He stood up and waited briefly for her to join him before scuttling off into the shadows.

It was difficult to keep up with him. He darted this way and that, in and out of the tight gaps between the containers on deck. Every now and again he'd stop and stand absolutely still before carrying on at an even more determined pace. As they approached the back of the ship, a shadowy figure emerged from behind an opaque sheet draped between a biobrick storage cupboard and the handrail around the edge. Moonlight reflected off the covering, creating the illusion of a pool of water on the deck, rendering everything underneath it effectively invisible. Alex whispered something to the figure. They nodded and slunk off into the darkness. He beckoned her to join him. Underneath the sheet was an identical biobrick boat to the one she'd been given. It was tied to some steps with a slug mucus rope. That was their exit. A climb down to the sea, an auto-constructing boat and Naomi waiting for them.

She grinned at him. "Does she know?"

He frowned.

"Naomi. To pick us up."

He shook his head. "Tell her."

Beth grabbed her globule from her pocket, squeezed and triggered the urgent rescue message. "She'll come," she said and exhaled.

Two insect-drones appeared. One was hovering so close to Beth's face that she could feel the breeze from its wings on her eyelashes. The other was practically inside Alex's ear. She froze. Alex studied the drones carefully. He gestured to Beth to stay still, a suggestion she didn't really need. Slowly, he reached down and took hold of two small transparent cloths, one in each hand. Gradually, he raised them until they were level with his head. He glanced at her and gave an almost imperceptible wink. Immediately she felt the heat of the cloth brush against her cheek as he swiftly smothered both insect-drones.

"Quick, before more arrive to find out what's happening," he said, and without waiting for a reply, he untied the biobrick would-be boat and stepped onto their escape ladder.

She glanced over the side of the ship, took a deep breath and followed him. The bottom of the ladder ended two metres above the sealine and without pausing Alex dropped the boat into the ocean and as soon as it had constructed itself, he jumped. Beth immediately did the same and when she landed he bit through the rope and they drifted away from the ship.

"You cut the rope with your teeth?"

"Human saliva weakens it." He laughed. "A little-known fact."

They were tossed this way and that. Rising and falling with the waves and clinging on to the boat as it was thrown around by the ocean. She was desperate to talk to him. She ached to ask him why, about so many things. Instead, they clung on for their lives and she made wish after wish that Naomi had received the message and would be with them before it was too late. She heard the drones circling around attempting to find them, but the opaque sheet that had deceived any curious drones onboard the freeship was draped over the boat, shielding them from detection. Despite their protective tech, she was beginning to lose hope. Alex was constantly spluttering, having inhaled significant amounts of saltwater and her hands were cold to the point she was finding it hard to maintain her grip. They were so close to being rescued, and yet with each watery wave a matching wave of despair washed over her. She made wishes. She said prayers to no particular god. She cursed the ocean. She swore voraciously, screaming her hatred at mother nature, and at the point of almost utter exhaustion, Naomi sailed their ship into view.

Beth collapsed, crying and sobbing, and laughing.

As soon as their ship was close enough, Alex leapt up to grab hold of the harness hanging from a drone and held out his arms to help Beth. She waved his arms aside and grabbed hold for herself. The drone hoisted them up and flew them across. The tears kept streaming and it took Beth all of her concentration not to slump into a heap in the harness.

Home.

Naomi was waiting for them and when the drone set them down she raised her eyebrows at the sight of Alex and then ran over to them. Grabbing Beth's head between her strong warm hands, Naomi kissed her with such a ferocity it made breathing difficult. It was a kiss that was a little too forceful, but a kiss that was full of hunger. It lingered on Beth's lips long after it had stopped. It was the best welcome home she could have hoped for.

"East Albion," shouted Naomi above the crashing of the waves. "Here we come."

40

ALEX CAME running from the front of the ship, where he'd been relishing his freedom by shouting obscenities into the wind.

"Come to shout at us, no doubt," said Naomi, rather unhelpfully from Beth's point of view.

"Hey, he's allowed," she replied, feeling weird to be defending her son to Naomi of all people.

Breathless, he stumbled into the cockpit. "Fuck. Fuck. Fuck," he blurted, his breathing calming down with each expletive. "Fuck."

"What?" demanded Naomi.

"Shit...should've... guessed," he spluttered through each gasp.

"What?" said Naomi and Beth together, each with a raised voice and an edge of impatience.

Having calmed down, he stared at them. "Owls. Snowy owls."

Naomi made a small coughing sound. "Unlikely," she said, with an undercurrent of a chuckle.

Alex bit his top lip, blinked, and then spoke slowly. "We are being followed by snowy owls. Bioengineered snowy owls. Snowy owls that can rip out your eyes and tear off your arm without even hesitating to say hello."

Without thinking, Beth stroked the back of his head. "Slow down," she whispered, assuming the Rejuve had already begun to wear off and that he was hallucinating.

He sniffed loudly, a habit from early childhood that he'd never grown out of. "On Freeship One," he said, "they have owls, snowy owls, that are part bird part bot. They are used to hunt undesirables, usually those who have left without permission, those who Kai thinks might sell his prototype technologies."

"Where?" asked Beth, taking a telescope globule from the shelf to her left.

Guiding her eyeline, Alex pointed her towards what looked like a tree floating on the sea, until she could see it up close. Its surface reflected the sunshine and appeared to be fizzing with tiny bubbles where it touched the water.

"Special nanodust," explained Alex. "Forming and reforming as required. Perfect for the owls to settle on."

Putting the globule back on the shelf, Beth turned to Naomi. "There's definitely owls and tech out there. Kai, for sure."

"So what? Guess we should have expected to be tracked."

"Naomi!" Beth was frustrated by her dismissal of Alex's warning.

"There's no time," said Alex, banging the wall with the side of his fist. "Bad things follow. Very bad things."

Beth grabbed his fist in hers. "Tell me."

"Flying fucking reptiles."

Naomi called across. "Pteranodon?"

"How do I know? Big sharp teeth, massive wings, tiny feet, hooked claws."

Letting go of his fist, Beth hesitated before she asked. "Did he resurrect them?"

"Probably. No idea. Like the owls, biotech mix. Nasty fuckers."

An owl perched itself on top of Beth's ancient deckchair, the one she used to relax and watch the ocean passing by below and the stars drifting by above. The owl's sinister yellow eyes were firmly fixed on the cockpit, on Beth, rotating its head in a lazy figure of eight. The large bulbous lump on the back of its head was where its bioengineered brain was kept, according to Alex. She shuddered and at the same time a deafening noise filled the air, the sound of a giant witch's broom sweeping the tops of the trees. It was as if Alex had summoned beasts from the depths simply by mentioning them.

"Alex, what do we do?" shouted Beth.

"I don't know. Maybe—"

"No need," shouted Naomi, hitting a red button with the R&R logo emblazoned on it. Beth hadn't noticed it before; it must be new. "Distress call to the alliance nearby," clarified Naomi.

"Bit bloody cross your fingers and hope," said Alex, snorting his derision.

"Oh ye of little—"

No sooner did she begin her sentence than at least twenty ships appeared of varying shape and size. Many of the smaller ones being dropped from the sky by large vintage style military helicopters.

Beth recognised the logos on some of them. "Ours?" she asked Naomi.

"Yes."

"Lucky," said Alex.

Naomi grinned at him. "Young man, that's not luck. They've been shadowing us, in case."

"Neat, but really? Against Kai? Don't underestimate—"

"I don't," snapped Naomi. "You can be sure of that."

The sky had turned dark from the sheer volume of flying reptiles, outstretched and obstructing the sun, made all the more frightening by the brushing sound of their mucus wings beating, to slow them down and to allow them to swoop. The deck of the ship was littered with snowy white owls using their bioengineered brains to twist their nasty heads and control the attack.

"Now would be good," screamed an uncharacteristically agitated Naomi into her globule.

"What would?" Beth shouted back, but Naomi was too engrossed to hear.

A sharp, hook shaped beak hit the window right in front of them and gouged a deep scratch, which repaired itself without any problem.

"You're gonna have to do better than that," screamed a manic Alex, thumbing his nose at the stunned reptile.

Beth hadn't seen him do that since he was about six years old. She wanted to hug him and tell him it was all going to be alright, but she just didn't have it in her. And, he was unlikely to listen.

Another beak chiselled a groove in exactly the same spot and this time the self-repair took longer and left a faint mark.

"As soon as you can," said a sweating Naomi into her globule, which she held so close to her mouth that she could have swallowed it without moving.

The voice of someone distracted by more important things replied, "Almost there. Contrann is finalising code now."

"Contrann?" asked Beth, but Naomi only smiled in reply.

Crack! The window had finally given way to the onslaught of flying reptile beaks. Beth grabbed the dust she'd kept with her from her freeship days and smeared it across the crack, hoping it would work out that a repair was needed.

An occasional owl could be seen between the flapping translucent wings, soaring gracefully from one perch to another, only to swivel its manipulating head to control a different set of attackers.

Naomi's agitation was adding to the stress of the assault.

A smear of blood materialised where the crack had been. Apparently, the dust had done its job. A shattered skull and a broken wing remained glued to the window until one of its fellow attackers grabbed the broken reptile it in its jaw, lifted it high and tossed it overboard. With its broken associate out of the way it flew up in a long arc, readying itself to succeed where its fallen comrade had failed. While it paused high in the sky, the other reptiles moved to the side, leaving a clear flight path directly to the compromised window. Beth gripped the console and noticed that Alex was also holding on tight. She tried to force a soothing smile for him, but it formed into a grimace of fear rather than a mother's reassurance. The hovering reptile drew its wings back into a dive position and fell out of the sky like a dart. It felt like an age was passing as it dropped towards them. She couldn't take her eyes off it or release her grip on the console. It pierced the sky, an arrow heading straight for its target. Alex gasped, but she couldn't tear her stare from the accelerating bioengineered reptile plummeting straight for their ship. Narrowly missing the assembled flock that had parted to give it precisely the amount of space it needed, it hurtled through them. She closed her eyes.

"Yes, you fucker," shouted Naomi.

Opening them as fast as she'd closed them, Beth could see the crumpled reptile on the deck in front of the cockpit. It had missed and crashed. "What happened?" she called across to Naomi.

"The coders cracked it. Contrann did its job. Look." Naomi pointed up at the sky and all the reptiles were in freefall. The owls perched around the ship were also behaving strangely, spinning their heads in erratic movements before they flopped sideways as if their necks had been broken. "Didn't expect that, you fucker, did you?" screamed Naomi, to what Beth guessed was an imaginary Kai.

"Are we safe?" asked Alex.

"Yeah, little man. You're safe," replied Naomi.

"We're safe," confirmed Beth, not knowing if that was true.

Shaking, Alex edged closer to her, inside her personal space but not quite touching. A wave of motherly warmth and anxiety swept over her. "It's over," she repeated, as much for herself as him.

Naomi already had her hand on the door. "Help me clean this shit up and let's go home," she said to Alex in a conciliatory tone.

He glanced at Beth and then at Naomi. Beth gave a tiny nod and a whispered, "Yes."

"Sure," said Alex, pulling Beth's arm as he took a step towards the door. "Why not?"

All three of them stood close to one another on the deck, each with a cleaning bot under their command. Lost in thought, they watched as the bots did their work from the single instruction to tidy the deck and dispose of all rubbish. Before long, all traces of the reptiles and their snowy overlords were gone.

"Is that it?" asked Beth once they were back inside the cockpit and heading for home.

"For now," replied Naomi.

Alex snorted. "Really? Don't think so."

Beckoning Beth over, Naomi rolled out a sheet of SlendTek. "This is our route back, and those ships…" She pointed at the flotilla surrounding them, "will provide a protective barrier."

"Forever?"

"Alex," snapped Beth, "Please, just listen."

He huffed, but kept quiet.

"Naomi, you were saying?"

"The ships are protecting us, patrolling the skies with their drones and alerting any sympathetic land-based friends we pass to keep an eye out for Kai."

"Hey, he'll be back though."

"Absolutely. And we want him to."

"What?"

"Stay in his face with the physical stuff while New Peterloo works in the background, shifting the protocol and undermining him from inside."

Alex chuckled. "Neat," he said and smiled for the first time since he'd left the freeship.

"Thank you," replied Naomi, taking a bow in his direction. "Eventually, the algorithms will prioritise the positive from New Peterloo and an upwards spiral will begin as other, real life, cities follow its example.

"Home," whispered Beth, feeling overwhelmed by the escape, the attack and the inevitable fight to come with Kai.

41

GERRY HAD met Beth, Naomi and Alex at New Tilbury Docks and they'd travelled overland to Cambridge and then by water to Boston. Silence was the watchword of their journey. Travelling unnoticed was crucial, and there was little to say and much to consider.

Beth sat close to Alex, aware of his presence and grateful for it, hoping that the emotional gap between them could be bridged, planning out in her head how best to breach their divide without breaking the delicate bond he'd created by rescuing her. He stared into the distance. Whether he was lost in the depths of his own thoughts or suffering the pain of diminishing Rejuve, she couldn't be sure. Whatever the source, she listened to his rapid irregular breathing with delight and with concern. Naomi and Gerry passed the occasional pleasantry between each other, and every now and again Beth would exchange knowing glances with Naomi. Theirs was an understanding that had built up over time. A relationship that had been given the space to grow into a natural and beautiful friendship, without the need to update each other with their latest news, of any kind. Small or significant. Terrible or trivial. They sensed each other's need for company and knew how to gift one another solitude. Beth cherished their deep companionship and suspected that any hope of something similar with Tam was lost forever.

Morgan was waiting for them in his Faraday caged basement, surrounded by sheets of SlendTek. Row upon row of jars filled with gel and with wires protruding from them, reminded her of Tam's computer. On closer inspection, she could see a mini-globule nestling at the bottom of each jar. Alex hesitated in the doorway, only to be nudged forward by Gerry, promising him help to counteract the Rejuve withdrawal.

Naomi shot across to a jar that was pulsating between a warm red and a neon orange. "You did it?"

Morgan gave Beth a sideways glance. "With help from Tam."

Her face softened and all she could offer back was a quiet thank you.

Alex, on the other hand, regained his teenage arrogance and snorted. Swearing under his breath, he questioned the capability of his father, suggesting that his stupid inventions were as antiquated as his decrepit body. He clenched his teeth and turned his head towards Beth with narrowed eyes. He screwed up his face as if he'd swallowed the most vile and sourest of foods. "Fuck the lot of you," he said through his still clenched teeth. "No fucking clue. At all. No fucking idea of what you're dealing with. Resist and fucking Regain. More like, pissed fucking shit stains."

Beth reached out to him, but he shuffled away with his head down and his left leg dragging.

"He's broken," said Gerry. "He'll mend. He's young."

"I hope so. I really hope so. That stuff with the birds really freaked him out."

Morgan broke the solemn silence that followed. "Look at this."

Gerry grinned. "It's epic."

"Sure is."

Gerry whispered in Beth's ear. "I'll check on Alex. You stay here with these two and enjoy the fruits of your handiwork."

Naomi was bent over the SlendTek sheet connected to the jar while Morgan was busy tracing patterns with his finger and explaining something to her.

"Hey," said Beth. "Can I join you?"

Morgan chuckled. "You need to ask?"

"What's in the jar?"

"That, my dear Beth, is Luscious and the New Peterloo. Here, let me show you."

He pulled her across to the SlendTek at the same time as shoving Naomi to the side, and proceeded to explain. "Luscious is housed on the mini-globule. It is a far superior version of the New Peterloo you had onboard your ship."

Beth was distracted by how long ago that all seemed, but Morgan continued.

"Protected inside the basement, we can experiment privately with the New Peterloo data, by adding new people, new areas, and altering the overall behaviour of the town. We can try out new things before setting them free. At a much more complex scale than you could on your ship. That way we can avoid the majority of unintended ripples across the world's Ls from our fake town."

She was only half listening, but he looked extremely serious as he went to great lengths to emphasise the fact that it wasn't perfect, but the risks were worth it. That it could never be perfect because once it was live it interacted with all the other Ls and there was no way to accurately predict their cumulative effect, or in the future what might interact weirdly and counter to their intentions.

"Look," he said.

On the sheet in front of them was a map of the town. Morgan slid his globule back and forth along the streets and the parks and hovered over certain houses to take a look inside. The three-dimensional human and animal characters inside his globule were magical. At home and interacting with one another. The clarity was so sharp that it was easy to believe that you were indeed looking into a tiny house and its occupants going about their daily lives.

Naomi made a strange noise, a hybrid sound of a cough and a laugh. "Genius."

"We're updating this," he said, and moved his globule to the high street. Inside, the shops were bustling with activity. From swapping clothes or furniture through to a baker with a massive communal oven and a café full of people cooking for themselves and others. "The trick is that the wealth of every resident is within spitting distance of each other and the businesses are thriving. Risk is shared. Reward and failure belong to everyone." He stepped back and let them examine the data stream scrolling down the side of the sheet. It was impressive. Not only was New Peterloo thriving, the happiness rating was sky high.

Beth play-punched him. "Hey, mister genius. This is extraordinary."

Naomi licked her lips. "And in the real world? What's changing?"

He shrugged. "Nothing. Yet."

She grimaced. "Beth risked her—"

He interrupted. "It's too soon. Give it a while. It'll happen." He put his hands on Beth's shoulders. "You may well have saved the world," he said and drew her close. "Thank you," he whispered.

"Hey. My pleasure. It was nothing. All in a day's work," she whispered back.

They were brave words, but she shuddered slightly at the memory. She was about to correct herself when a cube attached to the corner of the ceiling began to whistle and pulsate from a dense black to a blinding white light.

Morgan shouted. "Get back from the SlendTek."

Naomi stepped back abruptly and shouted back. "What?"

"Five-minute warning."

"From? Who? What?"

"Our spies on the freeships. It's about to suck in all the data and shove out all the updates."

Beth caught her breath. "Hey. Spies? On the free—"

He waved his hand as if to swat her away. "Yes. Spies. No. You weren't the only one."

"But—"

"Later."

He scurried about and as he tapped the jars with his globule they changed colour.

"R and R," he shouted to Naomi and threw her a second globule. "Each one a hacker helping out, making sure we're not detected. Tap them all."

Beth watched, frozen in her exclusion. Morgan and Naomi were frantically working their way along each row. Tap. Tap. Tap. The jars glowed and the SlendTek exploded with data criss-crossing its surface.

He shouted. "All done?"

"All done," Naomi shouted back.

"This is it. The new data is set free to do its thing."

He placed his hands on the top two corners of the sheet and directed Naomi to do the same on the bottom two. He indicated for her to wait and after a few seconds, once the data had stopped streaming into the sheet and the gel filled jars had all returned to their original colour, he told her to sweep her hands diagonally into the centre. He did the same. As soon as their hands touched, a loud klaxon boomed from the cube and it turned bright red.

"Cage off. Allow data trawl," he said to a console with a globule resting in it.

All three of them stood holding their breath. Beth rocked from one leg to the other. Naomi frowned at her, and Morgan's gaze skittered all over the sheet.

"I'm always worried it'll realise we're not real," he said under his breath.

The klaxon ceased and the cube returned to its transparency.

"Cage on," he said and relaxed.

He lifted Naomi's hands from the sheet and gave them a squeeze.

"All good?" said Gerry as he entered the room, closely followed by a more cheerful looking Alex.

"Yup," replied Morgan.

"Good. Council has been called. Convening in fifteen minutes. Anything I should know?"

"Not really. That last data had some traces of small, loud and smelly restaurants finding compromises with their neighbours, which over ninety percent of customers are happy with."

"It's a start," said Gerry.

Naomi folded her arms and spoke in a matter-of-fact voice. "Sounds like we still need big distractions to give it time to get a grip."

"We do," confirmed Morgan. "The bigger, the better."

Shoving his hands into his pockets, Gerry clenched his jaw and then spoke with little emotion. "Let's take the fight to Kai. Let's destroy him."

Beth recoiled, surprised by the scale of his hatred. Not knowing how to respond, she focused on the immediate. "I need to get Alex sorted, then I'm with you," she said, looking across at Naomi who raised her eyebrows and her shoulders in response.

Beth beckoned to Alex who dragged his feet across the floor as he walked to her.

"What?" he said quietly.

"Hey. It's time to go home. Time to see your dad." She grinned. "And, your baby sister."

It was a weak smile that formed on his face, but it was an enormous pleasure to see. If he was softening towards her, she could wait for as long as it took.

42

"I KNOW exactly where we need to go," said Alex.

Beth studied her grown-up son paying for their transport. Time had not been kind to him. Slightly stooped with strange bouts of temper tantrums, he was beginning to show the signs of someone whose Rejuve was running low, although his physical struggle was nothing compared to the battle between accepting his dwindling health and the desire to simply top up his Rejuve and get back on his game. And she was itching to join Naomi, to destroy Kai as Gerry had so eloquently put it. She needed Alex to be well, though. Resist and Regain needed Alex to be well. This trip was vital to all of their futures.

"Done," he said.

She was finding it increasingly difficult to accept that he had his fifty years of wealth, less the cost of his extravagant clothes, and she had nothing. He had his whole life to live and she was dead as far as the Leveller was concerned. Her transfer of wealth to Tam had failed and had been sucked back into the pot and redistributed via some fancy algorithm to the new tranche of adults. The irony of Alex benefiting from her death was a constant irritant between her and Tam. A source of humorous observation on his part and bitterness on hers.

"Let's go," muttered Alex as the airboat arrived. "Sooner rather than later," he added with the desperate sneer of a juver.

She helped him climb onboard without drawing attention to his attitude. The airboat automatically raised its slug mucus cover to keep out the rain and whisked them away. Flooded roads and stormy skies raced past as they sat in an uncomfortable silence.

Beth broke the tension. "Hey. I'm so glad you know where to go. I'm sure we'll get this fixed. I've heard it's best to come off slowly. You know, to let your body adjust over time. You don't want to take too much of a hit all at once. Imagine that. I reckon that would hurt."

"I'm glad you know so much about it," he said, closing his eyes and hanging his head so his chin touched his chest.

"Hey. I know the side effects are horrendous. I know most sensible people think it's to be avoided. Not worth the agony of addiction."

The cloying silence returned.

She resisted asking him how long the journey was going to be, instead taking in as much of the changes to the countryside as she could. It was a lot slower than taking a train and she was surprised that he'd chosen this method of transport. That was, until they reached the border and the airboat took a roundabout route to cross at a checkpoint with only one guard, a BP from a small sub-contracted security company working for the Leveller, one that took bribes as a separate income stream. Alex held the disc in front of the BP. It pressed a similar one against it and then slid to the side.

"Into England undetected," said Alex with a smug grin. "You're not the only one who can drop out of sight."

"Hey. I'm impressed. Who taught you that? Your dad? Morgan?"

He tapped his nose three times and then reverted to resting his chin on his chest.

Two and a half hours later they arrived at Free Trade Wharf, the place where Alex and Sadie had set up their stall to sell their blood before boarding the freeship. The display on the airboat confirmed their arrival. Woof. Drew. Patch.

"Here?" said Beth.

"Penthouse office. Illicit market. Taboo trading. All suits and sofas."

Beth chuckled. "Suits and sofas?"

He smiled. "One of Sadie's sayings. You'll see. A veneer of retro respectability. Aping late twentieth century fashion. If it's posh, it's legal. That sort of crap. Mind you, better than traipsing around in underground sodden tunnels to find some halfdead dealer. Eh?"

Beth thought she caught a glimpse of Kai watching her from the back of a vintage adjacket. She touched her nose. She must be wrong. She was about to join Alex at the front door to their destination when two hooded figures with long, black sleeves appeared in the window opposite. Her torturers.

Silently, they parted revealing the obnoxious Kai, his gaze fixed on Beth, transfixing as ever. "Beth. Molly. Coddler. Failed caster. Mother of a junkie. Taboo mother. Dead mother." He blew her a kiss. "Come with me," he said, in a sultry voice.

She shuddered, unable to reply or to move.

"We'd be great," he continued. "Become the mother of my children."

From behind her, Alex was shouting, "You fucker."

She signalled for her fragile son to stay where he was and turned her attention back to Kai. "Off a duck's back," she said, forcing a smile she didn't feel. "You think your sperm can actually swim?" she added, a phrase she'd heard Esme use.

"Oh, Beth," he said, blowing her another kiss. "Until we meet again." And with that, the torturers moved in front of him and they all vanished.

"Mum," called Alex. "Quick, in here where it's safe."

As soon as she was with her son, she wanted to reassure him. "Ignore Kai," she said, and then added without thinking, "It's only going to get worse once we really start on him."

"Thanks," he said with a smile. "I know. I'm ready."

Once inside Alex led the way, focused on the job in hand. The lift scanned his face, his eyes and his handprint and then dutifully opened. She followed him into the gold-trimmed space, feeling the softness of the deep pile carpet under her feet and sniffing the fresh air being pumped in from outside. It was subtly soporific, despite the threat of what Kai might do next hanging over her.

Alex noticed her yawn. "Calm punters are good for business," he said and laughed.

The respect she had for her son increased another notch. She'd known that he must have done some stuff that she'd rather not know about. Otherwise, he would have been one of the shuffling juvers on the freeship, not the herder of those sad souls. She figured that she was about to find out new aspects to him and she hoped they wouldn't be too much for her to take, that she wouldn't have to witness behaviour and hear things which she'd never be able to reconcile with her beliefs. To be caught between the love for her son and the ethics that framed her whole life would be too torturous to bear.

The door opened with a quiet understated swish, and the young receptionist beamed a warm, welcoming smile. "Come to see Kaela," said Alex.

The receptionist blushed and grinned at the same time. "Hello, Alex. You're looking great," he said. "Kaela's expecting you."

Alex smiled back without acknowledging the compliment, but there was a distinguishable lightening of his step. A door to the left swung open and Alex walked through. Beth followed. Feeling like an imposter, she stayed one step behind him.

Inside, it was as luxurious as Alex had said it would be, with three extremely well-dressed people and four large sofas. A woman indicated for them to sit on the sofa furthest from the door. She and her two fellow suits took up position on the other three sofas, blocking any quick getaway.

"Alex." she said in a soft, mesmerising voice.

"Kaela."

She turned her gaze on to Beth. "Dead mum?"

Alex nodded. "Long story."

Kaela and the other suits all laughed. "I bet it is. It's the Molly Coddle comeback. Pisses Kai off, no doubt."

Beth kept quiet. Alex knew what he was doing, and even if he didn't this was one of those situations when one brain carefully picking its way through a tangle of tripwires was much better than two.

"What can we do for you?"

"Rejuve's wearing off."

"And?"

"Need some micro doses. Withdraw with dignity."

She twiddled the buttons on the cuff of her jacket while rolling her bottom lip in and out of her mouth. She turned to her right and raised her eyebrow and then to her left and did the same. Her companions both scrunched up their faces. She pursed her lips.

"Alex, my friend. The trouble is—"

"Cut the dramatics."

All three of the illicit marketeers were shocked at his interruption. Beth couldn't work out whether it had been the right thing to do or not, but after a few seconds of silence, which seemed to stretch out for a lot longer, Kaela reacted with a series of small nods.

"Dramatics, eh? Accusations from a juver? Now there's a thing."

"I have taboo tokens."

He showed her the disc.

She shrugged.

"You know I'm reliable. I won't tell anyone."

"It's not that, really. Well, it is that, but it's more. You'll need one of your implants to be reconfigured to moderate the release of the Rejuve, which in itself isn't difficult. But, to do that undetected is, how shall I put it, challenging. Altering an implant in a young healthy…" She coughed. "…man such as yourself is going to show up as an edge case in the data. For sure." She paused with her eyes half closed. "Alex. I don't see how. Unless…"

"What?"

"Molly here. Dead Molly. Disconnected implants dead Molly." Kaela looked at her companions who both nodded. "We could extract one from Molly and insert it into you. That might work. Costly. In disc. Or in favours."

Alex gave Beth a look, which was so full of pleading that it made her want to hold him, there and then. "Hey. Why not?" she said.

One of the suits stood up and without looking at either Beth or Alex, told them to follow. They left the room through a narrow exit built into the wall. It had been invisible right up to the point the suit was less than a metre away and then slid open. It led into corridors of soft squidgy floors. Beth recognised some of the art that hung on the walls, and she was sure it was famous and lost. There was one piece that she remembered being in the news when she was young. A biological shape-shifting, pattern-changing piece of gel that sat in an ancient fish bowl of scratched and scuffed glass. It had been worth a fortune then, so who knew how much it would be worth if it was to come to light years later? There were artefacts hanging casually on those walls that the Leveller wouldn't know existed, outside of the economy and a rich source of unregulated, untraceable and untouched wealth. Neither the suit nor Alex seemed at all interested in this display of prohibited power.

"Molly. Strip," said the suit when they arrived in a white-tiled, sterile room.

"Hey. I could roll up my sleeve. No need for any more than that, surely?"

"Strip," the suit repeated. "Not sure where to remove it from until we investigate. You, too, Alex. Don't know where to put it yet, either."

Embarrassment didn't even begin to describe the feeling of taking off all of her clothes in front of her son and, judging from the look on his face, he felt the same about his own nakedness. She brought memories forward of the *Strip for Dignity* protest when Alex was a child. She looked at him now. A young man developing a body similar to his father's. He lay down on one of the two beds and blinked rapidly. She did the same and let the mattress shape itself around her curves, to hold her in place.

With a pair of tweezers, the suit placed a miniscule bot on Alex's forehead and the tiny dot crept down and into his nostril. "Anaesthetic," said the suit, touching her forehead with the tweezers.

The room faded and the next thing she knew was the sound of Alex snoring. She sat up and looked around. They were alone. There was a tiny red welt on the skin between her bellybutton and her pubic hairline. It itched, but apart from that there was no sign of any operation. Alex had a similar mark on his shaved chest just below his nipple. He looked so peaceful lying there and Beth couldn't help thinking about him and Sadie, wondering what she could have done differently and wishing she'd been able to steer the course of his young life in a different direction. Stupid and pointless to ponder, she knew. Her thoughts drifted to Naomi and their adventures and then to Kai.

Alex stirred. "I feel sick," he whispered.

"Come here," she whispered back.

They held each other tightly. To an outside observer they were seemingly oblivious to their respective nakedness. Beth ached for him to be the young boy. She ached to turn back the clock to that fateful birthday party when he and Sadie had become close. She ached to rerun the past.

"We have to go," said Alex, groggily.

"Hey, Son. We do."

They hurriedly pulled on their clothes and Beth followed Alex out of the room and back along the corridors. "You know where you're going?"

"Yup. Spent a fair amount of time here. One way or another. Best to keep your head down, your eyes off the walls and focus on leaving."

"Hey. You're the boss," she said and immediately regretted her patronising tone.

"Yeah," he said under his breath.

"Why do we need to rush? What will they do?"

"Nothing, most likely, but it's all a bit temperamental here at times. Best not risk it."

They weaved their way along the corridors and took a service lift at the back of the building down to the basement. From there they scurried through the underground storage tanks and ignored the occasional zeroed squatter until they surfaced fifty metres to the side of the building's front door.

"Home?" he said.

"R and R?"

"Resist and Regain," he agreed.

43

"Hey, you're sure he's in there?" asked Beth, feeling safe with Naomi and Alex either side, despite the fact that they were about to seriously annoy Kai. Or, at least that's what she was hoping for.

"He was spotted going in," replied Naomi, without taking her eyes off the front doors of the OS headquarters in Pancras Square.

Alex took a step forward so that he was facing them both. "Hard to believe. That fucker never comes here."

"Well, we'll see, won't we?" said Naomi, more dismissively than Beth would have liked.

She gently moved her brave son back into line and reminded him why they were there.

Huffing and swallowing rather too loudly, Alex thrust his hands in his pockets. "I'm ready," he said under his breath.

Putting her hand very obviously on the zip of her trousers, Naomi laughed. "Let's do it," she said.

It was a risk, that's for sure, but one they'd agreed to take. Tucked inside each of their trousers was a mucus bladder full of what looked like piss. The bladders had tubing with a valve that could be opened and closed by applying pressure from pressing their thighs together. The contents looked like a liquid when streaming through the air, but was in fact a special formation of the nanodust.

"We just have to draw him out and confront him, piss him off enough to keep his attention on us." Beth laughed at her own pun, but the other two either didn't get it or were too focused on preparing themselves for action. She looked to her left and then her right. "Go," she said, and unzipped her trousers, took out what to the casual observer would have appeared to be a penis and sprayed the pavement in front of her. The yellow dust etched the word, MARY, in the grey slab. Naomi to her left had written, GIVE, and Alex to her right had added, BACK. Before they even had time to tuck themselves back in, the BP from in front of OS HQ had begun to move towards them.

"Next," said Beth, and wrote KIDS.

As soon as the new stream of dust hit the pavement, the previous dust words fizzed and vanished. Naomi followed Beth with KAI and Alex added KLEPTO. The BP were doing their best to remove the graffiti, but the dust simply reformed after being brushed away.

"You!" shouted a female security guard from the steps of the building.

Naomi flinched.

"You know her?" whispered Beth.

"We've encountered each other," replied Naomi, equally quietly and through tightly held lips.

The woman marched across the forecourt, aiming straight for Naomi, checking her wrist as she went. She stomped on each of the three words – Kai, Kids, Klepto – before shoving her face into Naomi's. They stared at each other, and Beth wouldn't have been surprised to see each of them bare their teeth. As it was, they both breathed steadily and rarely blinked.

The security woman spat on the pavement. "Don't exist, huh?"

"You tell me," said Naomi with a wry smile.

In a drawl heavily laden with sarcasm, the woman spoke to Beth. "Molly Coddle," she said and clicked her fingers. The BP slid to her side. "And, Kai's favourite junkie," she said, touching Alex's cheek. She made a circle in the air with her finger and the BP surrounded the three of them. "In place," she said into her wrist.

Kai appeared from the side of the building, flanked once again by his hooded henchmen.

"Kiddie Klepto," shouted Naomi. "What happened to Mary?"

"And Esme," added Beth, going off script.

Naomi gave her a sideways glance, but didn't say anything. With a flick of his finger, Alex gave the signal that the R&R drone was in place, ready to stream.

"Hey, it's Beth here. Molly Coddle to some of you. I'm here at OS HQ and about to chat to Kai. Should be interesting, so stay on stream."

A six-metre-tall projection of Beth appeared on the side of the building. The security guard was frantically looking around for the drone that was responsible, unable to see it. This was Beth's cue to push Kai over the edge.

"Kai," she shouted. "Come here."

The woman took one step closer to Beth and then stopped. "He says he wants you for himself," she said into Beth's ear. "He says that your reaction to his nerve doll was exquisite and he's sure you'd like to go again with him."

"Bring it on," said Beth, pointing at the huge rolling footage of the boy with the gut plug streaming across the side of the building where her image had been. "Kai," she shouted, her voice being broadcast loud and clear around the square. "Remember him?" The drone then dropped its gaze to the pavement where the dust was still formed into the three words of Kai, Kids, Klepto.

"Turn that off and we'll talk," said Kai as he approached, his voice being broadcast through the BP.

"Call *them* off and we'll talk," shouted Naomi, pointing at the woman and the BP.

He moved his head rapidly to one side and the human and bot security surrounding them moved back to the building. In response, Naomi instructed the drone to stop its streaming onto the OS building.

"What do you want?" he asked.

Naomi tilted her head to one side. "Brave to be here alone," she said with a hint of threat in her voice.

"Oh, believe me, there's plenty of firepower trained on you three. The slightest move from you and you'll be history. For real this time."

Beth saw Alex stiffen and she wished she could reassure him. His Rejuve withdrawal had slowed down since the trick with the implant, but he wasn't fully out of the addiction yet.

Naomi continued. "We will destroy you," she said in such a steady matter-of-fact way that it sent shudders down Beth's spine.

Kai seemed unaffected. "Really," he said. "How quaint. The rouse and rest are on the move."

"Resist and Regain," corrected Alex.

Ignoring him, Kai carried on with his sneering sarcasm. "Like flies on the majestic lion."

"Removing toxins."

He grinned. "Good point. Spreading disease, too."

"Maintaining the ecosystem."

"Simply annoying and inconsequential."

Naomi chuckled. "We are everywhere. All over the shit that is you. We are anything but anonymous. We are coming for you."

"Why, sweet lady, why?"

"To remove the cancer that sucks the health from our earth, our planet, our species."

"Go on then."

"We have so much footage to release, stuff that will undermine you and your kind to the point that you'll run for your lives."

"Good luck with that."

"The fakery behind the regrow shops, for instance."

He raised his eyebrows. "Faked faking, eh?"

"Who knows, but if it casts doubt…"

"Do your best," he said. Pointing at their groins, he added with a smirk, "And put those away, before you hurt yourselves." Flanked by the BP with the security woman bringing up the rear he headed back inside the building.

Naomi turned to Beth. "Think we got his attention?"

"I'd say so. Alex?"

Her son nodded and took a deep swallow.

"Let's pack up and go see what Gerry made of all this," said Naomi, unashamedly pushing her pretend penis back in her trousers.

44

During their walk to the station, Alex kept looking over his shoulder, but they weren't followed. At least not physically. Silent and scared about being watched by unseen surveillance, they waited until the train was full enough to leave and then jumped on at the last moment. Once aboard, they each fell into their own thoughts. Beth's led her down the path of what Kai might do in response to their threat. She didn't relish taking him on, but if it meant that New Peterloo could quietly get on with infecting the Ls then it was worth the risk she'd taken on the freeship and the coming confrontation with Kai.

They arrived in Boston and headed straight for their rendezvous with Gerry in an area dedicated to the refugees. "Here we are," he said as they arrived and he steered them in through the gates of the open-air café.

Beth sidled up to Gerry. "Do you realise what we have done?" she asked.

"Not a clue," muttered Alex next to her.

Naomi scowled at both of them. "We threatened him with rumours about the regrow shops."

"And that we'd come for him, wherever he was," added Beth.

"Did he seem worried?" asked Gerry. "What about—"

Alex interrupted. "No, he fucking well didn't."

"Who can tell?" said Naomi. "He left as soon as we mentioned the regrow shops. That might be his weak spot."

With an overemphasised sigh, Alex stared at the ceiling. "It's the fucking kids, you idiots. Get them to leave him and his whole father messiah thing comes crashing to the ground, ego crushed."

Beth cleared her throat. "We're going after him, no questions asked. Gerry, we came to talk…"

A rather shoddy looking drone showed them to their table. It had obviously been repaired over and over again, either because of love or poverty, or maybe both. A few of the clientele lifted their faces away from their drinks and their chatter to acknowledge Gerry as he weaved his way between the tables, doing well to keep up with the battered waiter.

He ordered a drink that Beth didn't recognise and placed his globule on the table's indentation. The waiter arrived with glasses of a black, viscous liquid that smelled of tar and tasted of mint. Delicious. Tucked under the waiter's arm was a head-sized globule, which it placed on the table in front of the empty chair. Gerry thanked it, paid in the new refugee currency, gees, and cupped his hand over the top of his own normal-sized globule. It gave off an orange glow and then faded. At the same time the globule on the table began to glow and Morgan's head appeared. As Morgan moved his gaze from left to right his whole head moved, showing his ears and the back of his head as he did.

Gerry grinned. "Nice bit of tech, eh?"

Alex's whole body shook with excitement. Beth copied Naomi and nodded in agreement.

Gerry clicked his fingers to bring Morgan's attention back to the table. "I want to chat things through."

"Go for it," said Morgan, whose voice was as crystal clear and rich as it would have been if he'd been sitting there in person.

"First," interrupted Beth. "You need to convince Alex that this quiet, in the background approach to the Ls is going to work." She looked to her son. "Didn't you say you thought that the Ls would realise New Peterloo was fake?"

"Fuckers'll spot it a mile off."

Gerry leant forward. "That's where you're wrong. Morgan, care to expand?"

"Towns and cities are dynamic. They constantly change. They're not watching each and every one of them in real life to make sure they exist. That's the whole point of the dynamic ANNs. They react to the data they're fed, without question."

"It's their strength, and absolutely their weakness," added Gerry, sitting back with his arms folded.

"But, if it's an outlier, they'll focus on it to find out why," replied Alex, also sitting back and folding his arms.

Morgan's head spun in the globule. "It won't though. When your mum inserted it, the data looked like an average town. But we preloaded change to happen slowly and we've been revising the data ever since. We have been extremely careful not to get ahead of ourselves."

Gerry unfolded his arms and leant forward again. "It's one or two steps ahead of where others are following. Softly, softly, 'n' all that."

"Alex?" asked Beth.

"Maybe," he replied in a slightly sulky tone.

"Hey, you still up for fighting Kai?" she asked, resting her hand on his wrist.

He pulled away. "Try stopping me. Nasty, shitty narcissist."

Gerry gave Beth a knowing smile, but she ignored him. He cleared his throat. "Morgan. Any idea how it's playing out across the Loop?"

"Nothing to suggest it's being rejected as an anomaly."

"Good. Now tell Alex how we've made sure the refugees are well represented."

"New Peterloo data shows the long-term benefit of inclusivity. But we're taking our time, to make it look genuine. Like I said, we can't just push it through with no build-up or backstory. Incremental change is one of the tests the Loop uses to validate authenticity."

"Alex, we're well on the way. This place proves it. Naomi, can you pass the word around R and R? I want them to talk about it as much as they can and in as many publicly monitored places as possible. Make it seem like a groundswell is underway."

Alex leant forward. "I still don't see how that works."

"Meaning?"

"One town out of thousands. Millions. How is that significant? Why would anyone even notice this town, let alone copy it?"

"If we're right and this stuff from New Peterloo makes a solid difference, the algorithms will amplify it and the upward spiral of a feedback loop begins. Little by little they all change and we've re-engineered Kai's toxic vision, right under his nose."

"While he's too busy trying to stop us smacking him in the real one," added Alex, smugly and with an aggressive edge to his voice.

Gerry laughed. "One more thing, Alex. We introduced the ninety percent rule. Any planning decisions and any punishment tariff for taboo breaking must be agreed by at least ninety percent of citizens before it can be enacted. Like it?"

Alex gave a half-hearted thumbs up.

Morgan turned to speak directly to Gerry, so all Beth could see was the back of his head. "Darling, don't forget. That'll take ages. For ninety percent of the population to agree. It's completely counter to the efficiency of the Locals."

"For fuck's sake," said Alex under his breath.

Gerry ignored him and answered Morgan. "No doubt, but it was the right thing to do. With the introduction of iterative decision making, we're already slowing things down, making decisions more considered. Can you add in another radical step to New Peterloo, altering the balance of ANN to human? In favour of the human. Is there a way of doing that?"

Morgan closed his eyes and they waited in silence.

Alex scraped his chair as he leant back. "Mum. Beth. Molly? We have to go after him, now. Even if this wackbrained idea works, we must crush Kai, in person. You know that."

Beth was formulating her response, noticing that Gerry and Naomi were looking uncomfortable, when Morgan broke the silence.

"Yeah. I reckon there is," he said and then opened his eyes. "We have large, multifaceted, fake companies that come close to the complexity required. We could alter their board structures to mirror what we want the council to look like."

"Good," said Gerry. "It's time to introduce our own R and R currency, too. One we can continuously adapt to encourage the society we want. It can underpin an equitable East Albion. Can you get it up and running?"

"Mum!"

"Quiet, Alex. Listen."

Morgan continued. "We have Graebit, and it's ready to go. I'll get on to it."

"Include that rule about being able to bank your IOUs."

Gerry lifted Morgan's head off the table and he vanished.

Alex chuckled, not hiding his relief that the meeting was over. "Smart tech," he said, with what seemed to be genuine respect.

Gerry returned the chuckle. "Let's go home," he said.

All of them opened their mouths at the same time, but Naomi was the first to speak. "No. We take the fight to Kai. We're gonna take that bastard down, once and for all."

Beth and Alex grinned.

"If you're sure," said Gerry. "It's appreciated."

"We'll grind his stupid face in the pile of shit he calls his movement, his destiny, his legacy," said Alex, almost spitting out each word of his threat, as a promise.

At the door, Gerry thanked the waiter, returned the large globule and they dashed across to an airboat, which was waiting for them in front of the café.

45

"Hey. Shall we try over there?" said Beth, pointing at a small group of kids gathered around an old-fashioned virtual reality setup.

"What's this then, *kids*?" Alex asked them as soon as he was within earshot, barely able to keep the scorn he felt for them hidden.

A couple of them glanced at him, made a strange high-pitched sound and turned their attention back to the screen, which displayed what was happening inside the VR. Beth joined him and deliberately showed interest. They were in a war with lasers and flamethrowers. Whenever a laser found its mark on one of the kids a jolt was delivered to the implant closest to the hit and they doubled over, usually in a fit of giggles. Above and below them were powerful devices that sent targeted bursts of intense heat towards whoever had been scorched by a flamethrower. They laughed less when that happened.

She took a sideways look at Alex. The muscles on his face were taut, narrowing his lips into a horizontal slit. How she wished she'd managed to persuade the younger him not to board the freeship or had been able to help him escape sooner. She hadn't, and there was no point dwelling on what might have been. It was what they did from now on that mattered and they each had a bag of cash discs in the hope that the kids from the recently docked freeship would take advantage of their offer.

Alex pushed for attention, showing a handful of the discs to the kid nearest him. "If you leave the ship and come with us you can have one of these," he whispered.

The girl stared at them.

Beth stared back, remembering that Alex had told her that the freeship indoctrinated these kids with the belief that the masses were stupid for not realising that in the long run the exponential development of tech was humanity's only hope. Kids like these were encouraged to play with this old stuff, fed the idea that its flaws showed how superior they were to their predecessors and that they were the future.

The girl who'd been standing and staring, spat a purple ball of phlegm at Alex's feet, tugged the sleeve of the girl next to her and together they told Alex to fuck off back to his perv girlfriend, pointing at Beth.

He wasn't easily intimidated. "I was one of you. I escaped. You can too. I can help."

Four BP had moved across and were making it clear that they were observing. They were soon joined by the man who controlled the swarm of drones with the cones in his cheek. Alex looked sideways at Beth. She nodded. Together, they drifted off into the crowds.

Another group of kids were sitting in a circle chewing and spitting while playing spin the bottle, except it was spin the demobilised BP. It looked fun and Beth couldn't help chuckling as she overheard one of the kids challenge another with the dare to kiss their friend's thigh. She gagged when she saw that the girl making the dare was pointing to a boy with a nasty unhealed wound where the lower leg should have been. She moved on quickly, dragging Alex with her. The BP and the cone man with his swarm followed close behind. Beth and Alex wandered through the crowds, offering the discs to any child who would listen. None of them accepted. The eyes of a few lit up, quickly extinguished when they spotted the BP and the drones. Others hastily moved away, with a deep fear in their eyes. Then there were the young Rejuve junkies who Alex had more luck with, being able to use their slang language and convince them that he had been one of them. It wasn't enough though. A couple of them agreed to come, but as soon as they reached a certain distance from the freeship their bodies doubled up in pain and they lay on the floor clenching their stomachs and groaning. Alex was scornful, suggesting they should ride the pain and press on, but afterwards was less derogatory.

"They said that's what would happen if we left while we were docked," he said. "I didn't believe them. But..."

The cone man came closer and his swarm of tiny bots flew around Beth and Alex, creating a sound so terrible she couldn't think straight.

Alex pulled her away from the kids and the swarm retreated. "Let's keep moving," he said, still holding on to her arm.

They wandered with a diminished enthusiasm.

Glancing over her shoulder she could see the drones following, playfully swarming into beautifully choreographed patterns across the sky. Spectacular. Scary. The cone man wasn't going to leave them alone.

As if to prove the point a young boy ambled over to them. "A present from Kai," he said, handing Beth a toy octopus. "He says thanks, he really enjoyed himself."

The boy scarpered leaving Beth holding it. She was shaking. Was it possible that he'd seen her make the original purchase? Anything else, anything onboard her ship, didn't bear considering. She swallowed a few times and steadied herself. It was designed to intimidate and she was determined to resist, but she needed a break to recover.

"Hey, Son. Should we quit? Come back tomorrow?"

Alex shook his head. "No. It'll be the same tomorrow, the next day and every day until it sets sail again and we've missed our chance. We must do it today."

"You're right. Determined. Like your father. It's an attractive quality and one I'm glad you inherited—"

He interrupted her. "Over there."

It was the boy with the plug in his stomach, leaning casually against a wall chomping on a pink tube of something. His shirt was undone and he appeared to be selling glimpses of his insides to curious passers-by. She followed Alex across to the boy, both of them with a renewed bounce in their step. If they could persuade him then others would follow.

Alex spoke as soon as they were within earshot. "I know you. You're famous."

The boy looked puzzled.

"My mum here. She made you famous across all of England. And beyond."

When they were close enough, Beth spoke softly. "Do you remember me from the orphanage? I snuck into the tunnel and found you. We met. Well, we waved. You were young. How old are you now?"

The boy sneered and buttoned up his shirt. "Ten and a half," he said.

"Hey. That's about right. It was—"

"Who are you?"

"—a long time ago."

He chewed his pink food with his mouth wide open. Staring at her. "Famous, eh?"

Alex cleared his throat. "Molly Coddle. Know her?"

The boy frowned. "Might."

"Good. She was trying to help then, and she's trying to help now."

He showed the boy the discs in his hand. "These can buy you passage into East Albion. As a legitimate refugee."

"I don't need those."

"You do. They won't give you a chain-wallet until you're thirteen, so you'll need a decent amount of gees to live on."

"I want to go to England."

"Not happening."

"I hear the Leveller has a thing going where your money is worth a lot more in certain places. Live where it asks and you're rich."

"Hey," said Beth. "You're right. It's keen to get areas populated in a way that everyone living there has roughly the same level of wealth. Makes us all happier. It uses currency rules to encourage people to move. It won't let you in though. England is not open to refugees in the way that East Albion is. That's a much better place."

Alex handed him a disc. "Here, you can keep it, no obligation. We'll be around for the rest of the day if you change your mind."

They hadn't gone far when the boy caught up with them. He had changed his mind.

"What about the crippling stomach cramps I've seen other kids subjected to when they try to leave? Are you scared of those?" asked Beth.

"Those particular implants, the ones that are triggered to cause that reaction were removed from me when they inserted this plug."

"That's good," said Beth.

"I'm immune to the freeship's constraints. I've wandered outside their invisible perimeter many times," he said and puffed out his chest.

Alex gave him a second disc in case he could persuade another friend to come and they arranged to meet outside the Retro Bar in an hour.

Beth couldn't believe they'd succeeded and was pensive all the way to the bar.

Sitting in the Retro Bar, she and Alex waited in silence, not wanting to break the atmosphere in case their luck evaporated.

After two beers and a shared portion of shipworm, the boy arrived. Alone and smiling.

"Congratulations," said Alex as he poured some of his beer into a cup for the boy. "I knew you'd make the right decision."

The boy clasped his hands together and took a seat next to Alex who put his arm around him.

"Alex."

"Yoanis."

"Will you travel to East Albion with me? To Boston."

Yoanis uncoupled his hands and put an arm around Alex. He didn't speak, but he moved a little closer and his face softened.

Beth put a reassuring hand on both of them. "Hey. Go. Quickly. You really must get moving before that cone man comes after us. He will, I'm sure. If you're not here there's not much he can do is there?"

"Thanks," said the boy, and they stood to leave.

"Alex. Once you're there and Yoanis feels up to it, you must send footage of him enjoying his new life. I'll stay here and use it to persuade others. This is the beginning of something big. I can feel it."

Alex touched her hand and left the bar arm in arm with his newfound friend.

She finished her drink and snack and followed them out on to the street, having thanked the doorman for the return of her globule. A pavement advert sprung into life as she approached. It was Kai. She hesitated, wondering if she should turn around and take sanctuary back in the bar.

He spoke. "Is Robyn taboo? Is she yours? Did you kidnap her? Why not let my orphanage take care of her?"

With that, the image vanished.

Her legs wobbled and she sat down heavily, scraping the back of her legs on the rough fragment of broken wall. It was difficult to form clear thoughts. She couldn't see a way of telling Tam about this without causing him panic and a lifetime of fear. She had to keep the threat to Robyn to herself. Something inside solidified and her deep determination crystalised. She wasn't going to be bullied and with Naomi's help she wouldn't be deterred.

46

NAOMI PRESSED her globule and the dust from the bag she was carrying formed into a cage in which Beth could put the pile of discs and the recently acquired implant-blocking pills. Beth had no idea how necessary the cage was, but recently she'd been located by the freeship drones on more than one occasion.

She gave Naomi's hand a squeeze. "Hey, me and you back on the mission," she said and turned her attention back to the cage, ensuring she had all she needed before beginning the day's work.

"Shame about Alex."

"Hey, he needs to recuperate. And, he's doing a great job coordinating your alliance. Which, by the way, is kicking."

"Resist. Regain," said Naomi and grinned.

Nearby, a group of kids were competing about who had the strongest limbs by slamming their fists into a bench to see how long it took the dust to reform. The more severe the punch, the more disrupted the dust.

Beth looked sideways at her friend. "C'mon. Let's start the day with that playful bunch."

They strolled over, attempting to appear as casual as possible while still maintaining their gravitas.

Naomi sniffed the air. "Oh yes. The smell of nanodust hard at work," she said loud enough for the kids to hear.

One of the girls replied. "Oh yeah. The smell of do-gooders. Hard at work."

"Fuck you," said Naomi.

Beth took over. "Hey. Let's not get off on the wrong foot. Your game looks great. Can we watch?"

"If you must." The girl turned her attention back to the game and her fellow dust punchers.

As soon as the bench had reformed, a boy who had been limbering up stepped forward, pulled his arm back as far as it would go, pressed the side of his neck and then gave the bench the almightiest of punches. It burst apart into mist, as if it had exploded into its component atoms. Different segments of the bench reformed in the air before coalescing into one in the exact same place it had come from. "Fifteen seconds," he shouted. "Beat that." He rubbed his bleeding knuckles and they immediately healed. Beth gasped and the boy turned to face her. "Prosthetic fists, adapted blood and super skin. We are the future."

"No doubt," said Naomi.

Beth took a couple of steps closer to the girl who had spoken first and who seemed to be a little detached from the jeering throng of youngsters. "I can help," she said, and the girl laughed. Beth put her globule on the floor between them and, after an introduction from Yoanis telling them that no matter how deep in you were you could get out, she played the footage of a dozen young girls of the same age who had left the freeship for a new life in East Albion. It was a mix of explanation and enthusiasm. Each one talked about their life before, how they hadn't realised they were being brainwashed into staying, hadn't known there was an alternative. The footage of their experience of East Albion was the most compelling, showing normal everyday life in a way which conveyed how special it was. Each of them ended with warm encouraging words that appealed for others to follow.

The girl was captivated by the testimonies, ignoring calls from her fellow competitors to take her turn. "Can I speak with one of them?"

"Hey. No problem. Is there anyone in particular you'd like to chat to?"

"The one at the end. She seemed nice. She has the same pre-release enhancements as me."

Beth made a call and handed the globule to the girl. Wisely, the girl took it out of Beth's earshot and for a few minutes all Beth could see was the girl's expressions, which ranged between pleased, shocked, angry, and perplexed. This was a perfectly standard reaction, and as far as Beth was concerned nothing to worry about. The conversation came to a close and the girl returned the globule, confirming that she would like to leave the freeship and begin again in East Albion.

"Nice," said Naomi.

Beth drew the girl closer so she could give her instructions in private. The three of them would wander through the docks for a few minutes and make it look as if the girl was showing Beth and Naomi around. When they were at the edge of where she was allowed to stray, they would pause to see if any freeship sentries were paying them attention. Then they'd make their move.

"Got it?" Beth asked them both.

"Yes," whispered the girl.

"Sure," said Naomi.

The girl told her companions that she was going to earn some currency by taking Beth and Naomi on a guided tour and waved them goodbye. She was great at pretending. She kept one pace ahead and stopped every now and again to give a tourist commentary. She showed them the latest food on sale from the freeship labs, the youthful Rejuve advocates, and led them to a stall selling a cutting edge chimera virus designed to combat cell deterioration. It was fascinating and terrifying in equal measure.

All the time they were engrossed in the girl's tour, Beth kept an eye out for any unwanted attention they might be getting. None as far as she could tell. To anyone else they were as they appeared – interested tourists marvelling at the incredible technology on offer from the freeship.

They reached the edge of the enclosed area. "Swallow this before you step over the boundary," said Beth.

"Why?"

Beth drew a shallow breath. "It reacts with your implants and suppresses their ability to inflict pain. Believe me, you'll need it."

"Thanks," said the girl as she accepted the pill. Her neck muscles tightened.

"Hey. You'll be fine. Plenty of others have done exactly what you're doing."

The girl blinked a few times and was about to pop the pill in her mouth when the freeship klaxon boomed across the docks.

"Wait," said Beth.

Masses of drones were taking off from the deck, carrying sheets of slug mucus. They positioned themselves around the docks so that everyone could see at least one sheet. The klaxon ceased its piercing noise and Kai appeared on the screens.

Naomi took hold of Beth's hand.

"Good afternoon, citizens of England. It is a pleasure to be here again. A popular stopping off point for Freeship One from the beginning." He waited for the applause to subside. "Humanity moves on. That is what it is good at. Adapting. Taking advantage of the hand it is dealt. Influencing the rules of the game it is playing. Wherever possible, changing the rules to give it the best chance of winning. We are a species that succeeds. Above all else. We are dominant."

The roar of the crowd was deafening. He had told them what they wanted to hear, and sadly he had told a lot of truths.

"Today we are celebrating one of those great successes. The freedom poll, conceived and designed by the Ls. What a success, consistently improving our understanding of the protocol."

He beckoned the crowd to join in with his chant of, "More and better," and then clapped his hands above his head, giving the thumbs up to different parts of the crowd in-between each burst of clapping. It was a splendid display of how to coax a crowd into adoration. Not that he needed to work too hard at that. By their very nature, those who came to greet a freeship were generally its advocates or wanting to set sail on it.

He snapped his fingers twice in quick succession and the crowd quietened. "Finally." He waited a few seconds. "Finally, I am proud to announce that we can now accept an NFT that is your DNA. Invest in your children's uniqueness. Invest in your future and theirs. Spot the geniuses among you and get in on their success early. To all you zeroed, this is your opportunity to repopulate your dormant chain-wallets."

He waved goodbye and swaggered along the deck. As he was about to enter the door that would take him inside and out of view, he hesitated and snapped his fingers again. "Molly Coddle," he shouted. "I know the kids are leaving. Feel free. Nobody is forced to stay. Believe me, there are plenty of children around the world that are itching for a chance to join us. Your lovely little coalition is insignificant. What is it? Rouse and rest? I wish you all the best."

With that, he disappeared inside and the drones returned to the ship.

"That told you," said Naomi.

"Indeed," said Beth. She put her arm around the girl, gave her a disc and whispered in her ear to take the pill.

The three of them walked over the invisible border of the enclosed area and although the girl complained of some mild discomfort she continued to walk as if nothing had happened.

A few paces beyond the border they stopped, as if they had an unspoken plan.

Naomi and Beth looked at each other and grinned. The grins became giggles and then full-blown laughs.

"New Peterloo," said Naomi.

"New Peterloo," repeated Beth.

The girl looked puzzled and Beth side-hugged her.

"Hey," said Beth through her giggles. "He's bought into the fake town, hook line and sinker. The infected Loop is gonna eat away at the selfish shit and his toxic vision until it crumbles."

Naomi flexed her biceps and grinned. "He's fucked."

47

A LOUD buzzing filled the air. The cone man was back, accompanied by bots and drones of all shapes and sizes. Rubbing his face to control his hoards, he approached at a slow, methodical pace.

"Run?" suggested Beth.

"What?" Naomi scoffed, making Beth's simmering anxiety rise up her throat.

"Have you seen him?" she asked. "It's us that's fucked."

"Stay exactly where you are," commanded Naomi, repeating it to the girl and handing her a mini-globule. "Capture it all," she said. "You're casting as R and R."

"Her?" asked the girl, pointing at Beth.

"She's dead. Can't cast."

The three of them stood facing the cone man and his entourage. Aware of the rigidity of her body, Beth glanced at her companions to see if they were as falsely bold as she was. It was hard to tell. Naomi had her determined face on, but Beth thought she could detect a slight tightness in her jaw. The girl was completely relaxed, busy chatting into the globule as she moved it around to capture the scene. Beth leaned in close to listen.

"They're coming to get us," the girl was repeating, with a hint of exhilaration in her voice. "Abandon ship," she quipped every now and again. She was a natural.

Four of the BP stepped aside from their unit and surrounded Beth, Naomi and the girl with a slug mucus sheet, in the same way that Alex had contained the Rejuvers on the freeship. The only gap was guarded by BP and the hovering drones.

"Keep leaving the ships if you don't want this to happen to you," said the girl with less excitement than before.

The BP pulled the sheets apart and the cone man entered.

"You must abandon ship. Check out the Yoanis casts if you don't believe me."

Beth gasped in admiration. This girl was good.

Cone man stroked his face so lightly it was difficult to see if he was actually touching it. Staring at them, he grinned, he smiled, he raised his eyebrows, but said nothing.

"Strong and silent," said the girl. "Or dumb and dumbstruck."

Running his finger across his left cheekbone, he tilted his head to the side, blew her a kiss and shrugged. Half a dozen tiny drones shot forward and landed on her globule. Shaking her hand, she tried to dislodge them but failed. Interestingly, they didn't close it down and she continued to cast, albeit with sound only.

Their jailor spoke. "You'll be here some time, so here's my gift."

A large drone flew into the corner of their cage and dropped a pile of dust, which formed into a bucket shaped container. Another dropped a swarm of the bioengineered flies that Beth had encountered on the boat, the ones that were half machine half fly, and a third drew a mucus sheet around the makeshift toilet. He then turned and left, while the BP remained, keeping guard, and the drones retreated to hover above the edge of the sheet.

After a long time of forced standing, Beth's legs began to ache and she noticed the girl shifting her weight from one leg to the other. Beth wished this wonderful young woman would tell them her name, but no matter how many times Beth asked, she politely refused.

"I know," said Beth. "Why don't we use the toilet to rest? We could take it in turns."

"Each of us should take the casting globule in and continue to encourage the kids to escape," whispered Naomi.

"Me first," said the girl and she disappeared into the cubicle.

Beth could overhear her talking, and although she couldn't make out exactly what she was saying, her tone was insistent. Before long, the girl returned and handed the globule to Beth.

Sitting on the toilet, half-expecting the BP to come and stop her, she began her cast. "Resist and Regain here. I'm one of the captured. Imprisoned for daring to question Kai. To all of you out there who are similarly trapped, you can leave. Everyone else is. Floods of you are deserting him. It doesn't have to be this way. East Albion will welcome you. We will welcome you. Resist and Regain. And, don't forget, if you don't believe me, then check out the casts of Yoanis and his network of the liberated: We Are Not Anonymous."

With that she relieved herself, walked through the machine-flies with her eyes closed and handed the globule to Naomi.

The three of them repeated this cycle of casting, over and over. Occasionally a drone would hover above the cubicle, but the girl's tip of taking your trousers down and lifting up your top to expose your stomach worked beautifully; no sooner had you seemingly prepared yourself for taking advantage of the toilet, than the drones disappeared. Genius.

They didn't stop their casting cycle until the cone man returned some hours later.

"Right," he said, as the mucus sheet closed behind him. "I have some news from Kai."

"Fuck off," said Naomi. "Not interested."

"You will be."

Beth put her hand on Naomi's bicep and squeezed, hoping to remind her that no matter how physically strong she was, she could rely on Beth, her friend. Naomi responded with a light kiss on Beth's cheek. The girl watched with a look of curiosity.

"Listen," he said, with an edge of impatience. "Listen carefully."

"Didn't you hear? Fuck off."

"Naomi," admonished Beth, conscious that to move things on they had to get out of this situation as soon as they could. "Hear what he has to say."

"Good girl," he said.

"Hey, like she said, fuck off," snapped Beth.

He laughed. "Cute. Unhelpful, but cute."

Beth noticed that the girl was holding the globule inside her fist, presumably, hopefully, still casting. Beth stared the cone man straight in the eyes and through narrowed lips she replied. "Get on with it."

"Good," he said. "Now, Kai wants you to know that he's going to send a courier drone with the latest top-of-the-range Rejuve to your ailing son. Alex? A gesture of generosity that quite frankly he doesn't deserve."

The bastard. Beth took a step forward, but stopped herself reacting just in time. "He's clean, he doesn't need it."

"We'll see. Need and desire can be two different things."

Beth swallowed. The girl better be casting, otherwise this defiance of theirs was pointless, and dangerous.

Cone man turned his attention to Naomi. "Gerry," he said. "On the council." He paused. "But not if his brain is damaged, eh?"

Out of the corner of her eye, Beth could see her friend flex her muscles.

"Those implants can go wrong, you know? Terrible accident. Such a shame." He paused again, waiting for a reaction he didn't get. "Yoanis. Now, what would happen if the tech we left inside him was activated? Not pleasant, I'm sure. Oh, and what if we offered Tam a fortune for his eggbox thing?" He leered at Beth. "Or, maybe his tattoo suit."

"Like we said many times already, fuck off," shouted Naomi.

"These are only observations of what *could* happen," explained the cone man. "Kai just wants you to know the risks your family and your friends face if you lose his protection."

Without giving them time to respond, the cone man ordered the BP to dismantle the cage, to pack the dust away and to leave.

Standing in the same spot that they'd been standing in since they'd been captured, the three of them watched the man and his hoards return to the freeship.

"Fucker," said Naomi under her breath.

"Who gives a shit?" added Beth quietly.

"You should," said the girl. "He's scary."

Naomi pulled the girl towards her and the three of them hugged. "What next?" asked the girl.

"You cast all of that?" asked Naomi.

"Yeah."

"Good. Give it here." As soon as Naomi had the globule, she twisted it around and contacted Morgan. "Numbers?" she asked, staring at the surface of the globule in anticipation. "Massive increase. Exponential," she told Beth, and smiled for the first time in quite a while. "It's happening across the globe. We're in business."

With a heightened sense of elation, Beth kissed her friend on the lips and shoulder hugged the girl. "Fucker's finished," she shouted to the back of the cone man.

"Morgan," said Naomi. "Make sure Tam and Gerry see those threats. If they're prepared—"

Beth interrupted. "Morgan. Tell them I love them both. Tell Alex, too. Tell them we have to carry on."

With that, Naomi handed Beth the globule and they started walking away from the freeship.

48

"Not so fast, ladies."

Beth looked over her shoulder and there was Kai, flanked once again by the two hooded torturers. Only this time, they were accompanied by six BP and the security guard from the OS headquarters.

"Quite a gang you've got there," said Naomi, rolling her globule around in her hand.

The aroma of barbecued worm from the freeship reached Beth's nostrils as it wafted across on the light wind. What surprised her was how captivating the setting sun behind Kia and the evocative scent of outdoor cooking were. Admittedly, it was tragically beautiful, the way the cloaked and hooded figures with their long draping sleeves absorbed the daylight, emphasising the orange halo around Kai. He was a beautiful man, blessed with a strong physique and features so handsome they were on the verge of caricature. The BP had extra-long limbs and necks, as if they were from a super-race of bots. Beth couldn't help giggling at the thought that a graphic novelist would have been proud of this tableau.

"Coddle, snigger all you want," said Kai, holding his hand out to one of the hooded figures. Taking the doll with which he'd tortured Beth, he continued. "Such insignificance as yours yelps when cornered. Come here my sweet puppy."

Naomi put her arm across Beth's chest. "She'll do no such thing."

"In that case… You," he said, pointing at one of the BP. "Neutralise any casting tech she might have on her."

The BP glided forward, swept Beth with its extended arm and she felt her globule close down.

"How dare you," shouted Naomi. "On what authority—"

With a tiny snort, Kai replied. "Mine," he said. "Talking of mine, how's Alex? Robyn? Tasty Tam?" He swallowed and smiled. "Are you mine, Molly?"

Beth clenched her fists.

"Calm," whispered Naomi, and then louder, "She's mine," and landed a full-blown open-mouthed kiss on Beth's lips.

Without thinking, Beth opened her mouth to receive the kiss and with the tip of her tongue Naomi placed a tiny object inside her mouth.

"Now her," he said pointing at Naomi.

Using her own tongue to determine what this gift might be, Beth moved it around surreptitiously. What genius. Naomi had passed her an eyebrow camera similar to the one she'd used on the freeship between her teeth. She could record whatever was about to take place and so long as she could still operate its tiny buttons with her tongue she could cast as R&R to the world.

"The lovers that lost. Everything," said Kai through a low chuckle. "Does love conquer all, my failing fiascos?" He raised an eyebrow. "Apology for the tautology," he added and looking for affirmation from his companions he laughed loudly. No encouragement came.

"You're leaking," shouted Naomi, and both of the shadowy figures looked at the hems of their sleeves. "Not you," she shouted again. "Him."

"Ooh no, ooh no, I'm leaking."

She took one step forward, which was matched by the BP. "They're leaving you. All over the world, the kids are deserting you."

He shrugged.

"Don't believe me? Ask them." She pointed at the BP. "Data don't lie," she said and grinned at Beth.

"No problem," added Beth, using their secret code for New Peterloo.

Naomi winked. "Indeed." Turning her attention back to Kai, she repeated her earlier observation. "You're leaking."

One of the BP shifted so that Kai could read its visor. It was delightful to see his face turn from smug superiority to cautious uncertainty.

He licked his lips and grinned inanely at Naomi. "What of it?"

"You can see. Global R and R is mobilised. We're enticing them away in the thousands, right across the world. You're finished."

Kia smacked his lips and clicked his fingers. The hooded figures stretched their arms out, revealing their flesh. Each of them had a doll with its head resting in their palm and its body balanced on their wrist and forearm.

"A doll for each of you," said Kai.

The security guard behind him cackled and rubbed her hands together.

It was time for Beth to activate the camera and begin the cast. Surreptitiously, she took the camera from her mouth and held it pinched between her fingernails. "You stop us in a lonely back street and threaten us? All because we have the audacity to challenge you and help a girl escape your clutches." She twisted to her left, to cast Naomi and the girl, and then back facing front for footage of Kai and his entourage. "How dare you?"

"Oh, I dare."

With a faked tremor to her voice, Beth continued. "The dolls. The same ones you tortured me with on your ship?"

"The very same."

"He'll use the doll to activate your implants and deliver pain to your body," she said to the girl, making sure she captured the horrified look on her face.

"Swallow this," said Naomi, passing the girl a pill. "Cognitive blockers, courtesy of Alex. Cancels the effects."

Kai lifted his doll in front of him and the hooded figures copied. He sucked his lower lip and narrowed his eyes. "Girl," he said, grinning at the girl. "You don't want to renege on your contract, do you?"

She shook her head and Naomi gently guided her so that she was standing in-between her protectors, Beth and Naomi.

"Good girl," he continued, ignoring Naomi's intervention. "It is legally binding, you know. Only pain and loneliness will be your companions if you leave me."

"So says the boy lost and alone in a man's body," shouted Naomi, making sure that Beth's camera heard the insult.

He stroked his doll and signalled the hooded figures to do the same. "A little tickle to begin," he said softly. "To get you in the mood."

Naomi laughed at him. "Are you going to travel the world threatening every single child who wants to leave you? All of the thousands that are currently leaking away."

"No, my sweet." He set his gaze on Beth. "Ask Alex what lengths a Rejuve junkie will go to for their top-up." Returning to Naomi, he added, "Thousands of *them*, too, all wanting to help me." He stroked his doll's neck and spoke directly to the girl. "Now, my love, let's persuade you to stay where you belong."

He pressed hard on the throat of his doll and the hooded figures did the same. Beth felt nothing and judging from the unchanged faces of Naomi and the girl, neither did they. His piercing stare settled on Beth.

"Activate her implants," he said over his shoulder to the security guard.

"I did," she replied. "No effect."

Naomi clapped her hands in joy. "You're not the only one with the tech, cute little manboy."

Furious, he shouted at his BP. "Grab them. Bring them to the ship."

"Not so fast," said Beth. "Before you kidnap us…" She paused for effect, and, revealing her camera, she asked him, "Do you have anything to say to our audience?"

"How the—"

Naomi slapped the back of one hand into the palm of the other. "The great macho Kai, outwitted by a female caster, a non-existent woman and a girl." Taking hold of Beth, she turned the camera towards her and continued with an amused lilt in her voice. "Would you really place your trust in him," she said and laughed.

"I'm your only hope," he said rather more quietly than usual.

"Tell that to the kids you experiment on in the orphanage, you lump of shit," said Beth with as much spite as she could muster.

He laughed a mock laugh. "I'm done with all that," he said.

"Unlikely," she replied, resisting the urge to press for more detail.

"Served its purpose. Done its job." He hesitated as if he was wondering whether or not to say the next sentence. Slowly, a big grin took over his face and his eyes narrowed. "Remember your visit, Molly? What else was there? Go on, drag your memories."

She tried, but could only remember the kids and the animals, and she wasn't about to pander to his sick view of evolution by describing either of those. "Tell me," she said.

He opened his mouth and paused, while his eyes twinkled with delight. "The Star System Research Lab? Mars Section? Remember that?"

She nodded, unsure of where this was going.

"Think about humanity, think about its evolution, its destiny. Trillions of lives yet to be lived. That's what matters."

"That's—"

"Keep your fucking orphanage, cleanse it with the blood of your bleeding heart. I'm done with it. Job done."

"How—"

"Oh dear, the lady is confused. Let me spell it out. The only way this fragile species will survive is to leave this poxy planet behind to die its unnatural death. That's what the orphanage, the freeship and all this effort was about. I sacrificed so much, for the long-term benefit of humanity. You should be on your knees praising me, not crawling around snapping at my feet."

Grabbing Beth's hand, and at the same time putting her arm in front of the girl, Naomi inhaled loudly and then spoke clearly, devoid of emotion and anger. "Your barren soul will be a perfect match for Mars. We wish you a speedy journey and an indefinite stay."

"Rouse and rest policy?" he asked, looking increasingly shaken.

"Resist and Regain and all our friends wish you every luck in the world, all the bad, evil, fucked up luck you deserve."

The security guard tapped Kai on the shoulder and he swung round swiftly. "What?" he snapped.

All six BP were lined up with data flickering across their visors. Kai became engrossed in reading it. Every now and again he uttered a deep groan and an expletive. The hooded figures were busy studying their globules, gradually increasing the speed at which they were spinning them around in their hands. All three dolls lay abandoned on the floor.

"What—"

Naomi stopped Beth from speaking. "Let it run," she whispered.

The girl was frozen to the spot in shock, her anxious expression betraying a fearful anticipation.

With slumped shoulders, Kai turned to face them. "Seems like you have the reach," he said, and turning to the security guard, he added, "Care to enlighten us all?"

Standing as tall and straight as ever, she took one look at him and then cleared her throat. "All the ships at sea have mutinied. Freeship One remains alone. The kids are leaving in droves."

"Fools. These outflux of the fucked will simply die, and that will be on you," said Kai, his posture renewed to the arrogance Beth was used to.

"But they won't," said Naomi. "You see, the Loop is pushing for refugees to be seen for what they are, fellow humans to be welcomed as equals. First, we abolished slavery, then women were seen as equal and now it's the turn of the displaced."

The visors of the BP were showing a crowd of angry people gathering and blocking the gangway to Freeship One. Kai was visibly distressed and pulled his hooded henchman close. They talked in whispers and Naomi signalled to Beth and the girl to keep quiet.

After much gesticulating from Kai and head shaking from the hooded figures, the security guard took a step back and instructed the BP to join her. Kai grabbed a hand of each of the figures and staring at Beth, declared, "Give us safe passage to Freeship One and we will leave."

It was Naomi that answered before Beth had a chance. "The Loop. We'll trade you safe passage, for the Loop."

Kai stood and stared, not moving a muscle, not giving anything away, remaining static, holding his henchmen, staring into the distance.

Eventually, he smiled. "I'll trade," he said. "Safe passage from here to the Star System Research Lab. I'll leave the Loop at the orphanage with OS and you'll give my ship safe passage to my island off the coast of Cameroon. Deal?"

It was Naomi's turn to make them wait. She shifted from one foot to the other, balancing her movements with an opposing alignment of her head. She sighed, she sniffed, she coughed and she made clicking noises with her tongue. Beth couldn't work out if she was trying to decide what to do or simply winding Kai up. Whichever it was, he was getting agitated, which was disturbingly pleasing to watch.

Finally, she spoke. "Dust and regrow. Give us the tech on those and you have a deal."

He laughed. "You—"

"No negotiation. Yes or no?"

He stared at Naomi for what seemed like forever, not blinking, expressionless.

She shrugged.

That didn't make a difference. He continued to stare. Then, slowly he leant into one of the hooded figures and listened, and then did the same with the other. Turning back to stare at Naomi, he spoke in a flat no-nonsense voice. "Deal," he said.

"Deal done," said Naomi into Beth's camera. "R and R, take note. Clear the crowds."

Naomi grabbed Beth's arm and pulled her forwards. "Lead on," she said and beckoned to the girl to join them.

Kai and his crew followed, the security guard bringing up the rear.

Not one of them spoke as they walked.

When they arrived at the crowd, it parted with a cacophony of cheers and jeers. Kai held his head up high, telling anyone who could hear that the future of humanity was his, that evolution was in the hands of the grown-ups. The girl, who had fallen into step alongside him, made mocking gestures each time he spoke. It didn't appear to bother him at all.

At the base of the gangway, he shouted to the sea of cameras, streaming history. "You deserve each other. Petty, pathetic and poor." He raised his fists in the air, in defiance. "Do not come crying to me when your planet burns and you want to leave."

With that, he strode up the gangway, which then withdrew into the ship, and with its loud echoey klaxons, Freeship One left the dock.

Beth slumped down on the floor and Naomi joined her, beckoning to the girl to come, too.

"Did we do it?" asked Beth through gasping breaths.

"Absolutely. You were brilliant," said Naomi. "You, too," she added, cuddling the girl. "Taken his ship and fucked off."

Beth was crying tears of relief and tears of pain for all the children that were to be rescued and rehabilitated. "A lot to do," she muttered. "Such a lot to do."

"Yes, but take a few moments to be happy. We won. He's history."

"It's hard to believe."

"Check out the stats. Even the Rejuve junkies are leaving him. He'll be lucky to have enough people to crew his ship."

"And his Mars mission?"

Naomi laughed and laughed, not even bothering to hide her contempt for such an idea. Beth rubbed her eyes, blubbed a bit more and then stood up straight. Smiling, she blew kisses to Naomi, the girl and what was left of the crowd. They hadn't expected to defeat him so dramatically, but the combination of a changed communal psyche promoted by New Peterloo and Kai's spectacular confession and fall from grace had to be celebrated with as much joy as possible.

With quiet confidence, she suggested they made their way to the Retro Bar where their nearest and dearest were already gathering.

"Party!" shouted Naomi, as she began walking towards the bar.

49

WHEN THEY arrived at the bar, everyone else was already there. Beth walked alongside the conveyor belt with Naomi and the girl from the freeship in front of her. A lot had changed since she'd first made this walk but it still looked the same.

Naomi had changed, softened and sharpened in equal measure, her truest friend walking hand in hand with a rescued child, talking reassuringly.

Robyn was sitting in the alcove staring at the wonderful selection of food and drink passing by, enthralled as ever by her surroundings. A curious four-year-old. She picked up a bottle of lime green beer only to be lovingly scolded by Tam, his long, grey hair falling in front of his eyes as he leant forward to prise the bottle from her hands and replace it on the belt. He had proved to be a much better father than she was a mother, and despite her physical, mental and emotional wanderings, he had always been the one for her. She wasn't sure if he knew and vowed to make sure that from now on he would never doubt it.

Alex and Yoanis were deep in conversation, lost in the complexities of whatever they were discussing. She was proud of them both. Alex was on his final withdrawal from Rejuve. He had persevered when lesser men would have quit, and for that she was grateful to Gerry. Morgan and Gerry were sitting next to each other showing a rare display of their physical love for one another and Floella was sitting between them waving wildly. It had been a surprise when Naomi had adopted Floella, a failed experiment with photosynthetic skin, but as Naomi had pointed out, if Beth could do motherhood, then so could she. Beth wasn't so sure about her own ability to be a mother, but she was pleased for her friend.

It was family in action. It was community at its best.

Beth edged her way in beside Tam and gave him a kiss on the cheek. He smiled and she kissed him on the lips.

"Really?" said Alex, and laughed immediately.

"Hey, Tam. Can we talk?" she said.

He shrugged. "Sure."

"Outside?"

He stood up, patted Robyn on the head, grabbed a dish of berry caviar and two cherry beers, and walked towards the door. She followed, collecting her globule on the way out.

"Why do you need that?" he asked, passing her one of the beers.

"I want to show you something."

She squeezed it into life and played snippets of the footage from the children she'd helped escape the clutches of Kai. He watched closely, absorbed in the stories they were telling.

"Hey. I want you to know I love you. I know I don't always show it. Can't always show it. But honestly, I do. Intensely."

He kissed her. "And?"

She hesitated. "And, I have to help these kids. I have to sort out that orphanage. You can see that. Can't you? You know. Don't you? Do you remember how we met?"

He nodded.

"You started this. Crawling into that stinking seawall to rescue a kid you didn't know. Because it was the right thing to do. The only thing to do."

"What about your own kids? Don't they deserve you?"

He had a point. She had made choices over the years, some of which had not put her own kids at the top of the list. They had Tam. The kids she was helping had nobody. If she could have done both she would. It hadn't been possible. Robyn was turning out well, and she'd been there for Alex when he had most needed her. He was coming good.

"They're lucky to have you, their dad. A truly magnificent dad."

He smiled.

"Not to mention, a superb lover," she added.

"Thank you," he said with a small half-laugh.

They were in the middle of a passionate embrace when her globule buzzed, indicating an announcement from the Leveller.

Tam let go of her. "Shit, what now?"

"I don't know," she said, and pulled her globule from her pocket.

There was a simple yet far-reaching message. The Leveller had decided on a moment of atonement. A moment, which would take place in exactly forty-eight hours. It acknowledged its own shortcomings in terms of treating the data it held on its citizens with insufficient respect. In this forthcoming moment it would cleanse all the data to ensure that each one of them was correctly represented. The offer was also made to correct any mistakes or corruptions.

Tam nudged her. "You can come back from the dead."

"Maybe. Hopefully."

He laughed nervously, adding, what to her, seemed an irrelevant afterthought. "Reactivating your implants might even do something about your insomnia."

She didn't reply, but was pleased that he still cared for her.

The Leveller went on to state that all taboos on the current ledger would be nullified. They wouldn't be erased, that wasn't possible, but all chain-wallets would be reset. There would be no lasting stain on any citizen. A chance to start again. Except for serious crimes, where the individual would remain punished, paying for their own prison costs.

Tam hugged her and then set off for the bar.

She caught up with him. "What's wrong?"

"Nothing. Don't you see? I have to get home. I need to get things in motion to resurrect you and to make sure all of Alex's taboos are in his wallet and don't appear after the atonement. Yours, too."

"And come clean about Robyn?"

He nodded.

She watched him walk into the bar. At that moment she couldn't think of any way he could be improved. He was perfect. For her. For their children. For the world.

Gerry joined her. "Quite a scene, eh?"

"Hey, it's wonderful. Did you see what the Leveller did?"

"Yes. The upward spiral continues."

"When will you scrap them?"

"Them?"

"The Loop, the Ls."

"Why?"

"Wasn't that the point?" she said, astonished that he didn't understand.

"Let OS continue to host them while secretly we have the control," he replied. "We can accelerate our way out of trouble, change the world for the better."

"Risky. Unethical. Sneaky."

"Not so sure. We should keep it going, keep New Peterloo doing its stuff."

"But it's false. It's lying."

"For the greater good," he said and turned to go back into the bar.

"Wait."

Returning, he shrugged his shoulders. "It's still a fragile world, with plenty of kids and zeroed to look after."

"Hey, I know. But, it's dishonest to carry on with New Peterloo." She hesitated. "Unless, of course… You're going to tell everyone, come clean? A vote?"

"No. New Peterloo has to be real to be believed. How can we tell people? All that positivity lost, forgotten. Another spiral of trepidation, of worry and fear."

"Does Naomi know?"

"Yes. She's not happy, but she's a pragmatist." He moved conspiratorially close and whispered, "Don't tell Tam, and certainly don't tell Alex."

"I can't—"

But he was gone.

She followed him inside and there they were, her companions, her friends, and her family, doing life in their own unique ways.

She studied them closely. Each one of them had a future, and all of their futures looked bright.

Taking a long, considered breath, she clenched her jaw and, looking across at Gerry, she gave him the thumbs up, despite her misgivings. It was time for a fairer world and the sooner the better.

ACKNOWLEDGEMENTS

With thanks to all those whose work contributed to my background reading and research. Too many to mention, but I must explicitly thank Luke Robert Mason and his Futures podcast, Naomi Klein for *This Changes Everything*, Kate Raworth for *Doughnut Economics*, the late David Graeber for his insights expertly communicated, and Douglas Rushkoff for his unique perspective on the relationship between technology and humanity and those in control.

And a special thanks to those who read, commented and improved the drafts of the novel as it made its progress to the outside world. In particular, Hannah Kowszun, Jane Walker, Jared Collins, Paul Milnes, and Penn Smith for their reader feedback, and to Ben Greenaway for his help imagining future AI technologies and the potential means to take them down. Finally, to my editor Allen Ashley who expertly helped me improve the various iterations of what became *We Are Not Anonymous*.

ABOUT THE AUTHOR

STEPHEN ORAM writes social science fiction novels and short stories set in the near-future, exploring the intersection of messy humans and imperfect technology.

He is also a leading proponent of applied science fiction, working with scientists and technologists to explore possible outcomes of their research through short stories.

Stephen is based in the heart of central London and attributes much of the urban grittiness and the optimism about humanity in his writing to the noise, the bustle, and the diverse community of where he lives.

ALSO BY STEPHEN ORAM

Quantum Confessions
Fluence
Eating Robots and Other Stories
Biohacked & Begging and Other Stories
Extracting Humanity and Other Stories

www.ingramcontent.com/pod-product-compliance
Ingram Content Group UK Ltd.
Pitfield, Milton Keynes, MK11 3LW, UK
UKHW020343040125
453108UK00004B/188

9 781068 576409